"This novel is the vivid and gripping [...] brutal occupations: Sam is first a you[...] pation of The Netherlands in World [...] a colonial perpetrator as a Dutch soldier in the occupying army of Indonesia in the late forties. He suffers and then he deals out suffering. In this moving novel, Sam must search for a way to navigate his way through moral quagmires and find some kind of peace for himself and the ones he loves."

— ANTANAS SILEIKA, author of *Provisionally Yours*

"In this deft and deeply moving novel, Anne Lazurko disperses the fog of war to shine a light on one soldier's process of reckoning. As Sam confronts the enemy without and within, his creator honours the terrible vulnerability of our bodies, the essential balm of love and friendship, and the life-affirming beauty of the natural world, all the while lamenting the hell we so often make of this paradise we call home."

— ALISSA YORK, author of *The Naturalist*

"*What Is Written on the Tongue* is a gripping story of frailty and resilience. Anne Lazurko's novel is a fully engaged, deeply researched study of one man's struggle to retain his humanity amid the many tragedies of war."

— HELEN HUMPHREYS, author of *Field Study: Meditations on a Year at the Herbarium*

"Teeming with life and drama, *What Is Written on the Tongue* is an ambitious, sweeping, riveting story of war, immorality, love and family. Spanning The Netherlands, Germany and Indonesia during and after the Second World War, Anne Lazurko's novel serves as a grim reminder that the oppressed sometimes become oppressors. The novel hooked me on the first page and captured me to the last."

— LAWRENCE HILL, author of *The Book of Negroes* and *The Illegal*

What Is Written on the Tongue

A NOVEL BY

ANNE LAZURKO

Purchase the print edition
and receive the eBook free.
For details, go to
ecwpress.com/eBook.

This book is also available
as a Global Certified
Accessible™ (GCA) ebook.
ECW Press's ebooks are
screen reader friendly and
are built to meet the needs
of those who are unable
to read standard print due
to blindness, low vision,
dyslexia, or a physical
disability.

Copyright © Anne Lazurko, 2022

Published by ECW Press
665 Gerrard Street East
Toronto, Ontario, Canada M4M 1Y2
416-694-3348 / info@ecwpress.com

All rights reserved. No part of this publication may be
reproduced, stored in a retrieval system, or transmitted in any
form by any process — electronic, mechanical, photocopying,
recording, or otherwise — without the prior written
permission of the copyright owners and ECW Press. The
scanning, uploading, and distribution of this book via the
Internet or via any other means without the permission of
the publisher is illegal and punishable by law. Please purchase
only authorized electronic editions, and do not participate in
or encourage electronic piracy of copyrighted materials. Your
support of the author's rights is appreciated.

Editor for the Press: Susan Renouf
Cover design: Caroline Suzuki

This is a work of fiction. Names, characters,
places, and incidents either are the product of
the author's imagination or are used fictitiously,
and any resemblance to actual persons, living or
dead, business establishments, events, or locales is
entirely coincidental.

LIBRARY AND ARCHIVES CANADA CATALOGUING
IN PUBLICATION

Title: What is written on the tongue / a novel by
Anne Lazurko.

Names: Lazurko, Anne, 1964- author.

Identifiers: Canadiana (print) 20210343656 |
Canadiana (ebook) 20210343664

ISBN 978-1-77041-619-2 (softcover)
ISBN 978-1-77305-922-8 (ePub)
ISBN 978-1-77305-923-5 (PDF)
ISBN 978-1-77305-924-2 (Kindle)

Classification: LCC PS8623.A98 W43 2022 |
DDC C813/.6—dc23

We acknowledge the support of the Canada Council for the Arts. *Nous remercions le Conseil des arts du Canada de son
soutien.* This book is funded in part by the Government of Canada. *Ce livre est financé en partie par le gouvernement du
Canada.* We acknowledge the support of the Ontario Arts Council (OAC), an agency of the Government of Ontario,
which last year funded 1,965 individual artists and 1,152 organizations in 197 communities across Ontario for a total of
$51.9 million. We also acknowledge the support of the Government of Ontario through the Ontario Book Publishing
Tax Credit, and through Ontario Creates.

ONTARIO
CREATES

ONTARIO ARTS COUNCIL
CONSEIL DES ARTS DE L'ONTARIO
an Ontario government agency
un organisme du gouvernement de l'Ontario

Canada Council   Conseil des arts
for the Arts   du Canada

Canada

PRINTED AND BOUND IN CANADA   PRINTING: MARQUIS   5   4   3   2   1

For my parents,
Gerardus Theodorus Johannes Groenen,
who loved to tell a good story,

and

Anna Maria (Cisse) Groenen,
who loved to read one.

CONTENTS

"I am sure there are those who . . . feel that the dead have no voice. Theirs is a stone-age sensibility with a criminal blush." — PRAMOEDYA ANANTA TOER

PART I

"As a general rule, don't try to act macho and think you know better than seasoned inhabitants of the tropics."

— SCHEEPSPRAET (GUIDEBOOK TO LIVING IN THE TROPICS)

CHAPTER I

To Say This Is Mine

SURABAYA, ISLAND OF JAVA,
DUTCH EAST INDIES
MAY 1947

IT IS THE MEASURE OF A MAN, Sam thinks, to drop his pants on command and without hesitation as the army doctor shuffles down the line, head bent to inspect the genitals of each in his turn. Foreskin back, squeeze the head, firm grasp on the balls, the selected soldier asked to blow on the thumb he holds tight in his mouth like a drooling toddler. As a final indignity, he is then expected to turn and bend so the doctor can peer up his ass and discover whatever might be amiss there. Pecker inspections are a monthly occurrence. Sam watches the faces of men turn crimson as their dicks weep with the disease they've brought back from a few days' leave in Yogyakarta.

The generals say they need the men healthy for Operation Product, a planned offensive to regain control of the coffee plantations and coal mines from nationalist rebels who took them over when the last of the Japanese left the East Indies. A good case of VD makes a man vulnerable to capture or death, they say. A good case. Sam tries not to look at the others. It wasn't so long ago that he'd been horrified at the loss of his belt in the latrine at the Nazi camp, forced to choose between dignity and bread, shame at his

3

nakedness. But now his superiors ask him to wave it around like it's just another part of the uniform or a gun to be cleaned and working properly for this new goddamn war.

"Not sure why they're so concerned about our lul," Andre echoes his thoughts as they return to barracks. "It's the rebel bastards will get us. Them, or malaria, or this fucking dysentery. It's all the same. You're dead in the end." Andre is a big, thick, idiot of a guy, but good with his hands and sharp with a gun. He pauses long enough to look down at Sam's foot. "Jesus, what the hell is that?"

A chunk of flesh has come off in Sam's sock.

"Not as bad as Bart's." Sam nods toward a young man sitting on his pallet, wildly plunging a stick inside the plaster cast encasing his lower leg, a version of heaven on his face as the itch is relieved and then hell as bits of rotten skin come up with each stroke. It's a disgusting thing, but Sam's got his own afflictions to worry about. While the locals go about their business barefoot, the army doesn't understand the torture induced by leather boots worn in flesh-melting heat. He finds his Whitfield ointment, smears it between his toes, and wraps each foot in a light cotton hankie before sliding them into sandals. Such relief.

"Indonesia for the Indonesians." He mutters the guerrilla mantra under his breath. "They can have it."

Obliterated by Hitler in only five days, the Royal Dutch Army relied on the British to organize, train and even dress new conscripts like Sam. After six months of boot camp in the Netherlands, he was sent to the Indies and has spent another six deployed in Surabaya. His squad of a dozen men from the Twelfth Infantry has seen little of the country they're supposed to be fighting to reclaim. Day patrols and guard duty, sometimes twenty-four hours at a time, but mostly their lives are reduced to finding relief for ravaged feet, or from prickling skin rashes, or dizzying malaria. On a constant diet of rice and fruit and small amounts of meat of suspicious origin, men drop regularly from stomach ailments, the human enemy almost trivial.

Vices keep them sane when the advice of the *Scheepspraet* is not enough. The guidebook reminds them to forget toilet paper and use instead a small water dispenser to avoid anal fissures, instructs on the proclivities of ants and mosquitoes and how to keep them out of food and gear, offers techniques for boiling water to ward off typhus and dysentery. Cigarettes are a lifeline, the constant companion hanging lit from their mouths even as they raise their weapons. And they drink. A lot.

Feet wrapped, Sam heads outside in an undershirt and cargo shorts to smoke and share a beer with others in the squad. Andre is soon by his side, reaching for Sam's lighter.

"They're tough sons-of-bitches." The voice pipes up from behind Sam. It's Raj, his brown face looming out of the night.

"Who?"

"The pemuda." Raj jumps onto a barrel and rests his lean frame against the shack behind him. A bottle dangles from his hand, a cigarette from his lips, his dark eyes glittering. He's part of the KNIL squad stationed nearby, Indo-European soldiers in the Dutch colonial army, their clothing and attitudes, skin and song mixed up after two hundred years of their ancestors pretending not to love each other. Housed separately, the Indo eat at their own end of the canteen and have little to do with Sam and his full-blooded totok friends until they are thrown together on patrol.

"What does he know?" Andre nudges Sam in the ribs.

"I know they torched my family's printing business here in Surabaya in '45," Raj barks with contempt. "And, for good measure, they tortured and killed anyone who worked for my father. Most of them locals."

Sam recalls the newspaper reports: British soldiers liberating local populations from Japanese camps only to be horrified at the violence the Javanese inflicted on each other in their rush to fill the power vacuum.

Raj puffs smoke lazily into the air, but his voice is pained. "They kill their own as easily as they'll kill you."

"Jesus." The men scuff the ground with their toes or look toward the harbor.

"They're stealthy. Unpredictable. Fight like they're possessed. Like they have mystical powers." Raj jumps down from the barrel, sarcasm painting his words. "They wear a fucking amulet around their neck that makes them immune to pain and death. Or that's what they believe, what the villagers believe. They call them jagos, fighting cocks." He stumbles to the center of the group and struts about, flapping his arms in a drunken dance.

Sam holds up his hand, laughing. "Enough already. You'll scare the boys."

"They should be scared," Raj snarls, his eyes whirling across them. "You white boys don't know shit. Coming here. Thinking you're going to fight these animals in your short pants and berets. And with your good intentions." He raises mocking eyebrows.

"Well, you half-breeds weren't doing it by yourself, now were you? Dumbass." Despite his broken leg and the agony of the cast, Bart still wants to instigate. Sam groans.

"I can take any of you," Raj shouts, shaking his fist at each of them. "Come on." His friends slowly gather behind him. The blue-eyed Dutch stand behind Bart, who waves his crutch at Raj.

This is absurd. "We're on the same side here," Sam says quietly. "And we're not expecting we can do it all in our short pants either. It's the tanks and artillery that will run them over."

"Yeah, and then they die." Raj's tone is withering. "And become heroes of the revolusi." He says the last with a flourish of his hand, everyone laughing, the tension broken.

Sam turns and walks back to barracks and to bed. So many evenings turn into drunken brawls, men trying to settle scores that never change anyone's mind anyway. Since coming to Surabaya, the squad has been caught in the occasional skirmish with revolutionary forces in an alley here or a street there, but since he left home Sam feels he's accomplished nothing. Worse, there are reports of protests in Amsterdam condemning Dutch action in the East Indies. Condemning him.

And now Raj's indestructible jago. Sam wants to dismiss the native superstition for what it is, but if believing in supernatural powers gives the rebels courage to fight back, he has to admit he's a little awed by it. He wonders if things would have gone differently for the Dutch if there'd been less acceptance of the new reality brought to Holland by the Nazis, if they'd believed in their immortality; for the Jews had they resisted the transports. If, if, if.

Andre comes in and strips quickly to his shorts.

"So?" Sam asks.

"Same as usual. All talk."

Sam nods in the dark, watching Andre's bulky shadow kneel. Every night Andre prays, eyes closed, lips quietly murmuring as the rosary beads click through his strong fingers. He pockets the rosary and climbs under his bed net. Sam watches the faint outline of his friend's chest rise and fall as the chorus of mosquitoes whine around them.

"Lot of trucks and tanks coming through lately." Andre's deep voice startles the dark. "I imagine they're getting ready for the offensive."

"General Spoor says we could take them in a heartbeat if Van Mook would give the go-ahead. Where's all his negotiating got us so far? Pinned down around the edges of the island, eating dog meat for all we know. I just want to get out of Surabaya and see the countryside."

"Spoor is great. Did you hear he sent a recruit on leave so he could visit his mother before she died?" Andre sounds lovesick. "He cares. That's more than the rebels can say, sending kids in wearing rubber boots. Jesus."

"I don't know that anyone sends them," Sam says quietly. "I think they just show up ready to die for the cause. Sukarno is good. The man gives one hell of a speech. You gotta give him that."

His supporters call him Bung Karno. Brother. In the midst of Holland's liberation, news from the Indies filtered in. Encouraged and armed by the fleeing Japanese, Sukarno proclaimed an independent Indonesia, and the Dutch notion that they'd waltz back into the colony and begin where they'd left off quickly ended.

"I'm not giving the bastard anything." Andre's voice is hard.

Sam listens to Andre's breath stutter slowly to sleep. The cause is everything to Andre, his righteous words hinting at a violence Sam doesn't want to believe his friend capable of. The Nazi occupation taught Sam the risks of certainty, the choices his family were forced to make proving loyalty a nuanced thing.

The next morning the squad is called to assemble, Sergeant Major Mertens stumping to stand directly in front of the men, his glare daring anyone to comment. The man is career KNIL, an Indo officer who survived Japanese internment and torture by the infamous Kempeitai. His lower left leg balloons like a gnarly tree stump from his khaki shorts, the grotesque foot wrapped in white and encased in sandals, the leather stretched to fit. Sam has seen many career men with such afflictions, the elephantine foot acquired when the prisoners were infected with worms that caused blockages and swelling. Other vets have scars from pellagra and beriberi, and many suffer constant bouts of malaria. But they've all re-enlisted because this is their home. Sam tries to keep his eyes on Mertens's face.

"As you know, HQ is planning a major offensive to take back economic assets, but first they need to know the strength and location of the enemy," Mertens says. "We're going out with KNIL 47th to scope out the plantation area south of here. We're looking for members of the TNI, Tentara Nasional Indonesia, or rebels to avoid confusion. I imagine you've come up with your own creative names for them."

"Klompens!"

"Ploppers!"

"Hmm . . . surely you boys can come up with something more original." Mertens sighs into the silence. "They're hard to recognize. It's a soup: communists and liberals and Islamists, they're all looking to be in power. But it's the pemuda, young nationalist soldiers, who are the most dangerous. They work for Sukarno's Republicans when it suits them, independently when it doesn't. Mostly they are out of control."

"How do we know the difference?" one man asks.

"You'll know them when you see them."

Sam raises his eyebrows at Andre. "What the hell does that mean?"

"Green uniforms, barefoot, coming at you with spears. Those are the ones you shoot."

The men hoot their approval, rallied out of their fear by this picture of enemy incompetence. Sam snorts as he thinks of Raj's jago. Raj is full of shit. They head to barracks to get ready. Sam strips and washes, pulls on clean underwear from a box beside the bed, khaki pants and tan shirt, clips bars to the shoulder — a single yellow V with brown stripes running across. Corporal. The Dutch military deemed his few months of post-war agricultural college worthy of instant promotion, but the tropics don't consider rank, and his feet have certainly not been spared because of his stripes. He wipes more ointment between his rotting toes, carefully pulls on clean socks, and gingerly pushes his feet into his boots. Ready.

The men gather in the compound and the squad climbs into the back of a waiting truck, Andre slapping Sam on the back as he pushes past to sit.

"Just keep your eyes open," Mertens calls as they roll past. "They're out there trying to soften up the locals, just like you'll be doing for us. And you'll have no idea who got there first."

They leave the harbor, snaking through the streets of Surabaya and around checkpoints to escape the city and wind their way into the countryside. It's early but Sam's shirt is already plastered to his back with sweat. He sits up a little straighter, nervous as the road plunges into tropical forest, palm fronds and tall grasses slapping his head and arms, the truck bumping over roads pocked with holes blasted by grenades or mortar shells.

The truck hits a trench, sending the men straight up from their seats. Andre is at least ten centimeters taller than any of them and swears as his head whaps the metal frame used to hold the canvas roof. Rat-faced Freddy laughs too loudly. Sam doesn't like Freddy. He's too eager, too quick to speak, too loud. Freddy's sharp incisors work at his lips and even now he fidgets, running his hands nervously over the gun clenched between his legs, eyes in flight as though they can't find anywhere to land.

The forest suddenly gives way to an open field, and Sam breathes again. Brilliant green crops stretch out, water glistening through slender rice stalks. In the distance, terraces stagger up the mountainside, huge banyan trees studding the hills, their branches reaching out as though to anoint the heads of the workers who stoop and rise. Beyond them, a volcanic plume rises from the peak of Mount Arjuno. It hangs there an instant, dissipates, and the mountain belches again. They've been told not to worry about the volcanoes that dot the archipelago, their small eruptions, but Sam keeps a wary eye on them.

The men were told the British did a good job kicking the Japanese out after the surrender, soldiers like Sam told they were here to restore law and order and get things back to normal as the Brits withdrew. But with the country so strange, Sam doesn't know what normal is. Flora and fauna he doesn't recognize, tropical jungle suddenly opening up to large plantations. It's become clear they are here to reclaim it — tea and sugar and rubber, the oil refineries and coal mines — so the colony can provide Holland a means of recovery from the Nazi occupation. Except for the coal, Sam doesn't recognize any of it. He's a bit ashamed of his ignorance but can't bring himself to care; none of this has any relationship to him and he certainly doesn't want to die for it.

"My grandparents farmed these sawah." Darma's voice is soft

beside him. "I used to help with the rice harvest. Complained the whole time." He smiles, a flash of white teeth, and shakes his head.

"Where are they?"

"Died in a Japanese camp." Darma gestures to where pipes protrude from the hillside and distribute water that flows in channels among the terraces. "I'd like to come back someday."

Sam doesn't really know Darma Kemp. They've been on patrol together a few times, but Darma seems impossibly young to be a soldier, pimples marring his smooth skin, uniform drooping from his slight frame. He works quietly, keeps his gun clean and rarely swears.

Past the rice paddies the truck jolts along the broken road another hour, winds through more forest and breaks again into the open as they pass stately homes, battered, but still redolent of their former glory; two storied and sprawling with wraparound verandas and flower-studded yards. At first, he'd thought it a bit much, this decadence they want to reclaim so Dutch colonials can return to be pampered by houseboys and nannies. Holland is in ruins. What did these people expect? But out here in the countryside, the appeal is obvious: to sit and stare out at the orchards and fields, the flowers and trees, the lazy puff of the volcanoes on the horizon. To say this is mine. Such beauty. Who would give it up easily?

They come to a field of coffee stretching into the distance, a nearby orchard destroyed by grenade-blasted holes. The war has been here and the men are suddenly alert as they approach a small bridge. They've been told the whole area around Lawang is infiltrated, but none of them knows what infiltration might look like in a place so happily green.

"Fan out and walk from here," Mertens says quietly. "Road's too visible, so we'll head through the trees. Raj, Sam, take your men to the house and yard." He gestures to buildings about five hundred meters north and signals for the squad to move out.

Sam stays close to Andre and Darma and Hans Visser as they move crouched and listening through the dark canopy. When they reach the buildings, Sam puts the Sten to his shoulder so he is running ready while Andre eases himself along the back of a large building to check round the corner. He motions, and Sam slides around the side of the building, a sudden gasp and clatter sending his heart to his throat. Breath stopped, he fumbles for the trigger.

An old woman stares at him, her wide eyes the same brown-black of the coffee beans scattered now on the dirt floor from the basket she's dropped. Dust smudges her white blouse. They stare at each other and she slowly puts her hands in the air, shaking her head. There is a buzzing in Sam's ears so loud he can barely see.

"It's okay, man," Darma says, gently pushing the muzzle of Sam's gun toward the ground. "Just an old lady."

Sam turns to see Raj and four of the others watching him, loudly breathes out his embarrassment. He turns back to the old woman, who looks at the beans on the ground as she slowly lowers her hands to her sides. "Let's go."

They check the rest of the building. Raj knocks baskets of beans from a conveyor to the ground while five or six women stand watching with their backs to the wall. Sam wishes Raj would stop. What point is he making to these women? Darma follows and sets the baskets upright again. In front of the building, an old man dressed in white drops the rake he was using to turn beans laid out in the sun to dry. His face gives nothing away as the squad stumbles and slides toward him, coffee rolling underfoot.

"Ruining their whole damn harvest," Darma mumbles.

"Jesus, Kemp. Why do you give a shit?" Raj shouts at him, pushing the old man who wavers and then stands tall. "This doesn't belong to him. Not any of it. They're only here because the Japs threw their bosses in camps or killed them. They have no right to be here." He pushes the man again.

"Lay off, Raj." Sam surprises himself.

"Shut up."

"Still glad to get out to the countryside?" Andre asks wryly.

"You four come with me." Raj jerks his head. Darma, Andre

and two others head toward the house. "The rest of you pair up and check the warehouse and barn."

Sam signals to Visser and they head toward the barn. The door is open, the space so silent it makes him more uneasy than noise might have. Past a broken cart in the alleyway and an empty ox stall, Sam finds a ladder and creeps up the rungs to an overhead trapdoor. Visser's gun pointed at the opening, Sam swings his head and the Sten up and through, craning violently to scan the loft. Empty. He climbs up. The roof above him is bamboo trellis made solid with thick ivy growing through it. A pulley system at the end of a beam sticks out the loft door. Normally used to lower stored baskets of beans, a wooden seat now dangles from it to the ground and Sam pictures small blond children squealing their delight.

From the loft he sees the red-tiled roof of the house with its large open verandah, flinches as Raj pushes a young woman ahead of him so she stumbles before recovering quickly to stand tall. She glances toward the barn and Sam hesitates a moment, held in her gaze.

"Nothing in here," Visser says. "I gotta piss, bad." He blushes. The doctor kept no secrets about who needed treatment after the inspection.

"Go," Sam says as they climb down. "I'll check that shed in the trees. Keep an eye on me."

The shed is about fifty meters away and he approaches slowly, hopscotching between trees for cover, sliding along the west wall toward a door hanging slightly open from its one remaining hinge. He hears the clank of metal, then again, and a sound like someone humming. Slowly releasing his breath, he creeps forward on the balls of his feet, raising his gun as he moves toward the door, the hum louder.

A deep breath and he slides his head around the side of the doorframe to see inside. A man stands at a workbench, pliers in hand and a screwdriver in the back pocket of pants rolled up to expose muscled calves, his whole body wrestler squat and strong. Parts of a small motor are laid out in front of him, and he picks up a small shaft. Trying to push it into place, he shakes his head so fringes of silver hair escape the leather tie holding it back. He smears grease on the shaft and tries again. Sam has the urge to back away and leave the man to his work. But the squad was warned of homemade bombs. He shifts his weight and the door creaks. The man freezes for an instant and slowly turns. Sam trains his gun on the man's chest, sudden thirst like a sliver in his throat. His eye twitches.

"What are you doing?" he croaks, nodding at the motor.

"Fixing." The man gestures at his tools. "Fixing for my wife."

Sam steps into the room and the light from the door illuminates the space. Beside the motor is a stand with a bowl. The man is fixing a Mixmaster. Sam almost laughs out loud with relief. Instead he nods and looks around, the mess inside a blur. Odds and ends of every sort hang on the walls and are crammed into every corner, cords and motor belts, metal parts, cans and jars filled with screws and washers. It's just like his dad's shop back home, or their neighbors' down the road. A farmer's shop.

"I fix it, and she makes bread," the man says, grinning, friendly eyes dancing in the light.

"What's your name? Do you work here?"

The man's eyes cloud an instant. "My name is Amir. I am the boss."

"You know that's not true." Sam's voice in his ears sounds painfully inadequate; the man is twice his age. "You know this place belongs to someone else."

Amir nods thoughtfully. "My grandfather, my father, they worked here for the Hegman family. I worked for the Hegman family. Now, I work for myself." He stands taller.

"Okay." Sam lowers his gun and moves slowly toward the workbench, Amir moving over to make room. Sam uses his free hand to pick up the shaft Amir had been trying to fit into a small yoke. "Do you have a fine rubber washer?" he says and makes a circle with his thumb and forefinger, mimes placing it over the shaft.

Amir takes a paint can down from a shelf beside him. Sam chooses a washer and slides it over the shaft, handing it to Amir, who firmly pushes it into place. A clean fit. They look at each other and smile and, for an instant, Sam wants to stay in the shed and fix things with Amir. Shouts rebound in the distance and they both look up.

"We're the only ones who can protect you from the rebels." Sam forces certainty into his words. Amir nods, but his eyes shift with suspicion and Sam senses the rebels have been here promising the same thing.

"I just farm." Amir turns back to his bench. "Sukarno calls me a communist. You call me a thief. I just farm."

"My family farms, back in Holland — potatoes, sugar beets, oats." He doesn't tell Amir they grew thyme and basil and other leafy herbs before the Germans came with their demands for more practical production. No response. "Do you have a family?"

Amir inclines his head slightly and Sam wonders about the girl Raj pushed onto the verandah.

"We can protect them. Especially if you let us know what the rebels are up to in the area. It'll help your neighbors too."

"The pemuda find out, they kill us. I stay out of it."

"I think you know that's not an option."

"I just farm."

"You do what he fucking tells you to do!" Raj lunges through the door, grabbing Amir by his silver hair to torque his head around. "Tell us if the fucking pemuda have been here, you prick. Or we'll torch the goddamn place."

"Raj!" Sam grabs Raj's arm. "What the hell?"

Raj throws Sam off, twists Amir's arm behind his back and holds his pistol to the man's head. "I'll blow your fucking head off and *then* I'll torch the place. So ..." He wrenches Amir's arm higher and Amir gasps. "Tell me where the jagos are." Raj's voice is diamond cut with hatred, his eyes black pinpoints.

"They were here last night. Offered me weapons to protect myself." Amir huffs through his nose. "I didn't take them. Perhaps I should have."

Sam hears the change in Amir's voice, the perfect Dutch, the set of his jaw now as Raj slowly releases the pressure on his arm.

"Where'd they go?" Sam asks.

"East, across the river toward Mount Arjuno."

"Good boy." Raj's voice is cold, sarcastic. "See, Sam. They're spineless cowards. Give each other up for a good fuck. Let's go. And you," he spins back, pointing a finger at Amir. "We'll be back. Find out anything you can."

"I just farm." The words aren't out of Amir's mouth before Raj pounds the butt of his rifle into Amir's stomach so he crashes to the floor, curled and gasping, throwing a hard look at Sam. Sam sweeps his eyes once more round the shed and leaves, moving behind Raj through the trees and back to the yard.

"What the hell was that? How's that supposed to make him trust us?"

"We don't have time to wait for you to kiss his ass long enough to get information. He told us where they are. That's all we need." Raj stops and grabs the front of Sam's vest, pulling him so close he inhales Raj's rank breath. "You think Mertens wouldn't have done the same if he wasn't a goddamn cripple? Don't get in the way again or I'll report you."

Sam holds Raj's stare, exhaling slowly to stop from swinging a punch, wondering if the contempt in his heart is visible in his eyes.

For three weeks they travel through the region, cajoling and threatening those who might be inclined to support the rebels. Or invited to tea by local owners and landlords, adipati, who have profited from their relationship with the Dutch and expect the people to run into the streets to bow at the sound of their carriage bells. These Raj condescends to, patting the heads of their children and telling them they will be kept safe. As they move through the countryside, the squad sleeps where and when it can.

"That's how it's done," Raj says late one evening as they lean against the tires of the trucks and jeep parked out of sight in the trees off the road, chewing dry rations that stick in their throats. Beside Sam, Darma is already softly snoring, head on his chest and rifle propped against his knee. Sam reaches over and puts the safety on, leaning back again with heavy eyes.

"What?" he says, barely enough energy to speak. "Beat them up? Or kiss their ass?"

"Fuck off."

Sam braces for more. But Raj is silent. The wind shuffles through the dense bush. A twig snaps and something small scurries away. Mosquitoes whine around his netted hood but he can't be bothered to swat them. Exhaustion filters down from his forehead through his shoulders and into his groin and feet. His stomach churns. He's been battling some kind of bug he must have picked up from the water, and his rectum alternately itches or screams red pain from the diarrhea shooting out of him every hour or so. Trying to use water to clean his ass is harder than the *Scheepspraet* would suggest. Shifting, he finds a less painful position. His head nods.

The next day they are called back to Surabaya. On the way they pick up two men they'd left at Amir's plantation. As the truck drives in, the sun glints off coffee beans stretching across the yard in a collage of ripening yellow and red and green and brown. Sam wants to take a picture and send it to Marie. She won't believe these are the same beans she turns into strong black brew soothed with milk, *Product of the Dutch East Indies* right on the jar. The same old man in white tunic and pants grips his rake tightly this time, watching warily as he continues to turn the beans. Sam thinks he sees Amir's silver-haired head disappear inside the barn as the soldiers join the squad in the truck and the troop heads home.

The men are quiet. No one has slept much, convinced the locals have not told them everything. Ahead of them, a young woman on a bicycle moves to the side of the road to let them pass. She wears a scarf, wrapped to cover her head and shoulders, a basket on the carry-rack behind her seat, the bicycle moving easily as her long skirt billows behind. Wind from the passing truck lifts the scarf and she rides no hands to adjust it, pedaling with ease. Sam remembers riding that way a lifetime ago when the war at home ended, before this one began. He smiles at the memory and is startled when the girl smiles back, her eyes a deep brown so intense they seem to Sam to hold a thousand questions and as many answers.

"You like that one, Sam?" Raj jeers. "Special piece of ass under all that?"

"Shut up," Andre says.

"Who asked you?"

Sam turns and stares at Raj, eyebrows pinched in a question he doesn't know how to ask. Who is this man, with his small mind and his lust for vengeance? Sam turns away again, silent, watching the road behind them, the dark girl a speck in the distance as they round the corner. And how did Sam end up on his side?

Surabaya is uglier on their return. He's ignored his homesickness so far, but their stint in the countryside reminded him. The plantations, the crops, the clean emerald green of it all. If he had a choice, he'd stay out there and learn what Darma knows about rice and water and life in this place. Just stop for a while, maybe lay in a hammock in Amir's yard and listen to the sounds he'd been too nervous to hear, canaries in the garden, beans tumbling as they're turned, rattle of rain on clay shingles. Instead they return to a city unaware of the choices forced on people like Amir. He realizes with a wrench the man reminds him of Leo, or what Leo might have become; the tilt of his head, the courage in his eye. In another life Amir might be a family friend, or uncle. They could tinker in his shop, share a beer.

The squad gets back to find their shabby barracks teeming. Someone has left a single banana on a bench, blackened now with rot, and the ant infestation has spread. Hordes rove across the table and chairs, dive into the spaces around their gear, disappear into cracks in the floor and walls. Andre groans as he slides his locker from under his bed to find it not quite closed and the ants taking up residence. He fishes frantically amongst his possessions.

"Thank god." Andre triumphantly holds up a mason jar filled with Lucky Strikes, a pinch of tea leaves at the bottom to preserve their freshness. "The bastards didn't get my smokes!"

The others cheer as though his triumph is theirs. The Dutch blockade is designed to force the rebels to give up, but it means tea, tobacco and sugar are scarce for everyone. Including the Brits who, according to articles in *Bataviaasch Nieuwsblad*, are some pissed about it. Sam finds a can of boric acid and sprinkles it on all the surfaces and in Andre's locker.

"The book says that should do it," he says, then reaches into his own locker for a sachet of instant soup. He lights the Esbit burner, quickly boils water, adds the soup mix, opens a packet of biscuits and smears them with tuna spread. Brushing dead ants off the chair, he sits down to eat, the rations disappearing before he's even tasted them. Not that they have any flavor; his taste buds have adapted and he's happier now with sambal-hot rice and sweet fruits.

He pulls off his socks and boots and strips down to his underwear, the men around him doing the same, gasping as blisters tear open, groaning at their own stench. Cold buckets of water, ointments and gauze, and everyone is under their nets huffing and yawning. The steady click of Andre's beads slows and stops, the buzz of his inevitable snore filling the space between them. Usually it lulls Sam to sleep, but tonight it isn't enough to crowd out the questions.

He stares into the dark, head filled with images of Amir in his shop, Amir on the ground, images that mix with his memories of Leo until he is sweating with confusion. Amir wants to choose his own work and make some decent money off the resources of the land. It's not so hard to understand. Sam resented every minute of the Nazi occupation of Holland, every potato or kernel of corn the Germans took from them. Imagine two hundred years.

At least Amir has some claim, an argument to ownership and birthright. Not like the good Dutch Christians back home who wasted no time in taking over the homes of the Jews. Later they stared at those returning skeletons as if they had no recollection of the Elias or Berman families taken away two years earlier; no shame in the fact they'd waited across the road, imagining how they would make over the Jewish homes even as their neighbors were loaded up. In the end, people decided the Nazis had victimized everyone in equal measure so there was no extra compassion for those few who'd survived Auschwitz. It was unbelievable, really. He winces at the crassness, the cruelty. Yes, Amir has a claim.

And yet, Sam is afraid Amir won't be allowed to stay out of the conflict. Mertens said it, the countryside is running amok with all kinds vying not only with the Dutch for ground, but with each other for power. Amir will have to choose a side. After Raj's performance, Sam has a sense he knows which it will be.

The knot in Sam's stomach tightens, a coil of unease waiting for his attention. But he can't give it any. Doesn't dare. Instead, he pulls out the notebook his father pressed into his hands as Sam boarded the ship for this new life.

"Write it down, Sam. All of it."

He didn't know what his father was referring to, the war he just left behind or the one he was heading to. They'd simply looked at one another, nodded, and Sam was gone, left wondering if his dad thought the gift would somehow fix things between them. But Sam doesn't want to compromise his anger, can't forget that Hendrik was a collaborator. Or at the very least compliant. Sam pretends not to care about the notebook, trying to convince himself the thing is not beautiful, the smooth leather binding, the way his thumb ripples over the ridging of his name embossed on the cover. He hasn't written anything in it yet. Doesn't know where to start. And his words won't change what happened. They won't matter to anyone.

CHAPTER 2

If We Only Knew the End

JUNE 1947

HE WAKES TO THE SWISH OF BROOMS. Always the brooms, clearing streets, walkways, dirt floors and yards, a constant sweep as though the dust has changed from yesterday, as though it makes a difference.

Dust on the ground, water in the air, the humidity is heavy on his skin as he wraps a towel round his waist and heads to an open bath. A low concrete wall screens him from the street and buckets of well water drawn by hired locals stand waiting. He scoops the frigid water with an old tomato tin and pours it over his head. After three tins it feels like his head is shrinking and his balls actually do, such cold a rare pleasure in the tropics. Sam soaps up and splashes himself once more, then snugs the towel again before heading back across the small alley to barracks.

Flicking wet hair back from his face, he glances down, surprised anew at the adult breadth of his chest and taut stomach, a far cry from the awkward rope of adolescent limbs he'd gone into training with. Flexing a bicep, he reaches for the Whitfield, smearing a fingerful around his testicles to relieve the itch there.

"Yeah, I'm so impressive."

Dressed in clean khakis, he heads outside. The babu hired to cook for them serves breakfast in the small, open-ended canteen. Oona waves him over to the counter, her saggy triceps flapping from otherwise bird-thin arms, the etchings round her dark eyes deepening with her smile. She slaps food on Sam's plate, and he carries it to the far end of a long table away from the other men. He cracks the boiled egg and eats slowly, deliberately. The white is cooked to rubber. So good. He missed eggs during the Nazi occupation, any kind of egg. Something so simple amongst all the deprivations.

"Terima kasih," he says as he finishes and hands Oona his plate, pocketing one of the small teardrop salak from the basket next to her. Under its reptile-like skin, the fruit is firm like apple, refreshing like coconut.

"Sama-sama," Oona replies.

Every day she feeds him. And every day these niceties. Careful not to gulp the thick sludge of grounds at the bottom of the cup, he drains his coffee and heads outside.

"Hari baik," he says slowly. A hoot of laughter from Oona, and he wonders how he's managed to mess up "have a nice day."

At the Ophaalbrug, he watches the drawbridge rise to allow a small fishing boat through. When it descends, he crosses and walks north along the river toward Kalimas Harbor, the city awakening around him. Doors of warehouses yawn open, while families living upstairs emerge to sit on balconies overlooking the sewage-filled canals. Closer to the port, men scramble up three-meter stacks of rope layered in different sizes and braids and colors, heave down coils thick as a woman's thigh and twenty meters long, while others sort through pillars of sky-blue barrels used to take fish to market. The long prows of the Bugis pinisi boats angle across the pier as though stacked. At one, fishermen run up and down a narrow log propped against the hull, balancing nets and rope, barrels and gear they load onto the ship. Finally they jump in, throwing off the ties as they land.

"Hari baik," Sam calls to the watching crew and waves. They wave back, laughing and hollering something he can't make out. The ship makes its way out from the jumble of boats, hits open water and unfurls its seven sails to begin the run to Madura, or north across the Java Sea to Kalimantan, or east to Flores. He wants to go along and see these exotic places, the orangutan and Komodo dragons he's heard about, the pygmies and Dayak people. But those aren't the exploits he was signed up for.

Holland had never conscripted soldiers to the East Indies. Not in two hundred years. Not until now. Lucky him. At the office in Roermond, he'd signed the papers as instructed, told by a weak-eyed private that the tropics would be the adventure of a lifetime. But the Nazis had provided more than enough adventure. When he finally made it home from where he was forced to work in Germany, he'd wanted only to go back to school and date his girl, Petra. And he hated to leave his sisters to listen to their father's rage. Marie and Anika and himself, all of them wrung out by war and grief and all they could never understand.

Before he could hope to make sense of it, even before he finished his first set of exams, the Koninklijk Leger called, and he found himself celebrating his twenty-first birthday on a troop ship waiting for passage through the Suez Canal. Looking down from the lock, he'd been mesmerized by the hustle and colors of the market below, parallel lines of vertical rope dangling dark against the hull as buckets were hauled up full of goods and sent back down filled with money for the vendors. Still stunned, he crossed the Indian Ocean to land on the archipelago, expected to secure places like Medan and Yogyakarta from people named Hatta and Tan Malaka.

"Hari baik." He says it softly now to the ship cresting in the distance.

Shaking a Lucky Strike from the pack in his shirt, Sam lights it and inhales long and slow. Is there anything that will ever give him more pleasure than a first morning smoke? Sex likely will. Or that's what the other men say, acting like they've conquered all the women of the Indies when he knows they're mostly as afraid as he is. He doesn't tell them about Emma.

"Nice morning." It's Commander Hagen come up behind him with a mug of coffee. "Practicing your Javanese?"

"Yes, sir." Sam salutes. It seems an odd thing to do, off-duty and alone with the man, but Hagen is an officer. "But it's not very good."

"Keep trying. It makes things a bit more bearable when you can speak to them." Hagen pats absently at his pockets.

Sam hands him a cigarette and with one hand opens a pack of matches and strikes a flame, holding it to the tip, hoping the man doesn't notice his nerves. Hagen closes his eyes as he drags in the smoke, his large hand almost circling the cigarette he holds between thumb and finger. He's at least two meters tall, dark hair, baby blue eyes softening a moment as he looks gratefully at Sam and blows white rings into the still air. The sun warm on their faces, they stand looking east across the strait to Kamal port on Madura, the salt island, a desolate place where the stuff is mined and processed by Javanese workers.

Hagen's eyes jump to a large cruise ship anchored near the end of the wharf, the *Johan van Oldenbarnevelt*. With their navy wiped out by the German Luftwaffe, the Dutch have improvised for this new war. Just as Sam did on his arrival, a hundred new recruits scrub the decks of the ship that brought them here.

"Tired of these kids who show up and think they're on some kind of holiday because they've landed in the tropics." Hagen sighs. "I want you to go down there and hustle them up, make sure they're doing a good job."

"Yes, sir."

"And Sam, I'm trying to find common ground with the KNIL men. They're posted with us and we all need to be fighting the same war, if you know what I mean. Let Raj be in charge."

"Yes, sir." He hopes the colonel didn't notice his hesitation; Raj is proof the KNIL are willing to fight this war in ways Sam is not.

"You're not on duty yet. Call me Leo."

A breath puffs out of him. "Yes, sir."

Hagen laughs as he walks away into the brilliant morning light, the sun glinting off the island in the distance. White salt. Black coal. A brother named Leo.

Sam arrives to find Raj waiting at the wharf, has to admit Raj cuts a figure in his uniform, erect and confident, dark eyes above the wide Ambonese nose, long sharp-chinned face. Sam has steered clear since the encounter with Amir.

"Morning," Sam offers.

Raj ignores him.

Asshole. Sam moves quickly toward the ship, Raj matching his long stride until Sam is forced to slow down to stop the sweat gathering under his arms and running down from beneath his cap. More than fifty Javanese mill about, hoping to be chosen to work a day for the Dutch harbor master. Every day the same spectacle, skinny men — young and old, sick or healthy — rush to the dock to be assessed for their work value.

"Like a bloody slave auction," Sam murmurs. Raj gives him a sharp look.

A one-legged man stands tall and hopeful as though no one will notice the crutch he uses. But a harbor worker kicks it out from under him so he hops and flails, finally grabbing onto the shoulder of the man beside him, who quickly shrugs him off. Of the fifty, only ten are chosen. The rest melt away into the surrounding streets to wait another day.

The roar of the ship's motors is suddenly silenced, replaced by the shriek of seagulls circling overhead to land on the thick ropes holding the vessel to the wharf. They wait for the morning feast dropped from the bowels of the ship — foodstuff spoiled in the heat. A thick scum of oil covers the water near the docks, its green and blue swirls eddying into black, almost beautiful in the morning sun. Here an orange crate bobs, there a plastic tub. The stench of the harbor is unbearable, the combination of oil and effluent and rotting food filling Sam's nose.

The new recruits work quietly, some still puking up their sea sickness from the long voyage over, some pretending to be either bored or absorbed in their work, trying to ignore what might otherwise make them afraid. Sam knows how they feel, this bewildered introduction to a beauty and squalor they could not have imagined wanting or needing to defend. Raj strides between them, reminding them every inch of the deck must be clean before they'll move on to more important work for the army. The recruits glance sideways at Raj, to Sam for guidance; it's their first contact with a brown man giving orders.

From the deck, Sam hears a sudden splash and leans over the rail to see a small dark body cut through the water toward a loaf of bread suspended on the oily slick. Triumphant, the boy holds the loaf over his head as he paddles with one arm back to the ladder at the edge of a nearby dock. Two older boys are poised at the top. Before the swimmer has reached the first rung, the others have snatched the loaf and are running away.

"Hey, hey," Sam yells.

They look back once and sprint. The child clings to the ladder, sobbing. Sam bolts down the gang, hops the rail and hits the street running.

"Jesus," Raj shouts behind him. "What are you doing?"

Sam keeps running, sees a flash of bare feet slip round a corner, bolts down a side road after them. "Goddammit, little shits."

Anger spurs him, prevents him from noticing how silent the street has become, how it narrows into an alley, a walkway, a dead end. Until he slows up and knows he's lost, the rage replaced by trepidation. The boys are long gone with their trophy bread and Sam stands alone, peering through hanging laundry at small homes raised on short stilts. The smell from the aluminum gutters collides with his nose, the cross-hatch weave of the bamboo walls distorting his vision, doors and windows gaping. There is no sound, the air around him still, as though even the birds have stopped their chatter to see what he might do.

He tries to calm his breath, swiveling his head, skin tingling as he fingers the pistol at his hip and draws it. He has only one extra clip. An explosion of pigeons bursts behind him and he wheels around, gun pointed. An old man sits on a stoop, watching Sam from under hooded eyes. A woman stands frozen, head high and tilted, a small child held close. Sam breathes deeply, feels every rib expand.

"Hallo," he calls quietly and puts his weapon away. The girl suddenly clambers down from her mother and runs straight to him, grabbing at his hand, turning it over to trace her finger down the veins. Her touch is firm as though she expects to probe some treasure from his skin while her mother's eyes widen with indecision. Finally, she clutches her headscarf tight and rushes to pull the girl away, but her daughter's chubby hand clings to Sam's.

"It's all right." He picks the girl up and holds her in one arm.

The woman doesn't look at him, says something to the girl in a tight voice. But the child only cocks her head and stares at Sam's face.

"Selamat pagi," he says, trying to kill the quiver in his voice. The child smiles gleefully at his attempted greeting, tugging at the bars on his shoulders and pushing at the cap sweat-stuck to his head. He holds his free hand out and gestures around him, exaggerating his eyebrows in a question. "Tolong?" The woman seems to understand he needs help.

She looks round. "Tuan," she says, finally, beckoning him to come.

Tuan. Young sir. He puts the child down and follows. They walk between houses through a maze of small side streets, the woman leading, the child between them pedaling her legs fast to keep up. They zig to a dead end, zag into another narrow alley. He has no idea where he is and his scalp crawls; this far from the harbor, it must be a rebel-held neighborhood. She might be taking him to them now.

He fingers his pistol, the metal cold even in this heat. He barely knows how to use the thing, more familiar with a rifle. Most of his training for the tropics was with field guns, as though artillery weapons could even make it through these narrow passages. Stupid. He looks around. Tries to breathe. Not much choice now. And something about the little girl.

They turn a sharp corner, startling a woman who crouches against a wall, holding a coconut she was grating over a large tub of shavings. Her hair is wrapped high and loose in a violet scarf and she stares at him through dark eyes under fiercely arched brows. He glances at her bare feet, at the coconut in her hand, the multicolored peppers in the basket beside her, breathes the pungent smell of the lemongrass stalks propped in bunches nearby. The woman seems to have no age. She rests on her haunches, regal, beautiful with smooth skin, nose flared toward rounded cheeks. Small lines frame her mouth, which is pursed as though she is amused. Or maybe curious. He wants to still the fear, stop his running and sit with this woman, tell her how Oona likely buys these goods at the market, how fresh her food is. But he looks up and his guide has disappeared.

"Hari baik," he says quietly and rushes away. The narrow street opens out to a large bamboo structure, the air from inside harsh with the smell of kerosene. The woman waits for him to catch up before she enters, pulling her daughter behind. He swallows hard and ducks inside, blinking through the smoke. Nothing moves, wide eyes flashing between Sam and the woman, pen-size tools poised above fabric laid out on laps. Groups of three or four people squat or sit on the dirt floor, beside them blackened pots sitting atop small kerosene fires. He holsters the pistol, suddenly ashamed to be someone they are afraid of. The woman nods to him and the others slowly lapse back into their work.

He is safe for now, though he has no idea how to get back to the squad on his own. He wanders among the workers, girls so young they wear their sarong from the waist down, sweat glistening on the brows of women and old men. The bamboo allows air to breeze through, but even at this early hour the heat generated by the small fires is overwhelming. He crouches near a girl of about thirteen. She holds a small wooden tool, dipping the copper reservoir at one end of it into the wax heating in the wok beside her. She then applies the melted wax to the fabric through a tiny spout at the end of the tool, covering some of the dots and lines of the pattern penciled onto the fabric. Painstaking work. Looking up at him, she pushes damp hair from her eyes.

"Putih," she says shyly, pointing to where the wax has been applied to the silk. White. It is the color of the fabric. And him. She gets up and heads to where buckets of dye in various colors wait along the wall. "Tuan," she says and gestures him over. Plunging the fabric into amber-colored liquid, she swirls it a few times before wringing it out and opening it to show him.

The fabric is golden except for the waxed dots and lines, which will remain white. She hangs it to dry near an old woman who tends to pieces in other buckets, wringing them out and hanging them on racks outside in the shade, all at various stages of waxing and dying, a palette of subtle shades and colors. A boy of ten adds tree bark to a pot of boiling water. The perimeter of the building is lined with cornsacks and boxes containing jackfruit and mahogany bark, indigo leaves and small fruits. The girl points to each in turn and then to the dyes: gold, brown, blue, red.

All the sarongs and headdresses and baby slings he's seen come from such a place, even the tapestries in the government halls in Surabaya. He watches a white-haired woman work on an intricate piece, his frantic heart slowing with the pace of her quiet move-ment, the murmurs and comfortable silences of the workers, the occasional small laugh.

From light to dark, one color at a time, a million bits of wax. These artists know the end before they begin. It's an abrupt reali-zation. He has a moment to consider how life might be different if one knew without a doubt what they wanted and chose so carefully.

The little girl tugs at his arm and he bends to brush fine hair away from her face. Her deep brown eyes are slightly puzzled and she pulls his head closer to look right into the blue of his. Someday, instead of going to school, she will work here with her mother, inhaling the kerosene fumes and making beautiful things for little pay. He pats her head. She runs to her mother, who is speaking with a teenage boy in the corner, gesturing as though to convince him of something. The boy finally nods, but doesn't look happy as she leads him to where Sam stands, and then both of them out the door.

Outside, she points to the boy. "Wira," she says. Then she points to Sam and waves her hand back to where they'd first met. "Dia, tuan," she says quickly. "Kampong."

Sam understands that this boy, Wira, is to take him back to where he came from. He almost laughs. Wouldn't that be nice, home to the farm in Limburg, to de Kruidenteelt. He smiles at the woman, nods to the others and follows the boy into the street. Wira has hold of the little girl's hand and walks quickly, head down and just slightly ahead of Sam, the girl protesting as her feet barely touch the ground. Wira's reluctance to be seen with Sam is not a good sign. Sam's shoulders tense as he pulls the pistol out of its holster, flips the safety off and holds the gun loosely in his hand. A swift rush of adrenalin and the slow calm of the batik works is gone, everything around him taking on a new clarity. He's an idiot. He's put not only himself, but now this boy and small child in danger; if the rebels are watching, they won't forget.

He expects to see the coconut woman. But the boy has taken a different route, the doors of homes open to reveal bits of life, mats and laundry, tables and crudely carved toys. Twists and turns and narrow wandering alleyways.

"Jesus, isn't anything square in this country?"

The girl glances back at him. He smiles to disguise his growing panic. A rat runs across the space in front of him and he flinches as it dives into the gutter running alongside the street. A middle-aged man in undershorts stands in a corner made by two buildings and pours water over his head from a makeshift bucket shower, pausing to give Sam a long look from under bushy eyebrows. Two others look up from a bicycle they are fixing before slowly melting into the alley. He could die here and no one would find him. Sweat trickles between his shoulder blades, down his pants, runs from under his cap and into his eyes.

Suddenly they round a corner to a familiar intersection, the woman's house, the old man's stoop. Sam lets the breath he's been holding go. But Wira stops short at a ruckus down the street. Andre and Freddy stand surveying the area with guns ready. Raj waves his at the old man, whose hair now spikes wispy from his head, checkered sarong flapping loosely round his thighs, white shirt streaked with dirt. Wira drops the girl's hand and silently charges, trying to push Raj away.

"Little shit." Raj pushes back so Wira stumbles.

"No. Jesus, Raj."

The noise has drawn people out of their homes. Women and children stare from porch steps. And then, a collective silence, as young dark men move from the shadows to surround the soldiers. No breath, no sound. Raj slowly steps away from the old man. Sam sees everything large and in slow motion, Andre's finger wrapping more tightly round the trigger, Darma searching Sam's face for explanation.

"I was lost," Sam offers, spreading his hands in front of him.

Raj slaps them down. "Stop that."

The little girl's face is streaked with tears and before the old man can stop her she runs to Sam, throwing her small body at him and wrapping her arms around his knees, sending him off-balance so he stumbles and is forced to pick her up. The smell of her damp sweat is light in his nose, her plump thighs fleshy on his arm. The old man stares at Sam an instant, holds his hand in the air and makes a short speech, his Javanese quick and sharp.

"He's the local ulama," Darma says quietly from behind Sam. "He's telling them it's a misunderstanding."

Wira's eyes fire between the soldiers and the old man, and, as Sam watches, the boy takes a deep breath and makes a choice, jumping in front of the dark young men and turning to glare at Raj. Sam has a moment to recognize Wira's bluff. The boy is trying to convince the rebels of his loyalties. Raj grips his gun tighter. Andre raises his. The circle shrinks back a foot. The old man says something sharp into Wira's ear, but the boy stands tall.

The girl in Sam's arms bites her lip, eyes tearful and confused, finally struggling so Sam realizes he's crushing her and sets her down. She stumbles and runs to the old man, who gathers her to his side, eyes never leaving Sam's face.

Raj trains his gun on Wira, shouting at him to sit in shame in front of the old man, Andre and Freddy suddenly pushing the others one by one to the ground. Sam has a moment of clarity, sees these small men, boys really, dwarfed by the size and weaponry of the soldiers. Yet they do not look afraid. They sit quietly in the dirty street, hands clasped behind their heads and gaze at Raj with a combination of resignation and contempt. Jago. The word flashes through Sam's mind.

"If we find out you're with the rebels." Raj points his gun at Wira's head, mimics taking a shot.

Sam flinches.

With the men still on the ground, Raj pushes Sam ahead of him through an opening and they walk quickly away. The others follow, watching doors and windows, rifles ready until they are in familiar streets and finally reach the Dutch-controlled space of the harbor. Hustling him into the empty canteen, Raj shoves Sam into a chair and motions for the others to sit, lights a cigarette.

"Wish the whole unit had been there. A raid would have turned up guns for sure, a few arrests."

"I got lost, Raj. The kid helped me."

"That kid was nothing but trouble." Raj shakes his head, his voice hard. "A rebel, and the old man was protecting him. What the hell is wrong with you? First that fucking farmer. Now this kid? What do you think you're doing here?"

Sam stares at the floor, the salak fruit hard in his pocket. He wishes he'd given it to the little girl to soothe her fear. He pictures Wira's panicked eyes. What if those were rebels? Raj said they don't hesitate to kill locals suspected of helping Dutch troops.

He was careless. He'd let his anger carry him as he ran after the thieves and because of him they'd possibly made enemies of potential friends. He thought he might help a little boy who only wanted bread, thought he was doing a good thing. But being good is hard when everything is strange, when you can't know the consequences.

"Sam," Raj shouts and looks at the others. Andre is staring at him, Darma's mouth set. "Did you hear me? We're going to get cleaned up and take a rest just like every other afternoon. And then we'll meet up and go to the cantina as usual. Listen to some music, watch the girls. Everything is the same. Nothing has changed."

But Raj is wrong; something has changed. The grace in the hands of a woman shaving coconut, the trust in a little girl's eyes, the pride in an old man standing tall. Sam thinks of the woman choosing to help him, of her intricate art, art that asks him to think ahead, to consider how his actions here will help him to become what he wants to be — a good man. A small panic in his throat. How will he know?

The next day is Sunday, and the squad lounges on cots, writing letters home. They stare into space, considering what they might share with loved ones who have no reference point on which to pin an appreciation of this current hell. Nostalgia bubbles up, and they burst into spontaneous bouts of wrestling, Andre jumping on Sam, who feigns surrender only to push his friend from behind and send him crashing into Bart, whose leg has finally healed. Some of the men have already had their first drinks of the day, play-fighting quickly given a whiskey edge. Bart throws himself into the fray and ends up bludgeoning his nose on a table edge, ending the fight as the others jump over each other to get away from the blood.

Sam grabs Andre's arm. "Let's get out of here."

It's mid-morning as they head outside and wave to the men on patrol, ducking into the street to listen for the bell of their favorite street warung, where a local woman serves hot bakso soup thick with rice and vegetables. Her generosity with the sambal makes Sam's eyes water and hands sweat.

"We should go to Birth of Our Lady," Andre says. "I haven't done confession in a long time."

"Me either, but I'm not sure what I'd say." He is suddenly nervous, can't remember the last time he was in a church.

Andre glances at his watch. "We can get there before ten o'clock Mass."

"Mind if I join you?" Brother Keenan is suddenly at their side. "Saw you leave. Quite the ruckus back there. Glad I caught up."

Sam raises his eyebrows at Andre. They can hardly say no.

Keenan was assigned to the squad only a couple of weeks before, the cleric fresh-scrubbed and pious. Sam has avoided him, imagining the man will somehow guess his blasphemous heart. They head toward Kepanjen and the church, its double spires rising behind the hotel across from where the Dutch flower market laces the canal. He'd like to linger amongst the suspended baskets of color, potted plants and peat, but Andre hurries ahead of him.

Keenan chatters at Sam's side as they near the church. "Built late 1800s. She's a beauty."

Andre and Keenan plunge into confessionals, Sam hanging back to slide quickly into a pew instead. He can't imagine doing a confession. How could a priest understand his ambivalence about Amir, his doubts about Raj. Kneeling, he tries to pray, wishes he could, but his discussions with God are confused bits of anger and pleading all in one. He'd never prayed so hard as when waiting for Leo to come home after Holland was liberated, landing in a pew at the church in Heibloem almost every day. The priest thought such piety indicated a vocation and asked Sam if he needed help to resolve his doubts. Sam almost laughed, instead mumbling something incoherent and ducking out, unable to confess to the priest that his conversations with God included a great deal of cursing. He blames God. He hates God. He needs God. But he can't find him.

"Pillars are wood from Kalimantan," Keenan whispers as he and Andre join Sam to kneel and do their Hail Marys. "And look at those wall carvings. All teak. Stunning."

He feels Andre shake with laughter and elbows him. The Mass begins. As hard as he tries, Sam can't pay attention, fidgets with the hymnal, mouths responses by rote.

"Go in peace, to love and to serve the Lord," the priest intones.

"Thanks be to God." And they are on their way.

"What now?" Keenan's head puppy-wags as he looks from one to the other.

"Going back to write some letters," Andre says.

"Pasar," Sam says, and makes toward the market without looking at Keenan. He doesn't want company.

Their movements restricted to Dutch-patrolled areas, Sam hasn't had many opportunities for sightseeing, but he likes to wander the market. He walks, listening to the chatter of the sellers sitting behind fleets of bamboo baskets filled with chard and cabbage, chilies and peppers. He finds a stand where the vendor squeezes a hairy coconut, lopping off its top with a long knife before handing the fruit to Sam. The milk is fresh and clear and just sweet enough to be more than water, the white flesh peeling out in strips of slimy richness. Wiping his chin, Sam fishes a few rupiah from his pocket for the man.

"You didn't take communion."

He spins round. Keenan is ordering a coconut. What the hell?

"I couldn't. I . . ."

Keenan waves him off. "Come."

Shit.

The cleric leads him to a bench alongside a wall where the building's overhang provides a little shade, the open space beyond housing an assortment of pigeon apartments, some large, some small, all painted a variety of bright colors. The smaller cages have tiny windows with dormers carved above the door as though the birds might appreciate a view and some architectural nuance. Some of the doors are open, a few blue-gray heads and small sharp beaks protruding from the openings. The birds eye Sam as he passes. He will never understand the Javanese obsession with pigeons.

Sam tries to ignore the slurping and smacking of Keenan's lips, instead watching the bustling meat market across the street. Chickens and ducks, lambs and goats are stuffed in crates or tied by a string to the handlebar of a bicycle or the wheel of a cart. Local men smoke and visit, a Dutch woman among them asking after the most tender cut of goat, vendors shouting "Belanda, Belanda" trying to attract her money.

"They want her rupiah, but they don't much like us Belanda, do they?" Keenan sets his empty coconut shell down, wipes his chin.

"Some do. Some don't. Depends which side they're on."

"How do we know?"

"Apparently we don't." Sam pictures Amir's silver hair as he worked in the shed, Wira's defiance. "I think sometimes they don't even know."

"But they make a choice."

"Maybe they're forced to." He doesn't want to argue. "Have you met Raj?"

"Angry young Indo? Yes."

"He's certain. About the enemy, I mean. But I don't think it makes him feel any better to be sure. I think it's what makes him so angry."

"Hard for us to judge. I hear he's been through a lot."

As if Sam hasn't. "I heard you volunteered."

"Yes." Keenan pauses, as though deciding to trust Sam. "I sailed through seminary, thought I had it all figured out. But six months as a deacon and I just couldn't do it. Couldn't be ordained." He looks past Sam to where the market thrums. "All those people coming to church to grieve their losses from the war. A few others looking for forgiveness for causing them. I just wasn't sure what to make of it." He smiles wryly. "I guess I thought coming here might cement my relationship with God."

"And?"

"I remain a deacon."

Sam feels bad for the cleric, but what is there to say? He can't figure out his own feelings about God. Strange word, relationship. So far it's been a one-way thing, God calling the shots and Sam dealing with the fallout. He gets up and walks, wandering among the cackling and braying and crowing, amazed always at the variety of colors a rooster can be: bright oranges and reds, blacks and whites, hints of purple. The church spire gleams dark in the distance. It seems cold and lonely, out of touch with this life here on the ground, with what it means to eke out a living selling what you've grown or picked or slaughtered with your own hands.

Keenan is trying to barter for bananas, holding up fingers to show how many rupiah he's willing to spend. No one will look at him, distracted by a woman at his side in white kebaya and sarong with a flaming red headscarf. An indignant looking orange cock threatens to peck her hand as she smiles and strokes its plumage, calming the bird. She nods to the vendor, watching as he kills it with a quick twist of the neck. She pays the man and grasps the bird's feet so it swings from her hand. She catches Sam's eye; he can't look away from the satisfaction in hers.

He gets back to the rat-infested storage shed they call home. It sits at the edge of the wharf, a long wood structure with bamboo walls and clay shingles that rattle and pound when the rains come.

A row of tempat tidur run the length of the room, men in various stages of undress, some napping the afternoon away while others quietly talk, the morning melee evidently forgotten. Sam crawls onto his cot and scratches the rash behind his knee, trying to ignore the sheen of sweat that coats him through the day. Andre's breath is heavy with sleep, the letter he was writing abandoned on his chest, pen dropped to the floor.

Sam fishes the notebook from the trunk by his bed and fingers the embossed letters, the leather spine. *Write it down, Sam. All of it.* The family hadn't spoken much about the war and its aftermath. Not much for talking, the Vandenbergs, especially about feelings. He imagines it's because their mother died when he was so young and his dad hardened to granite, the sharing of emotions stifled by the heaviness of the air they walked through every day. Farming, food, money — that's what they talked about, not the important things that remained unanswered after the Nazis left: how it happened, why it happened.

Maybe his dad is right. Maybe words will help explain the war Sam left behind, perhaps guide him in this new one. They won't change what happened in Holland any more than the constant swish of brooms can change the nature of this country's dust. But perhaps he can see it more clearly from a distance, write it down, make his confession, the words a purging or a search, hindsight either gift or curse to those who lived.

CHAPTER 3

What if We Do Nothing

DE KRUIDENTEELT, LIMBURG PROVINCE, THE NETHERLANDS

APRIL 1943

EVEN MY NOTEBOOK WAS A SUSPICION. As though the writings of a teenager would be the final chink in the Nazi armor. I liked the idea though. Maybe I could share with the resistance. Become a hero. But heroics were hard with the Germans right in our yard. Early in the war, they'd decided de Kruidenteelt was a perfectly lonely and strategic place for a command center, and soon occupied the farm's outbuildings, their trucks and jeeps racing through the yard at all hours, men running in and out of the barn. I imagined them inside, spinning dials and pushing pins into maps, deciding who would die that day.

I envied them. Not their actions of course, but their freedom. We scurried and bowed while German soldiers not much older than me walked erect as though they were in charge of the universe. I suppose they were at the time. All I wanted was to get away from the farm and join the Allies on the Eastern Front or in Africa where *Radio Oranje* reported some success. I'd make a good soldier. Leader Groeneveld had given me the Jonge Wacht trophy for marksmanship. Breathe and keep both eyes open. I could do it.

But the Nazis had gone berserk, scooping up anyone they could find to work the labor camps, as though forcing people to pound rocks in a quarry would help Germany win. No telling when a person might be picked up, on a bright morning or in a midnight raid, or why. I was forced to hide from the Nazis. Sometimes I hid from the neighbors. The Hoedemakers were members of the Nationaal-Socialistische Beweging, fascist sympathizers who slob-bered over Mussolini and then Hitler, handing out NSB leaflets, "With Germany against Capitalism," "With Germany against Bolshevism." They hated everyone.

When the raids were on, the chicken coop became my second home. I always emerged hungry, yet heavier, weighed down by a slow accumulation of dread. It pissed me off. I should have been finishing Form II in school, growing. Instead, my brain was fogged with hunger and the mirror was a disappointing thing, all twig-thin arms and spindle legs. By that point in the war, even Leo was a slim shadow thrown against the wall, drifting through the house in the morning after his night shift at the coal mine. We'd catch brief moments to talk before he headed to bed or I headed to the coop for the day.

I remember a time he was happy, optimistic in an "it'll all work out" kind of way. Patient with me when I asked dumb questions Dad was too busy to answer, about building a fence, or why the boar's lul is a spiral and if that's why they call it screwing. He laughed and laughed at that one, rubbing my head hard with his knuckles. But then he told me about sex and how we only talk dirty about animals and not girls, that we have to respect them and be sure we are married like they say in church. Not long after, I caught him in the hayloft of the barn with his hand up the shirt of a local girl.

"I asked first," he said and cuffed me, laughing as he walked away holding her hand.

Then the war. Six months after the occupation began, Leo was sent underground to excavate coal for the Nazis, paid a small wage at first, and then nothing at all. And it made him more than pissed off, his face always tinged with anger, brooding through his days and shutting out even Anika, the one who could make anyone see things with a little more hope. Maybe Leo was right; maybe hope was stupid, a dangerous thing after so long a wait. But then the miners went on strike and everything changed.

I'd gone to the kolenberg with Marcel to scavenge for small bits of coal from the mountain of stones left after the loads were excavated and washed and sorted. We hoped to get enough nickel-sized pieces for Marie to start the stove and brew up some broth to go with the usual onion sandwich. I vowed I would never eat another goddamn onion sandwich if the war ever ended.

Even Marcel was losing his baby fat, forced to hide more often after rumors that his dad, Alfred, was forging documents. The Gestapo had crashed the door once already, his mother pretending she didn't know a thing while standing where Marcel and Alfred hid under the floorboards. Her house was trashed, and Marcel said she almost fainted when the bastards finally left. And he'd pissed himself. I knew Marcel almost as well as I knew Leo, maybe better. We'd practically traded diapers as kids, and told each other everything. Well, not everything — it was his mom told me he pissed himself. But Marcel did tell me he was worried about the lack of hair on his face and chest and other parts.

Jumping off my bike, I called, "Hallo," the word sliding deliciously dangerous off my tongue, acronym then for Hang All Traitors. "I asked Marie about the hair."

"Oh for Christ's sake, your sister?"

"She says you're fine. Everyone grows and changes at different times. Might be our lousy diet. Not like any girl is ever going to see it, anyway." I grinned.

"Shut up." He punched my arm. "I'm not really worried."

We headed north, our bike rims squealing like pigs going at it. Too much noise in the quiet dawn, but there was nothing we could do. War had stripped the country of rubber and the old garden hose I'd cut to fit the rims was quickly shredded by black chunks of bombed asphalt scarring the road. No matter how I weaved, the pocks in the road shoved the bike seat up my ass, vibrations shooting through the handlebars into my arms and rattling my teeth. I could hear Marcel grunting and caught him looking across the space between us.

"I'm surprised they haven't taken your dad," he said.

Excuses crowded my mouth. Dad had to run the farm and the Krauts took everything we grew. It's not like we asked for their base in our backyard where they watched everything we did, ogling Marie and Anika. I pedaled harder.

"Wait up." Marcel puffed behind me. "I didn't mean anything."

"So why'd you say it?"

"They took my dad on Sunday."

"Oh shit. Where?"

"We don't know. But he was staying close. Keeping out of sight. Makes you wonder." Marcel's pause was just long enough. Asshole.

We reached the kolenberg sloping high into the air. An old woman crouched at the base wearing cracked wooden shoes, scarf flapping round her face, grunting as she threw stones this way and that, glaring at us with watery eyes. Two small girls scrambled across the stones, bare feet and wrecked dresses, black dust swirling around blond curls. Other kids huddled over their loot, watching me with suspicious eyes as I climbed high, the stones rolling underfoot and tripping me up so I landed on my knee, a spot of blood blooming where my pants ripped. Shit. My only pair. Marcel was beside me again. A persistent asshole.

"I know it's stupid," he said.

"You actually think my family would give up your dad?"

"No." Marcel was always first to back down if we hit a snag, but this time he gathered the last of his baby fat up straight. "But Hendrik . . ."

For Christ's sake, we were just talking about goddamn pubic hair. I wanted to hit him, to shut him up. But God help me, I knew what he meant.

Hendrik, my hard dad. When the war started and tracers fired the sky and flak sparked, Dad hadn't offered any reassurances, not even to Anika, only eleven then and scared out of her mind. Marie stood by the sink, pretending to peel carrots while her shoulders shook, but Dad ignored all of us, ignored the fact of the war even as Dutch gunfire chattered through the yard in the brief fight for de Kruidenteelt and his family huddled in the cellar with the pickle jars and sugar beets. Two days in, Dad got tired of scurrying for the shelter. "Not running from the sons-of-bitches anymore," he'd said and stayed in his bed, risking a bullet that would leave me and Leo the care of the farm and the girls. But no bullet found him; instead a hole through the wall ten centimeters above his pillow. Some called it luck. But I knew. Dad thought he was immune. He'd believed Hitler's big words and loud slogans, trusted the Führer's promise to continue the Reich's traditional friendship with Holland. Instead Rotterdam was scorched, Utrecht threatened. And eventually they were shooting at us.

And afterward? It hit me what Marcel saw; Leo relatively safe at the mine, and Dad hauling supplies from Roermond twice a week for the German base in the yard, rewarded with the occasional half pint of whiskey or bar of soap for the girls. Dad flaunted these things a little too much, thinking he was better than everyone else.

"You know my dad." I shrugged. "He figures he can do what he wants if he just works hard and talks louder. I wish he'd just shut up."

Marcel nodded like he understood.

We filled our bags quickly and headed back home, stopping as a thrum of deep voices echoed over the squealing bike rims. Hiding the bags in tall grass beside the road, we pedaled north, straining to hear so I forgot the near dawn, the threat, and suddenly Marcel shoved me hard into the ditch. We landed in a heap just as a German truck whizzed by, a dozen soldiers in the back leaning ahead and focused on the road to the mine, guns ready.

"Holy shit." Marcel untangled his pedals from my spokes.

Leo was working. We dumped our bikes into a thicket of lilacs at the side of the road, sprinted west across a clover field and crawled to the lip of a ridge carved out of the hill by the excavation of the mine site. It was chaos below, fifty miners milling about at the surface. Cave-in? I scanned the group for Leo, but one soot-stained face was the same as the next.

Four miners in green uniforms sat with their hands bound alongside one wall of a shed. Bastards, Leo had said after his first shift, saying the Krauts gave them a uniform and a gun and they suddenly believed in their own importance. The rest of the men were all talking at once, the sound the same as we'd heard early in the war during the February Strike of '41. Protest words. Fighting words. I grinned stupidly at Marcel and punched his shoulder. He laughed, and his eyes softened a moment before we both jumped at a voice echoing against the ridge. It was Hans Elick, who'd been a lawyer in Heibloem before they sent him into the mine. Now he stood on the bucket of a payloader and hollered through a bullhorn.

"They want them all. Every Dutch soldier they captured and then released at the start of this fucking occupation." Hans's voice was even and strong, his words bouncing round the bowl created by the mine. "Expected to turn themselves in to be sent to labor camps." A few men hollered their disgust, but it was a tentative sound after the years of silence. "That's three hundred thousand men they want to send back to the camps to do their dirty work," Hans shouted. The number hung in the air. "Three. Hundred. Thousand."

"No!" the men shouted.

Hans looked out over them, chest heaving. "This coal fuels their war. Their factories. Their trains."

The murmuring of the men followed the flow of Hans's voice.

"Those men fought for us." The sound grew. "Now we'll strike for them." His voice boomed as he raised his fists in the air.

The men roared. Tools clattered to the ground, headlamps dropped in a pile so the glowing lights flashed across the dirt. Slapping backs and gripping hands, the men formed a loose line and walked away from the mine, their energy pounding up the hill. Gooseflesh broke over my skin as a bubble surged up from my gut into my throat and released like a cork, all the months of fear and dread ripping through so I jumped up and let out a long whoop. Beside me Marcel did the same and we slapped each other on the back. The men looked up and shook their fists toward us, a solidarity of intention.

One of the men held his arm higher, watched us an instant longer. It was Leo; his dirty blond hair, broad shoulders, long legs, the way he cocked his head when he was paying attention. My chest damn near exploded, as though Leo's awareness of my presence made me a part of what was happening below, as though I too was brave enough for action.

The men started chanting, black faces and straightened shoulders, fifty men scuffing up dust from the gravel yard and heading toward the road. And then the German truck rounded the corner and I froze, my hands suddenly reaching straight out like I could block the sound of the men from escaping into the air beyond.

"Germans!" I screamed, but the men couldn't hear.

The shooting started. Marcel flattened me into the dirt, but I had to see and chanced a look over the ridge. Men scattered, some trying to scramble up our hill. Others ran back toward the mine, taking shelter behind a warehouse. One sprinted east across an open field, falling suddenly face first in the summer fallow.

"Get up," I whispered, but the man didn't move.

Crouched behind the ridge, I was afraid to go, afraid to stay. Leo was down there and I couldn't do anything. The black dust of the mine swirled up toward us. I couldn't see. Sputtered. Thought I would cry. Where the hell was Leo? The shooting and shouting slowed and I lifted my head again, heart hammering in my ears. The dust cleared and I saw most of the men had vanished or run into the distance, but below us the German soldiers hovered over three captured miners. They screamed and kicked at the kneeling men.

An officer made his way from the mine entrance, pushing back his cap as though settling in for some hard work. He drew his pistol and I wouldn't look away, as though by witnessing I could change something. The crisp report of a gun, and the first man fell, another shot to the second. The voice of the third rose to the ridge. "My wife. My children. Have mercy." His face twisted, hands outstretched to where I watched as though I might gather him in. But the distance was too great. For a moment the air was quiet as a held breath. The miner ran. The pistol fired. This victim in flight, a single flap of hands, face thrust forward as he too landed. Another of the soldiers walked slowly to the twitching body and shot the man in the head.

I ducked out of sight, sat staring at Marcel, mind slowed, body numb. It was an impossible thing, the disregard. But those miners were dead. Someone should retrieve the bodies, deliver them to families, tell wives and mothers their husbands and sons were brave.

Leo. I'd watched his red-blond hair merge with the rest of the miners. Marcel pulled at my arm, pushing me away from the ridge so I turned and looked down at the clover and was suddenly running, slipping down the slope, sliding the last meters on my ass. Sprinting across the field, I gulped at the air, had to get home. I would find Leo at home. We reached our bikes, picked up the coal and rode like hell. But it was too slow, our tire rims clumsy, the bags too heavy. German trucks tore past, heading toward the mine, their lights sweeping past us, kicking up dust we coughed through. Reaching the lane to de Kruidenteelt, Marcel gave me an encouraging smile and headed east toward his farm.

When I burst in the door, Anika shouted, "They're striking. *Radio Oranje* says the workers are out in Hengelo. Philips factories shut down in Eindhoven."

"They shot four miners," I said.

Marie walked in from the back room. "What?"

"They were shooting at the mine," I said. "I don't know where Leo is."

Anika gaped at me. Marie's hand flew to her mouth. And Leo stumbled in the door, breath ragged, face red. The air flushed out of me. When our eyes met, he shook his head; don't say a word. The girls fussed, checking him front and back as though they couldn't believe there was not a single bullet hole in him. Marie turned on me.

"What the hell were you doing there? You could have been picked up." She looked, horrified, at the notebook hanging from my shirt pocket. "Or worse."

The men killed. The risk Leo took. I wanted to yell at her for worrying as though I was a child. Instead I asked Leo what he would do now.

"The leaders say we strike until the Nazis change their minds about taking all those men, or until the war is over."

Marie snorted. "Impossible."

"It could happen," Leo snapped back. "Hans Elick says the Allies are gaining in Russia and Africa. It's only a matter of time until they take back Europe."

"How much time?" Marie's words were clipped. "How many dead?"

"Too many." Dad stood in the doorway. "Radio says they're shooting at strikers across the country, anyone arrested sentenced to death."

"They can't kill us all," Leo said. "They won't have anyone left to work."

I wasn't so sure, wondering if Leo would talk so big if he'd been one of the men pleading for his life.

"You're not going back," Dad shouted. "You'll hide in the coop, that's what you'll do. You don't owe those bastards anything."

Leo ignored him, heading out to wash up at the well, Dad yelling behind until he turned on me. "Give me that goddamn thing." He grabbed my notebook and threw it into the coals in the open stove. I wanted to scream at him that at least Leo wasn't afraid to stand up. That he didn't kiss Nazi asses for a bit of moonshine. Instead I watched a small flame lick the cover of the notebook until it curled, and I slammed the stove door shut. I didn't need the damn thing to remember what I saw.

Following Leo outside, I watched the spray of water as he splashed it over his head and neck, squeezing the last of the coal-blackened water from the washcloth before using it to wipe inside and around his ears. I ached to tell Leo what I'd seen. Why he should listen to our dad. But I knew Leo's anger made him deaf.

For the first time Leo joined me in the chicken coop. We'd painted over the hinges of a small feed room at the end of the coop, disguising the inner door with small shelves for pails and hooks for scoops. I took one of the blankets Marie had piled as a mattress and made a bed for Leo beside me. We lay in the darkness, the space so narrow our shoulders touched. Listening to his murmured prayers, my chest was suddenly heavy.

"You won't go back, will you?" I whispered.

His long nose was profiled in the hint of moonlight coming through small cracks in the wall. He stopped his praying, the silence stretching long. "Do you know what I pray for?" His voice was clear beside me.

"The war to end?"

"No. I don't believe God will somehow save us from the Nazis."

Deliver us from evil. It's the only thing I prayed for.

"Before she died, mom told me God can't help us with anything but ourselves. He can't help us control what other people do or think, or whether it rains, or if we have money. Ourselves. That's it."

I'd been too young to have such conversations with our mother. And then she died. Suddenly I was five again, lying in bed with Leo after the funeral, confused by the priest's words, the hands patting my head, the sorrowful looks the neighbors didn't think I noticed. Dead was not my mom. She was the lightness that softened Dad's edges.

Leo had explained it to me. What dead was. "She'll never come back, Sam. Not ever." I couldn't imagine never, but a sob came up from my belly at the sadness and certainty in Leo's voice. He gripped my hand on the sheets between us. "But when we're done being sad, she would want us to think of her and be happy."

"Okay." My voice was small in the big room and I started crying again. Leo cried too, holding me and rocking back and forth until I slept. For god's sake, he was only nine. Where was our dad? Where was Hendrik?

"So I pray that I do the right thing." Leo's deep voice startled me back to the coop. "That I can be good even with all the shit happening around us. That I can be brave."

I almost choked. "I saw three men executed." My throat closed up. And then I blurted. "Praying sure as hell didn't help them."

Leo stiffened beside me. "You don't get it, Sam. It's not about saving yourself. It's about right and wrong and actually doing something. Standing up."

"But what if . . . ?"

"What if? What if? What if we do nothing and we die anyway?"

The question sucked up all the air in the tiny space. It was all just ideas. Leo was real. Solid. It felt like a brick sat on my chest and I pushed up on my elbow. Dad had chosen to be as absent as our dead mother, I couldn't lose Leo too.

"What difference can you make? Risking your life for a bunch of strangers? We need you here."

"Shut up, Sam. You don't know anything."

"Maybe not. But I know Marie is terrified." Leo's twin. It was the cruelest thing I could say.

"I know." His voice broke.

The next day a wave of workers rose up across Holland but was quickly suppressed. Except in Limburg. By the second day 40,000 miners were striking. The resistance supplied the workers with arms and for the first time since occupation, we were firing back. But it wasn't enough. We heard of fifty casualties, then one hundred and more, hundreds of other strikers made prisoners of war and sent to concentration camps. Leo set off to support the workers while Marie and Anika waited for his return, and I waited endlessly in the coop. I was angry with Leo in one moment, filled with admiration the next. Mostly I was numb, not letting myself think of the inevitable. But it was inevitable, and on the fifth morning the strikes were over and Leo didn't come home.

"Stupid son of a bitch!" Dad yelled. "Didn't I tell him not to go? What's all his talk worth now, hey? Hey?"

Anika cried quietly in the corner of the kitchen while Marie stared out the window, the tightness in her thin lips reflected in the glass.

"We have to find him," she said finally, and looked across the room at me.

CHAPTER 4

A Jew in the Chicken Coop

SEPTEMBER 1943

I FAILED MARIE. Spring of '43 slid into summer and summer into fall, the razzia more frequent so I spent more time in the coop nursing terrible visions of Leo and his fate. I'd thought the resistance might help find him, but they disappeared after the strike, as if Leo and all those others were already dead. Marcel figured there wasn't much anyone could do. Not for Leo, or for Marcel's father who'd been arrested for his forging and taken to Kemna, a camp near Wuppertal in Germany. We both pretended we hadn't heard how brutal the place was.

"Mom thinks he's alive, says she feels it," he said.

I couldn't look at the hope in his face. I'd seen Mrs. Bakker; she was wasting away. Made me wonder what she really believed. But then again I was doing the same thing, convincing myself Leo was alive and would somehow come home despite the odds.

I spent my days obsessing about how I might find Leo. Dad's solution was to swear at the crops. He seemed to shrink a little each day, raging at God and the war and Leo, sometimes so loudly

Marie shushed him, afraid the soldiers would hear and arrest him too. He blamed the resistance and the union as much as he did the Nazis. But I knew what I saw that day at the mine when Leo and those men shed their fear for something outside themselves, for three hundred thousand strangers. Leo wanted to be bigger, wanted his actions to count for something, wanted to be more than a cog in the Nazi wheel. Beside Leo, Dad was a coward. But then I'd done little to find my brother, nothing really. And the longer Leo was gone, the more likely he was to die. And if he was already dead, then he knew I was a coward too.

My sisters, however, were not.

As the war dragged on, the flood of refugees seeking shelter and food grew, people showing up with outstretched hands, children squalling in their prams, grandparents shuffling with bowed heads, all of them with eyes stunned blank by desperation. Anika looked defiantly at Dad when he hesitated, helping Marie turn scavenged beets into brothy soup, scraping the bottom of the bins for grain to crush into flour for bread dense as leather. But Dad drew the line at the evacuees, refusing to shelter any onderduikers with the Germans so close. No one from the underground. I was ashamed at my relief, comparing my reaction against Leo's actions, Dad's fear against Anika's resolve. She was only fifteen and tiny as a child, but suddenly I saw the tent of breasts under her sweater, the swing of her hips. She wasn't my little sister anymore and the determination in her eye made me afraid for her.

On a bright September morning, a shadow of a man stumbled down the lane to de Kruidenteelt, lurching forward a few steps at a time, suitcase bumping his legs. He was so tall and so lean I thought he might buckle under the weight of his own head. Running to grab his elbow, the sight of the yellow star pinned to his lapel was like a knife twist to my gut. A Jew. Fuck. What now? In my moment of hesitation, a bicycle turned the corner. It was Anika's friend Inga, hair flying free, scarf fluttering from the handlebars of her bike as she rode past.

"Raid." Anika appeared at my side, grabbing the suitcase and running ahead as it bumped against her leg. "Quick, to the coop."

No time to think. The man leaned heavily against me and I struggled to hold him up. Anika was already inside. The scrape of wood, a squawk. I looked back an instant and saw a German lorry turn down the lane, Marie drying her hands on her apron and squaring her shoulders as she walked out to meet it.

"Shit." I stumbled with the man into the hiding space and collapsed onto the blankets layered in the corner. The smell of stale vomit and loose bowels hit me and I scurried to the other side of the small space, breathing through my mouth.

He coughed hard. "Name's Daniel. They told me I'd be safe here."

They? Anika's daily bike rides, her constant meetings with Inga, heads together whispering; I thought they were being silly girls, talking about boys, maybe about me. But Inga arrived with her scarf around the handlebars. A sign. And Marie standing ready to take on the Nazis. My sisters were with the underground. They hadn't told me. I felt both left out and terrified. The penalty was death. But Dad had said nothing about sheltering the Jews.

Sliding down the wall, I sat on the straw-covered floor, listening with my whole body, heard a scratch like a fingernail running across the roof. Bird. Branch. Mouse. The man stirred on the makeshift bed. His clothes were loose and dirty, face darkened with stubble and black rings under his eyes, cracked lips. He was maybe twenty-five. Mumbling in his sleep, he shivered and tucked his hands between his legs. I suddenly had a terrible image of this man dying in the coop, his last breath clogged by the dank claw of chicken shit and straw.

Rustling outside. Heart hammering, I stared at Daniel as if that might keep him silent. The outer door creaked, footsteps, a strangled squawk. The disguised wall began to move, the scoops and pails clanging. Anika's pale face appeared in the light.

"They're gone." She came closer to peer at Daniel, hands twisting the sides of her skirt. "They searched the house. Didn't even bother with the yard." She gestured out the door. "Germans right there. No one suspects."

"What are we doing, Anika?"

She regarded me a moment, lips pursed in thought. She pushed her hair behind her ear and gazed at the man who rolled to face the wall. "Probably best if we keep this between us for now."

When I started to protest, she put up her hand. "We'll get him feeling better and then send him on his way." She closed the camou-flaged door behind us and adjusted the scoop on its hook. Walking through the coop she stopped just before the door leading outside, absently touching the last cage so the chicken jumped back.

"His name is Daniel," I said, hoping that by saying the man's name aloud it would make him seem less of a threat.

"Daniel," Anika repeated and stepped through the door.

Anika fed broth and the occasional vegetable root to Daniel in the first days. He slept a lot and didn't speak much. Despair clung to his skin and I didn't want to be dragged down into it so I spent my days reading books I'd read three times already, imagining how the Three Musketeers might have rescued themselves from my current hell. Every evening before heading to the house for the night, I dumped the pot we used for a toilet onto the pile of chicken shit outside. One night he finally spoke as I was ready to leave.

"Any news from the underground?"

"No." It came out a hiss. "But you'll have to leave soon." I hadn't known my anger was so close to the surface.

He peered at me through the gloom and slowly chuckled. "I think I like your sisters better."

I snatched his empty plate and cup, trying to remind myself this wasn't his fault. None of this was his fault. "What happened to you, anyway?"

His eyes clouded and he stared silently at the wall.

People said they cheated. Bought hogs low and sold them high. Controlled the banks and businesses. Folks stood back as the war went on and watched the Jews lose things to the Nazis — their businesses, their rights. By '42, we were watching them being loaded onto trains. Even in a place as small as Heibloem, we watched as the Germans took away neighbors we'd known our whole lives. And the bystanders waved — the women — waved from the platform, as though they believed the Jews were going to a better place, as though waving might make them feel better and stop their crying. I hadn't thought about what it meant.

"They took my wife and my baby," he said, finally. "Shoved them into a cattle wagon while I hid in the shrubs at the end of the street. All I could see were their hands reaching through the slats as it drove away." His voice broke. "All I can think of is the hands."

A moan escaped his clenched lips, but he quickly stood tall again, shaking his head. "The Dutch are fucking efficient, that's for certain. Run the trains on time." His eyes were piercing. "No one allowed to die too late."

Dying? What the hell was he talking about? He shook his head and lay down on the blankets, rolling to face the wall, dismissing me. Outside, I leaned against the door frame an instant, checking the night for sound.

"Sh'ma Yisrael." Daniel's voice was a sing-song whisper from inside. "Adonai Eloheinu Adonai Ehad."

I saw myself as a child of six, hands cradling the pillow under my head, rocking my whole body to soothe the absence of my mother. "Now I lay me down to sleep. I pray thee Lord my soul to keep. If I should die before I wake, I pray thee Lord my soul to take." Back and forth, back and forth. The glimpse of a connection opened up a crack in my breastbone. In the same moment I looked up to see the lights still burning in the barn, the Germans working into the dark hours. And the moment of sympathy evaporated, overwhelmed by the fear of what might happen if they found out about the Jew in the chicken coop.

"Shut up in there," I whispered and kicked at the door to the hiding place. The chickens squawked from their cages. "Fucking Jood."

A sharp intake of breath, Anika beside me in the coop. "Sam!" Her voice was pinched with disbelief.

In the flicker of her candle, she couldn't see the tears burning my eyes, how good I wanted to be, how scared I was, wanting nothing more than to run away from the choices the war forced me to make. Can a person die from dread? Fear comes in an instant, but dread lingers, insistent, conjured by the word Nazi, by the thought of vanishing like Leo, of endless hunger, of helplessness, of being prisoner to what moments like this demanded. For an instant I wondered if death might be easier than carrying the weight of all that dread.

Anika fell into step beside me as we crossed the yard and climbed the two steps to the porch. She didn't open the door, instead turning to look into my eyes, her face inches from mine in the dark, her breath yeasty. Anika had always held the sky in her eyes, wide and honest and hopeful. That night I saw the glint of tears gathering in their corners and had to turn away.

"He has to stay a little longer," she said, her voice still tinged childhood high, but her words determined. "He's still weak. And it won't be easy for him. You know as well as I, not everyone will take him in. It needs to be arranged." Her shoulders slumped as though suddenly tired, and I wondered what else she'd been risking.

"Is it worth it?"

"It?" Her brow furrowed and I couldn't escape the disappointment in her gaze. "He's a person, Sam. Like you. Like Leo."

"Leo's our brother. You can't compare a stranger to family."

"And where is Leo?" She threw her hands in the air. "You and Dad are just the same, carping on about him while everything is going to shit around us."

"What? You don't care about him?"

"That's just mean." She took a deep breath, held my eyes. "Don't you see this is bigger than us, bigger than Leo? This is about who we want to be through this hell, what the whole goddamn country wants to be. If we can live with ourselves when it's done. If we can live with each other."

I pray that I do the right thing.

"What if Leo dies because someone decides he's not worth it?" Anika's tears ran freely down her small face. "Daniel is somebody's brother too."

A flutter ran through my chest and stomach to settle in my groin. I took a hard look at Anika, wondering where my sister had found this new self, if she'd been there all along, floating unseen above where I was tethered close to the ground by the gravity of my fear, too suffocated to have the kind of hope required for courage. I drew a deep breath, reaching past all of it and finding air. I brushed her hand with my fingertips.

"Alright." I couldn't speak another word. "Alright."

CHAPTER 5

Depends Which Side You're On

SURABAYA, ISLAND OF JAVA,
DUTCH EAST INDIES
JULY 1947

WHEN SAM FIRST ARRIVED IN SURABAYA, the early morning keening of the muezzin set his teeth on edge, seemed more a call to war than a summons to prayer. But he's grown accustomed to it, now soothed by the bending vibrations of the local caller's voice as the people wake; a baby's cry, a mother's song, the phlegm-filled hacking of an old man. Over the past week, the reverberation of drums has pounded through each night as local Muslims eat their fill after a day of fasting for Ramadan. It's impossible to sleep, the noise receding only with the muezzin's morning call.

"I suppose it's like your Lent," Darma says.

Sam doesn't tell him Lent never required much real sacrifice. Give up sweets, smoke a few less cigarettes, sit your ass in a pew a bit more often. He knows fasting only from childhood Fridays when he was punished with a light meal of fish, a strange way to show deference to Jesus, but some things you don't think to question until you find yourself hungry in the middle of an occupation when fish is no longer a sacrifice, but a treat on any day. If there was food, you ate it; piety can only carry a man so far. Sam has to admire Darma's convictions.

This morning, the muezzin is followed by a sudden rap on the door, someone hollering at the squad to assemble outside barracks within five minutes. The men grumble, yawning and scratching themselves as they shuffle out, straightening up quickly when they see Commander Hagen.

"It's on," Hagen says. "Operation Product. A police action to retake the plantations and other economic assets. We're sending two brigades — seven thousand men — from Surabaya to the south and east. Other troops will come west from Bali, and north from a new landing on the south coast. Twelfth infantry is assigned to First Battalion, and they've put me in charge. I'm now Lieutenant Colonel Hagen, boys."

The men cheer; a battalion is six hundred men and they are happy to have a familiar face leading them. "We'll move out tonight. Have your packs and bedrolls ready. Clean guns and boots. And try to get some rest between now and then. General Spoor will broadcast at 1500 hours. Make sure you're listening." Hagen dismisses them.

Sam catches Andre's nervous glance, and they rush to the harbor to see Dutch troop transports pull close enough to drop their ladders. Men disembark in chest-deep water, holding packs and Sten guns over their heads. Hundreds of men come ashore as other ships move closer and open their maws to disgorge Vickers light amphibious tanks, jeeps and trucks and supply vehicles of various sizes and utility. Finally, all of the equipment is unloaded onto the beach and rolls into the streets of Surabaya. Sam's chest expands. He is finally part of something big, something he can name. A battalion. An army. A mission.

Back at barracks, Sam turns on the radio. At precisely 3:00 p.m., General Spoor's voice floats on the airwaves, deep with confidence.

He tells them they are doing their duty to Holland, and to the generations of Dutch and Indo who have built the colony. Sam pictures Spoor's straight back and the black sunglasses he wears as a nod to MacArthur's genius.

"You are not advancing to bring war to this country, but to restore peace."

And the broadcast is over. The men quietly fold underwear and socks, extra shirts and mosquito nets, and stuff their packs. Sam applies cream to the angry rash flaming behind his knees and in the crooks of his elbows, gently peels the dead skin from his toes and heels and applies fresh ointment and bandages. He packs his rations, a few toiletries, wraps his bedroll and lays down fully clothed on the bare canvas of the cot to wait. Seconds later he leaps up, checks that he's packed the Whitfield ointment. He'll die without the Whitfield.

At midnight, July 21, Sam shoulders his pack and joins Darma and Andre, Raj and Freddy, Visser and Bart and the rest of the squad as they say goodbye to the city. They join hundreds of others climbing into trucks and armored vehicles, hundreds more marching on foot. Air support drones overhead, while on the Java Sea, ships carry more troops and equipment to ports on the far eastern side of the island. The air is electric with intent. The precision and coordination, the number of men and the size of the tanks, the convoy of support vehicles — it all gives Sam a sense of imminent change, for him, for Amir struggling under the thumb of the rebels, for the batik workers in their poverty and for young Wira's future. At this moment anything is possible, his actions will solve something and move him out of his uncertainty. They have a cause. It's what he needs to believe even as his gut churns.

Sam's squad is ordered into an overvalwagen assault vehicle, climbing in through the steel door and stuffing packs into the space between the double plated sides. They stand six a side, the armored walls coming barely to their chests. Mertens is squad commander again and he climbs slowly into the box, heaving his stump foot forward as he ducks into the plated compartment up front. He takes Darma with him to drive and handle the machine gun protruding from a small port where a windshield would otherwise be.

They drive through streets lined with civilians woken by the noise of engines and voices and boots. Dutch, Indo, Chinese, Arab — all those who'd been driven by the rebels from their homes in the interior to port towns controlled by the Dutch — they wave and they cheer. Children run alongside the trucks, bold teenagers grabbing on to the bumpers as if to hitch a ride. Andre reaches down the steel side of the overvalwagen and grasps the hand of a small boy, lifting him in one motion so he lands in the middle of the men. His huge brown eyes are stunned for a moment, and then he is climbing up Andre's torso to peer out and wave at his friends. Andre laughs and in another single motion sets the boy back down to run among them.

"Reminds me of my little brother," he says and smiles at the pack of boys fading into the stretch of army behind them.

A prop plane drones close overhead and soon leaflets drop into the outstretched hands of the locals. Sam catches one. It tells the people to remain calm, asks them to refrain from retaliation, Spoor's signature looping across the bottom. The convoy heads south out of Surabaya on the narrow road toward Lawang, the same road Sam's squad had traveled on reconnaissance two weeks earlier. It is lined by trees and their battalion stretches round curves ahead and behind, men and tanks, trucks and jeeps as far as Sam can see. It begins to rain.

"Dry season," Raj snorts.

And it doesn't let up though sunrise tries to pierce through the dark pillars of clouds. The volcanic dirt of the road quickly becomes slick, slowing the convoy as the mud pulls at truck tires. Tank tracks spin a little deeper. The road is flanked by jungle, the tips of red tile roofs piercing through leaves and branches, deserted walking trails from distant rice paddies disappearing into the village. Clutches of large trees felled across the road are checked for mines, a dozer piling the trees on the side of the road like pickup sticks.

"Hope it's all that easy," Andre says.

"Don't count on it." Mertens's head pops up again, like a trophy mount on the truck.

A few more miles and they are split up, Sam's squad with Hagen's battalion heading south where forests open into rubber plantations and rice paddies backdropped by volcanic mountains. Peasants in the sawahs and on the slopes rise from their early morning work to peer at the convoy from under wide-brimmed hats. In the misting rain they quickly gather their baskets and slog hard through the mud sucking at their feet until they reach solid ground where their children wait. One last look and they run into the distance.

"We're not after them," Andre says.

"Might not be workers at all." Raj pipes up. He's been silent since they left, huddled in a corner with his rain poncho over his head. "They could be informants. Pemuda. You have to assume they all want to kill you."

Andre rolls his eyes. "Yeah, those little kids are gonna kill us. With what? Their crayons?"

A few of the men laugh. Raj shrugs and ducks back under his poncho.

It rains harder, the convoy creeping ahead on slick roads, a tank running in a field alongside the road suddenly hung up on the camouflaged stumps of sawed-off trees, a poor man's tank trap. The driver manages to seesaw the machine out just as three fighter jets roar overhead flying toward the city. A volley of anti-aircraft fire erupts from five hundred meters away. Sam ducks down in the overvalwagen while those walking dive into ditches. He peers east into a field of tea trees, a light infantry tank careening toward the spot and firing until the rebel's tripod crumbles, burying the rebels and their gun in the same pit in which they hid. White-knuckled, Sam shoulders his Sten, crouching again in the safety of the truck's armor. They push on.

The downpour has become a fine drizzle, the midday sun at last breaking to sparkle across the wet valley. He can't escape how beautiful it is. Except for his mission here. Except for the absence of life on the road. Village after village, they arrive to find the streets are deserted, only chickens left to squawk their discontent, the odd pig rooting in a garden it would otherwise be kept from. He grips his rifle closer, watching for movement in the dark recesses inside the windows of the huts, sensing the people waiting somewhere nearby. They'd expected a welcome from Chinese and Arab shop owners who'd stayed despite constant harassment from the rebels. But no one greets them. Only dogs running out from between huts to wag rope-like tails, a beggar's look in their eyes.

His shoulders aching with tension, Sam imagines opaque faces, whispers behind him, machine guns in the branches of trees. But the day unfolds with little resistance, the men grumbling; they have nothing to shoot at, no target on which to unload their anxiety. Daylight recedes again, the sun crashing behind the mountains on the west side of the valley so that darkness drops like a guillotine over the convoy.

A familiar road; they are near the plantation where Sam met Amir. All are quiet as they choke down rations, throw bedrolls on the ground and fish mosquito nets out of their packs. Just as Sam is about to release his feet from the stench of his boots, Commander Hagen arrives. The men jump up to salute.

"It's okay, boys," Hagen says, pushing his cap back to scratch at his forehead. "Been a long day, but Raj tells me he doesn't trust the plopper here. That we should make sure the rebels haven't gotten to him. Where is Raj?"

Raj groans from where he's already wrapped in his bedroll.

"He's sick," Andre says.

"Sir, I'll lead." Sam swallows the quaking in his voice. "I actually spoke with the man. Seemed like a good enough fellow."

Raj snorts and Hagen gives Sam a long look. "Okay. Be careful. Your friend might have had his mind changed. Take a radio. If there's trouble, we'll have reinforcements there in minutes."

Darma and Andre throw longing looks at their bedrolls, grumbling as they gear up with the rest of the squad, fixing bayonets a little tighter to rifles, checking belts for extra ammunition and pineapple grenades. Sam nods to the soldiers on watch, breathes the night air, exhaling hard to rid his stomach of its nervous fluttering. He leads the men toward the plantation, hugging the trees at the side of the road for cover, trying to pierce the black night with his eyes. His senses rage; the snap of twigs, the thick smell of damp moss as he ducks branches, steps over stones, crosses puddles. At the edge of the yard, he signals the men close.

"You four scout the perimeter, you the warehouse and shed." Taking charge clears his head. "Darma, Andre, come with me. The rest, spread out around the house and cover us. Godverdomme! Put out the cigarettes. Your head's a bloody target."

They move out, holding their Stens at the ready, the safeties unlatched long ago. Sam's group runs first to the edge of the warehouse and then to the house. He creeps up the verandah steps to the edge of a lit window, motioning Darma to the door and Andre to another brightened window near the back of the house.

Sliding his head round the edge, Sam peers through the curtained window with one eye. It's a dining room. Simple. Quiet. Flowers spout from a vase set on a lace doily in the middle of a teak table surrounded by six bamboo-laced chairs. Delft china is displayed on a side cupboard. With a start, he realizes a woman looks toward him from the sitting room beyond but doesn't see him. She is a tiny, fair-skinned Indo, her sarong cinched tight at the waist, a bright kebaya closed to the throat, hair piled on her head. She picks up a book on the end table and sits to read. Maybe it's Amir's wife. He wonders absurdly if her Mixmaster is working.

Just as he's about to go to the door, a scream flies out the open window, boots thundering as Andre rushes past Sam toward the verandah, stopping short at the door, a gun from inside pointed at his temple.

"Amir," Sam says, voice low. "Don't shoot him. It's me." He steps into the doorway, dimly lit from inside by a kerosene lamp.

"I thought you were done here." Amir's voice is hard as he waves his pistol at Andre.

"Just put down your weapon," Sam says slowly. "There's a squad of men out there and they won't think twice about shooting you. Amir, please."

Amir glances into the darkness and slowly lowers the pistol, silver hair haloing around his head.

"Okay. That's good." His fucking eye won't stop twitching, distorting Amir's face. He clenches his rifle as Andre slowly moves to the bottom of the stairs. "We're just here to make sure the rebels haven't been threatening you."

Amir only looks at him. Sam inches up the stairs to stand between Amir and the men in the yard. The woman from the window stands behind him still holding her book and staring at Sam. Beside her is a girl, probably eighteen, dark and beautiful, her face startled, but there is curiosity in her deep brown eyes. It is the girl he'd seen on the bicycle.

Sam raises his eyebrows. "Hallo!"

She ducks her head but regards him with a curious expression. "Hallo," she says quietly, her voice a soft slow chime.

Amir's face clouds.

"I'm sorry," Sam stumbles. "I didn't mean any disrespect."

Amir motions the women away with a hand behind his back. "Sari, go."

She doesn't move.

Sari. He has the absurd wish to impress the girl. "There's an action in progress and we just came to tell you to sit tight and wait." He speaks loudly, making it up as he goes. "When we have the area cleared, we'll station a patrol nearby to protect the plantation. And your family."

"Yes, well, your friend showed me last time the nature of the Dutch concern."

"You won't have to deal with him again. It'll just be a few men in an outpost nearby. You can carry on with the farm as usual."

"Except you will take what I produce to fund your war and leave my family in poverty." He looks directly at Sam. "You come to my joglo to tell me that I will again be forced to work for someone else. And I'm supposed to thank you for this?"

"Father," Sari says, shaking her head as if in apology to Sam.

Behind her, a blue plate hangs on one wall, an intricately carved screen against another, bamboo and teak accenting the room. A large doorway to the right is hung with sheer curtains and behind the curtains a bed on a dark wood frame. It is a Javanese home accented by Dutch. He's supposed to be here making things better. What the hell is he doing tonight? He almost buckles with the not knowing.

"For now, you just have to trust me. My name is Sam."

Amir gives him a long look, skewering Sam to the spot with a gaze that threatens to strip back his skin and reveal his uncertainty. The man nods, and quietly closes the door in Sam's face.

"All clear," Sam calls into the darkness. As he moves away the curtain at the window falls back into place, the outline of the girl just beyond.

The squad heads back to where the rest of the battalion sleeps. In the pitch, Sam sees the red cigarette dots of the soldiers on watch, a beacon to all comers. He finds Hagen and tells him Amir will give them no problems, though his eye twitches as he says it, his heart not as sure as his head wants him to be.

Finally he can crawl into his bedroll beside Darma and Andre and the rest of the squad. His exhaustion is sudden and complete, his bones melting as he lowers himself to the ground, his arms lacking the energy to get the mosquito net properly round his head and shoulders. He lays there with his eyes closed, but behind the lids he sees the girl. Sari. Sam wonders what her name means, pictures the wisps of hair dancing round her quiet face, imagines her brilliant dark eyes looking into his, dreams of her arms reaching for him.

He wakes to shouting and the smell of smoke. Disoriented, he sees the sun throw a pink halo round the distant volcano, the valley still bathed in its dark shadow. More shouting and Sam jumps up, kicks out of his bedroll and pulls on his boots. All around him the men drag themselves from sleep and pick up their rifles. Smoke hangs in the air, in the east an orange glow.

"Oh Christ, no." He starts to run.

"Wait." Andre grabs his arm. Darma and the rest of the squad arrive at the edge of the road.

Sam charges to where Commander Hagen is pointing and giving orders. "What's happening?"

"The bastards are burning them out."

"Because we were there last night?"

"Because we're staying."

"Jesus." He swallows hard. "Permission to take the squad and see if we can help, sir."

"Go. Watch out for them. It might be a trap." Hagen grabs Sam's shoulder. "You can't let it be personal, son. He might have torched it himself for all we know."

Sam nods, running to where the squad stands waiting. The men run, barely taking precautions against ambush, pulling up short as they come out of the trees and into the yard. They stare in awe. Everything is in flames. The smell of scorched wood and burnt coffee singes their noses, and in the distance, coffee trees burn like matchsticks, the entire plantation ablaze, dancing orange and red against the pink sunrise. It is glorious and heart-wrenching, beautiful and brutal.

Sam shouts at the others to cover him and runs bent double toward the house. Its windows are shattered, licks of flame lashing out. The back half of the house is already destroyed, the second story threatening to collapse on the rest. Anyone inside is long dead; Amir, his wife. Sam can do nothing but watch, a terrible awe constricting his throat. Sari.

Fifty men from the battalion arrive to dig trenches around one warehouse and a shed, hoping to stop the fire's spread and salvage something. A Bren gun carrier turns off the road and wheels into the yard adjacent to the house. The mounted machine gun lurches back and forth, the gunner searching for targets as he covers the troops working in the yard. Sam whirls around as the house collapses on itself with a whoosh of flame and heat he can feel from thirty meters away. The sound explodes in his ears, simultaneous with another behind him.

He turns again to see the carrier toppled forward, its machine gun pushed into the dirt. Men run to pull the gunner and driver from the wreckage, others crouched or splayed on the ground, Stens ready. Medics rush in with a stretcher for one man as the other sits up dazed, shaking the cotton from his ears. They are taken away to the hospital unit at the rear of the column.

The yard was mined.

Sam is stunned, pictures Amir's shop, frantically trying to recall the tools on the walls, the wire looped over a nail, what the man might have used. Amir did this?

"Nothing more to be done here," Commander Hagen hollers. "Sixth, you'll stay here to clean up. We'll set up a post to control this area. You'll get full orders and logistics later." He looks at Sam.

"I thought . . ." What did Sam think? That Amir gave a shit because Sam tried to be friends?

Hagen ignores him. "Twelfth and fourteenth, fan out and head south around the plantation. Watch for mines or ploppers. Meet the convoy back at the road" — he checks his map — "four kilometers south. Then we head to Malang."

They skirt the burnt fields to walk in the taller grasses, fanned out with a few feet between each of them to create a human net. Sam watches for ambush from the trees adjacent, searches the ground before each step. Halfway round the scorched area, Darma yelps and stares at the ground. Sam swims through the grass, pushing Darma aside to see the old woman who sorted the coffee beans and the old man who turned them with his rake. They lay side by side, their white sarongs muddied and askew, throats expertly slit so only a ribbon of blood trails down the sides of their necks. Their eyes are wide open with horror. Andre and Raj arrive.

"What the hell?" Andre's question hangs in the air.

"Rebels must have thought they were on our side," Raj says, staring at the gruesome scene.

"Maybe they were." Sam kneels beside the bodies, shuddering as he gently runs his hand down over their faces to close their eyes, crosses their limp arms over their chests. His own aches. Are these two dead because they trusted Amir? Or because Amir trusted Sam? Goddammit.

"Let's go," he says.

Andre shoulders his rifle and trudges back to where the others wait. Darma continues to stand over the bodies, the rope of muscle in his throat taut. "They should be buried."

Raj nods, surprising Sam, who looks to a distant road where the convoy moves away from them. "We don't have time," he says quietly, then steels his voice. "Now. Let's go."

Raj throws him a grateful look, as though for once Raj has been spared the need to be an asshole, as though perhaps they are a little more alike now. Jesus. Sam looks down at his boots and moves out with the rest, scouring the grasses with a new intensity. But he has no idea what he's looking for. Raj tells him peasant workers might have done this. Mertens tells him to watch out for barely clothed men with spears. He should know the enemy by the evil in his eyes, but he hadn't seen that in Amir.

They find no one. Whoever torched the plantation and killed the old couple have somehow melted into the landscape. The squad catches up with the rest of the convoy and they jump into the over-valwagen and head south again, jittery now with the thought of the jagos watching them from the trees.

Darma sits beside Sam.

"Reminded me of my grandparents," Darma says.

"I'm sorry. Someone will find them. Bury them."

Darma is silent for a long time.

"What happened?" Sam asks.

"Dad was KNIL. Once they'd occupied the country, the Japanese let him go with all the other native soldiers. But my father didn't trust the Japanese and their talk of Indonesian autonomy. He was caught trying to sabotage one of their ammunition sheds. They killed him. And came after us."

"Jesus."

"We were all in that camp, watched my grandparents fade to ghosts. My mother, well, she did what she had to do to keep us alive."

Darma tells Sam of his once beautiful mother, ordered to provide "comfort" to the Japanese camp commander. The extra food she managed to get as a result saved her children. Just before British troops liberated the camp, the commander killed himself, but not before shredding her face with a knife, telling Darma's mother that he loved her and couldn't bear the thought of sharing her with the leaders of the next occupying force who would undoubtedly behave as badly as he. But they hadn't. A British medic put her face back together as best he could.

"And she was grateful. Even after all of that," Darma says quietly. "I don't think I'm as brave as my mother."

Sam can't think of one thing to say.

CHAPTER 6

Give a Thing a Name

JULY 1947

THE CLOUDS DISSIPATE AS THEY push on toward Malang, the air cooling as they climb higher into the mountains where orchards and small flower gardens create a patchwork of color. Sam enjoys a moment of bliss at the sweet crunch of an apple's dark red skin, streaks of pink bleeding white into the flesh. He's brought back by the howl of three Dutch fighters, their machine guns opening fire on targets on the west side of the city, the flak from anti-aircraft guns ricocheting back. Tossing his apple core, he holds his ears as the fighters circle back and buzz the convoy.

"We're taking out the airport and some warehouses held by the rebels." Mertens tells them. "Ploppers torched the rest themselves."

Flowers and apples give way to destruction. Malang smolders, its people like ghosts wandering through a surreal scene. Nuns mill about the smoking remains of a large two-story convent, their faces blank with despair and fear while small children peer at the convoy from behind the sisters' black skirts. Sam feels like part of a strange parade. The town hall is completely destroyed and the high school still burns. Further down the street, an elderly Chinese man sorts through what remains of his tobacco shop. Stopping to run his hands through thin black hair, the man looks up at the advancing troops in bewilderment — they have come too late.

"Every time, it's the Chinese."

"Because they run the whole economy like it's their own," Darma snorts.

The Chinese work as middlemen with a reputation for buying low and inflating the price on resale, merchants always on the hustle. Sam has to admit it jangles his nerves. Yet the Chinese have trusted the Dutch to restore order, have stayed despite terrible suffering at the hands of the Japanese. Apparently they suffer still.

Beyond the sad skyline stands a tower topped with a huge metal horn. It is an air-raid warning system, one of many all over Java built by the Japanese. It has no purpose now, nothing and no one left to protect. The rebels torched the plantations and now the cities — Sam wonders if this self-destruction is happening across Java and the other islands, wherever Dutch troops advance. He'd watched the helmeted goose steps of the Nazis through Heibloem and could never have imagined his family and neighbors burning everything in advance of the Germans.

They pass the grand entrance of the Tugu Hotel, its marble pillars scrawled with graffiti: *We hate the Dutch* and *Merdeka: freedom or death*. In a quiet street, children play in the dirt in front of a clapboard and bamboo house, a stinking gutter nearby carrying away both the waste of their lives and the monsoon floods when they come. Opposite the children's home are an abandoned tennis court and open-air clubhouse where an elderly Dutchman sits on a piano stool looking into the distance, perhaps into some future he can't quite see, or maybe at a past he can't believe is gone.

At the center of town, the battalion is called together. Commander Hagen tells them they will be dispersed, squads and platoons sent in various directions to rebuild infrastructure and to guard any assets claimed in the advance. A regional control center will be set up in Malang from which Hagen will run the field operations.

"Remember, this is about law and order, about keeping the rebels under control so the people out here can live their lives without harassment and fear," Hagen says. "But it's also about protecting our assets. So if they blow a road or a bridge, we fix it. And we don't give back a goddamned inch of what we've got. Spoor wants to press on to Yogya and get rid of Sukarno and his bunch. Decapitate the movement as it were. This thing could be over in a week. But the politicians back home think securing the assets is enough. So . . ." His pause is full with what he cannot say, his mouth pinched. "I guess it has to be enough."

Sam's squad is sent east of Malang as part of a platoon of thirty men, a steep climb taking them past small farm huts hugging the road, their back doors hanging absurdly over the mountain prec- ipice below. They descend again into lush lowlands, green crops glistening into the distance as a slow double line of peasant traffic comes and goes on the rutted dirt road. Women walk single file, some so poor from endless war they wear cornsacks for sarongs, shoulders straight in spite of the great packages of goods balanced on their heads. In the sawah next to the road, peasants stoop to thin the precise rows of fresh green rice shoots growing alongside paddies almost ready to harvest. Sam is filled with a sudden ache to go home. He means nothing to this ancient culture molded by millions of plantings and rains and harvests, by their belief in the power of the natural world.

"It's like they've been standing there for a thousand years," Sam says. "As though whatever we've done before, what we're doing now makes no difference at all."

"Maybe it doesn't," Darma says quietly.

They follow a muddy tributary of the Brantas River. It boils round giant boulders, disappearing further downstream into a swamp edged by brilliant green bamboo thickets, dropping suddenly into a crevasse it has carved into the volcanic loam. Mertens drives ahead in his jeep, the trail narrowing until they are forced to move single file down the road, a minesweeper pushing ahead. But there is nothing to find. Nearing the village of Ngadipuro, they find the bridge into it obliterated, not a rebel in sight, the village quiet on the other side.

A few men patrol as the others hunker down to rest and eat and get their bearings. Sam waits with Andre and Darma, Raj and Bart and Freddy, stretching out on the riverbank, soaking blistered feet in the cool water. Mertens finds them there, pulls off his oversized shoe and unwraps the bandages from his stump-like foot before lowering it into the water. He closes his eyes and a smile cracks across his broad face.

"They're sending in materials for a Bailey," he says after a minute. "Should be here first thing tomorrow. It'll take two, three days to put together."

"Will it make a difference?" Sam asks.

"Word is Van Mook is negotiating a ceasefire and we'll be restricted to the areas we already hold," Mertens says. "That village is friendly. We have to build the bridge and push a little further or those people will be left to the jago."

Three women emerge from the trees across the river and downstream, setting down their baskets and plunging their laundry into the river. Naked children splash beside them, ignoring the remains of the toppled bridge, chunks of its wood trellis bobbing in the water around them, the acrid smell of explosives weighing down air drenched in heat.

Jago: Mertens used the word. Sam won't. Saying it out loud will somehow mean he believes in Raj's story of the invincibility of the pemuda, their lust for death by freedom fight. Give a thing a name and it has potential. Say it out loud, you make it real.

"Bridge is here," Raj shouts in the morning, prodding the squad out of their bedrolls, everyone expected to work until the construction is finished.

They are camped along the riverbank and fifty meters off the road. One of the villagers has been persuaded to take Mertens across in a shallow-bottomed boat to negotiate for someone to cook for them and do their laundry. The young woman who arrives is hunched into her worn and loose fitting kebaya, shrinking back when some of the men edge too close, avoiding their gaze as she slops porridge into their camp bowls and pours dirt-black coffee into the tin mugs they hold out to her. The powdered milk disappears into the murky depths without a trace. Sam wonders if he dares to drink the brew, thoughts of the dysentery he's finally conquered still fresh in his mind.

"Selamat pagi," Darma says quietly, taking a small banana from a basket.

Beside him, Andre nudges Darma. "What did you say?"

"Just good morning." Darma grins at him.

"Selamat pagi," Andre says awkwardly, holding his mug down to the girl who is half his height. His cup shakes a little as she pours, and she looks up at him a moment, her face relaxing into a smile that makes her eyes dance. She moves on to the next bowl, the next mug.

"Holy shit, she's beautiful." Andre sits on the running board of Mertens's jeep to eat. "I wonder what her name is."

Raj bursts out laughing. "Likely married off to some old man with a few goats."

"Jesus, you're an asshole."

"Yeah, well, at least I'm not looking for love in the Javanese jungle."

"Shut up, Raj." Andre is on his feet and moving toward Raj.

"Okay, settle down," Sam sighs and stands between them, facing Andre. "You're right, she has a great smile. And Raj is an asshole." He hears a snort behind him. "Now can we just have our coffee? It's going to be a long day."

The Bailey bridge helped the Allies win the war in Europe, the structures quickly built over crossings destroyed by the retreating Germans. They might be ingenious, but Sam's afraid his back will break from the work of building one. Quarter-ton welded trusses, sledgehammers to slam the pins home, steel connectors and four-meter wooden slats for the driving surface. As each section is completed, a small dozer pushes it toward the other side of the river, the nose pointing upward and slowly reaching across open water. The villagers of Ngadipuro watch silently from the other side, and Sam can't tell if this feels to them like rescue or invasion.

They break for lunch. Sam sinks to the ground with a bowl of bakso ayam, soup containing chunks of pepper and bits of yellow-looking meat they're told is chicken. A banana leaf filled with steamed rice completes the meal. Andre sits beside him, glancing at the girl often, sometimes staring as he wolfs down his food. He heaves himself up to ask her for more.

Sam laughs. "Wonder how much he'll have to eat before he gets up the nerve to talk to her."

Beside him, Darma doesn't respond. He's leaned back in the grass, helmet pushed back and mouth gaping. Sam watches him a moment. Asleep, Darma's features seem even more refined, cheekbones high, nose long and slim like the rest of him. Even his hands are slender with tapered fingers and finely shaped fingernails rimmed with dirt. Those hands. Sam feels suddenly and strangely protective.

Andre thumps down again beside him. "Wake him up." He points his broad chin at Darma. "I want him to ask her name."

"You know what they told us about fraternizing."

"Yeah, whatever. You can hardly tell she's native."

How much native is too much?

Mertens hollers. They groan and go back to building the bridge, straining, pounding, pushing. The roar of the dozer drowns out all sound. Sam holds a panel alongside Andre, hammers pounding in his ears, vibrations running through his straining biceps and rattling his body.

"Don't know what the hell the rush is," Andre huffs beside him.

Sam wonders the same. Just as he bears down on the iron bar to lift another panel into place, the world crashes into silence. Craning to see, he watches the dozer driver fall forward over the steering wheel, slowly tumbling sideways off his seat and to the ground, rolling down the riverbank into the water. Blood trails down his face from a hole in his forehead.

"Sniper!"

The panel Sam's holding tips as the men scramble, Andre pulling him away as he narrowly misses being crushed. The dozer at the end of the bridge erupts in an explosion, shrapnel whistling past Sam's head. He crouches beside one of the side panels for a moment. Holy shit. He ducks, runs behind Andre over the roadbed, jumps into the water, slips, splashes to shore. Sniper fire bursts in the air around him. A shriek just as his feet hit the bank and he dives for cover under Mertens's jeep parked there on the road.

Andre rolls in behind him. "Jesus. Holy. Fuck. How did that happen? How'd they rig the dozer?"

Sam's chest heaves. He fumbles for his pistol, crawls forward to peer out. He'd taken his shirt off to work and stones dig into his ribs, his elbows. In the distance, rat-faced Freddy crawls away from the bridge, dragging his left leg. Mertens covers him, standing in the center of the road firing his rifle. Sam scans the trees above the river, the rocks along the bank. Nothing except the dozer driver's body bobbing face down, riding the slow current at the edge until it picks up speed in the middle. The noise subsides. Touching his forehead to the ground, Sam gulps hard. "Jesus, holy, fuck," he says quietly and looks at his friend.

Neither the sniper nor the body of the man he killed is found. An unexploded aircraft bomb had been strapped to the dozer, the sniper exploding it with his second shot. Freddy's leg was only grazed but he was hustled off to Visser, who has proven useless at almost everything, and so was given a little training and made camp medic. It seems an impossible thing to have happened right under their noses and they suddenly understand the rush to finish the bridge.

The number of men patrolling is doubled and Raj volunteers to cross the river and scout the village for rebels. Sam sees him haranguing the women who continue to beat their laundry on the rocks as Raj waves his arms, impatient with what he believes they are not telling him — that one of the villagers is the sniper, or the guy who rigged the bomb. Sam doesn't want to believe it, hates that he watches the locals more closely, looking for signs he doesn't know he'll recognize.

All the men are jumpy, impatient, with nowhere to unleash their nervous energy. Darma alone is completely civil, politely nodding his appreciation to a heavy woman who takes their stinking laundry and paddles it back to them under the watchful eyes of the patrol guards. Each day he thanks the babu for his food. They've learned her name is Bonita.

"Bonita." Andre says slowly, rolling it off his tongue like a prayer.

On the third day the nose of the bridge touches the other side and is secured. Mertens does a test run with his jeep and the men finally have something to cheer about. Someone starts singing the Dutch anthem and they are somber for a moment as they sing. A man lost his life for this bridge, for these people. They've done a good job. They should be proud. At the final words, Andre does a dance, leaping and flailing, splashing in the water before falling on his back to float there an instant as the men roar with laughter and smiles play around the mouths of the villagers. Sam watches Bonita's tight face open ever so slightly, a silent laugh shaking her ample breasts.

CHAPTER 7

Cash and Starvation

AUGUST 1947

"MERTENS INVITED THE VILLAGERS TO the party. Is he crazy?" Raj
paces the ground in front of Sam. "What if...?"

Sam turns to walk away and stops. Enough of this bullshit. He
can't stand what it's doing to the men, to him. He walks back to
within inches of Raj.

"If Hagen decides to leave us here, we're going to need those
villagers on our side." He looks directly into Raj's eyes and leans in
close. "So don't fuck this up."

Raj pulls back, a moment of bewilderment in his face. Quickly
recovering, he snorts as though Sam is an idiot, and stalks off. But
it's too late; Sam has seen the uncertainty, and in that hesitation,
maybe even a little fear. He has a brief flash of pleasure at this
unexpected weakness from Raj, followed quickly by a deep sense of
unease he can't quite explain.

He's quickly distracted by the excitement of the party, assem-
bling with the others on the riverbank just as a parade of villagers
appears on the other side of the bridge. Two men carry a freshly
slaughtered goat on a pole while women in bright kebaya hoist

assorted baskets of fruit and cones of colored rice called nasi tumpeng. Others arrive with clay bowls of incense and soon the air is choked with the mingled scents of jasmine and charred meat.

"Selamatan." Darma grins, looking at Sam. "A feast to safeguard the bridge."

The crowd parts to create a path for a wizened man who shuffles along on bowed legs. The old man wears a white tunic over black pants, the peci on his head fringed by snow-white hair. He flashes Sam a toothless grin from under a trimmed mustache and goes to stand beside Bonita. She puts a protective arm around the old man's shoulders and the other villagers smile with great affection.

"Bapak," Darma says, bowing his head slightly.

"Who is he?" Andre asks.

"Likely the dukun," Darma says. "A medicine man."

Sam snorts. "Really, Darma?"

"Really."

The old man holds up his hand and silence falls over the villagers. Some of the soldiers are confused, not about what is expected from the raised hand, but about how to respond; the old man is black as pitch and not even an officer. But Mertens raises his hand and smiles, and the men do the same until the sound of the trees and moving river overtakes their voices. The last to close his mouth is Freddy.

"What the fuck?" Freddy says and laughs. Raj frowns.

The dukun bows his head to say a few words, his voice cracked with age, and the villagers murmur a response. After a momentary silence, the man sweeps his hand toward the bridge and village and smiles widely, his voice strong in some kind of declaration. Or dedication. The villagers applaud. The soldiers look at one another an instant and erupt into shouts of approval, raising their fists high. The party is on.

Bonita and two other women float through, passing out the nasi tumpeng and portions of meat. Slowly, the village men move in from the edge of the circle to join Darma and the other Indo soldiers, their shared language creating an uneasy alliance. The women chat at the water's edge, the younger girls glancing quickly at the men and then away. Before long, the beer and whiskey flow, a whiff of opium hanging in the air.

As the sun sinks, Sam watches Andre take a deep breath, grind his cigarette into the ground and walk to where Bonita stands. Andre finally speaks, waving his bottle in the air as he talks with his hands. This raw display is very un-Javanese, likely rude in some inexplicable way, but Bonita doesn't seem to mind. She laughs discreetly and finally reaches up to take his waving hand in her own. They stand beside each other, pretending a quiet contemplation of the water. Sam sees a smile spread across Andre's face as the sun disappears and darkness drops.

Everyone moves in close as kerosene lanterns are lit. The beer makes Sam's world tilt a little, and he catches himself grinning stupidly through a fog of happiness. He hasn't felt this good in a long time. Across the crowd a familiar form swims into focus. She is tiny, hair piled high on her head, the curve of her neck the same as when she read her book in the plantation house. Amir's wife. He makes his way toward where she stands with a group of women.

"Permissi?" he says quietly, hoping he doesn't sound drunk. She jumps and looks at him warily. The other women fade back. "It's okay. I recognized you from before, at the plantation."

"Yes." Her dark eyes glitter in the light of the lantern. "I am Fatil." She turns and clambers up the riverbank to the road.

"Wait."

She stops and turns back. "What do you want with us?" she says in perfect Dutch.

"I, I don't want anything," he stutters. "I saw the fire. I thought you might all be dead."

"Well, you can see I am alive."

"And Amir?"

"He is not here." It could be Javanese for dead, or simply a fact of his absence. Sam doesn't want to press. "But Sari is here. Come."

He is surprised by the sudden weakness in his bones. He throws his beer into the bush, takes a last puff of his smoke and follows her. From the corner of his eye, he registers Freddy watching from the edge of the party. Sam stumbles behind Fatil as they make their way between two rows of bamboo-walled houses, the narrow dirt path lit by the light flickering from their windows. A baby cries. A dog barks somewhere close by. Wira and his grandfather flit through Sam's mind. A sudden terror. He flips the cover off his pistol holster, wondering if he can see straight enough.

Fatil turns and shakes her head impatiently. "You are safe."

At the far end of the village they come to a larger house, its roof tiled, a verandah wrapped round and dotted with containers overflowing with flowers. He almost trips over a small basket containing bits of rice and red pepper, a square of batik, a wilting flower. These offerings are everywhere, in the doorways of shops and homes, on the handlebars of becaks. Darma told him they're offerings to the gods. Hindu traditions amongst the Muslims, Buddhist amongst the Christians. One can never be too careful, Darma said and laughed.

The dukun is whittling in a chair on the porch. He looks at Sam with mild surprise.

"Bapak." The word is awkward on Sam's lips as he dips his head and climbs the steps.

Fatil ushers Sam into the house, motioning him toward a chair in the sitting room before disappearing to the back of the house. He stays in the doorway, sweat gathering under his arms and trickling down his back. A small statue of a fat-bellied man with an elephant head stands in the corner by the door, its neck draped by a garland of fake orange flowers, its trunk resting in a small bowl it holds on bent knees.

"Ganesha," Sari says from a doorway off the sitting room. "Guardian of entrances, and remover of obstacles."

"Should I be worried?" He hopes she can't hear the tremor in his voice.

"No. He also presides over knowledge. So I don't think he'd object to us talking."

"Hmm . . . not sure what you might learn from me. But I've already learned something so we should be okay."

Her face opens right up when she laughs. She is as beautiful as Sam remembers. But her left foot and lower leg are bandaged, fiery red blisters visible at the edges, and she walks with difficulty to an armchair. He follows to sit across from her. He doesn't want to stare, focusing instead on the dip in her chin where a small scar extends to her lip and becomes a fine white line to her nose. She has a small pink mole on her neck where her breastbone disappears into a dark kebaya. He waits, not sure if there is a custom for introductions, if he should shake her lovely hand with his sweaty palm.

"Sam," she says, and laughs as his eyes widen. "You introduced yourself to my father. He was very rude to you."

"Well, it wasn't the best of circumstances." He rushes on, "I'm sorry about the fire. I thought . . ."

"Yes, we lost everything." Her eyes mist for a moment. "We came here that night. Ngadipuro is my mother's village."

"You were injured," he says, stupidly waving at her leg. "Are you all right?"

"The dukun has done what he can. I will be fine."

"And your father, Amir?"

"He is not here."

The same answer, but Sam won't ask. Relief sweeps into his lungs. Amir wouldn't have caused his family this pain. Sam wasn't wrong about Amir.

Fatil comes back with tea and Sam jumps up. "Sit, sit," she says impatiently and takes the chair across from him, pouring tea and handing him a cup. "Now, you have built your bridge . . ." She draws herself tall. "We need a medical clinic in the village."

Sari starts to interject, but her mother rushes on.

"The dukun can do much, but not all. We need western medicine for the things he doesn't understand. And Sari is a nurse. She can help."

He's stunned, suddenly convinced this tiny woman might wring his neck if she doesn't get the answer she wants. "I don't have any authority," he falters.

"My mother is very blunt. I apologize," Sari says quickly. "The children here suffer a great deal. Malaria, beriberi, infections. If your medic could help?" She leaves the question hanging.

"And they are too weak from hunger to fight disease," Fatil adds, her voice low and hard. "Because of your blockade."

He looks at her, incredulous. Fruit hangs from the trees in this country, rice and beans everywhere.

"Rice was our currency. Good currency and always available. Now it's sold only on the black market, only to the highest bidder. And the children go hungry." She shakes her head.

"Maybe once we've secured the area," he murmurs. "Set up our post here. But I just don't know." God, he sounds like a schoolboy.

She snorts. "You Dutch, you bring cash and starvation all in the same wallet."

"Mother," Sari says curtly and sighs as her mother walks out of the room. She turns to Sam, smiling as if joining him in a conspiracy. "She gets upset. The women ask too much of her. They all want something. Equity with their husbands, a ban on child marriage, to hold political office. My mother thinks none of these things will matter if we are not healthy and educated."

"And what do you think?"

"Does she look like someone to argue with?"

"I see your point."

"Never mind. It's only the clinic we ask your help with, not the entire war." She laughs, the sound throaty and warm, and in that moment Sam wants desperately to give her what she asks for. "You can do this," Sari says, her eyes wide with hope. "I saw you with my father. You're not like the others."

He has no idea what she means and doesn't know how to ask.

Her mother returns with a houseboy at her side. "He will take you back to your party now. Please think about what we have asked."

He's been dismissed. He walks himself to the door. Sari gives him an encouraging smile, and as he passes her chair, she brushes his hand with hers, the touch tingling in his fingertips. He follows the boy outside, through the maze of village paths and back to the party. The locals have gone home and most of the soldiers are drunk, the happiest singing loudly, the unhappy complaining at equal volume of their mosquito-infested, rice-eating, miserable lives. Sam finds Andre in their tent, humming drunkenly before shouting into the air and falling back onto his cot, his snores soon filling the space. Sam pulls a net over his friend and crawls into his own bedroll.

The clinic is a good idea; it will connect them with the locals and help build trust. And Sari is here. He's not supposed to feel this way about a Javanese girl. He grabs himself under the blankets, forcing himself to think instead of Petra's flirty blue eyes. Before long he moans softly, realizing too late it is Sari he imagines, her impenetrably dark look, the way she cocks her head so the soft skin above her collarbone is exposed. *You're not like the others.* His cupped hand catches his efforts, his breath ragged as he cries confused and lonely tears.

The platoon is left stationed in Ngadipuro, thirty men charged with keeping the village safe from the rebels who lurk across the demarcation line only six kilometers to the northeast, a no-man's land stretching between. Andre doesn't hide his joy at having more time with Bonita. "If we have to be in this place, might as well be here." He gestures to the jungle and the village as though they are a palace.

Sam is kept from thinking about Sari by more immediate needs. The men build a defense post in a bluff high on the riverbank and accessed by a steep bamboo ladder. From it they can see both the bridge and the village perimeter strung with barbed wire, a gateway across the entrance road. Access from the far side of the bridge is controlled by a sandbagged roadblock. They modify a low tin shed near the post for barracks, sweltering at night on their cots until

Darma and Sam cut holes in the tin for circulation, covering these jagged windows with pieces from a mosquito net. Bonita cooks breakfast and supper for them, taking their laundry back with her to be washed.

Within a month, rebels ford the river at night to dynamite a section of the bridge. And the men rebuild. Two weeks later, the rebels attack again.

"So much for safeguarding," Sam says.

"We're alive." Darma shrugs.

Hagen sends more troops from Malang to help reinforce the perimeter and they bring with them two machine guns. The bridge secured and the rebels finally quiet, Mertens comes to roll call in so much pain he can barely walk. He beckons Raj to stand next to him. "Well, boys, I protected the colony. Fought the Japs. Spent two years in their camp that left me with this." He grimaces at his leg. "And now this lovely time with all of you. But they're finally letting me retire."

Sam's stomach clenches.

"We're set up here now," Mertens continues. "You just keep the bridge intact and these villagers safe until the rebel bastards get their asses kicked out of Yogya. Then you'll be going home too."

The men cheer.

"Colonel Hagen will be in Malang for the foreseeable future. And I've promoted Raj, so he's in charge now."

Everyone hears Darma gasp.

"Raj deserves this," Mertens says, a moment of pity in his eyes as he puts his hand on Raj's shoulder.

Raj flinches, doubt creasing his face. Or perhaps what Sam sees is dread.

Mertens straightens and slaps Raj on the back. "I know he'll do well by you. Besides, would you rather I put Andre in charge? The one who falls in love with the first pair of local tits he sees?"

The soldiers laugh and Andre turns first white and then brilliant red. Sam feels the heat in his own neck as his thoughts go to Sari.

"You boys need to understand something." Mertens voice falls so they lean toward it. "You might think the color of your skin doesn't matter, if you're on the same side, and in love." He rolls his eyes. "But it matters. Your mommas back home won't accept a native girl and consorting with you can get these people killed. They'll just as likely cut off your white balls as accept you as a son-in-law. So stay away from them." He shoots a withering look at Andre, who stands taller but cringes just the same. "You're good men. Use your head, keep it in your pants and shoot straight. You'll be just fine."

"But Raj?" Darma whispers.

Sam elbows the younger man to be quiet. He'd thought he might be put in charge after Colonel Hagen's attention. But Mertens is Indo, Raj too, and it is their country to reclaim. Mertens's confidence in Raj seems real, like he's giving Raj a chance to step up and be more, to make the right choices.

CHAPTER 8

The Hope Required for Courage

DE KRUIDENTEELT, LIMBURG PROVINCE,
THE NETHERLANDS
OCTOBER 1943

I DON'T KNOW IF MY choices came from courage like Anika's, or from being young and stupid. But I was suddenly pissed off at the swastika waving from the peak of our barn, Nazi jeeps and trucks parked outside like they owned the place. I had to see inside. Maybe I'd discover some vital thing about how the war was conducted, what distinguished a Nazi from a regular German from a Dutchman, what convinced them to hold themselves so straight and believe so completely that they would slaughter miners like pigs and whisk Jews away on trains. Courageous or stupid, I spied on them.

Climbing to the branch of an old oak, I looked inside the barn through the knot-holed wall, the Germans inside dimly lit by a bare bulb. Where I expected ramrod straight bodies and murderous faces, there were only men at ease, jackets off, shirt sleeves rolled up. An officer showed up, spinning knobs on a radio and listening to shouted orders coming through the static, and I had a moment to wonder who they were planning to bomb that day.

Suddenly the officer was looking straight up at me, and I was sliding to the bottom of the tree, jumping the last few feet and walking fast around the side of the barn. Running got people shot. It was a sign of guilt, as though lung-crushing fear had nothing to do with a person's inclination to flee. About to head across the small creek separating the outbuildings from the main yard, I felt a strong hand on my arm, another on the collar of my shirt.

"Well?" he said, the German sending a shiver of fear up my spine. "What's your name?"

"Sam." My voice squeaked like a girl.

He chuckled softly and let me go. "Konig," he said, holding out his hand. "Rudy Konig."

I didn't know what to do, stared dumbly at his hand.

"You're supposed to shake it."

The bone in his long fingers, the warmth of the fleshy part of the heel, the lines etched and dry in his palm; it could have been Dad's hand, or my uncle Matt's, or Father Demetrius's. A tremor passed through the officer's hand and I pulled away, didn't know what to think when I looked up and saw his open face, gentle eyes crinkling at the corners. He seemed more curious than anything, like we'd just met at a coffee shop and might want to have a chat about the weather or the crops. Normal.

"No school today?"

Why would he ask? No one went to school anymore. Not after the bishop's letter was read from pulpits across Holland, telling students they had no moral obligation to sign the declaration of allegiance demanded by Hitler. Most students refused to sign, the older ones heading underground, the clergy arrested.

"No, sir," I said, trying to keep the stammer out of my voice.

"It's Rudy. Come with me."

My stomach lurched. I'd seen too much. The radios. The maps. Jesus, I was an idiot. Stupid. Spying. Idiot.

"Come on." He waited, watching me so I forced my legs forward, barely able to feel my feet, surprised to look down and see them there. He went to a small bluff of trees and rummaged around the base of one. Looking for what? A rope? Christ, he was going to hang me. I scanned the trees for a place to hide, considered the distance. Maybe I'd run. Sweat trickled under my arms.

He drew out a tackle box and two rods. "You fish?"

My breath rushed out in a strangled laugh. I swallowed hard, mouth too dry to spit. "Sometimes."

He led me to the edge of the canal, carefully folded his tunic and laid it on the grass. His suspenders were snapped over his undershirt and he rolled his pant legs up to the knees before pulling off his boots and socks and squatting under a tree at the edge of the canal. A Luger was holstered at his hip. The warblers chattered above as he picked a leader from the box and tied it to the line, slipping on a hook before handing the rod to me. We were actually going to fish.

"I like fishing," Rudy said. He prepared his own rod and sat on the edge of the canal, feet dangling just above murky water blasted to sludge by bombs and grenades.

"You catch anything?"

"Ha! Nothing yet. Not likely to, I suppose."

"Then . . . ?"

"Doesn't matter. I just like it." He closed his eyes, smiling like it was the best moment of his life. "Just let your mind go fishing." His booming laugh echoed in the still air, and I ducked without thinking. "And what about you, my friend? What do you like to do?"

At first I didn't even know what he meant, like maybe I was missing one of the fractional differences in our languages. I said the first thing that came to my head.

"I like Jonge Wacht meetings." I wanted to suck the words back. The meetings were illegal, the Gleichschaltung shutting down any non-Nazi organizations, as if by signing a decree they could make me forget how Leader Groeneveld made me feel like anything was possible. I laughed a stupid sound. "I *liked* the meetings."

"What do you like about them?"

I told him how we learned wilderness survival, to chop wood and start a fire. But I didn't tell him I'd learned how to clean and shoot a rifle or that I was a crack shot. I didn't tell him the Jonge Wacht had taken over the empty chicken coops of Holland, the birds long ago sold or eaten with no grain to feed them after the Krauts took it to make their bread. Groups of boys across the country cleaned out the coops and made them into clubhouses, papering over the windows for nighttime meetings where we played table tennis and shot billiards, sang songs about Holland's history, told stories of the Boer War. The occasional prayer. The meetings were a bit of defiance, something to look forward to.

"I liked my leader," I finally said, and it felt right. "Strict, but kind too."

"The best leaders," Rudy said with a nod.

I couldn't help raising my eyebrows. The man worked for the Führer.

We sat jigging our lines, Rudy's eyes half closed under monstrous eyebrows, his long nose silhouetted as the sun slowly dropped and the evening birdsong faded. Light shadowed the field. It was kind of beautiful. Strange to be thinking such a thing with a Nazi officer beside me, but I felt lulled, safe somehow in the circle of his authority. The thought made me suddenly nervous; out of sight behind the barn, what I was doing might look like collaboration. Maybe it was a risk for Rudy too, fishing with a Dutch boy as though we were family. Or maybe Rudy was setting me up to get information about the resistance or to find out what the girls were up to. I thought of the notebooks hidden behind the headboard in my room since Leo's disappearance and grew light-headed. I wanted to run away, thought instead of Marie and Anika working with the underground, Leo's act of defiance despite the danger. This was my chance to do something to help Leo, my moment. I sat there with the fishing hook barely below the surface of the water, stomach fluttering, breath shallow, deciding. Looking hard at Rudy, I sat up straight.

"I was wondering, sir. Maybe you could help me."

"If you call me Rudy, maybe I can."

"Rudy, then." A deep breath. A picture of Leo at the mine, nodding at me, recognizing the courage it took for me to be there, to witness. I closed my eyes. "It's my brother." It rushed out in a whisper. "He disappeared after the strikes."

Rudy exhaled loudly. "A miner?" When I nodded, his chin dropped to his chest.

The words were out, hanging there in the still air. Rudy was silent. What had I done? I started to my feet.

"Sit down." It was a soft command. He looked up over the canal. "No idea where he is?" I shook my head.

"What's his name?"

It was a risk. If Leo was hiding, the Germans would know who they were looking for. But if Leo was already arrested, it was the only way Rudy could help. If Rudy planned to help. I watched him, looking for clues, but all I saw were suspenders and rolled pants, his bare feet dangling in the water like a child's.

"Leo. Leo Vandenberg."

He nodded, nothing more. Still as stone, my line in the water, I waited for the man to say something, took one quick breath and another. Jesus, I'd just trusted a Nazi with Leo's name. I looked at him, at his tunic and boots on the ground. The Luger. And suddenly I was back on the ridge at the mine, remembering the outstretched hands and wide eyes of dead miners. I jumped up and thrust the rod at him. He startled.

"I forgot," I stuttered. "I have to help my dad unload the wagon. At the shed."

"Go then," he sighed. "Go help your father."

I turned and heard his voice soft behind me.

"Be careful, son."

The hair stood on my neck. God knows I wanted to run, but I didn't. Instead my senses flamed, the autumn leaves brilliant against the dark gray-blue of the crumbling concrete along the canal, the smell of dank rot coming off the water, the crisp yelp of a dog in the distance. I chanced a look back. Rudy sat on the bank of the foul creek, jigging for fish that weren't there.

I never used Rudy's name, never told anyone about the German it was hard to hate the way I was supposed to. Soon the pull of war was stronger than my confusion. The job of survival was all-encompassing as winter wandered in, gray and wet, my hunger acute as I shivered about, stuffed into suffocating layers of clothes and bone chilled in a house without heating fuel.

We survived another occupied Christmas, subdued by the absence of gifts, of joy, of Leo, celebrating the birth of a savior who hadn't thought to save us. Anika tried to rally, baking banketstaaf though she had to improvise with so little spijs in the center that the pastry barely tasted of almond. We pretended it was wonderful, pretended at normalcy, relieved when the New Year rang in and we could finally return without guilt to our former gloom. The weather obliged with thick clouds and wet fog hanging just above the ground for days, the sky hammered bleak by war and winter.

On such a day I stood outside watching the dark silhouette of our horse, Netti, and caught sight of a lonely figure at the canal, staring into the distance as though waiting for someone. Maybe for me. I needed to hear something about Leo. Even an answer I didn't want was better than what I imagined at night, or the guilt when I woke with my legs splayed onto Leo's empty side of the bed. I stood a distance away, shocked at how small Rudy had become in only a few months, shoulders tented by his uniform, belt notched tight.

He stared into the frozen canal. "Come."

I jumped across a narrow bit. The edge of the ice cracked, splashing frigid water into my wooden shoes as I scrambled up the other side to stand beside Rudy where we'd fished on a late summer day.

"You've grown." He coughed hard.

I stayed quiet, senses alert, the hush of winter broken only by the murmur of voices from the barn, a rare moment of peace I couldn't appreciate. Maybe Rudy wasn't waiting for me after all.

"He's in rough shape," he said, so quietly I strained to hear. "He was sentenced to death."

Alive but going to die. I doubled over with a soft moan.

"Stop that. I had him sent to Lager 21." He looked into the distance. "He's safe for now."

A camp in central Germany. I wasn't sure how it might be safe. They were called reeducation camps, but everybody scoffed that starvation and back-breaking work would educate the politics out of anyone. I didn't understand what it meant for Leo and was too afraid to ask. I should have thanked the man, but the words stuck. Leo was alive — it was the news I wanted — but I couldn't help wondering what Rudy had saved Leo for. Rudy hummed to himself, staring into the distance again. I knew I'd been dismissed and this time he didn't stop me leaving.

"Who told you?" Dad was instantly suspicious.

"I can't say, but he's at Lager 21. That's all I know." There was no point telling him about Leo's health and the narrowly missed execution. Dad didn't want to believe I knew anything, let alone that his oldest son was in a camp.

"You can say. He's my son, dammit. You tell me now." His fist was under my chin.

"You're going to hit me?"

"Leave him alone." Marie stepped between us, thrusting her wide chin at Dad. "We don't need to know. It's more dangerous for all of us if we do."

"There's nothing we can do?" Anika's voice broke. We all knew the answer.

CHAPTER 9

Blinded by Loss

FEBRUARY 1944

DAD WAS ALL JITTERS, SMOKING more than he ate, clothes hanging ragged on his back. His rage had turned to silence — not a word about his increasingly frequent trips to Roermond except to say that because the city flanked the border, it was a front line of German defence and things were tense. But on a cold day in February he came home with a broken arm. A large crate had fallen on it while loading and I was expected to help on the next run. He tried to hide the worry in his voice, but I was terrified to think of venturing off the farm. Allied successes in North Africa and Italy had sent the Nazis into a frenzy, conscripting more of their own men and boys and prompting a wave of raids in occupied territories to supply their labor needs.

"They'll give you papers." Dad gestured to the German base at the barn. "It'll be fine."

"But Dad."

"We don't have a choice." His voice was soft, the change more alarming than if he'd shouted as he used to.

We wrapped ourselves against the cold morning. Marie pushed a thermos of weak coffee into my hands and when I cracked the reins over Netti's rump, for an instant there was no war; I was just on an outing with my dad. Maybe we would talk awhile, about important things for once. But we hadn't gone far before I realized I'd have to speak first.

"What are we hauling?"

"They don't tell me a goddamn thing," Dad snapped, holding his splinted arm close to his side. "Food. Fuel. Weapons. That's why they send me. Not as likely to be targeted."

"Targeted?"

"Allies. Resistance."

"Jesus."

"What? Did you think this was a milk run? I don't ask to do this."

"But they give you stuff." I was surprised by the hurt in his eye and wondered what else he kept to himself.

An early morning fog hovered over the road. Shrouded shapes rose out of the gloom ahead, people walking, refugees using the weather as cover to search for food and safety. An elderly man waved his cane as if we might stop and offer a ride, but when I slowed the horse, Dad shouted to move on. Slack-jawed, the man watched us pass.

"Stop for one, they'll all be climbing in," Dad said, shaking his head at my protest. "We play by the rules, we'll be all right. Krauts want us there for the noon train so we can't piss the time away."

I looked at Dad, at his constantly trembling hands which fumbled now to light a cigarette. I took it and did it for him, watching his profile, nose thin and hawkish, stubble a dark field against pale skin, eyes ringed in black. Haggard. I felt a sudden surge of pity for him, for all he'd lost and was still losing. Perhaps Dad could be forgiven his disregard for others.

Near Roermond, the road was flanked by a web of small lakes created by the mining of gravel from the banks of the Maas. The fog hovering over these puddles dissipated as the sun rose, and the refugees melted away leaving the whole area deserted. But there was an edge in the air, a sense of unseen faces, held breath, strangers hiding in vigilant watch of Netti's plodding progress. The silence was shattered by the approach of a German jeep, a platoon of marching soldiers behind, a checkpoint in the distance.

Dad tensed, his jaw working as he sucked on the last dregs of the cigarette before tossing the butt into the ditch. Sitting up straight, he breathed deep, coughed. "Just stay calm."

No time to ask questions. The jeep stopped in front of us, the driver and another soldier jumping out to stand on either side of the wagon and point semiautomatics at our heads, my hands frozen on the reins. Two more of them threw back the tarp covering the cart, swept mine detectors under the wagon, behind the wheels. Netti danced nervously and the men shouted and jumped back. I pulled hard to bring her to stand, felt Dad's broken arm rest against mine, grateful for its steady pressure as Netti's eyes rolled and her nostrils flared. I could barely breathe. Dad handed over the papers to a third soldier, who scanned the documents and came round to look at me. The bastard was younger than I was.

"Where'd he come from?" he snapped at Dad.

"My son." Dad gestured to his wrapped arm. "He's helping me."

I was scrutinized for so long it felt I must be guilty of something. The young soldier was confident, certain of his authority and of my weakness in the face of it. I recoiled a little and the soldier raised his eyebrow, a kind of challenge, though we both knew I would do what I was told. Something was written in a ledger and the papers were handed back to Dad.

"Soon as the arm is better, we'll expect him at the labor office."

"Of course," Dad said and shot me an encouraging look.

"Oh, yes," I stumbled, voice cracking. "Of course."

The young soldier sniffed, nodding at us to move on.

I barely twitched the reins and Netti pulled hard, her nerves matching mine as the cart lurched away from the checkpoint. The platoon marched past, eyes straight ahead as though we were invisible. Jesus, how quickly fear makes a man weak. At least I could have sat up straight and looked the bastard in the eye instead of cowering. But even Dad bent to the soldier, and I wondered at Dad's silence all those months. Maybe it wasn't about Leo at all.

"You made them nervous," he said quietly.

"They're the ones with the guns."

"Yes, but they like everything to go exactly as planned. You are not part of the plan."

"What plan?"

"Just drive."

We crossed one damaged canal, then another, finally reaching the Maas. The long stone bridge spanning it was bruised, stone railings crumbled and driving surface pocked by shells. Dad breathed hard beside me, clutching the seat with his good hand as though waiting for the whole thing to blow, eyes fixed on St. Christopher's Cathedral looming in the distance. Atop the white spire, its patron stood with hands spread, anointing the deserted square below. As we passed beneath the holy gaze, I couldn't help mumble a grateful prayer for having made it this far while, beside me, Dad crossed himself. The streets of Roermond were deserted, the walk-ups shuttered though it was daylight, flowerpots and window boxes filled with withered stalks, not a bike or wagon, not a child or adult. We maneuvered down the narrow medieval streets, gothic wooden shutters closed over broken windows, doors bolted.

"Where is everyone?" I asked.

"Hiding from Ulrich Matthaeas." Dad inhaled. "Son of a bitch ordered a massive draft, but everyone hid. So he sent his paratroopers door to door, and anyone found was forced to dig their own grave and then shot." A stream of smoke escaped his nostrils. "Examples."

"Jesus."

Around another corner, the quiet was broken by a babble of voices, unfamiliar words and accents rising from where people rebuilt a road. Women stooped to dig, their shovels throwing dirt on a growing pile while Green Police stood watch. The workers' hands were wrapped in rags, faces hollow under the handkerchiefs holding back their hair. Something broke a little inside me, some sense I'd had of the rules of a sane world. One woman looked up at me, her face blank with exhaustion. She smiled an instant, vaguely aware, as though I wasn't quite real.

"Who are these people?" I whispered.

"Russians. Poles." Dad looked around warily. "Krauts never have enough workers and they bring them here."

Suddenly the guard was on top of the woman with his baton, striking at her shoulders and head. She did nothing to protect herself, just kept smiling at me. The guard looked up and waved the baton to hurry up. "Ga verder," he hissed. Move on. It was a Dutchman doing this. A goddamn Dutchman. A bolt of anger threatened to send me off the wagon to wrap my hands around the guard's neck. I wanted to feel it pulsing there, to get an answer out of him, but Dad put his hand on mine, forcing me to snap the reins over Netti's back, the wagon lurching forward.

"It wouldn't have helped," Dad finally said.

We passed the steeples of Minderbroeders Church, Netti picking her way until the narrow street opened onto the station square. It was furious with activity, the sudden noise jolting. Talk was a flurry of words and gesturing hands, orders hollered over a loudspeaker as men ran toward a train rumbling in at the platform. Netti skittered in her harness as the engine thundered by, brakes squealing.

"More workers," Dad said.

German guards took up positions, their dogs barking and lunging at the end of heavy chains. The steel latches of the rail cars clanged, stunned faces peering out as the doors rolled open, eyes adjusting to the light. Thin men jumped down to the platform and turned to help the women, their voices soft with languages I didn't recognize. The guards were quickly on them, herding the men away in groups. They looked back, their faces twisted, their wives and girlfriends and daughters standing transfixed by their departure. A young girl of about eleven cried out for her father and was quickly silenced by a guard's backhand to her face. She clutched her cheek and looked right at me, eyes wide and confused.

I was startled back by a German soldier demanding the papers from my dad and directing me to a low-roofed shed at the far end of the train station. Inside, wooden crates had been loaded onto a trolley I pushed to the wagon, heaving them up as Dad sent an encouraging nod, a nervous smile, pointing to where each might fit best. When I was done, I tarped the load and started to clamber to the wagon seat, but Dad's hand on my arms stopped me.

Three women were pushed from the train platform toward the wagon, the young girl trailing behind. The soldier behind prodded the women, gesturing to the wagon and barking an impatient command. They responded with a flurry of harsh words. Before anyone could move, a guard hit the oldest one across the face with his pistol barrel and she crumpled, the soldier screaming so the others stopped themselves from helping, watching horrified as she staggered to her feet, blood running down her face from a gash above her eye. Subdued, they all climbed up to sit at the back end of the wagon.

"What the hell?" I breathed it out. Dad wouldn't look at me.

When the women were on board, the soldier motioned for me to go, but I froze at the terror in the women's eyes. The butt end of a rifle crashed into my ribs and I doubled over, gasping for air, while Dad finished tucking the tarp behind the women with his good hand, grunting with the pain in his bad.

"It'll be okay," he said quietly, threading rope through the side slats of the wagon. His voice was gentle, coaxing. "It's okay. Just do as he says."

The women seemed to understand his meaning if not his words. I climbed up, hoping to catch the eyes of the women, to reassure them of our good intention. But I had no idea what our intentions were. The women quiet, the load tarped, we waited on the seat while the soldier stamped the papers and handed them back. I slapped the reins across Netti's rump so she strained against the harness, the heavy cart lurching forward. We made our way out of the square and back through deserted streets, rolling through the shadow of the church where I hoped St. Christopher was blind to our work.

"South after the train bridge." Dad's voice was low in my ear.

I obeyed, the silence suffocating. I had the astonishing thought that Dad was with the underground, and we were taking the women to safety. It's why he wouldn't speak of his work. That was it. I was filled with a new kind of nervous excitement. And relief. Such relief. I couldn't wait to tell Marcel.

Four more kilometers and Dad told me to stop. Thick bluffs of trees flanked the road, the land rolling up and away from the river. I helped the women down. I thought Dad would tell them to run, wondered how they would survive, how Dad would explain this to the Gestapo, to the young prick who signed the papers. Instead Dad walked toward an embankment two hundred meters off the road. The women followed and I hurried to catch up, but Dad shook his head. "Stay with the wagon."

I watched, baffled, until I couldn't see them anymore. "Good girl." I stroked Netti's neck. "You're a good girl." I rubbed her ears, scuffed the dandruff under her mane so she leaned into me. My ribs hurt where the rifle had hit and I massaged them, glancing anxiously into the trees, too exhausted to focus. I imagined Dad meeting with the underground, negotiating safe passage for the women. "What's he doing, hey girl?" I was certain the horse had been down this road before, that she knew the answers to the questions rattling in my head.

Suddenly Dad appeared over the embankment, awkwardly holding his broken arm with his good one, his hurrying step become a stumbling run.

"Go," he said, clambering into the wagon.

I jumped in. "Where'd you take them? What's going on?"

"Go." He stared straight ahead, his words quaking with tears. "For fuck's sake, Sam, just go."

It was a voice I'd never heard from him, not even when Leo disappeared. A chill ran down my spine. My left eye spasmed sharp and quick. I whipped the reins over Netti's back and she pulled hard, knowing she was going home. I dared a look back as we rounded the ridge to where people trudged over a mound of earth, another mound in the distance, and another, all of them teeming with people digging and prying. I'd seen it before. They were constructing artillery bunkers for the Germans. We'd delivered those women to dig for the Nazis.

I stared at my dad. "She's a little girl."

He nodded. A tear dropped onto his cheek.

"What the hell?" My breath came hard and fast, stomach swirling.

"I don't have a choice. You know I have to do what they say."

"Bullshit."

"Sam."

"Shut up. Just shut up." I pulled on the reins, jumping down before the wagon stopped. "You fucking coward," I yelled.

"Coward?" Dad looked back toward Roermond.

"If you had half the backbone Leo did, you'd let Netti die." I waved at her head and she balked. "You'd chop the wagon to kindling and tell the Nazis to go fuck themselves."

Dad breathed deep, his voice soft as he looked toward where the women blended into the swarm of people digging on the hill. "You think that doesn't kill me?"

"Then don't do it."

"You don't know everything, Sam." It sounded like a warning.

I stumbled to the edge of the road, turning to look at my dad helpless in the wagon, a shell shrunken and cracked. He could refuse. I had a moment to think of the guns pointed at my head, the terror, and for an instant wondered if I could do what I expected of my father. But I didn't want to let the thought in, wanted only to see him as a monster who would save himself by delivering women to be worked to death by the Nazis.

"Fuck you," I hollered. I'd walk the distance home before getting into that wagon again. "Fuck you."

Rudy was a German I was supposed to hate. And I didn't. I was supposed to love my dad. But I hated him. I hate him still.

PART II

"Truth is in everyone; it is not far, it is not near; it is eternally there." — JIDDU KRISHNAMURTI

CHAPTER 10

Befehl ist Befehl

NGADIPURO VILLAGE, ISLAND OF JAVA,
DUTCH EAST INDIES
DECEMBER 1947

MIDNIGHT JUNGLE IS BLACK AND deep and raucous with the throated rumble of frogs, the whir of cicadas, the pitched crackle of geckos. Sam and Andre keep watch from the post high in the trees, the whistle and grunt of the macaque sounding above the constant tumble of the Brantas River below. Sam jumps as a gutted scream pierces the night.

"Like a baby on a pitchfork," he mutters. He's learned the sound comes from a harmless bird, a huge white cockatoo. It shouldn't terrify him anymore, but every time the bird shrieks, Sam's breath seizes in his throat. Andre snores lightly beside him.

"How the hell do you sleep through that?"

"Huh?" Andre jerks awake, fumbles with his binoculars and pretends to scan the area.

"Sorry, I got back late from town."

"Town? You mean from making out with Bonita."

Andre grins. It's been a month since Sergeant Mertens left and Andre has ignored the man's advice, sneaking out regularly to cross

107

the bridge into the village, offering cigarettes and booze to bribe the night watch not to shoot him when he signals his return.

"They've sent guys to other units, Andre." Sam scans the bridge through the machine gun sight. "Court-martialed some. Why would you risk it?" Andre tenses beside him. Sam has watched his friend change, settling down as he spends more time with Bonita.

"So have you done it? With Bonita, I mean."

"Not any of your business, but yes." Andre's eyes are plugged into his binoculars.

"What's she like?"

"Jesus, Sam."

When he sees Andre and Bonita together, it's like they've never been apart. Easy. Natural. The way they look at each other and laugh. "What if she gets pregnant?"

"Sam."

"Sorry. It's just that, what Mertens said. What would you do? Where would you live?" He has a sudden vision of Sari, pictures her swinging his baby in a sling on a plantation porch while he sips a beer nearby, watching his wife, his child, his farm. He grows hard.

"Sam, shut up." Andre is completely still, his binoculars trained on the river below. "East end of the bridge, four o'clock, two men."

Sam's hard-on evaporates as he catches their movement, the sinew of his neck and shoulders suddenly taut and tingling. A sliver of moon glints off helmets and he quickly trains the machine gun on the spot. "Sight me."

Andre grips the binoculars. "Four-fifteen, now twenty, just past the second set of panels."

"Got 'em." Breathe. Squeeze. Staccato fire erupts into the night and rattles the helmet on his head. He fires another four-second round, stops, listens. He thinks he hears a splash just as Raj and the others burst from the barracks, shouting.

"Bridge, east side." Andre's voice is loud into his radio. He looks at Sam. They wait, scanning the village and the river, the taut voices of the men bouncing across the water, stretching up from the bank to where Sam and Andre are perched in the trees.

"They got one."

"Good shot in the dark."

"Leave him there till morning."

Sam whistles out his breath. He's killed a man. He thought perhaps this moment would somehow, miraculously, not occur, that he'd live out this war without having to shoot someone. But a man is dead. He waits to feel something but can't tune in to any particular feeling. Just emptiness. It was a shadow on the bridge, no scream, no cry, just a splash like fish jumping; an illusion of a man in the distance can seem like nothing at all.

In the morning the body is gone, and he lets himself imagine it didn't happen.

"Jesus, they came back for him. Even with the machine gun." There's a hint of admiration in Andre's voice as he scuffs his boot through the trail left by a dragged body.

"Jago." Raj arrives so silently they both jump. Raj laughs and then frowns. "They can't come in here and terrorize us. Try to blow up our bridge. Hide." Uneasiness settles over Sam just as Raj leaps up the riverbank and gazes at the village. "Andre, get the squad out here. We're going on a tour."

"Where?" Andre asks.

"I've got a feeling." Raj jumps into the jeep Mertens left behind weeks ago with instructions to take good care of it. "Get in."

Sam, Darma and Freddy clamber in, Andre riding shotgun. The others pile into a truck behind. They thunder across the bridge and through Ngadipuro, the children screeching with glee as they run alongside, pointing at Andre.

"Tuan Andre, kasih sayang, Bonita," they sing.

Sam watches the lobes of Andre's ears turn red under his helmet. Raj glares straight ahead and manhandles the jeep out of town and over the rutted road toward the village of Sugro, ten kilometers into rebel-held territory.

"What the hell are we doing?" Andre looks at Raj.

"We're going to flush the bastards out."

"I thought we were supposed to hold our positions, stay inside the line."

"Well we can't hold anything if they're hiding out here and coming at night to blow up our bridge, can we?" Raj guns the jeep so they're forced to clutch the sides.

Andre swings his head round to peer over his sunglasses at Sam, who raises his eyebrows and shrugs in return. Despite last night's attempt, there have been fewer attacks and the slow double line of traffic streams to and from Ngadipuro again. Ahead, a gray oxen sways under the center pole of a cart, its driver slouched under the straw canopy; a man jog trots with a long pole stretched across bony shoulders, balancing the weight of baskets of goods at either end; in the distance, a small pony pulls five people in a tiny cart. The demarcation line is imaginary; on either side, the country and people are the same.

The traffic thins out as the road does and soon they can barely see the trail, arriving finally in a kampong of scattered bamboo homes deep in the bush. One woman quickly shoves laundry from the line into a basket and beckons her children. They rush to cling to her skirts before being herded away. Other women scatter from where their shuffling feet turn harvested rice drying on tarps. Raj runs the truck over their work, scattering the kernels. Sam jumps out of the slowing jeep and joins the squad rushing ahead to the center of the village, guns high while Raj points and shouts instructions. They spread out.

Sam's not sure how to recognize what he's looking for as he heads down a small side street with Darma and Andre. All the doors and windows are shuttered, the thin bamboo walls of the huts almost transparent. Darma hesitates, pushes a door open. A woman shrieks as he and Andre disappear inside, Sam keeping an eye on the surrounding homes. Two small children come bolting around a corner of one hut and stop short, eyes wide.

"Hallo!" he tries to sound friendly.

They smile tentatively before trotting away, looking over their shoulders every few steps and sprinting off down another alley, their bare feet kicking up dirt. Andre pushes a boy of about sixteen out of the house. Skinny, pimpled, he watches Sam through the smudged lenses of his glasses, like the bookish boys Sam and Marcel teased in school, their distant stare containing the next big idea. Darma pats the boy down and asks him a question in Javanese. The boy shakes his head hard. Darma and Sam exchange a silent agreement and let the boy go. They continue down the path and search two more houses.

Sam wants to avert his eyes from the people in these homes, embarrassed to burst into their lives in such an obscene way. In one, a couple jumps up from their breakfast table, the man's terrified eyes taking him in, gauging the distance between Sam's gun and two staring toddlers on the other side of the room. The mother's eyes are on his face, her baby grumbling as she pulls it from her breast and pushes it in its sling around to her back. The house is one room, sleeping mats and rumpled sheets on one side, a crude table and chairs and small counter on the other. The earthy smell of brewed coffee fills his nose and he wants to sit at the table and cradle a warm mug in his hands. He pushes his weapon so it hangs from his shoulder behind, smiles at the children and glances briefly at the mother.

"Maaf," he tries. Sorry. She looks puzzled a moment and he leaves, shaking his head at Darma and Andre. "Nothing."

They continue down the narrow street. Approaching a low tumbledown shed, Andre points to his ear. He's heard something inside. Sam and Darma fix bayonets to the ends of their rifles while Andre pulls a knife from his belt, crouching beside the door and slowly putting his hand to the latch. He nods to Sam and throws it wide. Jumping into the opening, Sam thrusts his gun forward, the bayonet extending it to twice its length. At first his sun-blinded eyes can see nothing in the dark interior. The stench of piss hits his nose, his vision adjusting to see an old man sitting on the dirt floor, the front of his sarong drenched, hands held trembling in front of him, mouth open in mute terror.

"It's okay." Sam steps closer. "We're not going to hurt you."

The man raises his hands higher, tears streaming into the papery folds of his skin. His egg-white eyes are blind with cataracts, wide with fear. He whispers words quiet and intense and Sam knows the man is begging for mercy, for Sam to spare his life. Stunned, Sam slowly puts his rifle on the ground and squats, pulling a Lucky Strike from his shirt pocket and resting it on the bottom lip of the man's open mouth. The man's hands slowly descend to his lap as he closes cracked lips round the cigarette.

Sam strikes a match. "It's okay," he says again, holding the flame to the tip as the man inhales a shuddering, grateful breath. Sam keeps his head down a minute, an immense sadness closing in as he lights another for himself. The man's hands still rest in his wet lap, the skin mapped with raised veins, the knuckles opaque. A lifetime in those hands. Sam can't resist touching the back of one of those ancient hands. The old man's slender fingers wrap slowly round Sam's a moment, squeezing slightly as though in recognition of some shared sorrow.

"Bapak," Sam says, a catch quivering in his throat. He looks up. Darma and Andre watch from the door. He turns back to gaze at the old man a moment.

"Jesus Christ," he whispers, picks up his gun and gently closes the door of the shed behind him. He waves to the shed, to the houses they've just been through. "What are we? The fucking SS?"

"Befehl ist befehl," Andre mutters. An order is an order.

Sam stares at Andre a moment before walking down the street, head down and silent, the stream bubbling happily beside them as they catch up to the rest of the squad who have four men lying face down in the street. Raj has no idea if they are pemuda, but one carried a machete, another a bamboo spear. The prisoners protest that these are tools for cutting cane and for hunting, but the soldiers bind their hands and feet and load them into a flatbed truck, Sam and Darma ordered to take them back across the line to the detention center in Malang.

They pick up their kits from barracks in Ngadipuro before bouncing their way out of the jungle, Darma driving while Sam rests, the vision of the old man haunting the space behind his eyes. Have they become Nazis? The question rings through his head amidst the scratch of words on a wall at the labor camp, it seems an eternity ago, when he would have had a ready answer. He's brought back by Darma nudging him as they near Malang. He looks back at the men, who sit on the hard floor of the truck box, their feet and hands tied with twine and rope, remembers the women he'd helped his father haul for the Nazis. And he is not sure of anything.

They arrive as the town emerges from its afternoon rest. He'd forgotten what the city feels like, its heat more urgent without the jungle shade, whitewashed walls stark against ancient blue sky, the efficient line of street and sidewalk. Much of the burned rubble has been pushed back to make way for new enterprise, corrugated tin shacks a temporary replacement for storefronts and homes.

"You picked these guys up in Ngadipuro?" Colonel Hagen asks when he meets them at the army garrison on the edge of town.

"No, sir. In Sugro," Sam says. "Other side of the line."

Hagen looks up sharply but says nothing further. "Well, you won't make it back before dark so you might as well enjoy a good bed for the night. Quarters are in the back side of the Tugu. Second floor, first door on the left is yours. Canteen just down the street." He smiles at them. "Enjoy yourselves. Come see me tomorrow morning."

"Yes, sir."

They stare in awe as they enter the old colonial hotel. Stone tile floors sparkle beneath their dirty boots so Sam finds himself walking on his toes. The ceilings are four meters high and he wonders dumbly who manages to paint them and how. A huge portrait of a young Queen Wilhelmina with her daughter, Juliana, hangs on an expanse of wall, the girl staring out as though daring Sam to enter under the ornately carved moldings of a tall, wide doorway. Bouquets of hydrangea and chrysanthemum and lotus flowers flash blue and yellow and red against the blinding white marble. Everything is white, including the pressed linen suits of the men in the foyer who glance his way with a quick frown as they hurry on to the next room. Other men in full uniform look at them with raised eyebrows and Sam imagines how he and Darma must look in their short sleeves and khakis, dirty socks and ragged boots. A wide marble staircase ascends to the right, its carved wood railing burnished soft by many hands.

The chandelier has captured Darma's attention. Glass domes cascade down, the bottom fringed by small glass tubes swirled into a sparkling vortex. Sam wonders again at the decadence they've come here to preserve, aware that the only locals likely to have seen the inside of the place are those who clean and cook for the men in white. As if to prove him right, a small Javanese boy rushes in from behind the staircase. He wears dark shorts, a white sarong with long sleeves and a black peci so large it almost doubles the size of his head. He nods to Sam, grabbing his kit.

"Hey." Sam moves to snatch it back.

The boy points and pads up the staircase in bare feet. Sam leaves Darma to stare at the crystal glow of the chandelier, following the boy, who leads him to a room with high ceilings, a dressing table, separate water closet and real beds. It's all a bit surreal after the squalor of Ngadipuro. He glances down at his dirty clothes and turns to close the door. The boy stands waiting.

"Terima kasih," Sam says. He fishes a few rupiah from his pocket, dropping them into the outstretched hand as he shuts the door. Alone. It's the first time he's been truly alone in months. He stoops to unlace his boots and step out of them, gingerly peels off socks wet with sweat and blister fluid, finally padding his abused feet across the cool sheen of tile to the window.

Flamboyant with the colors of cassia and plum, a groomed courtyard stretches between the two buildings, a large, screened gazebo in
the center. Sam closes the shutters and heads to the bathroom. Two
buckets of water wait for him in a small tiled alcove with a drain at
the bottom. He quickly sheds his clothes, steps in and pours some
of the tepid water over his head, soaping himself all over with a bar
from the ledge before rinsing with the rest of the bucket. He leaves
the other for Darma. Finding a comb in his kit, he slicks back his hair,
reaches in again for the Whitfield ointment and applies it to crotch
and armpits and elbow creases, the backs of his knees — anywhere
blood comes close to the surface of skin and the itching is unbearable.

Relieved, he flops on his back on one of the beds. He can't
remember such comfort. Before he can think about the cracks running across the ceiling, he is fast asleep, waking only when he hears
Darma laugh.

"Well, you didn't waste any time."

Sam rolls to his side, groaning with pleasure. "God, this bed is
great."

Darma flops down beside him.

Sam is suddenly wide awake, scrambling up. "Hey, get off. You've
got your own bed."

"But it's clean. And I'm not," Darma laughs.

Sam's laugh sounds as false as it feels. He sits in the chair by
the window, watching as Darma gets up and strips off his clothes,
throwing them into a twisted ball on the floor. Darma is skinny,
lean biceps in rope-thin arms, meatless thighs, bony buttocks.
"God, you're like a starved chicken."

Darma looks back at him and shrugs. "With a big cock-a-
doodle-doo!" he says, throwing his hand in the air as he arches his
neck and takes one long stride to disappear behind the bamboo
screen hiding the shower area.

Sam chuckles, but his stomach churns. Sometimes Darma
acts like a little boy, as though he has nothing to prove. Sam was

always anxious to grow, as though height and muscle would make him a man. Even with the threat of the razzia and forced labor, his single wish then was to become a man and prove himself to Leo. A wasted wish. Twenty-two. It's a number that should make him a man. His body has filled and his shoulders broadened, yet he feels equal parts young and old, naïve and ancient, like he knows nothing and everything in the same measure. But Darma seems to have no such confusion. He's kind, never uses words like plopper or klompen, doesn't talk dirty about girls the way most of them do. Darma treats everyone exactly the same. It's strange and it provokes the other men, their eyes narrowed when they look at him, as though his ability for kindness is a threat.

Darma comes out of the shower rubbing his hair in a towel. Suddenly Sam feels free to loosen the tight grip he's kept on his thoughts. This hotel room seems far from the war, a place he might find some perspective, find a way to control what is to come.

"Do you think it's true? Befehl ist befehl? Those families. The bapak in the shed."

Darma tilts his head. "I think," he starts slowly, his eyes distant, "we need to listen to the dead."

Sam looks up quickly.

"They're with us." Darma is matter-of-fact. "They influence those of us left behind."

All those lost to war, dead from bullets and bombs or gas chambers or bad luck, dying so Holland could turn around and send him to wage a new war on people who only want the same freedom he'd longed for throughout the occupation.

"It's why history is important to us. Mengeti — the writing of history. Not your kind of history. Not dead, like a story from the past. But living, history a kind of prophesy, a way into the future we want."

Sam thinks of Ngadipuro, the jungle and its fecund green sponging the rain out of the air to nurture more bamboo and sandalwood. Maybe he hasn't been paying attention. Maybe if he does, he'll find the voices of those he lost, absorb them like the trees absorb the rain, create a future that is better than he is right now. Mengeti. Sam nods at Darma, struck again at his friend's quiet grace. Perhaps Darma is the only one among them who is not ugly.

CHAPTER 11

Saints and Monsters

JANUARY 1948

SAM AND DARMA ARE SILENT as they dress in light pants and long sleeves to keep the evening mosquitoes at bay, slip into sandals and head outside, the sun setting swiftly behind what remains of the hotel. Small streetlights guide them to the cantina, where a babu beckons them in and sits them at a round bar table, scooping huge amounts of fried rice and fish onto plates and plunking beer down in front of them. Sam pulls on the bottle and sighs, digs into the meal and doesn't look up until his plate is clean. Beside him, Darma does the same.

He hears a snort and a high-pitched laugh so familiar that the hair stands on his neck. He glances around the smoke-filled room, watching the profile of one man, the deep dip in the bridge of his nose before it curves down hawk-like over full lips. He is tall now. Not a pound of baby fat left, thin arms clutching a beer, nervous eyes darting about until they rest on Sam and widen in disbelief.

"Marcel?" Sam says it quietly, not quite believing. Marcel had vanished during the war and hadn't come home before Sam was shipped out. Everyone thought he was dead, yet without knowing for sure there was no real way to grieve. And now, here he is making his way to Sam's table where they grip hands and hug hard before Marcel steps back. It's like seeing someone risen.

"Holy shit, Sam."

They leave Darma and the cantina and begin to walk along the nearby canal. Marcel lights a cigarette and passes it to Sam, lighting another for himself as Sam takes in his friend's simple white tunic and dark sarong, the sandals on his feet.

Marcel notices Sam watching, grins and shrugs. "Hell of a lot more comfortable," he says, as though comfort is the point and not the importance of distinguishing themselves from the locals. "How long have you been here?"

"Just over a year." Sam can't quite believe it himself.

"Same. I was stationed in the East near Bali, until recently."

"Ha! Tough orders."

"I know. It's beautiful. I do love this country."

They exchange glances as they walk, eyes moving across one another's adult faces and changed bodies, questions forming without being asked. Where have you been? How was your war? What did you come home to?

"I'm sorry about Leo," Marcel says softly.

"Well, I guess you know what it's like. I'm sorry too. About your dad."

"His body was never found. Mom didn't get to bury him."

"How is she?"

"People think she's a bit touched now. Maybe she is."

Sam shakes his head in sympathy, exhales smoke in a puff.

"Heard the last year was pretty rough on you too," Marcel says. "Anika told me you were in Germany. Pretty beat up when you came back. Angry."

Had he been so angry? "More tired than angry, I'd say." Sam sighs. "What about you?"

"I almost made it out. Needed one more connection through France. But they found out and sent me to Vught."

"Shit."

"Yeah. I try not to think about it too much." Marcel closes his eyes as though the remembering hurts them. "I joined the BNV when I got home. Hunted down collaborators and war criminals in Amsterdam and Utrecht. Guess I was angry too."

Sam remembers a flurry of arrests and retributions, even some killings. People walked a wide berth around anyone suspected of collaborating, while those like Sam's neighbors who were once tied to Hitler through the NSB pretended they had no part in the Nazi plan. He thinks of his dad and the women, looks hard at Marcel.

"I thought you were dead." It rushes out. He glances at the scar running down Marcel's left arm.

"I should have sent word."

"I was an ass. You didn't owe me anything."

"What are you talking about?"

"Hendrik. You were right about him."

Marcel stops walking and looks at Sam like he's crazy. "Your dad was a hero."

Sam snorts. "I saw what he did. He was no hero."

"I checked, Sam. Felt like a son-of-a-bitch for still thinking the worst. But I had to know. So I checked BNV records." He pauses. "When he hauled those loads from Roermond, he altered the documents the Nazis gave him and always took some of the goods to the Heibloem resistance before taking the rest to the German base at your farm. And if he was hauling people, well . . . same thing. For every person Hendrik delivered to the Reich, he took another to the underground."

Sam can only gape.

"He didn't tell you?"

The woman beaten in Roermond because she'd taken a moment to smile at him, the little girl forced into Hendrik's cart. His dad had let Sam believe he didn't care, or at the very least was too big a coward to stand up for them. Sam had kept the image of those women in his memory, easily retrieved to keep his anger alive. And the picture of his dad too, anxious and unable to eat or sleep. Distant and cold and hard. He'd thought selfish fear drove his dad to do the unthinkable, but the demons haunting his father were something entirely different. And Sam hadn't asked. He'd held on to his anger too tightly to ask. Rudy. Hendrik. Saints and monsters.

His head is suddenly pounding, and he stops to lean against a retaining wall. The sound of the city recedes as the light dwindles, and then as it does in the tropics, darkness descends and the red glow of their cigarette tips is all that distinguishes them from the night. Lamps are lit to illuminate the small homes along the way.

"Thought you should know," Marcel offers.

"Yeah, of course, I'm glad you told me. It's just that afterward, I was so hard on him. We barely spoke and then I was shipped here." How different things might be if he'd known what his father was doing, if he'd let Sam help him.

"Maybe it was just too hard to talk about," Marcel says. "Can you imagine the choices he had to make; who to save, who to sacrifice. Even worse than the ones we're expected to make now."

Sam raises his eyebrows.

Marcel gestures around them. "Do you know which fucking ploppers are supposed to be the enemy?"

"Spoor says they just have no discipline, no strategy."

"Well, they have a cause."

"So do we."

"Do we? Do you actually give a shit?"

"Jesus, Marcel."

"I don't know, Sam. I thought I knew what we were doing here. But all I've got to show for all this work is dysentery and skin diseases. And dead friends." He looks around, gestures to a window where a woman stands over a stove preparing the evening meal. "These people just want to live their lives. Like we did. We just wanted the Germans to get out, to leave us the hell alone. Do you ever think of that? That we might be to these people what the Nazis were to us?"

What are we? The fucking SS? He's worked hard to keep the answer at bay. And now his dad's a hero. And suddenly nothing seems impossible. Even here. It's all too much. He just wants Marcel to be his friend from home, the person worrying about baby fat and missing pubic hair. He cocks his head, shuffles.

"You always did think too much," Sam says finally.

Marcel's eyebrows shoot up and he begins to chuckle. Sam knows what's coming, a high-pitched wheeze, then chortling and finally from deep in Marcel's belly, a loud booming laugh, hands on thighs as he huffs to catch his breath.

"I think too much!" Marcel hoots. "Yes, I do."

And he's off again, Sam quickly catching up, laughter a foreign taste in his mouth. He draws air down into his belly, all the tension of the past months expelled through his laughter into the tropical air. They gasp and wheeze until they are spent. Sam sways, a little lightheaded.

"Haven't done that in a long time." Marcel draws a shaky breath to come back to where they stand in the street, swatting at mosquitoes arrived with the cooling dusk. "Let's go have a drink."

They head back to the cantina and order another beer. Sam introduces Darma, but before they have a chance to exchange a word, a man in short sleeves and black pants straddles a chair at their table.

"You fellas just in for the night?" he asks. "I'm Albert. This is Braam." Another man sits down heavily. "We're in administration here." Both are in their forties, hair slicked back, identical trimmed mustaches.

Sam nods hello and takes another swig of beer, Darma launching into an explanation of the prisoners they'd brought, how he believes the four men innocent, but you can't be too sure, right? The two men nod, bewildered. They have no idea. The one named Braam signals the bartender to bring another round. Sam starts to protest, but Albert claps him on the back.

"Least we can do. Where'd he say, Ngadipuro? Securing our interests out there, right? Fighting the devil bastards. I'd say we can buy you a drink."

Securing Dutch interests. A mirage on a bridge, a blind old man in a shed. His skin crawls and the beer doesn't slip quite as easily down his throat. He can't look at Marcel.

The place fills up: servicemen, civilians, Dutch, a few Indo. Three Javanese women lounge in wicker chairs, the honey brown skin of their shoulders attracting Sam as one raises a frosted glass to her lips and leans in to listen to a younger one who tucks a stray tendril of hair into the dark bun piled on her head. They rise and make their way around the room, dipping toward the men to speak into their ears. The young one looks right at Sam, a slow smile spreading across her face as she lifts an eyebrow. He blushes and looks away. An image of Sari bursts into his mind.

"You always could attract the women with those smoky blue eyes," Marcel laughs.

"I think you should go after her," Albert says, eyeing Marcel's tunic and sarong. "More your type?"

Sam bristles, but Marcel ignores the jibe, sipping his beer, watching as four men take the stage. One sits at a piano, another holds a violin, the third slings a saxophone strap round his neck. Sam almost doesn't see the fourth, only an upright bass cello, the instrument's neck like an extension of the man's head. The man doesn't move, has no expression, eyes closed. His white hair matches the perfect pearl white of his suit. And shirt. And tie. And shoes. Everything white. Even his skin, the man so old it is as though the blood has prematurely left his face and hands.

The piano starts softly, the violin coming in, the sax filling in behind the melody. The old man grips his bow lightly, holding it poised above the strings, eyes still closed. Sam leans forward as sound eases out of the cello, deep and resonant, then light and keening, arching over him.

Sam has no idea what he's hearing, only that the sound builds around him as the cello threads between the spaces, the sax moving forward then back, the violin piercing through first plaintive and then demanding. The harmonies soar. He imagines the music is for him, about home and longing and confusion and love. The last notes fade. The old man has barely moved so Sam can almost believe he didn't just hear the beauty of the cello.

"Who are they?"

"Austrian. Czech," Braam says. "Those men lived in the tropics their whole lives, even played with symphonies abroad in their time. Like the old man. I heard him once in Vienna."

Sam looks around, sees men pulling on opium pipes, others on whiskey bottles. The young woman sits on a soldier's lap. The crowd has barely noticed the music. But it is the most beautiful thing Sam has heard in a very long time and he looks to Darma to share his appreciation. But Darma isn't watching the stage. Or the women. Instead he sips his beer, eyes fixed on the corner of the room. Sam follows Darma's gaze to a soldier who stands bare-chested, his beret cocked over Dutch-blond hair and a strong jaw. The man's foot is on a chair in front of him and he holds forth to those gathered round. But his eyes are riveted on Darma.

Marcel catches Sam's eye, raising his eyebrows and clowning a what-the-hell kind of face. Sam shrugs, shaking his head, an uncomfortable thought interrupted by an officer joining their table. The officer shakes hands and buys a round of whiskey that burns Sam's throat. Sam listens to the music and sips his drink, catching bits of the conversation around him, throwing covert looks at Darma, whose focus has returned to their own table. Maybe he was imagining things.

"So is it true what they're saying?" Albert suddenly asks the officer. "About Turk Westerling?"

Sam's heard the rumors. The villagers of Rawagede wouldn't give up a rebel who'd been ambushing Dutch bases, so Westerling ordered his special forces to take the men and boys to a field and shoot them. One by one. Dutch radio calls it an incident.

"Four hundred villagers." Braam says quietly, leaving the number to hang in the air.

The officer is suddenly searching the room like he'd rather be anywhere else.

"Sounds like a massacre to me," Marcel says quietly. "Westerling's an animal."

The officer frowns. "Soldier, that's enough."

"Right."

Sam tries to catch Marcel's eye, get him to shut up, but Darma suddenly stands and wheels around, almost knocking the glasses off the tray of a waitress. "Gotta piss," he says as he sidles behind Sam's chair, squeezing Sam's shoulder as he heads to the door.

"You should be more careful," the officer says to Marcel. "We're all on the same side here."

"We've just had a few bad days, sir," Sam interjects.

"Tell me about it. We're trying to set up logistics. Men and equipment, supplies, communications." The officer shakes his head. "In rice paddies and jungle."

"I've learned a little about working in the jungle," Sam nods, keenly aware of the itch in his crotch, his blistered and cracked feet.

"You shoot anyone yet?" Albert asks, his voice a slur.

The question startles Sam so he puts his hands out, desperately wishing the whiskey wasn't making the room spin. Four hundred. The splash of one body. And his dad is a hero. His stomach swirls and he pushes past Marcel to charge out of the canteen and round the corner to spew. His throat burns and his nose runs. He wipes his face with his handkerchief. A buzz has started in his head and he closes his eyes, opening them quickly again as the world starts to spin. He sees movement in the shadows. The outline of a long lean body.

Darma is pasted face to the wall by the shirtless Dutch officer. What the hell? Sam makes to hurry down the alley but pulls up short. The older man is grinding himself against Darma's bare backside. Sam turns abruptly, turns back. What's he supposed to do with this? He spits and wipes his mouth again. Suddenly there's shouting behind him and Marcel swoops past, grabbing his elbow and rushing him toward Darma, a half dozen Dutch soldiers in pursuit. In the alley, the two men look up in surprise, the white officer sprinting away, Darma left to clutch his pants as Marcel shoves him toward Sam.

"Get him out of here," Marcel hisses and turns to face the angry soldiers.

Sam pushes Darma ahead of him, behind them the men's voices. "Fucking little faggot."

"He's not hurting you." Marcel's voice.

"You one of them too? Dressed like that. Are you a faggot?"

Sam shoves Darma through a small opening that leads to a side street. "Run," Sam says and turns back to help Marcel, arriving just as the last boot hits his friend in the ribs and the drunken soldiers turn, leaving Marcel curled in the road.

"Fuck, Marcel." Sam helps him up. "What the hell?"

Marcel spits blood. "Assholes." And he laughs.

Sam looks at him, incredulous. "Why didn't you run?"

"Because I know their kind." He spits again. "I survived Vught, Sam. Those little fucks were nothing."

"Jesus."

"Your friend got away?"

Sam nods, breathes deep.

"They might have killed him, you know. It doesn't matter that he's KNIL. No one would have asked questions. Because he's dark. And different." Marcel's voice trails off.

Sam walks Marcel back to where his platoon is staying in an old colonial house. They clasp hands. "Can't believe I found you here, but I'm glad I did." Sam squeezes Marcel's upper arm with his other hand and looks into his friend's eyes, trying to ignore the swelling bruise on his cheek. They stare at one another a long moment and it's all there — the kolenberg, the lost brother and dad, the answers they don't have to the mysteries of this new war. Sam's nose flares. "We'll be all right."

Marcel's nod is vague, like he wants to believe Sam, but knows neither of them have any idea how this war will go, and what the outcome, and who they will be when it's over. Marcel smiles sadly and turns to limp into the house, his dirtied sarong trailing.

Sam breathes deep, trying to quell the sense he will not see his friend again. He walks back toward the hotel thinking of Darma, the look of ecstasy on his face, and then the terror as he ran. To live such a life. Why would one choose it? And what is Sam supposed to do with what he saw? Surely he's supposed to report Darma. It's a crime, after all. To be a homosexual. Hard to think the word, let alone say it about a man he thought was his friend. Yet Marcel took a beating for Darma, a virtual stranger.

Back at the room in the grand palace, the houseboy waits cross-legged on the floor outside the door, head on his chest, asleep. Inside, Sam kicks Darma's things together onto the other side of the room.

Darma slips in as the sun rises, quietly closing the door behind him, but Sam is wide awake and meets his gaze as he turns.

"What happened to you?"

"I know some people."

"Hmm . . ." Sam rolls over to face the wall. His head hurts and he hasn't the energy to ask. He listens as Darma showers, watches him dress and quickly pack his kit, hoping Darma's movements or words will provide an explanation, even as he tells himself he doesn't want one.

"I'll get something to eat, meet you at the truck after you've seen Hagen." Darma says. Like everything is normal. He stops, head down. "Your friend . . ."

"He's okay."

Darma nods, biting his lip, but Sam sees it quiver.

The backs of his eyes and temples pounding, Sam showers and readies himself for his meeting with the colonel. Outside, the boy waits in the truck pretending to shift and steer, sliding across to the other side as Sam gets in.

"Jesus, kid, you gotta go home sometime." He tousles the boy's hair and the boy smiles, eyes flashing in the rearview as they drive a few streets over to the command center.

"Did you have a good night?" Hagen asks, ushering Sam into his office.

Sam pictures Darma with the officer. It can wait. "Yes."

Hagen is in full tropics uniform, white linen jacket, the gold chain of a watch visible at the breast pocket. White pleated shorts, long socks held up by garters. Sam imagines himself dressed the same at the post at Ngadipuro and almost laughs. Hagen looks up from searching his desk drawer. "What?"

He nods at the colonel's suit. "Just not sure how you keep it clean."

"Ha, well I only wear it in the office and on official business. Separates us from the native troops. Ah, there it is." Hagen hands the boy a chocolate bar, sending him to wait outside. "Where'd you find him?"

"He just kind of latched on to me."

"They do that. Try to make a little cash for the family." Hagen pours Sam a cup of coffee and motions him to sit in the chair across from his desk. "How are things in the village? The bridge is holding?"

"Seems to be, yes. I think the people appreciate our protection, for the most part, anyway."

"Your barracks, food, everything okay in that regard?"

"Yes, sir." It's pointless to complain about the heat and the bugs and the constant diet of rice. The colonel can't change anything. And he has a sense this is not the information the man is looking for.

"So Raj is working out, then?" Hagen nods encouragingly, hurrying on before Sam can answer. "It's been a hell of a time. Too many experienced officers discharged. But they needed out after what they've been through. You saw Mertens. Wrecked. I'm one of the oldest now and I'm only thirty-five, hardly any experience. Fought Hitler for five days and spent the rest of the war trying to stay out of his reach. Before that I played football for the national team." He shakes his head, pensive for a moment.

Sam doesn't move.

"So Raj is okay? Mertens seems to think so."

Hagen hasn't mentioned their raid of Sugro inside the line. Maybe the brass doesn't care about a few mistreated ploppers. Or four hundred. Marcel's questioning eyes flash in front of him.

"I think the men would like to know — I would like to know — what exactly it is we're doing."

Hagen laughs a loud snort. "Wouldn't we all?" He looks past Sam to the window. "Spoor's orders are to hold our assets and try to flush out and arrest any rebels who might threaten them. But Spoor's not in the field. It's like football, sometimes the coaches can't see what's happening out there during the play." He pauses. "Tell me, do you know what they look like? Do you know how to find them?"

"No sir, to be honest, I don't. Those men we brought here could have just been villagers, like they claimed. No uniforms. No guns. They had spears and machetes but so do the women and the old. They use them for everything." Sam shakes his head. "Raj seems to think those men are rebels in the jungle at night and villagers by day."

"I think he's right. It's brilliant, really — hiding among civilians. And if the village refuses them shelter and food, they burn it down." Hagen sips his coffee and looks out the window. "It didn't start out this way. In the beginning, the pemuda were young, educated in the Dutch H.B.S. They had a vision of independence for this country. I understood that. We just came out of occupation. How could we not understand?"

Sam sighs with relief. The man has put into words thoughts he didn't think he was allowed to have.

"They wanted to negotiate," Hagen continues. "But that takes time, and Sukarno didn't want to lose the momentum he had when the Japs left. So the pemuda became something different, uglier. Young men with no education and no goal other than violence. You've seen it; they have a complete disregard for life. But we care. Ironically, it's our moral code that makes us weak."

"I suppose."

Hagen cocks his head, eyebrows raised. "Drafted, right? Don't want to be here. Don't care about this place. Girl at home."

Sam blushes.

"Me too," Hagen continues. "A wife and newborn. But just remember, there's a lot of suffering here that we can help avoid if we maintain the peace, provide stability."

It's his chance. The words rush out of him. "I've had a request from the villagers." He breathes deep. "They'd like us to set up a medical clinic in Ngadipuro. Their children, you know, malaria and infections."

"Beriberi," Hagen adds.

"Yes." Sam nods enthusiastically. "The post is right there, so we could treat soldiers and villagers all in one spot. It would help to gain their trust. Make them more willing to help us."

"It's a great idea. Make it happen, Sam."

"Me?"

Hagen laughs and motions Sam toward the door. "Let me know what you need. I'll tell Raj and the medics your plan. Keep me posted."

Sam salutes and the door is closed. The breath rushes out of him. He didn't tell the colonel about Darma, but Darma hasn't hurt anyone, hasn't jeopardized the squad. It's a sin and a crime and something Sam doesn't understand, but he pictures the fire of hate in the eyes of the soldiers who chased Darma and beat up Marcel. He will keep the secret. His decision makes him feel better about himself in some obscure way, like he is protecting his friend from unseen and unmentionable forces, like maybe he's becoming a man.

The boy still waits in the truck and Sam pokes at him, teasing until he fights back and they are a tangle of limbs and squealing. Darma arrives, jumping in and pushing the boy to the middle of the seat.

"He can't come with us," Sam says.

"Sure he can. Doesn't have family. Do you?"

The boy averts his eyes and shakes his head.

"He can do odd jobs," Darma says. "Clean up the place for us, take our laundry to the village. That kind of thing."

"I don't think it's allowed."

"Sam. It's fine. I'll be responsible for him if it makes you feel better. Let's go."

They ride home through the brilliant morning light, Darma drowsing against the window with the boy curled between them. Sam glances at them, chest tightening with a protective instinct he doesn't understand.

Visser gives him another smallpox injection when they get back — a needle every time a soldier travels from one region or city to the next. Just in case. He wonders if too much vaccine can actually cause the disease. But he puts out his arm as directed, suffers the shot and carries on. At least it's not as bad as the malaria treatment. Every few months the same routine, two pills a day for a week, suffer the nausea and cramps and headache, wonder if the prevention is worse than the disease. In spite of the treatments and bed nets and long sleeves, men succumb regularly to malaria, KNIL sent home, the Dutch to a military hospital.

The boy's jaundiced eyes look up at him. At least the soldiers receive the treatments; if he gets the clinic built, maybe the locals will too. And he wants to do it for Sari even though he's a little afraid of his feelings for her. Why can't he get her out of his head? Sari, Darma, this boy, all various shades of native, a strange troupe he seems to have gathered into his life, leading him down an unknown path.

CHAPTER 12

Walking as Men

LIMBURG PROVINCE, THE NETHERLANDS
OCTOBER 1944

ABEL GROOT WAS KING OF potatoes in the Heibloem area. But, since the occupation began, every one of his harvests was taken to feed German forces, and every year, in a small defiance, Abel invited his neighbors to take their chances and scavenge what they could. One early October morning, I joined others in a field surrounded by trees and shrouded in fog, feeling safer than I had in a long time, safe enough to focus on the hunt, chapped fingers scrabbling to pry small potatoes out of the near frozen dirt. A few boys shared news of Allied successes as they worked the rows, their words clear in the space between the ground and the blanket of wet air.

While Normandy had changed everything for some, it changed nothing for us. So much hope on that bright day in June when the radio quaked alive to the excitement of the Allied landings and promises of liberation by Christmas. Bombing raids at the German border with Limburg came closer to the farm, and we wrapped up in blankets to wait out the long nights in the cellar, empty jars rattling like skeletons when the bombs dropped close. But when the Allies finally entered Holland in September, they managed to liberate only a small corridor from the Belgian border to Nijmegen, *Radio Oranje* reporting failed tactical and strategic planning and huge Allied casualties. And we knew the war would not be over in time for Sinterklaas.

"Hallo."

I looked up to see blue eyes, deep as sky and flecked with cloud. She smiled, her lips full, teeth slightly gapped, an upturned nose. Her brown hair was bobbed and held back from her face with barrettes. I took her in with a breath, standing awkwardly to offer my hand before remembering how dirty it was and rubbing it on my pants. She laughed, looking me up and down, her open face inviting me to do the same. She wore overalls cinched at the waist with a man's belt, pant legs rolled so her wooden shoes peeked out. When I looked at her face again, her head was cocked.

"Hallo," I stuttered.

"I'm Petra," she said, glancing around. "Are you from around here?"

"Yes."

"I'm from Arnhem."

"Oh."

"Do you always speak in single syllable words?"

"No." My face flamed, stupid, such a relief when she laughed. "I'm Sam." It felt like my whole body was awake to the girl.

"Aren't you afraid to be picked up?" she asked suddenly.

"Well, yes actually. But I'll leave before the fog lifts."

"Where do you hide?" She carried on like she hadn't just asked the unaskable question, looking at me with raised eyebrows. "Oh, come now, would I be here picking potatoes in the fog?"

Her whole face smiled, nose crinkling, cheeks lifting under laughing eyes. I wanted to trust her, wanted to keep this beautiful girl talking. I looked around. No one was paying any attention to us.

"I've heard things are bad in Arnhem," I said.

"They are. Abel's my uncle." She crouched to dig again, and I joined her, our hands inches apart. "I was sent here because it's safer. But my mom stayed. My dad and brother. I should be grateful, but all I want to do is go home."

I wondered if I'd ever feel such desperation to be with my family. Perhaps if Mom had lived, if Dad gave a shit. "They say the Allies will take Arnhem soon."

"I don't know. The resistance is helping, but . . ."

"But what?"

"Well they wrecked the airport, so the Germans shot the mayor. Someone always pays, but it's never anyone from the underground. And then the onderduikers ask us to hide them."

"And do you?"

It was her turn to hesitate, watching me through a silence thick as the gray mist around us. Her shoulders relaxed like she'd made a decision. "It almost happens without knowing it. They come and say this neighbor boy will be drafted in the next razzia. Or that Jew is headed for transport. What else can we do?" She looked at me like I had the answer.

I didn't. Courage was hard to define: a bed for a stranger, a forged document, everyday acts of defiance sometimes more dangerous than blowing up a bridge. Because *what else can we do?* I thought of Marie walking out to meet the Gestapo, Anika's tired, determined eyes. Perhaps all women were brave.

"I wish my brother had found someone like you to help him," I said quietly. "Last we heard he's in Lager 21. More than a year now."

"I'm sorry. I really can't imagine."

"I try not to let myself imagine."

"What's he like?"

I felt a sudden panic. I couldn't quite conjure Leo and frantically searched my memory for fragments — red-blond hair, the blue of his eye, the scar above his lip — until finally the parts began to congeal into a face, a voice. Relief flooded in and I looked up to see her watching. She reached across the gap between where our fingers rested in the dirt to cover my hand with hers.

I looked into her sympathetic eyes. "Leo's a good man." It came out a whisper.

"I think you must be too." She squeezed my hand and something fluttered in my stomach. She looked around and started. The fog was lifting, the scavengers heading for the nearby forest to make their way home, pockets heavier with half-rotten potatoes.

Abel came to where we lingered. "Better get going," he said, glancing back and forth between us, a small grin on his face.

My ears grew hot and I smiled at Petra, desperate to say something and drag out my leaving.

"Good-bye then," she said, her smile shy again as she turned to walk across the field to the house.

A dog barked in the farmyard. I turned just as camouflaged paratroopers emerged from the haze like ghosts, as though the fog in my brain and the shadows of the men walking were an illusion. Worse, I couldn't tell if they were Allied or German. A hail of warning shots and guttural shouting and I hit the ground, face in the potato dirt, Abel thumping down beside me.

His eyes peered into my own. "I think we should run."

Which war did the man witness to think this crazy thing? The paratroopers had their guns ready, but Abel jumped up anyway and ran toward the trees behind us, slowed by age and dirt-caked wooden shoes. A single shot rang out. He screamed and clutched his thigh, staggering a few more steps before collapsing at the edge of the bluff.

The paratroopers hollered for everyone to get up slowly and put their hands over their heads. Two went to Abel moaning in the bush, grabbing me and gesturing to bring the wheelbarrow sitting at the end of the field. Reaching Abel, the troopers were surprisingly careful with the older man, twisting a tourniquet above the hole in his bleeding leg, bracing the side with a stick before wrapping the whole mess round and then heave-ho into the wheelbarrow. I helped push it round the edge of the field and to the house.

His wife opened the door, hand to her throat as Abel started to mutter and then to cry, gesturing to his leg and shouting they were animals, wounding an old man. I was embarrassed for him. So was his wife. She cuffed him and told him to shut up, that he shamed her acting like a baby in front of the Germans. Still shouting, she pulled Abel inside, dragging his leg and silent now while the paratroopers laughed. Past them, I caught a glimpse of Petra's stricken face. I stood tall as our eyes met, her smile small and sad as she raised her fingers to her lips, sending the kiss toward me just as the door closed.

They lined us up. Dread was gone. Instead I was numb, my body certain this was happening to someone else and I was just a spectator. There was little noise, no talk. Eventually, a German officer walked down the line, calmly telling us we were going to a prison camp where we'd pay for our evasion of the draft. The lucky ones might eventually make up for their sins working in a factory or on a farm. We left the field, and I was taken home to collect some things, allowed one small suitcase.

Marie and Anika met me at the door, whispering questions to one another about what a person might need in a camp, scurrying ahead to hand me things. Underwear, socks, a shirt and pants, a belt. Marie shoved a thin blanket on top before I closed the latch. She put her hand on mine and squeezed. I couldn't look at her. But Anika caught my eye, hers wide and too honest, saying what we were all thinking: I would disappear like Leo. At the door again, Anika hugged me hard and stood tall.

"You'll come back," she said.

I smiled at the sky glistening in her eye. Nodded. Marie didn't speak. Her hands shook as she looked from me to the soldiers on the porch and back again, the heavy brow over her square face arched, nose flaring with the effort to stop from shouting, perhaps from lashing out. She gave me a piercing look. Nodded once. Yes.

We were loaded into a cattle wagon, young men and boys, some of them neighbors, reaching down to help me up as though we were going on a Jonge Wacht trip and this would be an adventure. The grind of gears, and we grabbed at the stock rails and each other to stay upright. I was near the tailgate, watching my sisters watching me. As I slid my fingers through the slats, I thought of Daniel's anguish. Now the reaching hands were mine and I had a sudden rush of anger, wishing Dad was there to see that all his terrible efforts had made no difference. I didn't want his imagination to console him, to lend the moment some kind of hope it didn't warrant.

The truck passed the barn and I saw Rudy standing with arms crossed, face unreadable. For the briefest moment I wondered if he would stop the truck and save me like he had Leo. But Rudy lowered his eyes, turned and walked into the barn. I let go of the rail.

The truck wound its way to Roermond, where we were herded onto the station platform, a gathered crowd watching. I looked into their eyes, recognized no one; absurd to think I would. The onlookers watched, expressionless under the scrutiny of the guards, just as I'd watched the new arrivals a few months ago. No one could do anything for me now. Prodded into a box car, I was pressed up so tight against others that my feet almost left the floor. The stench hit me and I threw my head about, searching for a way out, but there were only two tiny barred windows at the top of one wall. Lungs crushed, I couldn't breathe, started to shake, felt my eyes bulge, elbows thrashing so I jabbed the ribs of the man next to me. The world spun. Strong arms came round from behind and held me hard. A voice, coaxing. Focus on the voice. Breathe. Slower. My chest stopped heaving and I stood, still crammed, but calm.

"I'll let you go now," the voice said, and the arms faded away from me. "Name's Pete."

I couldn't turn, my body controlled by the actions of the others, an appendage to the mash of flesh. Cranking my head, I caught a glimpse of red hair at my shoulder, a collar. A small man then. And a priest. I was suddenly aware of myself.

"Thank you, Father," I stuttered. "I don't know what came over me ..."

"It's alright," he said quietly and patted my forearm where it rested against his own. "This is a hell of a thing."

"Yes."

"Keep your wits about you and don't give them an excuse to send you to Vught. Nobody comes out of there."

The train lurched and, as one, the carload of men almost toppled backward and then swayed upright, shuffling until we were a stable mass again. I was stuck fast, the priest behind, my nose almost pressed between the shoulder blades of a tall man in front. Surveying the little I could see, I caught my confusion and fear mirrored in the wide eyes of another boy from my school. I tried to smile reassurance as the train rumbled. Some of the men murmured, but mostly it was a group lost in silence.

Fifteen minutes later there was shouting as the train slowed and stopped with the sharp crunch of the couplings. Wailing from outside, and we were suddenly drenched in daylight as the door opened. Scuffling and cries of fear and more men were pushed into the jammed car. They were skin looking for flesh to wrap itself around, their cheekbones ridged through translucent skin, eyes swallowed in sockets, heads shaved.

"Escapees," the priest said behind me. "When they catch them, they shave their heads to show everyone else what they have attempted is impossible."

I had a terrible image of Leo.

The sun was cut off as the door closed. We waited an eternity, watching the shadows shift against the dark interior. Again without warning, the train started up and I was thrown into the back of the man in front, the priest's body pressed hard into me from behind. The car rattled and shook, swaying round a bend, the whole group writhing like snakes in a pit, claiming space. Moaning and more cries, angry now, and I felt the priest's chest expand and push into my back.

"Everyone, shut up." The voice boomed in my ear. More angry shouts and the priest yelled again. "Shut. Up."

"Who the hell are you?" The question came from the other side of the railcar.

"Father Pete, here."

A hush fell. The only sounds were the small, pained moans that had been coming from the far end of the car since I boarded.

"It looks like we'll have to get along in here if we're hoping not to suffocate one another," the priest said with the slightest hint of humor.

"Tell that to the goddamn Jood shitting in the corner!"

The reek of it hit my nose and I heard others sucking in breath through their mouths.

"All right, no need for that." Father Pete's voice was sharp. "Imagine he's been in here longer than us. Sick too. I suppose we still have room for a little pity." His voice lightened. "Besides, we'll all need to shit at some point, so we'll just save that spot for it."

More grumbling, but our full bowels reminded us it was true.

"Just cooperate a little. It'll all be fine."

"Fine? How the hell is this fine?" The tall man in front swung his head around to direct his quiet question at Father Pete, catching my eye and lifting his brow like the priest must be crazy.

I shrugged. "Not much else we can do."

"It's not that, kid," Father Pete's voice was soft in my ear. "We could throw the poor bastard off the train so we don't have to put up with his stench. It's not like anyone would notice. Or care."

The stunned faces of people emerging from the train in Roermond, the little girl reaching for her father.

"But it's what the Nazis want us to do." The priest paused. "It's what they've been having us do all along."

I was suddenly filled with a terrible awe. "They run on time."

"What's that?"

"The trains. They run on time. Always leave Roermond station on Tuesday at ten. Filled with Jews. And now us."

Silence.

"Why hasn't the resistance bombed the tracks?" The question hung there in the spaces between the men.

"Shut up, kid." The shoulders of the man in front were suddenly taut. "You'll get us all shot."

I lowered my voice. "And the men running the trains, they're Dutch."

"Everyone's afraid." Father Pete's voice was tired. "They keep us afraid so we forget how to trust our best instincts. We do their dirty work and pretend we don't know. But we'll all pay something in the end."

I thought of Daniel's anguish, his words. "No one dies too late," I whispered.

"Nobody's dying today, son. Let's just get through this, okay?"

But the priest was wrong.

Dusk fell. I could just make out the top of a row of trees through the slats. Countryside? A sharp pang seared my ribs imagining I might never see de Kruidenteelt again. Eyes closed, I stretched up toward the small window as though a smell or a sound would help me know where I was. The train jerked to another stop. German voices outside and we were blanketed in darkness, a cover thrown over the car just as the sound of bombers came from the distance. A nearby blast shook the car, forcing me to lean hard into the priest.

"What the hell is this?"

"Allied," someone shouted from across the car. "They're bombing the tracks."

The sound crashed through the car and everyone hunched down as though it would help to be closer to the floor. Fear mixed with the stench to constrict my throat and loosen my bowels. I didn't care about our destination anymore. I only hoped to survive the journey. I tried to focus on the place between the shoulder blades of the tall man, tried not to think. But pictures flashed through my head: Marie washing dishes, Anika scattering grain for the chickens. The morning walk to the potato field seemed distant already, meeting Petra a dream, and I imagined everything changed at home, that somehow everything familiar was gone. But I knew it was only me that had vanished.

In the corner, the Jew went into convulsions, those around him backing away and jamming everyone else further. Limbs and torsos parted long enough for me to make out the large yellow star still pinned to the breast pocket of a shirt that hung from a skeleton, to witness the man slip into unconsciousness and slump to the floor. No one moved, the silence in the car pulsing.

I felt fear around me. And then I felt something else. The air was bloated with loathing. The sick man had become a creature not quite human, but human enough to remind us we were all one long train ride from the same fate. And the men detested him for it. I detested him for it. Within minutes, everyone had turned away, all of us waiting for him to die so we could focus on survival. I should have felt ashamed, but god help me, I didn't.

Suddenly Father Pete was squeezing past, grabbing my hand and pulling me along to weave and squirm through to where the man lay in his own shit. The priest crouched, a cross in one hand as he laid his other on the man's head, wisps of hair poking through his fingers.

"Per istam sanctam unctionem ignoscat tibi Dominus quicquid peccaveris sive deliqueris."

The men were a wall inches from where the priest administered the sacrament. They eyed me as though I was an accomplice, and I took a quick step back.

"He's a bloody Jood!" someone muttered from the back.

"This man has nothing. And no one." The steel of Father Pete's voice cut through. "The least I can do is to send him off with a blessing. Even if it's not one he knows."

The men rumbled behind me. And the man lying on the floor in his own filth took one long staggering breath, and died. Father Pete crossed himself, then ran his hand down over the man's face to close his eyes and quietly motioned me toward the dead man's feet. Horrified, I gingerly held the man's boots, expecting the dead weight of a slaughtered pig. Instead the limbs were thin and fine like a bird's and we easily set the man just beyond the designated bathroom area, his face toward the wall. Tears prickled the back of my throat.

"It might have been for the best," the priest said softly. "We've been hearing terrible things."

I pictured Daniel watching as his wife and child were loaded onto a truck. Father Pete pulled me back so we stood behind the tall man again, claiming the spot as if it were home. Another blast shook the rail car and the men hunched further. One man retched not far from where I stood, his vomit staining the boots of another.

"For fuck's sake!"

It launched something primal in the men, an opening to a chorus of abuse directed first at one man and then at the lot of us, shouts about trodden toes and jabbed ribs and sweat and stink. Before long men were sobbing questions to the air. Someone began to pray. "Hail Mary" rung out across the car. "Our Father, if you are in heaven," odes to sweethearts, prayers for the protection of those long dead. I stuck my fingers in my ears. I was going to die in this mess, amidst the wailing of these wretched people. Tears streamed down my face and I couldn't stop the sob belching up from a gulf opened inside. When Father Pete's hand closed round my upper arm, I imagined it was my mom's hand, her breath warm in my ear.

"Enough praying," he hollered. "Let's sing."

He drew the rancid air deeply into his lungs and a clear low tenor sounded in my ear, quietly at first, strains that for years had only been hummed.

"Waar in 't bronsgroen eikenhout, 't nachtegaaltje zingt.

Over 't malse korenveld, 't lied des leeuweriks klinkt."

The men sniffed back tears, the spew of angry words and fear-stoked prayers ebbing away. The silence radiated outward as though the song were a stone dropped in water, until there was only the sound of the priest's voice singing the anthem of Limburg. Our anthem. It rose above us and pierced through the crash of bombs dropping nearby. Others slowly joined him, their voices coming out of the dark until a wave of song resounded through the railcar, the final note suspended an instant before retreating into a profound silence. I reached for Father Pete's hand still gripping my bicep and covered it with my own, grateful for this man and his courage. He wasn't ready to quit. I expected a hymn from a man of the cloth, but instead he started up a bar song, the words as rank as the smell around us, all of us laughing and joining in with an energy that kept our minds occupied. And then the priest launched into "Piet Hein":

"Piet Hein, Piet Hein
Piet Hein, zijn naam is klein."

Some tried a harmony or two. It sounded terrible, but we sang anyway. We stood and we sang as though life depended on it. Just as I became conscious of the quiet from outside, the cover came off the train and a gust of fresh night air came in through the window. The whole group breathed as one.

"Shut up in there," a guard yelled. "No more singing."

The train lurched forward.

"Zijn daden bennen groot
die heeft gewonnen, gewonnen de Zilvervloot!"

We laughed and sputtered and for an hour we swayed and sang together. Even as some dozed, even as the sun rose, the singing continued. Finally the train slowed and our voices trailed away as we sighed with relief. Father Pete continued loud behind me and I wanted to shush the man, his defiance become suddenly dangerous. A long whistle sounded and I caught sight of rooftops through the small windows. The thick metal latches on the car clanged loudly, the door squealing open even as the train lurched to a full stop, commands to quit singing shouted by men I couldn't see. Stunned by the light and uncertainty, I moved out with the others, slowly at first, finally spilling ragged and stinking out of the car and onto the platform, shielding my eyes from the sun and finding balance on ground that didn't rock.

Father Pete carried on loudly, purposefully, while the rest of us shuffled, eyes shifting to one another, ashamed to abandon the priest in such an obvious way, increasingly terrified at what might happen if we didn't. I watched an agitated German guard fix his eyes on the priest whose head was thrown back, singing like he was oblivious to the danger. The guard rushed toward him, gun drawn. I wanted to step forward, to intervene somehow. Before anyone knew what was happening, the guard spun the priest around and pushed the gun into his back, marching him down the steps of the platform. Father Pete stumbled, caught himself and continued to hum, the guard poking him in the back and barking orders.

"Stop," I whispered as much to the priest as to the German.

Soon I was prodded by the barrel of a gun and swallowed my horror, walking the platform to join more men emerging from other cars, all of us shuffling off the platform to form two lines as instructed. Caught in the surge of bodies, I hustled to do what I was told. A pistol shot sounded. I swung round in time to see Father Pete crumple in the distance, the priest's shock of red hair sending up a burst of dust as his head hit the ground.

For a moment I couldn't breathe, couldn't move, eyes riveted on the priest's lifeless body, my vision shrunk to the impossibility of the red hair on the ground. A hard shove from behind finally forced me into the forming line of men. One word reached through. Prisoner. Yesterday morning, I dug for potatoes. A man was just murdered, and I was the prisoner. My shudder caught the eye of the tall man, who had somehow remained at my side.

"Just do what they say," the man whispered, lightly touching my hand. "That priest was crazy."

Before I could respond, we were ordered to move out. The sign marking the station said Ommen. I was in Overijssel province, near the German border and far to the north of Limburg. We were prodded forward, expected to march quickly and efficiently. It was nearing noon again and I'd had nothing to eat or drink for a day and a half, but such complaints were puny beside those of the escapees with their shaved scalps and sallow skin. Head down, I concentrated on the boots of the man in front of me and tried not to panic. When I looked up, the sun was a brilliant reflection of the fields of heather, remnants of their fall bloom stretching pink to the horizon. A sheep bleated somewhere in the distance. I was sick for home.

I thought of Father Pete, dead for what? The right to sing? Perhaps the tall man was right. Perhaps the priest was crazy. But I knew it wasn't true. On the train, in the center of our fear and panic, Father Pete saved us from behaving like animals, saved us from our darkest selves so we could walk as men. Prisoners perhaps. But men. I was swept by an overwhelming gratitude and a wish for such courage. I heard Anika's words, imagined faint threads of the priest's tenor floating in the air around me. And I walked forward.

CHAPTER 13

Pray for Us Sinners

NGADIPURO VILLAGE, ISLAND OF JAVA,
DUTCH EAST INDIES
JANUARY 1948

THEY'VE NAMED THE BOY TAUFIK, meaning "good fortune" —
Darma's choice, and Sam's not sure it fits. The boy's constant
presence is unnerving, the way he materializes out of thin air, ever
aware of Sam's needs — water for bathing or polish for his boots.
But it's Taufik's silence that bothers Sam most. Maybe because it's
clear the boy can speak, but chooses not to. It seems such silence
is a kind of judgment, though the boy looks at Sam only with a
reverence that Sam might have once held for Leo.

Today they walk into Ngadipuro to check on the clinic. The
squad had built it in the previous days, sinking stilts into the ground
for the raised bamboo platform, the locals pitching in to cover the
clinic with a red-clay shingled roof. When it was finished, Sam
helped Sari arrange a couple of stretchers doubling as permanent
cots, a table, some chairs and shelving for drugs and first aid supplies to be replenished from a locked shed out back.

"I knew you could do it," she'd said, and smiled up at him with
such gratitude he thought his chest might split with pride. Hagen

even assigned a real doctor to the village, Paul Appeldoorn, a staff sergeant who outranks Raj, but just barely.

Raj had muttered through the days it took to build. "You better be right about this, Vandenberg," he said. But he seemed more excited than angry, consulting with Appeldoorn on every detail and scolding the men for small imperfections. Sam wonders if the threat the clinic might pose is less a concern for Raj than the fact it wasn't Raj's idea, Sari and her mother telling the population of Ngadipuro that the clinic is Sam's doing.

Now as he approaches, a woman nods brightly to him from a porch where she swings her baby in a large fabric sling, its ends knotted and attached by ropes to a bamboo ceiling beam, each gentle pull on the rope sending the baby in an ever-widening arc. On another front step, three tiny old women peer at him through eyes sunk like thumbtacks in a wrinkled roadmap, their toothless mouths gossiping so fast he wonders if any of them hears a thing the other has to say. They watch him pass, smiling without stopping the flow of words.

At the clinic, he sees two heads bent together in intense conversation over some instruments on the table. His heart flops. Sari and Appeldoorn. They don't look up until he coughs from a few meters away.

"Sam." Appeldoorn jumps down to stand beside him and survey the site, his upper lip glistening with sweat, his short blond hair curled a little with the humidity, pecs rippling under soaked shirt. "I hope you and Hagen are right about this. Don't get me wrong, I'm all for trying to gain their trust, just not sure it'll work. Sure, they'll use our services, but I don't imagine that will induce them to give up their sons and brothers in return. It'll help the kids, though." He looks down at Taufik's jaundiced eyes. "You need a round of quinine." He ruffles the boy's hair and heads toward the shed.

Sari sweeps her gaze to the clinic around her and smiles, pulling syringes and bandages from one of the trunks and arranging them on a small cart. Her head tilts as she admires her work and Sam feels a rush of desire so strong he almost swoons. Gathering his courage to speak to her, he starts up the stairs just as Appeldoorn comes from the other side of the platform, Taufik in tow. Appeldoorn says something to Sari and they laugh together, nodding at the boy, who beams up at them. It's embarrassing how they leave Sam out of the exchange. He turns as though suddenly remembering somewhere he has to be, walking out of the village and across the bridge back to barracks.

Grabbing paper and pen from his trunk, he slams the lid and flops onto his bunk to begin a love letter to Petra, filling the page with his undying devotion from the other side of the world, his desire to hold her, vaulted talk of common destiny and fate, of how his love has grown only stronger with distance.

"What bullshit!" He throws his pen to the floor where its parts scatter under the bunks.

"What's up?" Andre is playing solitaire on his bed.

Darma makes his way over from his bunk at the other end of the room. They've kept their distance. Perhaps Darma doesn't know how Sam feels about what he saw in Malang. Sam has stayed away because he doesn't know either.

"Bad news from home?" Darma picks up the parts of the pen, puts the cartridge back together.

"No. Never mind." He takes the pen from Darma. "What do you know of Appeldoorn? I mean, he seems a good enough guy, right?"

"For Sari?" Andre says and chuckles. "Come on, Sam, it's in your moon eyes every time you look at her."

"She won't have anything to do with Appeldoorn," Darma chimes in. "She's very traditional and way too smart to get mixed up with him. He's kind of creepy don't you think? So damn perfect. But don't you have a girlfriend?"

"I thought I did. But she hasn't written in weeks. Even after all I've told her."

"Well, it'd be hard for her," Darma says slowly. "Her life hasn't changed and she has no idea what yours has become. And no idea how much you need her to give a shit."

"That's why I've got Bonita," Andre whispers. "She knows what's happening. She's in the middle of it. Even washes our stinking clothes. And she still wants to be with me. Me." His grin is huge with joy.

A homo and a man in love with an Indo. These are his friends. And they are getting more love than Sam's had in his life. Or at least more sex.

"Shut up, both of you." He stomps out of barracks and slips all the way down the bank to the river, kicking at rocks as he walks up and down its banks until his anger ebbs. He skips a few flat stones, stupidly pleased when one skitters seven times and a young boy on the other bank cheers in appreciation. Finally Sam sits on a large flat rock by the river until the sun disappears and he is cloaked in darkness. He should go back to the post, but can't bring himself to leave, instead watching the stars sparkle awake one by one.

He tells everyone the clinic is for the kids. Help the kids and the parents will support us, he says, but in his mind the clinic is his gift to Sari. And now that goddamned Appeldoorn.

Suddenly a hand on his arm.

"For shit's sake, Taufik."

The boy puts a finger to his lips as he hands Sam a note.

Please come. Sari.

Just like that. Sam rushes to the clinic.

Taufik leads, hugging the bank of the river, thick jungle shielding them from the post where Sam's own men watch. He strains to hear over the river's tumble and splash. They walk a hundred meters before the boy stops at a quiet spot where a small bamboo raft is tied to a tree.

"What the hell?" Sam pulls back. "Taufik, they'll think we're ploppers. Shoot us."

Taufik shakes his head. Jesus, Sam wishes the boy would speak. He feels the crumpled note in his hand and climbs onto the raft, Taufik poling it across while Sam crouches, swiveling his head to peer into the growing darkness, waiting for a bullet. He looks back. It shouldn't be this easy, the post so vulnerable; he'll have to tell Raj so they make some changes.

The raft hits the other side with a thump and Taufik takes Sam's hand in the dark, leading him down a narrow path through heavy jungle, the steady hum of the river fading behind them. Entering Ngadipuro through a side path, they snake their way between the dark, quiet homes. As they approach the clinic, he hears murmuring voices, a low groan. He's only got his pistol. Fuck, such an idiot. He looks hard at Taufik. The boy disappears around the edge of the clinic platform. Sam feels naked in the night, a target standing in the street under the light of the full moon.

Sari appears from behind the screen. "Oh, Sam, thank goodness. Come."

His doubt vanishes at the relief in her voice and he jumps to the platform, startled by the dark silhouette of a soldier sitting in the corner. The man wears a dark beret, two grains of rice the insignia on his shoulder patch, a round of ammunition worn like a necklace. A Lee–Enfield is strapped to his shoulder and rests across his knees. Sam freezes as the realization hits. Jago. Sari grips his arm hard and gestures to a stretcher where silver hair halos another man's face. It is Amir.

Sari returns to her father's side, dipping a cloth to wipe his face and neck and chest, Amir motionless, the muscles of his wrestler's body shrunk and hollowed, eyes closed in a face gray with pain. A tremendous stench wafts from Amir, reminding Sam of offal from butchered hogs. His head swings from Amir to Sari to the rebel soldier. He wants to run away, doesn't know what's expected of him here.

"The burns on his hands are infected. It's spreading." Sari's voice is pinched.

"I'll get Appeldoorn."

"No." She points her chin at the soldier still silent in the corner. "No. I need you to get into the supply shed, find disinfectant and bandages. And penicillin."

"Sari, I can't. I'd be court-martialed."

"You agreed this clinic could help the local people."

"Locals. Not the enemy."

"He's my father." She stares at him, searching for words. "He's a good man, Sam." He doesn't respond and her voice hardens. "Besides, Paul treats everyone, even when he wonders about their allegiances. This is no different."

"If Paul is so great, why not get him to help?"

She looks at him in surprise and he blushes. There's a gun pointed at them for Christ's sake. She gestures to the soldier, who continues to gaze at Sam without expression. "Because Paul might draw the line at a uniform."

"And me? Why shouldn't I draw the same line?"

"You promised my father protection." She thrusts her chin in the air. "And this all happened because you and your men showed up that night."

He's stung. It's an impossible thing. The soldier in the corner sits upright and statue quiet. The man is graying like Amir, face creased and hollow. He meets Sam's gaze, eyes deep with patient confidence, dark with the certainty that Sam will eventually do what Sari asks. All of a sudden, Sam sees what is happening; the safety on the man's rifle disengaged, the gun cocked and aimed ever-so-slightly toward Taufik and Sari. Sweat collects on Sam's upper lip and he sucks it in. Clarity is swift and merciful; he will do what he is told.

"I'll need Taufik to watch for the patrol," he says quietly, hoping to get the boy out of danger, terrified to leave Sari. She sighs with relief, catches his hand and squeezes it. Either she has no idea or she's a good actor, and they will both pretend Sam is making a choice.

"Yes, take him." She glances toward the soldier. His nod is almost imperceptible.

Sam leads Taufik away from the clinic and toward a small shed a few meters away. "Go wait at the raft for me."

Taufik shakes his head hard.

"Taufik, go." He pushes the boy toward the alley.

Two soldiers are stationed to protect the clinic and the supplies. Sam's breath comes hard and fast as their headlamps push light into the dark streets. He will be shot if he's caught, either by his friends thinking he's a rebel, or by a jury of his peers. How the hell is this happening? A picture of the rebel's gun. Sari's face. The headlamps fade away from him and he runs toward the shed. He has no way to break the padlock on the door and hurries to the back, spots a window under the eave, too high and too small.

A hand on his arm. His bowels drop. "Christ, Taufik," he hisses. "What are you doing? I told you to wait for me."

Taufik points to the window and lifts his leg for Sam to boost him. When Sam hesitates, the boy gives him a long look; they both know what the solider will do. Sam checks around the corner of the shed for the patrol, boosts Taufik to the window and hears a soft thud as the boy lands. "Disinfectant, swabs, bandages," he whispers through the bamboo wall. "And penicillin."

Taufik grunts and something drops inside. The headlamps turn toward them.

"Hurry." Silence from inside. "Taufik?"

Suddenly the boy's face appears at the window and he drops packages down to Sam one at a time, scrambles after them and jumps to the ground, sprinting away toward the river as he lands. Sam tucks the bottle of penicillin into his pocket, shoves the bandages into the waist of his pants and pulls his shirt over them. Stops. What is this choice he's making? He could simply run away and let Amir die. Sam would be the only one to know, the only one to care. It wouldn't change the course of this war. Or even of his life. He has no idea what Amir is; could be a rebel leader for all Sam knows. But he can't get the picture of Amir in his workshop out of his head, Amir the farmer. Amir, the man who reminds Sam of Leo.

And the rebel will kill Sari. He knows that for a fact. The army would say she's just a Javanese and not worth this treason. But he can't even think it. He runs out of time before answers and finds himself at the foot of the stairs leading to the platform. He climbs. The rebel hasn't moved but his teeth glint in a slight smile; he knew what Sam would choose.

Amir's hands are covered in infected oozing pustules, fusing together like frog web. Sari swabs them with the disinfectant, her father's eyes startling open with recognition, quickly fading back into fevered vacancy. She wraps thin strips of bandages around and between each finger to keep them separated, the white cloth quickly turning yellow even before she begins to wrap each hand in larger, more protective swaths. Sam watches her, glances toward the rebel, who has closed his eyes.

"I think he's hurt too," she whispers.

"Why did he bring your father here? What has Amir been doing?"

She continues her work as though she hasn't heard. Attaching a needle to the end of a small syringe, she draws penicillin from the bottle and plunges it into Amir's arm.

"Sari, I need to know. You can't ask me to help you if he's going to come back and kill us."

"My father hasn't killed anyone. But they want him to." She grimaces as her father moans. The soldier's eyes open and he fingers the trigger on his gun, eyes fluttering closed again. "They were coming to the farm long before you or the TNI, promising land reform. My father just wants to farm. But he has influence in the area. The PKI want him to do more."

"PKI?"

"Communists." She glances at the soldier.

Sam is struck again at his ignorance. He thought it was simple: him against the rebel forces who might look a little different but are all fighting the same battle, all the same degree of enemy. But his efforts are like a sideshow, just an annoyance to all the interests vying for power. His thoughts rattle, anger bridging between them. Why is he doing any of this?

The rebel is awake now and watching him, certain of Sam's impotence, just like the punk at Roermond. Rage soars up from Sam's gut and he wants to crack the man's neck, holler so the patrol comes and puts a bullet into his smug face. But the Lee–Enfield stops him, the soldier pointing it directly at Sari as he recognizes Sam's rage and smiles slowly, shaking his head. Motioning to Amir, the rebel speaks intensely to Sari, the singsong of his Javanese incongruous with his filthy hands.

"What?" Sam asks. "What is he saying?"

"He's taking my father with him." Fear catches in her voice. "His men are outside. They'll kill you if you follow."

"Jesus."

He watches them leave, the soldier almost buckling as he heaves Amir's limp body over his shoulder. Blood stains the man's right thigh and he winces as he walks. But his rifle is cocked and aimed at Sam as he backs down the stairs and turns into an alley. Sam follows him a few meters and watches as they disappear into the night jungle.

"Sam," Sari whispers behind him. He turns to see the tears in her eyes. "You have to believe me. He's a good man."

He hears the two men on patrol, a short laugh, murmured conversation. They have no idea. Hit by a wave of guilty panic, he leaves Sari without a word and makes his way back to the edge of the village. Taufik steps from behind the trunk of a palm tree.

Sam jumps. "Do you have to scare the shit out of me every time?"

The boy simply takes his hand again, leading him back to the small raft at the edge of the river. Sam crouches in the middle, wondering if guerrilla fighters have their rifles trained on him right now, if he will die here looking up at the glittering stars. Pray for us sinners, now and at the hour of our death.

Taufik looks amused.

Sam didn't mean to pray aloud. "Amen," he says, and they scramble up the side of the bank, hoping the jungle hides them. He cringes as the door to barracks opens and Freddy emerges, rubbing sleep from his eyes and heading to the toilet.

"Where the hell were you?"

"Toilet, same as you."

"Hmm ..."

Freddy looks at Taufik with vacant eyes, back at Sam, but seems not to make a connection, hurrying to the open-air toilet surrounded by stone walls and moaning a little as the diarrhea shoots from him. Sam tells himself the man is too sick to remember what he saw. He crawls into bed and falls into nervous sleep.

"Shit, Sam. Were you sleepwalking?" Andre stands in his underwear beside Sam's bed.

Sunlight from the small window singes Sam's eyes. He can barely turn his head, neck and shoulders knotted. He's tracked river mud to the side of his bed, his boots caked in it. His clothes are rumpled and he quickly shoves the corner of a bandage back into his pocket, glancing up to see if Andre has noticed.

"Couldn't sleep. I went for a walk."

Andre raises an eyebrow. "Okay."

"Sorry for the mess. I'll clean it up."

His friend throws puzzled glances at Sam as they dress. Sam sweeps and mops the wooden floor between their beds, then takes his boots outside to scrape off the mud and polish them.

"We've got patrol this morning," Andre says, passing by him. "I'm going for breakfast."

"I'll be right there." He wants to find a way to tell his friend what happened, but it will implicate Sari. And Taufik. Him. No one was hurt. And Sari is safe. Only a few supplies. Besides, it's like Sari said, Appeldoorn treats everyone who comes to him. Last night was no different. Suddenly he understands how his father could be made angry and small by the depth of the choices he was forced to make.

Finished with his boots, Sam dresses in clean khakis and makes his bed. On his way to the low shack where Bonita serves them breakfast, he sees the recent days of sun have dried the mud around barracks. For the first time in weeks, there is no mud.

Appeldoorn is in the shack, shouting at Raj, demanding doubled patrol numbers in the village. "Sons of bitches broke into the shed, came right into the clinic. How'd your men not see them?"

Freddy speaks behind his hand to Raj, Sam trying to still his face as Raj looks across the shack to meet his gaze. Instead of rage, Sam sees disappointment crease the corners of Raj's frown. The one time Raj trusted anyone with anything, and Sam let him down. Good god, if someone like Raj is disappointed in him . . . Sam watches Raj turn to follow Appeldoorn, tiredly haggling over the number of men he can spare. Freddy throws Sam a satisfied look, slowly turning his gaze to hover over Taufik. Sam's skin crawls.

"Sari must be scared," Andre says quietly to Bonita as she serves them.

"She's sick. Tuan Appeldoorn asked my help." She sighs. "I'm a cook. No good with blood."

Andre laughs and catches Bonita's hand a moment before returning to his eggs. Sam pretends he hasn't heard.

They patrol, they eat, they sleep. They hear reports the rebels are more defiant, bold, coming down from the mountains to infiltrate the villages and forcing the civilians to supply food and shelter or risk being burned out or executed. Close to the demarcation line, Ngadipuro is at risk. Sam claims the village like it is home and he its protector, guilt like a toxin in his blood so he works as though his commitment to patrol and paperwork will earn him forgiveness for stealing the supplies and putting members of his squad at risk.

He's avoided Sari, angry at himself for being drawn into her family's problems, but angry at her too, those expectant brown eyes and that shy smile. He keeps to himself, staying away from the clinic and watching from a distance as Sari and Appeldoorn work separately or together on soldiers and those men claiming to be villagers. Sam holds his gun a little tighter at any resemblance to the rebel who brought Amir to the clinic; his only wish is to confront the man and shoot him if necessary. He wills himself strong, refuses to allow the quaking in his heart to reach his hands or face, refusing to feel small again.

Two more men from the squad are killed by snipers, Joost and Hans taken out as they patrol the bridge and road into the village. Raj is relentless, working the rest overtime. Sam casually mentions the inadequacy of the sightlines from the post to the riverbank and the men chop down the offending trees. From there, Raj sends Sam, Andre and Darma to check the fence surrounding the village for weaknesses. They find two places where the wire was cut and burrows scraped to crawl under.

"Hey man, slow down." Andre shuffles to catch up as they walk the perimeter, slashing at undergrowth determined to grow fast enough to outpace their machetes. "We gotta do this all day; no point killing ourselves the first hour."

"Just pisses me off." Sam waves at the jungle, flinging sweat from his hand. "They could be watching us right now."

Andre shakes his head. "Yep."

"I've got my eyes on, Sam," Darma says from a half-fallen tree he's climbed, surveying the jungle as the other two work. "Nobody'll snipe you on my watch."

"Yeah, right," Sam mutters. "Your prissy little ass is gonna save mine."

Darma stares down at Sam.

"Whoa, Sam," Andre says. "What the hell?"

"Just saying."

"Saying what?"

"Saying is he man enough?" Sam wags his little finger in the air. Andre's eyes narrow as Darma sucks in his breath. Sam can't stop. "Or you." He whirls toward Andre. "What if one of them was Bonita's brother? You be able to shoot him?"

"I don't know what the fuck is wrong with you, Sam, but you better shut the hell up."

They stare at each other. The cicadas hum. Tall bamboo sways.

"We've all got each other's ass." Andre's words are even and measured. "If you don't have ours, I don't want you here."

Sam looks at the ground, then up, throat closing at the disbelief in Darma's face. Shame fills him. What is wrong with him? He nods once and then again, swallowing hard. "I know . . . I don't. I know." He looks up at Darma.

Darma closes his eyes, breathes deeply and opens them again. Nods.

"Okay." Andre looks back and forth between the two men. "Okay." They get back to work.

Sam is an asshole, turning on his friends to deflect his guilt, to measure his actions against something. Because he's afraid he is a traitor now. Or is that only true if Amir is a rebel? Maybe there's some other label for what he's done. No one seems to call things what they are anymore, words slipping the knot that ties them to their meaning so no one is forced to judge. Not a war, they say, but police actions. Not a massacre, but an incident. As though the name makes a difference. Not a traitor, but a . . . humanitarian? Right.

They've heard news of a real traitor, a Dutch conscript who deserted his platoon after Rawagede, saying he has a philosophical disagreement with colonialism and how the Dutch are suppressing independence. No one can believe a man would switch sides like that. Shoot at his own. How is it possible? Sam pictures the Dutch soldiers who chased Darma. Would they have killed him as Marcel said? And what had Sam done by helping Amir? If he's not a traitor, he certainly is an asshole.

CHAPTER 14

This Strange Family

FEBRUARY 1948

THE SKY THREATENS TO DROWN them. The Brantas River roars with the deluge of rain, ready to suck felled trees and debris down its length and toss it all up on the boulders downstream, threatening to sweep away the village and the post. It thunders on the tin roof of the barracks while Sam sits inside, sweat dripping under his arms and gathering at the waistband of his shorts, the humidity stuck to his skin and crushing his lungs.

He finishes writing in the notebook and lies back, arm over his eyes. He doesn't write to Petra anymore. What would he tell her? That he's starting to believe in witch doctors and spirits. That he has a homosexual friend who treats Sam as though he hasn't been an asshole, making him feel even smaller than before. That he can't tell friend from enemy, the lines so blurred they shade the space between right and wrong.

Sari only wanted to help her father in the clinic. He understands that. But he wonders what more she is doing, who else she is helping with her beautiful brown eyes and her gift for healing. He knows the power of such people. Like his sisters, or Father Pete.

Even Rudy. Do these people choose to do good? Or are they some-how chosen? He sighs and pulls on his flask. He's drinking too much. He should talk to Father Keenan, but knows he won't.

On a rainy Saturday, Andre and Darma corner him, sitting on either side of him on his bunk.

"There's a woman that opened a pub in town last week. We're taking you for a drink." Andre is excited at the prospect of this new thing. When Sam protests, they simply heave him onto his feet and push him out the door. "Oh come on, Sam. Whatever it is, let it go. A few beers won't hurt you."

They run through the rain, sliding into the muddy village and ducking through the door of a low building. On the outside it's like many village buildings — three-quarter bamboo walls, red tile roof, a wood floor — but inside it's filled with round tables, a bar at one end and a small dance floor at the other. A radio plays a loud and crackling "Lili Marleen." Darma and Andre lead Sam to sit at the bar, *Welcome to the jungle* carved into the wall behind. They order double whiskies.

"Well, you're starting hard." The accent is unmistakably Limburgish. A blue-eyed woman surveys them from behind the bar, crashes three more shots down and motions for them to drink up. Sam slugs one back, sputters, eyes watering. She smirks and sets a beer in front of each of them. "That'll hold you a while."

A short woman, she is thick and strong, breasts almost bursting the buttons on her shirt, dark stains under her arms. She wears a skirt, and sandals with a heel, the men watching as she struts away to bang a tray full of beer onto a table, leaning in to whisper some-thing to four attentive soldiers who burst into laughter around her as she walks back. She seems too old for this.

Sitting down beside Sam, she sighs and lights up a fat kretek, the cloves within crackling as their smell combines with tobacco to waft over him. He quickly reaches for his own pack.

"Not that shit," she says, pushing her kretek between his lips and lighting another for herself. He inhales deeply, the dark taste steaming through his mouth and into his lungs, his delighted sigh blowing the fragrant smoke into the air. It is pure, unfiltered joy. He takes a swig of beer and feels himself let go of the tension in his shoulders and the clenching in his gut even as he tries to hang on to his vigilance. He's so tired. He only needs a little rest, this chance to relax before taking up his gun again, his duty.

"There you go," she says, as if knowing his thoughts. She puts a hand on his knee and Andre gives him a sidelong glance before wandering off to sit with Darma.

Sam leans away from her, but doesn't want to seem rude. "What's your name?" he asks.

"Cora. And don't worry, I'm not after anything. You just seem like a nice young man is all." She leans back a little, takes him in with a calculating eye. "And handsome too."

He blushes. He likes this woman, Cora, her large voice and attitude, wonders if she's hiding something behind it all.

"Why are you here?" he asks suddenly.

"Jesus, you get right to the point, don't you?" The whiskey is warm in his belly and he's happy to wait. She gazes at him through the smoke spiraling around them. "I grew up here. Well, not here, but in Malang. My father came to make his fortune with the VOC."

"What did he do?"

"Trader. He was away most of the time, sailing the Indian Ocean, looking for markets." She looks up. "Damn. Right back." She slips behind the bar and pours liquids from various bottles into an array of glasses, then hustles the drinks over to where Appeldoorn sits with Raj and a few others at a side table. Bart pats her ass and she cuffs his ear.

"Where was I?" she says, breathless as she slides onto the stool beside him again. "Oh yes, lovely childhood and all that. Nannies and houseboys, gardeners and cooks. I was a spoiled little bitch." She laughs when he cringes. "But somebody decided they could handle it, and married me. A company man just like my father, only Franz was into oil. It was the next big thing, and he made a fortune.

Until the government blew up the refineries to keep them out of the hands of the Japs." She pauses. "He killed himself."

"Shit, I'm sorry."

"Yes, well, don't be." She grabs a rag to wipe the bar, then folds her hands in front of her. "They were coming for him, for both of us. He knew he'd end up dead in one of their camps so he decided to beat them to it. He was a weak man." Her voice is sharp. "Left me to face them alone."

The whiskey turns sour in his belly.

"But he didn't know I'd been fucking the gardener while he was away. Oh don't look so shocked. My husband had other women. In Singapore, Malacca, Siam."

"Why do you talk like that?" Sam asks, his words slurring out of the whiskey fog building in his head.

"Don't be such a child," she says, but her voice softens a little when he blushes. "The gardener saved me from the Kempeitai, forged documents for me. His mother took me in when she found out I was pregnant with her grandchild. And so I lived in the village. And now I have this place."

"What's his name? The gardener."

"What is it with you and names? Hasan. His name is Hasan." Her hard edge evaporates an instant. "I haven't seen him for two years."

"Jesus, he's not with them?" Sam pulls away from her.

"I don't know." She sucks on her cigarette and blows smoke rings into the air as though it's not a critical question, as though loyalties don't matter.

"But you're Dutch . . . ?"

She cuts him off with a wave of her hand, stands up and goes behind the bar to pour a whiskey and open a beer. "I've lived here my whole life. I know this place and these people. My kids are Javanese, and the Dutch want to keep them in chains. You don't know who I am." Before Sam can register her words, Andre and Darma are by his side and her face masks over. "Well if it isn't the other two musketeers."

The three get very drunk.

The music slows. Native women materialize. Some hold up soldiers who sway with their arms wrapped round the girls' waists, happy for any kind of contact. Everyone pretends they see nothing, know nothing of wives and girlfriends at home, a collective understanding that this place is not home and so the rules of home do not apply. One of the women is older than the rest and she sits on the lap of a young recruit who blushes at the erection she encourages with her slow movements. In the light of the kerosene lamp, her expression is far away from this place and unaware of the increasing frenzy of the young soldier under her as he struggles to stave off the inevitable, not wanting to embarrass himself in front of his peers. She doesn't care, is here for the money he will leave, anticipating that her success with him will encourage others to pay for her experience.

Darma stumbles to the edge of the small dance floor and sways alone, clutching a beer in front of him, smiling softly and eyes closed. His head tilts a little as though he hears something in the music meant only for him, oblivious to the noisy bar and drunken men around him.

"He's a poof, that one."

"Right bit of faggot," someone jeers.

"Get him out of here."

"Leave him alone," Sam says. The words hang in the silence a minute before descending like an accusation.

"You should all get out of here," Cora says, flicking the sound system off. "I'm closing up, boys."

The men protest, but she ushers them out anyway, leaving Sam, Andre and Darma until last. Darma is so drunk he can barely stand. "Does that boy have a death wish?" Cora shakes her head. "You gotta tell him to be more careful."

Andre gives Sam a sharp look through narrowed eyes. They prop Darma between them and stagger back to barracks, dumping him in his bunk and heading back outside for a piss.

"What the hell was that?" Andre asks. "Is he a homo?"

"Does it matter?"

"Well, Christ yeah, it matters."

Sam stands pissing and swaying, thoughts muddled in alcohol. Why does Darma make the other men so angry? Why anger, as though Darma has betrayed them, as though he owes them his manhood. Sam gazes into the night, picturing Marcel's bruised face.

"You told me we have each other's backs, no matter what," he says into the night. They all have secrets now. "You've got your own shit to hide. Just let it go."

Andre nods, but looks skeptical as he heads to his bunk. He doesn't kneel or pull out his beads tonight. Sam hopes it's because his friend is too drunk, but he wonders if they are all fading away from themselves, losing connections to things they once thought important, unsure if any of it means anything anymore.

The rain is loud but it keeps the rebels quiet. Finally, the heavy clouds thin, blue breaking through to rope across the sky, the sun casting light back over the past dark days to lift Sam's spirits. He wants to get away from the post and the village, and he wants to do something to show Darma that Sam is not like the others, that he can be generous like Marcel. The unit gets a day leave and Sam hits on an idea; he will take Darma fishing. By the time it is arranged, Andre and Bonita and Taufik are included as well.

"If I had a day off, I'd go to Malang and get laid." Young Willem looks up from his book, glasses hanging on the tip of his nose.

"Right," Sam laughs.

Andre throws a blanket in the back of the jeep, raising his eyebrows suggestively. Sam grins, fills a flask with whiskey and a jug with water and they drive into Ngadipuro, a flock of children running to catch them, envious of Taufik beaming in the back seat. One more stop for Bonita. Sari is with her. Bonita gives Sam a mischievous smile and he mumbles hello as she swings an overflowing basket into the jeep and climbs in the back with Andre and Taufik, Darma riding shotgun with Sari snugged between.

They head further east into relatively safe Dutch-held territory, their Stens resting in the far back. In the mirror, Sam watches Taufik absently stroke the barrel of one weapon, eyes flicking back and forth as the jungle races past, opening suddenly into sun-warmed fields. Villagers take advantage of the break in the weather to descend the trails from their homes and check on rice paddies that will soon be harvested. Others pick tea leaves. He catches Taufik's eyes and they grin at one another as he settles behind the wheel to enjoy the feel of the wind in his face.

"It's a fine day for fishing." He sneaks a glance at Sari, blushing when she smiles up at him.

The rains have flushed the countryside clean, forcing flowers full, creating a vivid splash of yellow and red and orange and blue against the sparkling greens. The sun is intense, the breeze from the moving jeep unable to cut through the humidity. Sam drives off the main road onto a small trail that leads to a tributary, the water shimmering in the jungle heat. Unloading their picnic, they set up in the shade of a huge jambolan, its leafy foliage reaching thirty meters into the air, decaying orbs of its blood-colored fruit on the ground. Taufik takes off to the edge of the stream, stripping down to his shorts and hopscotching across the rocks and into the water to float lazily on his back. Sam joins him, and they are quickly splashing and dunking one another until Andre and Darma join them in a free-for-all. Bonita and Sari laugh from where they sit on a large rock and dangle their feet in the water.

"Must be fish." Andre points downriver to where they can make out the silhouette of a man standing in the middle of the confluence of this stream and another, line flashing in the sun from the rod stretched tall in front of him, head bent to where his hands clasp the spool.

Taufik pokes Sam, handing over the two rods Sam made from bamboo and equipped with line he managed to buy in Ngadipuro.

The leader is wound from trip wire, simple J-hooks made from surplus ends of the village's perimeter fence. He attaches a pill bottle with a couple of rocks in it for a weighted bobber.

"Okay, let's go," Sam says to Taufik.

They stand on a rock where Sam casts his line and watches it flash across the water to land in the middle of the stream and float with the lazy current. The whole rig works remarkably well, and he feels an unusual contentment. He outfits the other rod for Taufik, shows the boy how to cast and sends him to a spot a few meters away to avoid their lines tangling. After a few minutes, Sam sits, the rock cool against his legs, the rod held lazily in one hand. He doesn't really expect to catch anything, happy to jig and let his mind go.

He watches Andre and Bonita side by side on the blanket. Their lips move in quiet conversation and he feels a wave of envy, a sudden longing for that kind of intimacy. He doesn't remember it in his own life, Anika the only one in the family able to show her feelings. It's sad, he thinks now as he watches his fishing line tugged by the river current, to have lived his life so long without such expression.

His chest aches with wanting as he watches Sari. She sits on the riverbank, leaning against a tree, book forgotten in her lap as she stares into the distance. She suddenly looks at him and, on impulse, he beckons to her, surprised when she smiles and comes to sit on the rock, arranging her sarong, her thigh a hand-width from his. He isn't sure what to say to her, hasn't spoken with her since the night he helped with Amir. He's imagined how he might explain why he ran from the clinic, imagined apologizing, but how to be sorry without giving the wrong impression of his loyalties. The silence is long.

"I'm glad you came," he says finally. "I would have invited you but I wasn't sure ..."

"How are you?" she asks, a little breathless. Maybe she's as nervous as he is.

"Fine," he says. "And you?"

She nods.

"The clinic is busy."

"Yes, it's been so good for the village. The children."

Good for Amir too, he thinks, and wonders again why he can't control the mean thoughts in his head. He is desperate to ask her what it all meant. For her. For them. But he can't. Not without asking her impossible questions about her father. Not without telling her the rebel at the clinic made him feel so weak and small the memory turns his thoughts to violence. Not without telling her that in the dark jungle nights he's wondered if it would have been easier just to walk away and let the rebel make the choice about her life. And here she is so close. So beautiful. He watches his line and bobber as though, in this moment, catching a fish is the most important thing in the world. Butterflies whirl in his stomach.

"I'm happy for her," Sari says, nodding to where Andre and Bonita sit. "There was a time I envied her light skin. When I was ashamed of my own, embarrassed by my father and the work he did for the Hegmans."

Sam listens with his whole body. "But your father seems a proud man. And you . . . you are beautiful." He feels his face redden.

She looks at him gratefully. "Perhaps, but we lived in servitude. To her family."

"What?"

"Bonita is a Hegman, Sam. Indo. And when the Dutch were in control she had everything I wanted, the best toys when we were children, education in the best schools, freedom. We became friends in spite of our differences — good friends — and they treated us well, but I knew I'd never have the opportunities she did and that she'd leave me behind."

He knows nothing, embarrassed again at his conceit that he might make a difference in this country.

"The Japanese came. And her light skin didn't protect her anymore. They sent her parents with the romusha, worked them to death. And kept Bonita. It was unimaginable what they did to her."

Her voice breaks. "My mother found a way to get her off the plantation and hide her here in Ngadipuro."

"Dear god." Sam looks to where Bonita sits laughing quietly with Andre. "Does Andre know?"

"Does it matter? Look at her."

Her words so tender he can't stop himself turning to see the sadness in her eyes radiate through the fine features of her face, such compassion he can barely breathe. He swallows hard, looking to the river. The sun is high, bright jewels of light bouncing across rivulets of water.

"I'm not ashamed of my father anymore," she says. "It was terrible what the Japanese did, but they let my father run the plantation, gave him independence even before Sukarno proclaimed it. He came alive then. Before the Dutch came back it felt like we all had a real future."

The Dutch.

"I thought we were here to help, to secure a future for everyone in this country," Sam says quietly. He remembers Amir in the shed, a man comfortable in his own skin, hoping only to be left alone to fix a Mixmaster for his wife and grow coffee for his livelihood. "But I don't know what we're doing."

She sighs her agreement at his ignorance. "Sam, I need to thank you."

"No." He says it too quickly. "Please, don't thank me. I'm still not sure I did the right thing."

She's quiet again.

"I know how that sounds, but it's just . . ." Raj's disappointment flashes through his head.

She nods. "None of us knows what's right. But you did save my father." She moves to cover his hand with hers on the rock between them, her small fingers pressing into the tops of his. "And me."

He saved her from the rebel. He did. This beautiful, gentle girl. And suddenly, he can't think of anything he's happier to have done.

He lifts his hand so their fingers twine. Eyes on the river, he moves his thumb across her palm, up the length of her fine index finger. She doesn't move. Finally he turns to see her eyes are closed, the brown glow of her face lifted to the sun. His fingers touch the inside of her narrow wrist, feel the pulse there as her breath catches. His doubts evaporate. This is all he wants. Just this. Her hand in his, with the sun warm on their heads. He wonders if he might kiss her.

A splash from Taufik startles them both and they let their hands go. Taufik's bobber has disappeared and his line is taut as he jumps with glee so the downstream fisherman raises his arm in salute. Sam throws Sari an apologetic glance.

"Go," she says, kissing him lightly on the cheek. "I'll help Bonita with lunch."

Sam pulls in his line and scrambles to Taufik's side, winding the line the boy pulls in hand over hand until a small barb flops onto the rock beside him. It thrashes and flips on the end of the line a couple of times before lying spent and still. Taufik stares at it.

"You want to keep it?" Sam asks, and reaches to hold the fish just under its gasping gills, working the hook free with his other hand. He holds the fish close to Taufik for a moment, the boy reaching out carefully to stroke its slimy surface, stumbling back as the fish thrashes again. Sam loses his grip and it jumps out of his hand and back into the water. Stunned, it rests in the shallows a moment and then with a sudden splash of its tail, flips out of sight amongst the rocks. Sam claps the boy on the back. "Well done."

Eyes shining with excitement, Taufik unwinds his line, re-aligns the bobber and casts again. Sam realizes Taufik had likely never left Malang before coming to the village, never seen a fish caught. He goes back to his rock, casting his line again just as Darma comes to sit on the bank in the shade nearby, relaxing back so his hands cradle his head. They both watch the boy.

"Wonder why he doesn't speak," Sam says.

"Traumatized, I guess."

"Lots of bad stories out there. Doesn't make everyone mute."

"Well, maybe if he starts to speak, he won't be able to stop. And then he'll have to remember. Saying it will make it real."

Sam thinks of his dad's silence, of all that was misunderstood until it was too late to say anything at all. How different things might have been if his father had told Sam what he was doing, how perhaps he saved other little girls from a Nazi fate, the choices he made. The bobber blurs in the distant water, and Sam looks up to see Darma watching him closely, holding his gaze an instant. He needs to say it now or he never will.

"I'm sorry, Darma."

"For what?"

"Before. Being an asshole. You know."

"You're not the first."

Sam thinks of Marcel. "Yeah, but I'm supposed to be your friend."

"Then be my friend. That's good enough."

He is surprised by the lightness rushing over him.

Bonita calls to them and Andre gestures toward the blanket where she's laid out the picnic. Sam smiles gratefully at Darma, winds in his line and calls to Taufik to do the same, but the boy doesn't budge. They gather, sitting cross-legged on the blanket to share sticky rice wrapped in cones of banana leaf, curried fish, boiled eggs, papaya. Darma fills an open banana leaf with food and sets it on the rock beside where Taufik continues to fish. No one asks where Bonita managed to find food for such a feast.

Stomachs full, the others stretch out and snooze a little in the shade while Sari sits beside Sam, her leg just brushing his own so it seems every pore of his skin reaches toward her.

"This was a great idea," Andre says, absently stroking Bonita's back as she sits beside him, watching Taufik fish.

Sam thinks of Darma's easy forgiveness, of Taufik's joy, and the pulse of Sari's heart under his thumb. He realizes with a start that he would do anything for these people. Like family. He needs them. Why can't this be his family? Strange, but his. Such contentment in the thought, he's less disappointed when the sun begins to dip and they load into the jeep to make their way back toward the village where they will be soldiers and cook, nurse and houseboy again.

CHAPTER 15

The Distance Between
Truth and Luck

CAMP ERIKA, GERMANY
OCTOBER 1944

THEY WALKED US THROUGH FIELDS of fall heather to Camp Erika. Trees lined the road, a simple wooden arch spanning the entrance, the lane opening into a large compound with rows of barracks and, beyond them, row upon row of white tents stretching into the distance.

The lagerführer of the camp was Karel Diepgrond, an Amsterdam-born policeman, and most of the guards were unemployed Dutchmen who'd been given a green uniform and a rank in the German police force. Like train workers, cleaning ladies and street sweepers, in the first months of the occupation, the Reich actually paid Dutch police a portion of what they'd received for the same jobs before the Nazis came. It kept things efficient and orderly. It lulled people; maybe things wouldn't be so bad. Until there was no more pay, and all that remained was a surreal system organized around fear, a system escaped only by hiding or death. And so it was in Camp Erika. Fifty Dutch Green Police watched three thousand prisoners while the Germans manned the corner posts themselves, sweeping their searchlights across the fences.

But a prisoner's main preoccupation was avoiding the attention of the few prisoner–guards given extra rations and treated a little better in exchange for their work. Responsible for pods of about twenty men, they were fierce because they were threatened with their own death should anyone escape while at work pounding rocks into dust at the nearby quarry. Random executions at the shabbily built gallows in the center of the compound kept everyone in line. Fear created discipline, created more fear and more discipline, until a perverse peace settled in.

Shuffling through the days, I worked hard enough to avoid the guard's baton, but not so hard I would collapse, and waited for the next meal. Stayed away from the fence. Filtered out the cries of the political prisoners housed in tents beyond the barracks. Blended into the gray. Everyone was hungry, prisoner and guard alike and one small slip could mean giving up rations for the day. Food was an obsession, my body shrinking as I waited to be placed somewhere else to work.

Two bunk-mates were hit with dysentery in the days before Christmas of '44. I held them up as they stumbled to collect their crust of bread or cup of broth. Something in their bellies was better than nothing, even if their bowels often erupted before they could make it to the latrine. Pushing them through their delirium kept me pushing past my own aches, the scratch of fleas, the cold.

Just as they began to recover, I sat shivering one day in the stink of the latrine, thoughts wandering as always to home and the girls, wondering about Leo, reliving those few lovely moments with Petra. I wiped my ass with the rag kept for the purpose and stood up too fast, catching sight of my belt as it slowly slipped through the last loop in my pants. So slow my gasp had time to suck every molecule of rank air out of the space. So slow I saw my hand flutter, helplessly hovering above the hole as if it might catch the belt. But it twisted and plunged buckle-first into the filth to lie across my watery shit and sink, slowly, away. I stood there holding up my pants and staring down the hole. The rules for collecting rations:

rice or bread in one hand, broth or tea in the other. No exceptions. I considered diving in after the belt, dying in excrement better than living through slow starvation.

That evening I lined up with one hand clutching my pants and caught the knowing looks of the other prisoners. The mess officer only smirked, asking which of the rations I was giving up. Fuck him. I wasn't hungry enough. Not yet. I looked the man in the eye, took only the bread, and walked away with my head high. But later as I lay in my bunk, stomach rumbling and twisting, I cried for the first time. For home. For food. Because I might die in this place for the lack of a goddamn belt.

Two days later I took the tea in my right hand, stomach clenched with hunger.

"Could you put the bread on top of the cup?" My voice quivered. No one ever spoke in the lineup.

"No."

"Please," I whispered, glancing quickly toward the guard standing at the side of the line.

"No."

"Son of a bitch! Give him the fucking bread."

The voice came from a few feet back and I knew it instantly. I dropped the tea, the line of men frozen behind me. As quickly as I turned, the guard was whacking at the man with the butt of his rifle.

"Stoppen." My voice sounded like it came from somebody else.

"Stay out of it, kid." An urgent whisper in my ear.

The man on the ground grunted as the rifle butt hit him between the shoulder blades.

"Stoppen!" The word spilled out. The guard looked up in surprise, then anger, raising his rifle again.

"Stoppen, stoppen, stoppen." I grabbed my head, the blood pulsing in my throat so I couldn't breathe, pants dropped round my ankles. Everything blurred and spun. I rocked on the balls of my feet tangled in the pants, stepped forward, tripped, fell hard on my face, dust choking mouth and nose. Blackness.

I opened my eyes to look across a small space between two cots at Leo. Tears ran down the side of my cheek and into my ear. It really was him, but he looked like an old man, scalp caked with blood, right eye bruised and swollen above sunken cheeks. I swallowed hard and brushed tears away, wincing as my hand touched the scrapes where my face hit the dirt.

"You put on quite the show." He opened his eyes and smiled. "Good distraction, dropping your pants."

The sound of his voice was overwhelming. "We thought you were dead," I said finally.

"I thought I would be by now."

"But how . . . ?"

The question was too big. There was too much to share, too much lost. I looked around to see we were in the infirmary, a few filthy bunks in a separate room. Most of the others slept. Only prisoners they believed would recover were taken there so they could be sent out to work again, those without hope left to die in barracks or drop dead at the work site, their mates forced to take the bodies out and pile them.

"Well I thought I was done after the strike. But then out of the blue they took me to Lager 21," Leo whispered. "And now I'm here." His smile was thin.

"When did you get here?"

"Two days ago."

"Are you okay? He beat you pretty bad."

Leo fluttered his hand in the air, eyes closed.

"You didn't have to do that."

"Shut up, Sam."

Silence. I stared at him, expecting him to disappear as quickly as he'd appeared.

"Marie okay?" he asked, the briefest catch in his throat.

"She's good. Worried, but good."

He sighed with relief. And in spite of everything, I was suddenly grateful for Dad's protection of the girls, no matter the cost.

"And you wouldn't know Anika. She's hiding a Jew, feeding the evacuees, she's . . ."

He was asleep.

The next morning we were sent back in time to collect our half bowl of watery porridge and tea, Leo bent and hobbling, his back and legs bruised and aching. I still held up my pants. As we lined up, a stranger came close beside and pushed a length of thin wire into my belt loop. I pretended to be engaged in conversation with Leo as the stranger navigated the wire round my waist until I could twist the two ends in front like a knot for a fence, left hand free, and my chance of survival increased by exactly fifty percent. A Christmas gift. I turned to thank the man, but saw only a shadow melting into a group standing a distance off. Stranger become savior. Only in such a place.

Leo's barracks were at the far end of the camp and we nodded to each other at morning parade, caught moments together walking the perimeter of the camp, occasionally working alongside each other at the quarry. There was so much to talk about, but too few words. Or not the right ones. I knew only that Leo spent months breaking up and loading hot slag for the Goring Reichswerke.

"Ruined my hands," he told me on a frigid evening as we huddled together over bowls of broth, breathing the steam into our lungs before swallowing the warmth into cold, empty bellies. He looked down at his fingers. They were pulled into half-moons by the raised scars warping the backs of his hands and palms and running down to his wrists.

I was impatient with his silence. I wanted more: to talk about home and Dad, to tell Leo everything so I could gauge my actions by his response. But he was a shrunken version of the man I'd watched at the mine when the strike started, when action had given us possibilities. The truth about Hendrik might flatten Leo entirely. I wondered what he'd seen to drive him to such silence, though I was losing my own battle against a kind of submission to doom, trying to take heart every time Allied planes droned overhead and the Germans were forced to turn off their searchlights.

"It'll be over soon," I said.

"Yes, well." He waved at the gallows in the distance.

We were forced to witness the executions, standing in front of the emaciated and shaved body swinging from the rope, watching it kick slightly until it didn't anymore and other prisoners were sent to take it down. I learned not to let my eyes focus on the hangings, the beatings, blurred the scenes so I could remain numb.

"You have to keep hope, Leo. You've made it this far."

"I still wonder about that."

I hesitated, unsure if he'd want to know how his life was spared.

"What is it, Sam?"

"There was a Kraut at de Kruidenteelt. We were so desperate for word of you. I asked him to help."

Leo's mouth dropped open. "Jesus, Sam."

"I trusted him. I don't know why. But he found you, had you sent to Lager 21."

I waited, expecting perhaps he'd thank me. But he was mute, shoulders slumped, hands shaking, his silence frightening; maybe his secrets were worse than my own.

Finally he spoke in a voice distant and pained. "We were kept in a dark cell for months. Let out once a day. Rats. Lice. Barely anything to eat. And then suddenly one day we were in a cement courtyard. We stood in the cold for hours. I wanted to die then. I really did." He searched my face as though I might understand.

"No, Leo." A lump in my throat. I hadn't yet wanted to die, had held the idea far away. I leaned toward him like I might shelter him from the thought.

"But then Hans Elick and five of the others were executed right in front of me. When I saw them hit the ground, I was suddenly terrified to die. Not the dying so much. But dying in that way."

Gunshots, eyes looking up the hill and staring into my own. I had a flash of anger. I'd warned Leo. Told him not to go back. I started to say it, but his tears stopped me. "You shouldn't feel guilty."

"I wish I did. All I felt was relief it wasn't me." Leo stared into the distance. "I didn't know why I was spared. And then sent to Lager 21. Thought it was dumb luck." He tilted his head at me. "But it was you."

I tried to smile but had to look away, my big brother become so small. I remembered his question, what if — *what if we do nothing and we die anyway*. But what if you act and you die anyway? Father Pete. Hans Elick. Marcel's dad. They'd been brave, even noble. But is that any consolation to the dead or the living left behind? They're still as dead as the next sniveling coward. Maybe even more likely to be dead than someone like Hendrik who stayed alive, kept me and my sisters safe by doing the opposite of noble. Refusing to help him, hiding in the coop, I'd felt better than Dad, righteous, like somehow it would warrant God's special protection or something equally absurd. But there we were near dead in a camp. I wanted to ask if Leo would still ask *what if* in the same way.

"Dumb luck I asked the right kraut," I said instead, trying to laugh.

"Brave, I'd say."

I needed something. Listening to the men around me pray for deliverance, for food, for the Allies to win, I tried talking to God, but the deity seemed difficult to reach, my lack of faith likely putting me at a disadvantage. I'd tried to buy into the gospels and the sacraments, hoping someday they'd mean something. I went to church and took the host, confessed my sins and never stopped doubting. In the camp, with nothing to hold on to, I was terrified to fall into the desperate gulf opening inside, a hole yearning to be filled with some kind of meaning.

On a cold January morning, a new prisoner who slept across from me shouted a mix of surprise and recognition. "Well, holy hell, it's still here," Mark said, as he scraped away paint carelessly splashed on the wall behind his bunk.

Truth Is a Pathless Land. The words appeared as the paint flaked away.

"I carved this here as a kid," he said, telling the story of how his family spent every summer in the camp when it was used by a group called the Order of the Star. The savior they craved was supposed to meet his followers there when he'd grown old enough to be their leader. But when Jiddu Krishnamurti finally showed up, he said he didn't want the job, told them to go home and think for themselves. Mark scraped away more paint.

Who but yourself can tell you if you are beautiful or ugly within? Who but yourself can tell you if you are incorruptible?

I read the words once, twice, and again, the questions washing around in my head, rubbing up against what the war was doing to Leo, to Dad, to me — the little voice in my head that might have once given me answers mute from fear and the gradual acceptance of things unacceptable. Could ugliness in the air stick to form a new skin, camouflage whatever existed before so a person might not know which he was, beautiful or ugly?

The news came over the loudspeaker: a truck in the compound would take the first thirty men with farming experience to work on German farms. I grabbed Leo and we ran, jostling with fifty other men until one of the guards came down the line, pounding on heads with his baton and yelling to shut up. We stood eyeing our chances, those at the farthest end grumbling as they walked away. Mark was one of them, but he searched the line and nodded encouragingly to us where we stood somewhere in the middle. I started to count.

"Some of them don't know shit about farming. Look." Leo pointed to two lean men from our block, accountants in their former lives, their soft hands raw now with work. Sure enough, the guard laughed and sent them away. A foreman surveyed those who remained, "interviewing" each in turn. The line tightened.

We answered the guard's questions about farming background. He looked us over and let us stay.

"I think this might be my last chance," Leo said quietly.

"What are you talking about?"

"Look at me, Sam. I have to get out of here."

I stared down the row, quaking inside at how close it might be, looked at Leo and truly saw him for the first time. He strained to breathe, hair barely begun growing back, the sockets of his eyes black above sharp cheekbones in a thin face. His hands shook and he grasped them together. "You'll be fine," I said.

"Twenty-nine." The guard pointed to the man ahead. "You're thirty," he said to me, hollering at Leo and those remaining, "Line up for the quarry."

"No," I stuttered. "He has to come too."

"Shut up. They said thirty. Let's go."

I stayed put, looked at Leo, heart pounding.

"What are you doing?" Leo hissed. "Get out of here."

"Take my brother." It rushed out in one breath.

"No, Sam, you can't . . ."

"Go. Go." I pushed Leo toward the men bunched by the truck.

"What's going on here?" It was the foreman standing in front of me with arms crossed.

"We grew up on a farm, sir. But my older brother is more experienced, and I'm number thirty-one. So . . ."

"Your brother looks like shit. I want you."

"No." I said it too loudly, lowered my voice. "Sir. Take him." Leo stood hunched by the truck. I looked directly into the foreman's blue eyes. "Please."

He squinted for so long it felt the earth was rocking under me. But the man's eyes opened ever so slightly.

"What the hell." He shook his head and hollered to the guard. "We're taking thirty-one."

What is the distance between truth and luck, between luck and goodness, between goodness and fate? But for a number, a look, a question? While I managed to get Leo out, I wondered if he had the strength to work at all. The foreman seemed to have the same worries, sending Leo to a munitions factory in the heart of the Rhineland where he could stand in an assembly line as he worked. I was put on a truck headed for a farm north of the industrial circle. A quick embrace, a word of encouragement and, just like that, Leo and I were separated again.

CHAPTER 16

An Ugly Wave

NGADIPURO VILLAGE, EAST JAVA,
DUTCH EAST INDIES
JUNE 1948

HE WRITES, HE SLEEPS, HE patrols, but mostly Sam is desperate to hang on to the buoyancy he'd felt fishing, the memory of Sari's hand in his. He forgave and was forgiven, and now this sense of a family, people he cares for and who care for him. But he is deflated by army life, some of the squad restless to get out of Ngadipuro and do real soldiering again. These men puff out their chests, finger their guns too often, laugh too loudly. Others shrink back, wanting only to protect the village and wait for letters from home, wait for an end. Snide comments, the occasional brawl — besides drinking and smoking too much, the one thing they all have in common is they're becoming assholes. Sam worries he will drift into the malaise around him.

Too many of the squad openly display contempt for Darma. Sam arranges to patrol with him whenever possible. On a moonlit night shift, Sam, Darma and Raj step onto an unfamiliar path winding through tall trees and suffocating shrubs, emerging into a clearing containing a bamboo structure with one small door and a tiled roof.

They pull their weapons tighter, ears tuned, eyes scouting the jungle for movement.

"Might be a weapons stash," Sam says, attaching his bayonet. "I'll go in. Cover me."

Raj stands back as Darma crouches beside the door. It creaks as Sam shoves it open and moves past sticky wisps of cobweb, an incredible smell of dank rot filling his nose as he pushes into the blackness. Suddenly, the moonlight spills through the doorway and bounces across the inside of the shed. A scream clogs his throat. Shrouded figures lean against the walls, tightly wedged together and propped as though having a party conversation.

He backs away, heart pounding even as he tells himself they aren't real, turning to see another body by the door, bent forward at the waist and ushering him out. His bayonet knocks it soundlessly to the floor, a soft billow of dust as he rushes past it and scrambles to hide behind a tree at the edge of the clearing.

"Sam, it's okay." Raj comes toward him.

The bastard is laughing. A flutter above, and Sam glances up to see a piece of white cloth shrouding another figure wedged in the crook of branches, a smaller bundle propped on top. He takes a wild shot, misses. Bayonet extended, he backs into the clearing away from the building and the tree. A hand on his shoulder nearly stops his heart, Raj laughing so hard he can't speak, Darma behind him, doubled over, shoulders shaking with great hiccups.

Sam wants to punch them. "What the hell?" He points his gun at the second figure in the tree, but Raj pushes the muzzle down.

"Dead." Raj chokes on his laughter. "They're already dead."

"I can see that." Sam tries to calm his breathing, looks around in the growing moonlight to see other figures in other trees, shrouded like the first. "What the hell is this?"

"A death pavilion."

"Well, yes. It certainly is."

"They're waiting to be buried."

"What?"

"It takes three days for the dead to realize their situation," Darma chimes in. "In between they're resentful of the living. Families try to confuse the soul so it won't haunt them."

"So they put them in a tree?"

"No." Darma's laugh barks into the night. "No. After three days the soul leaves the body as an insect, maybe a bird. But it will only pass to the land of the ancestors after a proper celebration with offerings, feasting, dancing. Death is complicated. And expensive. Families store the body like this until they can afford the funeral." Darma gestures at the shed, the bodies in the trees. "The war has made people poor."

"Seriously? That's crazy."

"Everyone has their way of the dead."

Andre, Freddy, Willem and Bart burst into the clearing behind them.

"What the hell?" Andre hollers. "We heard a shot."

Out of the corner of his eye, Sam catches the horror on Bart's face as he registers the figures outlined ghostly white in the moonlight. Freddy and Andre follow his gaze and before Sam can stop them, the men are firing into the trees. Shrouds and bones and bodies flutter to the ground, hitting not with a thud, but gently like angels, or demons. The men ignore Raj and Darma yelling at them to stop, instead firing blindly into the trees as though making up for every rebel they've been unable to find, every suspect villager they didn't shoot, unloading their anxiety and fear and anger on the already dead.

They shoot until exhausted, Freddy and Bart finally lying down in the center of the clearing to look up at the moon, high and bright overhead, the silence profound. More men come running from camp, wide-eyed at ten bodies in various stages of decay scattered on the ground.

"Fuck." Raj looks at Darma.

"They have no idea what they've done," Darma says, picking

up bones and shrouds and bundling them into the shed. Where laughter had been, his voice is taut with anger.

"Not the end of the world?" Sam says hopefully, an unreasonable fear growing in him as he rewraps a skull and some random bones, shuddering as he helps pile the bodies.

"We've desecrated the dead," Raj says. "You tell me."

Night shift over, they get back to barracks as the sun is rising, the men shouting and laughing about the death pavilion, mocking Darma for caring so much about a bunch of dark bones and skin, staying clear of Raj. They are soon under their nets and asleep, but Sam's head is filled with images of dead men, real and shrouded, as though the ghosts of his friends killed by war are no different from those he only came across in their long wait for safe passage to the next world.

Unable to sleep, he pulls on sandals and heads outside, walking without looking at anyone, considering Darma's world of ancestors. When his mother died, he imagined her in church heaven where all the good people went to be with Jesus and float around in a wispy-clouded paradise. He was only ten when he called that one, knowing instinctively that adults should have more to go on than an image of wings and clouds and passively smiling faces, a place of perpetual boredom it seemed to Sam. Until the war. Boredom might be a kindness to those who suffered. But the death pavilion, all those souls waiting to be released. He imagines them now, sucked into a giant whirl of energy made up of all the good souls, all those shrouds and bones. The more good souls, the greater the energy until the people, the animals, the plants, the entire world succumbs to that kind of purity, that kind of honesty. Heaven on Earth. Maybe that will be the final truth. Just that.

He has reached the small market and haggles a price for overripe bananas, tossing one to Taufik, who has tailed him all the way. There is little on offer these days. Locals continue to stream down the road with great bundles on their heads or the backs of bikes, but the rebels now intercept and take what they need, while those in the countryside eat what's left. More people in the village are hungry. Sam and other soldiers escort supplies from Malang to the post, but even these have been reduced, so Bonita is forced to find ever creative uses for rice and to stretch meat and fruit until the next truck comes.

He reaches for a bag of dried mango to take back as a treat. A squeal erupts from between the stalls down the aisle and Sam rushes to take Sari's elbow and look into her stricken face. He can't believe his luck.

"A rat," she says in disgust, shuddering and adjusting her umbrella as a soft rain starts again. She is beautiful, her agitation making her less aware, and giving Sam a chance to admire the sharp line of her clavicle, the soft round of her breast. "Ran right over my foot."

He laughs.

She starts to tell him off but grins instead. "I know, just a rat."

"I hate them too. It was just the look on your face."

"I'm glad I ran into you," she says, suddenly serious. She picks up her basket. "Come."

He hesitates before taking her outstretched hand and letting her lead him through small back walkways. Taufik trails behind. Disembodied hands reach from doorways to pull baskets of drying brown rice out of the rain. Small offerings at the gates of homes disintegrate and wash away. She slows as they reach her home, searching his confused face.

"My father is here."

The clouds clap. A frog croaks its pleasure while fat raindrops ping in the stone fountain in the yard, their spray dancing round the water lilies. Sam's shirt is soaked through, water dripping from his cap. He can't do this. All he's wanted to do is forget, to move past his treasonous actions and be a good soldier. But he desperately wants justification for having helped Amir, absolution of some kind. Terrified he won't find either, he follows Sari into the house, wiping his shoes and slapping the rain off his jacket as he enters. The houseboy takes his coat, giving him a towel to wipe his face and hair before grabbing Taufik's hand and pulling him to the back of the house. Ganesha still holds his bowl in the corner, still wears a necklace of flowers.

Sari leads him into the same sitting area where she'd sat the first time with her bandaged leg. Today, Amir sits in the chair. He is thin, his long wiry hair almost completely white now, but his muscles are still sinewy, eyes steely gray and commanding.

"Sam." Amir's voice rattles in his chest as he gestures to the chair across from him. His hands are no longer bandaged but they are bloated and scarred purple, his fingers unnaturally flexed. Sam looks at Sari.

"They had to amputate one finger." Sari's voice is pained. "The others mostly atrophied from lack of use while they healed."

Amir coughs, phlegm gurgling in his throat until he spits into a handkerchief.

"He isn't well," Sari whispers.

"Stop fussing," Amir says, and Sam hears the confidence he remembers. "Sari, will you bring us tea?"

She frowns, then disappears. Sam hesitates a long moment, feels inclined to run back out the door into the rain. Amir leans forward to gaze intently at him, silently and for so long that Sam's eye begins to twitch. Finally satisfied, Amir sits back.

"I didn't trust you. Perhaps I should have." Amir glances down at his hands, ruined now like Leo's. The rain pounds on the roof. "Please, sit."

"I'm sorry." It's all Sam can think to say. He goes to the chair to sit across from Amir. "If we had come sooner, better protected the area."

"No. You could do nothing to stop them." Amir's smile is sad, resigned.

"If they would just wait, we'd set up an administration. A proper government."

"Is that what your people tell you?" Amir shakes his head. "I learned at H.B.S. how the Dutch view the colony."

"You went to secondary school?" The fluent Dutch. The crafted arguments. It makes sense now.

"The Hegmans sent me years ago so I could become a good manager. A good foreman. But what I learned is how history is written so the Dutch are always right." Amir studies Sam, as though judging his ability to understand. "You lived under the Germans as we do now, under occupation."

"That was different. Holland is our home. We built this colony."

An amused smile plays around Amir's lips. "No, my friend. We did. For two hundred years it was our backs and hands did the hard labor so the Belanda could take our resources and live fat."

They eye each other warily.

Amir sighs. "The men who fight for independence, they won't wait."

"Are you one of them?"

"That's not the important question here." Amir cocks his head, a little impatient now. "The question is how many people will have to die."

"Have to?"

"When men hate, when they fear the other, they see no choice even when one exists."

"But you don't hate me, or I might be dead now."

"I could say the same. You saved my life."

"And that makes a difference?"

"Of course."

He knew Amir as a farmer working in his shed, with guns trained on him in the night, and vulnerable when the fever had taken hold. Without those encounters, would Sam have chosen to save Amir's life?

"And you care for my daughter," Amir continues.

Sam blushes deeply.

"I am an honest and patient Hindu," Amir says without a trace of pride. "I know that everything has its place in this world — my body, this house, the village, the smallest rice stalk in the field. I've never hurt anyone. Yet here I am, forced to make distinctions, to choose what matters most. As are you."

"I'm not forced. I know what I believe."

Amir waits.

"I believe in God, helping the suffering, in heaven." Trite bits he conjures from Mass refrains.

"Ah yes, heaven." Amir shakes his head. "I think you redemptionists are all the same. Muslims, Christians. You all live for something greater than what is here and now. But if transcendence is the only goal, then connection to this world is tenuous, yes? Making it easier to destroy things in the name of a greater power? Easier to kill?"

"I want to do what's right." Sam feels the argument slipping out of his reach. He understands but he doesn't. "That's what I believe in. Doing what's right."

"And do you know what that might be? Here? In this time and place?"

Sari comes in with tea. "Father, it's enough Sam is here. You don't need to confuse him with your philosophies."

Amir laughs, coughs until he is out of breath and smiles again. "Only a bit of conversation."

But Sam is unsettled. "Amir, I don't know why you wanted to see me. I'm glad you survived the infection, though I see it will be difficult for you to farm." He looks pointedly at Amir's gnarled hands. The man frowns. "But I have to go back to the post now. I've seen what the rebels are capable of. So I'll fight with my squad, and I'll do it willingly. I hope you stay out of it for your own sake, and for your wife." He doesn't include Sari. He will ensure Sari's safety himself.

"And do you think I will give up my country because you are a nice young man?" Amir looks down at the useless hands in his lap. "You helped set up the clinic in the village as my wife asked, helped me with this. I thought . . ." His voice fades. He coughs and looks up, dark eyes burning with intent. "Be careful, Sam. There are too many forces, too many angry voices. They've been whipped into dendam. Revenge. And it's an ugly wave you won't be able to stop. I like you. I'd hate to see it make you ugly in return."

Amir gets up slowly and walks to a side door. He looks back, his face unreadable. About to say something, he changes his mind and vanishes behind a teak wood screen carved with dragon heads and angels.

Sam goes to the porch to stand with Sari, watching pools form in the small garden.

"I don't know if I'll see you again," she says.

"What? Why?"

"My father will go back into hiding. He only came here to ensure my mother got away safely. The TNI is after him because they think he's with the communists."

"Is he?"

"Sam!" Her whisper is harsh. "Don't you understand? It doesn't matter. It's what they believe. My mother has already left and will meet him near Madiun. I'm to follow when I get a chance."

"Let me help you." He holds her arm and she doesn't resist.

"How can you help me? Being linked to a suspected communist is bad enough. Being seen as a collaborator, well that would get me killed, wouldn't it."

Collaborator. So he really is the enemy. The occupying force. It's all happening too fast. All he knows for sure is he doesn't want her to leave. But he has no words, no way to change anything. She hugs him then, softly at first, then tight, and he closes his arms around her, pressing his cheek into her hair and breathing her in until she draws back gently and looks up at him.

"I think you will do what is right, Sam. I think you are a good man."

He smiles, blinking away the blur in his eye. She kisses him then, her mouth soft and full, touching her tongue to the edge of his lip. He would give anything to stay suspended in this moment, but she pulls away to rest her head on his chest. A deep breath between them and then he steps back, touches her cheek and walks off the porch into the rain.

Taufik suddenly pulls on his hand, thrusting his chin toward a side street where pigeons fly up from a stone wall thirty meters away. Freddy sits watching them. Warm rain runs down the back of Sam's shirt, chills on his skin. The knot in his stomach twists tight. A slow smile spreads across Freddy's face as he pats his rifle, stands and jumps down the other side of the wall to disappear.

By mid-afternoon the squad is ransacking Sari's home. Sam pretends, moving things around, watching helpless as the men overturn the kitchen table, hurl the delft platter so it smashes on the wall above the bed. All he can think is that she is gone. Andre pulls everything from the cupboards as though a hint of Amir's whereabouts could be located in a flour sack. But Sam suspects Andre is mostly angry for being put in this position. Sari is Bonita's friend too. They find nothing. Raj finally gives up. Local informants have told him Amir is fighting against the Dutch.

"But he's an invalid. And maybe only a communist." The words aren't out of Sam's mouth before he sees his mistake, Freddy and Bart coming toward him with suspicion in their eyes. Raj jumps in front of them.

"Jesus, Vandenberg, it doesn't matter who he's with, he's our fucking enemy. And you let him go." Raj leans in so their foreheads almost touch and then jerks his head at the men. "Do they need to worry about which side you're on?"

There is a moment when Sam searches for words to explain why he likes Amir, even trusts Amir. How they are all being forced onto sides that don't have to exist. But he catches sight of the other men watching, waiting for his response: Andre's face filled first with hope and then concern Sam will somehow answer incorrectly,

Darma's shrouded, Willem and Bart and Visser confused. His breath catches. "Of course not."

"We're gonna find that son of a bitch." Raj signals. "Let's go, Freddy."

"He's a little trigger-happy," Darma says quietly.

"Maybe so." Raj looks calculatingly at Sam, as though unleashing Freddy is Sam's fault.

As if on cue, Freddy fingers the pistol in his belt, pats the rifle slung across his back. "Sons of bitches," he says to no one in particular.

Sam winces at the anticipation in Freddy's voice. From Sari's wrecked home, they move further into Ngadipuro, the locals first confused, then frightened.

Raj shouts at the squad to fan out and check every home, every outhouse. "There" — he points — "and that one," he says, pushing the men toward the buildings.

Sam grabs Darma's arm and pulls him along toward one of the houses, a shack, really. It's still early and a small child emerges, the words he was about to say swallowed as his sister grabs him and thrusts him behind her skirts. She stands aside as they enter, then takes a broom outside to begin sweeping the small dirt area out front, eyeing the door the whole time.

Darma goes to check one of two small bedrooms, quickly looking in the door of the other. He comes back to where Sam stands in the kitchen area, a rickety wood counter made of scrap boards doubling as a table, two wooden stools the only places to sit. Out back they discover a small room open to the air with a laundry tub and a water-filled drum on a platform that gravity feeds into a large basin for bathing. Sam gingerly pushes the door open to an enclosed toilet that flows out to a channel dug to carry the waste away.

"What are you doing?" The accent behind him is unmistakable. Cora's face is plain without the line of kohl round her eyes, her button-bursting shirt and tight skirt replaced by a simple housedress, wild hair tamed into a single braid down her back. He has a sudden urge to tell her about Sari and Amir. How he's caught in something he doesn't know how to stop. But Cora's face is hard, her blue eyes piercing. "There's nothing here for you."

"Of course not," he says, uncertain now, remembering Cora's mixed allegiances. "We're looking for ploppers."

She is silent. He looks around her home. The walls are unfinished, made up of an assortment of overlapping planks, with cracks between them big enough to let in wind and insects. The floor is pieces of wood laid side by side. They wobble as Sam walks across them. The house has no ceiling, the roof made of straw and palm leaves and held up by heavy beams.

"You live here?"

"Is that such a surprise?"

"No. I mean . . ." He doesn't know what to say. This shack is far removed from the woman slinging drinks in the bar and talking about the suicidal husband she so confidently despised. "We just want to protect you."

"Really?" Her voice is amused. "You need to leave now."

"What the hell?" Sam's mind swirls with confusion as Darma pulls on his arm and they back out of the house and into the street.

"My mother lives in a place just like that," Darma says. "After the Japanese, she doesn't trust anyone. And no one else will have her."

Darma is interrupted by a shout further down the road. Some of the squad have taken several young men and lined them up in the street. Most of them wear only white shorts and they are all barefoot, tiny compared to the soldiers who stand over them. Each is patted down for weapons and then forced at gunpoint to sit crosslegged in the dirt.

As Sam approaches, Freddy drags a man out of a nearby house and throws him into the street in front of the others. A splash of mud as his head hits the ground, and for an instant Sam sees Father Pete's red hair. He runs up just as Freddy kicks the man in the ribs with the hard toe of his boot. Then again, and again. The man on the ground moans, barely strong enough to put his hands out to protect his face and head. A small woman of about fifty hurries up, tripping over her sarong as she tries to pull Freddy away from the man on the ground. Freddy sweeps his arm and throws her to the side of the road like a rag doll. She begins to weep and crawls forward on her knees, begging him to stop.

"Freddy!" Sam says tersely.

"Bastard. Tried to run out the back door. Probably going to warn his rebel friends. Probably a fucking jago."

"Freddy, enough."

"Cocksucker, think you can get away with it? Warn 'em so they can ambush us. Not this time, you little bastard. Not this time."

"Sam," Darma says, his voice even, steady. "He'll kill him."

The man on the ground has stopped moving.

"Jesus Christ!" Blood pours from the man's ear. Sam reaches out his hands, the woman's screams vibrating in his head. The men move closer, shifting in their boots to lean in, eyes dark with excitement. Raj arrives just as Freddy gives one more boot to the man's head.

"And so we are infinitely reduced," Raj says, watching Sam as though waiting for him to do something. A challenge. Or a wish. What the fuck?

"Enough." Raj finally roars with the cracking of the man's skull. The sound breaks Freddy's trance and he wheels round, fists raised, gun dangling from his shoulder. Freddy stares at Raj as though suddenly confused as to who he is and why he is there. His eyes shift to the young man on the ground, the woman crawling forward to wail over the body.

"Freddy." Sam's breath heaves out of him. "Go to the truck."

Panting, Freddy staggers off as though drunk, weaving his way over to slump against the wheel.

"So, this is how you will protect us. By beating a simpleton." Cora stands in the road, hands on hips, defying Raj to come near the man face down on the ground. The little boy clings to her leg. "He is, you know. The village idiot. I'm sure we are much safer now."

The men stare.

"Rebels here?" Raj's voice is loud in the stillness.

She snorts. "They're everywhere, you asshole." She looks Raj straight in the eye, her gaze shifting to Sam, her disappointment saved for him.

Sensing an end, Darma rushes in, speaking Javanese to the woman, trying to hold the man's head together with his hands.

Early evening, and the laneways and porches of the village are empty, the citizens of Ngadipuro avoiding the squad as they walk through and back across the bridge to the post. They'd told these people they were bringing safety to the village, and Sam had worked to build their trust with the clinic. That will all be gone now. Along with Amir. And Sari.

Through the turmoil in his head, he drifts past the rest of the squad returning to barracks, slips down the bank to sit at the river's edge, peeling off boots and socks to dangle his rotten feet in the cool water. Dusk deepens the weight of the air around him. Darma wanted it to stop. Even Andre. And Raj? He'd waited for Sam to act, to stop Freddy from doing this unthinkable thing. But Sam had failed. And an innocent man is dead.

Steps behind him. He knows without looking that it's Raj.

"Don't really want company."

Raj ignores him, settling onto the ground, leaning back against a tree as he sighs and sits peeling a salak. "The rebels are stronger than you think," he says quietly. "Better armed anyway."

"So much for spears."

Raj chuckles, an uncharacteristic sound, low and affable. "You believed that shit, did you? Jagos, mystic powers."

"I thought you did."

"Just wanted to scare you little white boys." He shifts against the tree, his voice musing. "Maybe I used to, when I was a kid. My mother was superstitious, filled my head with ideas of spirits and black magic and curses, but my father would have none of it. He wanted me to get an education and sent me to seminary in Flores so I would see things for what they are."

The dark provides cover for Sam's surprise. "What did you study?"

Raj snorts. "Philosophy."

"Not much use out here, I guess."

Raj is silent. An overcast moon has come out, sending an eerie glow over the river, the cascading banyan roots like green-tinged tentacles floating toward earth.

"It doesn't help to understand why men behave the way they do," Raj says finally. "Why they think in the ways they do. If they are blind, understanding their lack of sight won't change them. Sometimes they need to be made to see what's right."

"But who decides?" The words jump out of his mouth. Raj will surely question his loyalty again. "I mean, the Germans thought they were right and look how that turned out."

"Hmmm, the Japanese too. Do you think we're wrong here?" Raj's voice has lost its usual goading.

"What Freddy did today was wrong."

"But you didn't stop it."

"You're the commanding officer."

Raj snorts. "Oh come on, Sam. Don't be a child. You think they're listening to me anymore?"

His skin burns with embarrassment. Is he a child? A nice young man as Amir told him? Maybe an idiot, like the man killed today.

"There's something big coming," Raj says slowly.

An ugly wave. Sam shudders. "I just wish we could talk with the rebels. If they were patient . . ."

"They won't wait, Sam."

"Amir says the same thing."

"Why do you think he's any different from the pemuda? That he wouldn't kill you if he had the chance?"

"Because he had the chance. And he didn't. Because I met another man, a Nazi, who did the same."

"Maybe just trying to find redemption."

The word is a surprise. He thinks of his father's constant walking after the war as if trying to get away from the memory of what he'd done, the choices he was forced to make. Hendrik and Rudy and Amir making their careful choices in a careless world. The silence grows as the jungle pulses, pushing thoughts to a space deep inside his head, the idea of such redemption growing so it tinkles like a drop of water in his thirsty brain.

"The pemuda destroyed more than my father's business in Surabaya." Raj's voice is pained, and he inhales deeply as though gathering his words. "I hid in the shop while they took him outside and tied him behind a jeep. They dragged him through the streets for an hour, neighbors running behind, screaming, 'People's Sovereignty! People's sovereignty!' And then they stopped. And took a machete. And cut off his head."

"Oh, Christ."

"They never asked." Raj's breathing is suffocated by the effort it takes to push the words from his throat. "My father supported independence of some kind. But they never asked. He was Ambonese. He had money. An education. And they killed him for it."

"Jesus, Raj, I'm sorry."

"I hid for days as the murders went on. When I finally came out, I remember the dogs wouldn't stop barking," Raj says softly. "And you'd see them, their bellies collapsed like bicycle tires because no one thought to feed them. Their owners were too busy killing."

They sit in silence. Sam stares into the forest surrounding them, trying to absorb what Raj is saying, the hell it must have been to watch his father die such a death. He pictures Raj picking up bones in the Death Pavilion. So many voices, so much terror. So many things Raj might become as a result. Saint or monster.

"Siiiiaaaaap." Raj' voice drifts high and haunting into the dark night. "Get ready. They called it each night, before the killings. Always, get ready."

A chill passes through Sam.

"Siiiaaap."

It hangs in the air.

PART III

"I am going on strange unknown ways, which will lead toward heaven, but must first take me down into hell."
— RADEN ADJENG KARTINI, *LETTERS OF A JAVANESE PRINCESS*

CHAPTER 17

A Flash of Gallows

NGADIPURO VILLAGE, ISLAND OF JAVA
AUGUST 1948

TWELVE DEAD MEN. JAAP, LUCAS, Adrian, Eric, Cees . . . in two months, twelve men lost to sniper fire. Even Raj wasn't ready. Commander Hagen sends replacements — Adam, Garrett, Frans, Levi — as though the men killed are only names, as interchangeable as spare parts. Discipline suffers along with morale, the men angry at the rebels and even more at HQ for the lack of direction and support. Under such brazen attacks, a no-man's land has opened up between the post and the village and with nowhere to aim their anger, the men aim their guns, prone to shooting first and asking questions later. Or not asking questions at all, claiming as Raj once did that they are all rebels.

The squad drinks too much. A few have gained an opium addiction and others persistent venereal diseases. An older soldier known fondly as Dad has fathered a baby in the village, but no one acknowledges it, least of all the father, whose dread at confronting the existence of his offspring is as palpable as the devastation his wife in Amsterdam would feel if she found out. Raj was right, he has little control of the men anymore. When Colonel Hagen finally visits, he offers no advice or guidance, only warnings of their duty to both country and family. Meaningless words.

Sam receives a bundle of letters dating back months, an apology enclosed from HQ for having lost them somewhere along the way. He is barely able to read those from Petra, her stories childish and naïve. He knows it's not fair. She can't know.

Most of the letters are from Marie, her familiar cramped handwriting a relief. She tells him it is a struggle to keep the farm going without him and they've been boarding a local boy in exchange for his help. Sam thinks of de Kruidenteelt a world away, how he'd pined for it when he was in Germany, nearly bursting with the need to be home. The sensation tingles in him now and he pushes it away. A hasty postscript added by Anika tells him she's gone back to school to become a history teacher. She wants to ensure Holland's children know what Hitler did, she says, confident such knowledge will prevent it from happening again.

"Jesus Christ," he says aloud. Andre looks up from his bunk. "It's already happening again." Muttering, he goes back to reading.

Marie tells him of the Nuremburg trials, victims of the Nazis providing testimony of staggering brutality. But Sam has the uneasy feeling those war crimes come from another life, the distance between it and this jungle so great he almost questions if what the Germans did was so bad. His memory tells him yes, but memory is slippery, the current situation distancing those discomforts and fears and replacing them with new ones. Marie asks if he's heard of the protests in Amsterdam against "his" occupation of the Dutch East Indies.

"Listen to this," he shouts at Andre. "My sister says the Americans are threatening to cut off recovery funding if we don't get out of here."

"What the hell?"

"Apparently, they've decided communism is now the greatest threat to humanity. Sukarno is killing the communists here, so they figure he's one of the good guys."

Andre laughs.

"And colonialism is so passé," Sam reads. Andre frowns. "You have to know Marie."

Or she believes it. He can't tell, though her letter qualifies this information with a pledge of support for him and his "friends," as she calls them. Just a bunch of guys, pal-ing around the jungle, bringing goodness and joy to the locals.

"None of them are going to get it, are they? What we're doing here. What we've done."

Andre says nothing.

"No one."

He won't write back until he can figure out a way to explain how heat rash blisters the skin, or how a grenade can turn leafy bamboo into lethal shrapnel, or how a man can be smilingly alive in one moment, face-down-dead from a sniper's shot the next.

The squad receives orders to cover a wider range around Ngadipuro, to flush out guerrilla fighters who blow up buildings, bridges and roads in Dutch-controlled areas despite signed agreements promising to stay on their side of the Van Mook demarcation line. Dutch forces have countered these incursions with artillery fired into villages where the rebels are suspected of hiding in ambush. But artillery means more civilian casualties and the radio announcers tell them the protests in Amsterdam are getting louder.

They've heard that the man who deserted after the Rawagede massacre is now collaborating with rebel forces, using his uniform to walk into Dutch bases and collect arms he turns around and hands to rebels in the jungle. One report says he's shooting at his former Dutch mates. And they know his last name: Bakker. Marcel's surname. *Do you ever think* . . . No, it's a common name.

The traitor is a target for the men's anger.

"Fucker, wait till someone gets him in their sights."

"Oh they'll want a long hard interrogation of that one."

"I'd just kill him," Andre says with such certainty it makes Sam wince.

This violence surprises Sam an instant, and then it doesn't. Andre is loyal. Always loyal. War is strange and dirty, and the only predictable thing is the shared knowledge they are watching out for one another, will perhaps even take a bullet. He can't imagine any one of them choosing otherwise, choosing something beyond that certainty.

And yet.

Somewhere in his head, a voice is screaming. The sound builds when he tries to sleep or is on patrol at night, when silence needs filling and there is too much space for thought. Boots to the head of an idiot, an old man pissing himself in a shed. And Amir, always the vision of Amir. Sam can't shake the sense Amir is what Leo might have become. It stifles his breath as he stares into the dark, waiting for a gunshot or a grenade, or listening to the snoring of men around him. It is all building into something he can't stop, something he will not be able to justify, deep where his silence is just able to snuff out the screams, to suffocate all he holds true. Or once did.

They maintain regular patrols, their senses ground to fine points, every bird whistle or shadowed movement gauged for threat level, while outwardly they slouch along as though they don't give a damn, the body's urgency flattened by heat, and lazy as the jungle in its summer stupor. Darma tries to distract them, picking a teak leaf to rub between his fingers until the green dissolves into a blood-red paste he uses like war paint. He succeeds in looking like a clown. Pinching a red hibiscus flower, he pulls off the blossom end and sucks the juice from the tip, handing one to Sam. "Have to do it at just the right stage or it'll be so bitter you'll want to cut off your tongue." Darma laughs.

Sam is surprised at the clear sweet nectar.

"He likes the flowers," Freddy taunts, his voice high. "Do you like the flowers too, Sam?"

Blushing, Sam drops the flower quickly, ashamed at his silence.

Darma moves light and confident ahead, unaware of eyes narrowed in disgust as he comments about the dew on the tip of the water lily or the stubborn nature of the orchid. Did Darma learn nothing from the incident in Malang? A shiver of worry passes through Sam.

A fleet of monkeys assails them, more than twenty macaques arriving to scold the squad as they walk. Sam watches the profile of an old male who sits hunched beneath the hanging aerial roots of a huge banyan tree, long fingers peeling a salak. The short, dense fur is smooth on its head, suddenly rounding to create a shelf over its brow. Its small ears twitch at a fly. Suddenly, it looks up as though it knows it's being watched, close green eyes staring right into Sam's with a wry impatience, like an intelligent old man who can't quite comprehend the stupidity of a youth long forgotten. Still watching Sam, it grabs a vine in one hand and fruit in the other, swings to a branch and is gone. Sam smiles and bows a little. Bapak.

Stefan tries to feed a younger macaque, coaxing it to eat from his hand, the monkey tentative at first, eyes darting like it might be a flight risk. Stefan pulls the cracker away, but the monkey bares its teeth, jumping on Stefan's forearm and grabbing the cracker out of his fingers, climbing to wrestle his cap off, frantically clawing when Stefan tries to take it back.

"Fuck, stupid asshole," Stefan hollers and flings the monkey off, taking a good long scratch down the back of his neck.

"Teach you," Raj says, laughing. "They're not goddamn pets."

The group of macaques takes off in a squabble of voices, jumping between branches to disappear as quickly as they arrived.

"Wouldn't it be great?" Andre says, staring after them. "Imagine what you'd see."

"You're fine," Visser says, looking closely at the scratch on Stefan's neck. "Been scratched deeper by a pissed-off woman."

"Yeah, but at least you'd get a fuck out of her first," Carl interjects from where he walks a little behind the rest of the group, blushing when the group turns on him.

"Like you'd know."

Carl fades away from them, face on fire as the men harass him, but he's brought it on himself. He's too new to the group to make such comments. He doesn't fit in because he can't, because he hasn't seen what they've seen, or done what they've done. Sam feels sorry for him a moment, but envious too; maybe the war will end before Carl too is damaged.

Sam sucks back the last of the water in his canteen. He's been so thirsty and is happy they're almost back to the post, where he can drink his fill. He can just make out two men, tiny in the distance, shuffling back and forth to patrol the bridge. It's a shitty job; no shade from the blistering sun, never anything new to see but so much to watch out for. The nose of the machine gun pokes out of the guard post above. The squad shouts to the two on the bridge and Sam sees one of the stick figures is Willem, his eyeglasses flashing in the sun as he turns to wave. The same instant, Willem's head jerks back, arms out as if on marionette strings as he does a puppet dance and topples forward into the river. The splash of spray and the reverberation of the shot happen simultaneously, an odd acoustic echo in Sam's stunned head.

The men jump back into the jungle and out of sight, Raj's semi-automatic firing into the trees, the blast rattling through the river gorge, careening off the rocks. Return fire. Sam scans the trees but can't find the source. Silence. The squad surges forward, watching as Jesse runs the length of the bridge back toward the post. Jesse, a pink-faced new recruit who likes to angle his head into the sun every morning as he tries to pass off his peach fuzz as facial hair. Always hopeful, always laughing at razzing from the others.

"Get down," Sam whispers loudly. "Get down."

The words aren't out before another rifle report flattens Jesse. The squad gasps. More fire from Raj. Sam and the others open up on the trees, the huts, the air. From the post, two men duck and run toward the bridge, crouching beside Jesse and heaving him onto their shoulders and out of the way. A flash to Sam's right. Past a stand of bamboo, Willem's body floats face down in the river. Sam shouts and wades into the churning water. Reaching the body, he clutches one of Willem's hands, flailing as they're both carried down stream. Sam leans into the current and pulls the body toward him, boots reaching for a hold as he rolls Willem over. Willem, spectacled and a reader of serious literature, is dead, a bullet hole in the forehead. Poor guy never got laid — a strange thought. Rocks on the bottom, he loses his footing again. Hang on, hang on. Where's the shore? There.

"Dive!" Darma shouts.

The rifle shot reaches Sam's ears just as the water explodes beside him. He dives and tumbles in the current, losing Willem. He surfaces and brushes water from his eyes. Another shot. Dive again, swim toward the bank, lungs pushed up into his throat. Pain shoots down his arm as he crashes into rock, but he grasps the boulder and crawls behind it. He's lost his rifle.

At the top of the riverbank stands a man. In an instant, Sam takes in the dark beret, the insignia — two grains of rice — the Lee–Enfield pointed at him. Heart in his throat, he takes a step from behind the rock to stand fully exposed to the rebel and his gun. The rebel who was either Amir's friend or enemy, who made Sam small. The gun that threatened Sari at the clinic. The gun that has now killed Willem. The same gun, the same man, the same slow, confident smile on the bastard's face. This man who has power only through his weapon. It's laughable. Sam snorts even as he knows he is going to die here. Son of a bitch.

"Fuck you." He breathes hard, refuses fear, anger pushing into his head, calming him. Glaring into the rebel's eyes, Sam's nostrils flare as he holds his chin high. Louder. Confident. "Fuck. You."

"Sam."

Darma stands a few meters away, pointing his gun at the rebel who points the gun at Sam. A triangle of waiting, they stare, daring each other to flinch.

"Walk away," Darma calls to the rebel in Dutch, but the man clearly does not comprehend. "On three, then." Darma's voice is deep and solid. "But go on two."

Jesus.

"One, two . . ."

Sam dives behind the rock. Shots ring. Silence.

He scrambles up the bank. The rebel stands stunned, blood blossoming red across his chest as he drops, Darma's rifle still pointed.

"Darma?" Sam goes to his friend, checks him for bullet holes and blood. Nothing. Darma's skinny arms shiver with goose pimples. They look at each other, breathing hard. Darma shoulders his rifle, Sam yanking the Lee–Enfield from the rebel's clutched fingers.

Blood paints them both as they heave the man up between them and drag him back along the riverbank toward the bridge. The squad shouts as Sam and Darma emerge in the clearing and drop the rebel to the ground. He moans and tries to get up. Sam kicks him back down, crouches at his side, listening to the ragged breath. The rebel's eyes clear an instant. Sam expects to see fear. Instead a complete fire of hatred flames the dark irises. The man smiles the same slow challenge. Shouting and jeering, the squad swoops in and carts the rebel off while Sam and Darma collapse on a rock at the edge of the river.

Sam looks at Darma. "Thank you." His voice is thick.

"You would have done the same."

He doesn't know. He was ready for the bullet, even as Darma was angling in on the situation, risking his life to save Sam's. His friend had been so calm, so confident. It was Sam who let his judgment be clouded by anger. Again.

They are quiet a moment. "Why on two?"

Darma chuckles a little. "Because he didn't understand. I thought maybe 'on three' is a universal thing. Took a chance we'd surprise him."

They laugh together and it feels good. Darma smiles once more, closes his eyes and tilts his head to the sun, whistling breath out loud and long. A shout from the bridge. The squad has put a rope under the rebel's arms and around his chest, tossing its end over the railing to haul him up. He hangs there, spinning slowly, the men below cheering as those on the bridge let the rope slip a little so the body lurches downward, then up again. A flash of gallows. The men call, waving a gun toward Sam and Darma, their intentions clear. Sam looks hard at Darma, who shakes his head.

"You have to try, Darma."

"It won't make any difference."

"One shot. He's going to die anyway."

"You think that makes it okay?"

Sam looks at his friend and has a moment of such profound sadness he can't speak. He wants to turn and walk away. To shed his gear, his gun, his uniform and walk. Away from the squad, the rebel hanging there, away from all the war has asked him to be. All the things he's afraid he might become. The others call again. Looking at Darma, the man who saved his life, Sam knows, in this dark place, what he has to do. For both of them.

The men hoot their excitement as he makes his way to the bridge where someone thrusts a gun into his hand.

"You get the first shot."

"Yeah, the bastard would've killed you."

"Go ahead, Vandenberg."

Raj watches carefully as Sam steps forward without a word.

"You know I have to." Sam searches Raj's face for agreement, but finds instead an unspoken question in the tilt of his head, a pain in his eye before he walks away with Darma. Shrouds and bones. Desecrating the dead.

Hanging from the bridge, the body turns like a wind chime in the breeze, the faces of the men lit with expectation. Sam breathes deep and raises his rifle. He is a marksman. He doesn't miss. The men go wild as the body swings violently, spraying blood. The men take turns firing, one after another after another, each report like a chisel into Sam's head until thankfully what is left of the shredded body falls from the rope into the river and is swept away.

It's over. Sam stares down river at four boys of about ten. Skinny naked bodies, hands held to soapy hair as the sun glistens off the water and the jungle rises up behind them. They watch the rebel's body float past, a swirl of river current pushing the bloody mass toward the boys who screech with horror, splashing to the bank, their stick legs churning, tiny sacs bobbing as they scramble away. Sam should feel badly, wonders briefly about Taufik — no small boy should witness such a thing. But he feels nothing at all.

He goes to the alley behind barracks and stands under a bucket shower. Sam soaps and rinses, soaps and rinses, exhaustion curtaining his thoughts. He gets back to see Darma on his cot in only shorts, the curve of his ribs rising and falling in sleep, mouth slightly open, hands tucked together under his cheek. He is once again the frail young man who loves plants, the homosexual Sam does not understand but to whom Sam now owes his life. Resolve floods his bones. He has not been paying attention, worn ambivalence as his cover, but no more. This war is real; his actions carry consequences just as they did in the last war when he was too stupid to understand. He is filled with sudden purpose, pictures Darma and the rebel faced off with Sam's life in the balance. Marcel saved Darma. Darma saved Sam. Sam couldn't save Leo, but he will keep Darma safe.

CHAPTER 18

This Simple Thing

LEO WAS SENT FROM CAMP Erika to a munitions factory in Essen that would be under almost constant Allied bombardment until the end. Saved from a particular kind of death in the camp, he faced it at the hands of the people trying to save us. A fucked-up world it was. I was relieved to be sent to a farm perched on a small knoll by the Ems River near Munster.

The house was small, a barn and broken-down corral behind it, sheep grazing in a small pasture beside. As I passed, the nose-clogging smell of the chicken coop almost made me weep; this wasn't home, but something like it. A woman stood drying her hands on the porch steps, two small children clustered round her skirts. She said nothing until I reached the bottom of the stairs, then let out a nervous sigh.

"Your name?"

"Sam."

"Hmm . . . you're pretty skinny, but I guess you'll have to do. This is Simon and Martha." The boy watched intently while the girl giggled from behind. "I'm Emma."

She was small and compact, her arms muscled and hands raw, her shirtdress buttoned so the dip between her breasts was just visible. A rolled scarf held back curly brown hair. She directed me to the corner of a dark back porch where a single bed was surrounded by milk cans and barn coats and rubber boots that stunk of manure. Some of them were men's things, though Emma told me she had no idea if she was a wife or a widow. Gone for two years, Franz was on the Eastern Front, and everyone knew how that was going. She gave me a long look when she said it, as though I might understand.

The two children ran about the kitchen as she explained what was expected of me: chores, fixing, lambing.

"Where are you from?" Simon asked. He was seven and bold.

"Heibloem."

The two children burst into giggles.

"Where is your family?"

"Why are you here?"

"Never mind," Emma said, shooing them out to the backyard. "And don't you try to run," she turned on me, her voice a little shrill as though not used to giving orders. "I'd have to report you. Otherwise I'd be in trouble myself. Just do the work. We all have to do the work. I think most of us are as scared as you."

I doubted that. The despair lurking on the other side of the German border was missing here. They seemed to have no idea what they'd done, indignant at Allied incursions, as though the German people were suffering a kind of discomfort that was beneath them. Her mind seemed a little scattered and her kids cowered when she yelled, but Emma did not appear unkind.

After six weeks on her farm, the air of early spring reminded me I was human, the sores and scabs from scratching at lice and flea bites in the camp finally healed. Twine replaced the wire belt, raw spots from its sharp edge a reminder of the temporary nature of luck. Emma fed me as well as she could, and I'd even gained back some of the weight lost in the camp.

"Can't expect you to keep the farm going if you're hungry," she said, as she slapped another plate of food on the table in front of me. The longer I was there, the more the change in her voice, softer, less gravel in it as she listed chores for the day. I thought perhaps she wasn't such a bad person, gulped down the porridge or thin stew she fed me each day, and went to work.

I didn't mind it, especially when I considered the alternative was dying in the rock quarry at Camp Erika. The farm felt more like a real job if I forgot that I was forced to be there, threatened with execution if I ran away. I checked the ewes in the barn close to lambing, the pasture where those already lambed stood in pairs under trees, cobbled together new fence for the corral with remnants of scattered and broken posts.

I never had Leo's skill for fixing. He should have been there in that crisp March air instead of slaving over an assembly line. If he was still alive. I tried to suck the thought back into the barrel it came out of, imagined hammering down the lid. I couldn't let myself consider it. Leo was alive and thinking of things like fences and sheep and pigs and the best time to cut the hay. Thinking how the two of us would one day take over the farm. We'd do a better job than Dad. I pounded the last nail and stood back to admire my work; the fence was a pathetic crosshatch of posts and nails, but there was satisfaction in knowing the flock would be safe. The sheep in Germany were just sheep. I could care about them without guilt.

Back at the house, Emma handed me a sweater from a pile of clothes growing by the door, items for the Volksopfer, a depot for such things. I'd seen a sign on the side of one of the collection trucks. *The* Führer *expects your sacrifice for Army and Home Guard.*

"They're still sending them to the front. Children, really." She shook her head. "And they're still asking for boots and jackets. Even when we don't have anything left to donate. I think we've sacrificed enough," she grumbled.

I didn't say what I thought, that her sacrifice paled in comparison to what I'd seen. I changed the subject. "Do you have other family?"

"One brother." She snorted and shrugged angrily. "But he's disappeared, same as my husband."

"Must be hard."

"Oh, don't try. I'm not stupid. I know how you feel about them. About me." She said the last with the faintest smile.

For a moment I could see she might have been beautiful in another place and time, younger than I'd first thought, maybe thirty-five. The war waged itself on all of us, Marie and Anika and Dad, all of us made ugly in a gray kind of way. I must have looked to Emma like a skinny kid in rags.

"You want to go home," she said. "But we both have to make the best of this."

She walked slowly behind me and ran her hand down my arm, fingers stopping briefly where my wrist rested against my thigh. Gooseflesh popped and I yanked my arm away, turning to stumble back out the door, Emma's laugh soft behind me.

What to make of it. Maybe she only touched me because we'd had something like a real conversation, a little bit of connection. But that didn't explain the flutter in my stomach or the hardening in my pants at the thought of my skin tingling under her fingers. It was a sin to think about doing it, and likely an even bigger one to be thinking about doing it with a German. I did the evening chores, piling hay into the mangers and distributing small buckets of grain, imagining the lazy eyes of the sheep laughing at my sorry confusion. It was late when I dragged myself back to the house.

Emma came from the washtub, her face scrubbed and hair damp, housecoat tightly wrapped. "Those sheep will be lambing any time, so you'll have to get up at least once every night to check them." She headed for the door to her room, the children long asleep in theirs. "And get me up if there's any trouble. Gestapo is suspicious if I lose any lambs."

I nodded, not daring to look into her eyes.

A week later I was exhausted from the nightly trips to the barn and from waking to Allied bombs dropping close one night, more distant the next. I had acquired Dad's skill at gauging their distance and stayed put in the house or the yard or my bed, but with every explosion Emma's eyes jumped with fear as she rushed the children to the cellar near the house. Smoke billowed from fires raging in nearby towns and every night the roar of planes broke the dark, a whoosh of shells, the pock of ack-ack guns in the distance. The countryside was relatively peaceful — a small mercy — I hoped for Allied success but didn't want to die as a result of it. I did my chores, ate the meager meals, and fell into bed in a blind repetition of the day before and the day before that.

Another week and I'd lost track of the days as I came in for lunch to the unusual absence of small voices. "Where are the children?" I asked through a mouthful of bread. I liked Simon and Martha. They accepted me as though my being there was normal. It gave me a little hope.

"I took them to visit my sister in Munster. She promises them ice cream." Emma smiled. "I'll fetch them tomorrow." Her gaze was soft as it lingered on my face a moment.

I blushed as she turned away to lift the edge of the towel covering the dough rising on the counter. She punched the dough, turned it and punched some more. Watching, I had a moment to wonder about her life. Was she lonely? She rarely left the farm and never had other women over. No one came by except the German who picked up sheep to be slaughtered to feed the soldiers. He leered at her and she always put him off with a good-natured shove. Faithful to Franz, I supposed, or turned off by the meat cutter's bloodied apron.

I studied her profile for a clue to her thoughts, the small nose, full lips above a chin ramping away to a fleshy neck, the only unattractive part of her. Eyes roving over her breasts and waist and buttocks, I thought of her hand on my inner wrist, embarrassed again at the reaction in my pants. Why the hell did I care if she was happy? She was German. Any hardships I endured were because of her.

Later, the bombs woke me with their thudding explosions as they hit the ground about two kilometers away. A crescent moon dangled high in the sky, providing enough light to check the sheep. I'd washed my underwear and hung them to dry on a hook by my bed. Dragging pants up over my naked ass, I picked my jacket off the floor, pulled on boots and headed to the barn. The racket of the shelling was louder outside, scaring the sheep milling in their pens. The power knocked out long before my arrival, I stumbled in the dark barn before finding a lantern to light, swinging it high to see the two round-bellied ewes I'd put in box stalls the previous evening. They were showing signs — lack of appetite, huge udders.

Despite the noise of approaching explosions, one ewe lay on her side, panting and straining, the bright red bubble of her water bag broken into a puddle behind her. Instead of two small legs coming from the sheep, there were four. I took my jacket off to keep the sleeves out of the way and knelt beside the ewe, gently winding my fingers up the side of the small legs and inside. Two heads, but through the slickness it was impossible to tell which feet belonged to which nose. The lambs weren't moving. A bad sign.

I was startled by a hand on my naked shoulder. Emma looked down and smiled, her long hair hanging round her face, her housecoat loosely tied, a hint of her plain white shift underneath. I hoped the shadows hid the rush of blood to my face.

"They woke me," she said, nodding toward the door and the distant thunder of shells. "Looks like she's having trouble." Emma dropped to the straw by the ewe's head and stroked her ears. "It's okay, love."

I'd never seen her so gentle. "Two at once," I said quietly. "I can't figure out which feet are which."

"Here, let me." Nudging me out of the way, she pushed up the sleeves of her robe and reached into the sheep, pausing a moment as her fingers slid past mine. She looked to the ceiling, concentrating as she moved her hand slowly round the ewe's cervix. "Okay. The feet on the right need to move over and to the left near that one's head. Then push it back a little so the other can be born first."

She could have done it herself, but made way for me, lighting a cigarette and sitting back on her heels to watch as a teacher might. One tiny hoof nicked my index finger as I slid my hand over the soft down of hair on the leg, pushing it over the rounded bump of the other lamb's head, so the baby was absorbed back into the ewe. Carefully, I pulled on the two remaining legs and the nose of the lamb appeared, the head suddenly out and the rest of the baby slipping onto the straw on the floor between us. Emma smiled and nodded toward the ewe, where the second lamb was born easily and the mother quickly up and licking the slick film of birth off the twins, wary now of her two human midwives.

It made me happy. This simple thing.

"Good." Emma pushed herself up with her hand on my shoulder again, letting it linger there. We watched the lambs clumsily nurse.

"I learned from Franz," she said quietly. "He was good with the animals. Patient. With the children too." She was silent for so long, I was tempted to leave her with her thoughts, but the warmth of her fingers stopped me. "I don't think he'll have survived the front." Her hand dropped to her side.

The lamp flickered across the sheep and I glanced at her, surprised at a moment of sympathy. I suddenly wanted to ask about her husband, their life before the war, what she thought would happen to me. But she was somewhere far away and would have likely only laughed. She did that, answered questions with a laugh and a wave of her hand as though either the question or the answer was too absurd to be spoken. Perhaps it was crazy to wonder about such things; perhaps no one knew anymore.

We left the ewe to do what new mothers do and walked toward the house. I pulled my jacket on just as a plane droned overhead. A whistle and a thud paralyzed us both before a split second later the air ricocheted with sound and the force of the blast. I landed face down in the dirt beside her. Jumping up, I grabbed her hand and sprinted across the yard to the cellar. She plunged down the steps and I pulled the door closed over us, falling into the hole and landing on top of her with a grunt. Another explosion ripped through my ears and blew the cellar door off, throwing dirt onto us, the sky above lit like daylight.

"Stop it," she shouted. Clutching at me, she buried her face in my chest. Another crash and she screamed. "Stop it, stop it, stop it."

I grabbed her roughly. I needed her to shut up. Her screams were infected with fear, slicing me through with it. I didn't want to die. Managed to outlive the occupation. Survived the train. The cruelty of the camp. It couldn't be Allied bombs that would kill me in the end. I pulled her closer, grasping at her, holding the solid presence of her body against mine. She bent toward me, pushing her breast and pelvis against me so the blood surged to my groin. She ran her hands over my chest, her mouth following, running her tongue down between ribs to navel. I moaned and she grabbed my hands, forcing my palms against her breasts, her nipples taut under the thin dress. And then she wasn't forcing anything. I wanted this. I didn't know anything, but I wanted it just the same. Wanted the blood pulsing through me to mean something.

Running my hands down her sides, the round of her hip, I pulled her shift up and over her head. She startled again as another explosion lit her body, naked beneath me. Her nipples at attention, the small black mound between her legs: it was beautiful. It scared me. I didn't know what to do with it. If I should do anything. I reached out and ran my hands over the softness of her belly, roughly thrust myself against her. She pulled at my pants, pausing at the lack of underwear, and I had a moment to wonder what I was doing. But then she had me in her hand and was rubbing and coaxing sensations out of me so I didn't know anymore what caused the pulsing vibrations in my head. Another explosion, the sky lit.

"Stop it. Please." She wept at the sky.

I felt huge and stupid. I wanted more but didn't know how. She touched my hand, guiding it to where she was slick and pulsing and arched toward my fingers. When she cried out I pulled my hand back quickly, scared I'd hurt her.

"No. More," she gasped and rolled me on my back, straddling and guiding me into her warmth. We rocked together. And wept together. Until a great shudder ran through me and she reared back before collapsing onto me and moaning into the night. Another shell struck and light blazed like sun into the cellar, revealing her face bent toward mine. She kissed me, her tongue a faint lick at the side of my lips.

It was the taste of her cigarettes that startled me from the desperation. I pushed her off, scrambling to sit and then stand, pulled my pants over my wilting dick and grabbed my jacket to run up the stairs and outside. She screamed something I couldn't hear as another shell struck close, throwing dirt into the air. I ran across the yard and into the house, flinging myself under the bed.

"Oh god. Oh god. What have I done?" I lay rigid amidst the shattering of glass and splintering of wood. When silence finally came, I dragged myself out from under the bed to lay boots and all on the hard foam, the quiet as deep as an accusation. Where was Emma? She'd screamed as I ran away, but I'd run anyway, left her alone with the bombs still dropping, ran even as I could smell her in my nose and taste her in my mouth. I felt I might vomit, yet was aroused at the same time, and shame smothered me, sitting on my chest so I thought I'd stop breathing. The sun rose.

"Sam, get up." It was Emma calling from the kitchen.

She couldn't be serious. I struggled up to walk slowly across the porch and forced my legs around the corner and into the kitchen, where a bowl of porridge waited on the table. She stood at the stove with her back to me, still wearing her housecoat, dirty and crumpled and torn up one side. I didn't sit, lifting the bowl and mechanically shoveling the mess into my mouth, finally noticing the shards of glass on the floor, the cracked ceiling beam, the dust settled on everything.

"I'll start cleaning this up." Her voice was hard. "Check the barn."

"Yes, Frau Emma."

"Really? So formal now?"

The silence was agonizing.

Still at the stove, she seemed to hesitate, then spoke to the wall again. "You know, I could report you, tell them you raped me." That was it. I'd be executed for my lust. I imagined all the ways they could kill me, looked down at my boots and pictured them swinging like those of the prisoners hanged in the camp, couldn't quite get a picture of my own body and face attached. I wanted her to look at me. Show me what she was thinking. At the same time I didn't want to know. She finally turned. I expected anger, saw only disappointment. Anger would have been better.

"I thought, perhaps . . ." She paused and pushed her hair behind her ear, resting her hand at her throat an instant. But her eyes hardened, and she laughed without smiling.

I kept my eyes on her face, trying to guess what she wanted me to say, suddenly remembering the feel of her mouth, her body, a hot flush spreading from my neck, nose flaring in embarrassment. She'd expected me to be a man. I'd run away like a boy.

Puffing out a soft breath, she shook her head, eyes softening a moment as she finally pointed her chin at the door. "It's a mess out there. See what you can do."

I bolted outside, shocked by the sight of the farmyard. We were lucky to be alive. Craters sculpted the yard and were filling with a hard rain that must have started in the brief time I'd slept, marooning the barn so I was forced to duck around the back of the house to get by the mess. Walking past the shattered kitchen window, I saw Emma inside at the table, running her index finger over the handle of her coffee cup and staring out at me though she didn't seem to see. Suddenly she jumped up to smooth her hair and wrap a scarf around her neck, pushing her arms into the sleeves of her coat as she came out the back door. She saw me, looked puzzled a moment and then began to walk.

"Emma?"

"The children."

I nodded, gut churning. The moment was rife with choices. I could swallow my embarrassment and run after her to apologize, say something to make her feel better. I imagined she might smile at my courage. My honesty. It had a certain romantic appeal. But a sudden anger cut through me. Such bullshit. How could she expect anything from me at all? I was her prisoner. And it was too late anyway. Excuses came easily as I watched her walk away, but I also knew something happened in the night that I didn't understand.

I made my way to the barn. The loft door threatened to drop from where it hung at an angle from its hinges. Inside, daylight streamed through a huge hole in the roof, rubble piled in the door-way to the stalls. I scrambled over it to find a lone ewe alive. She chewed her hay as though she hadn't almost been killed like the mother and her twins pinned under the weight of the bales and floor and roof that had crashed in on top of them in the adjoining pen. I pulled the wreckage off the small bodies. The twins had been nursing, waiting innocently for whatever life handed them. I should have been happy the Allies were punishing the Germans, elated they'd finally come to deliver me from that hell. Instead, I sank to my knees, pushed my fists against my eyes to stem the grief and shame and longing that streamed out in my tears, nose running so I tasted the mingled salts on my lips. Only hours before I'd tasted the same on Emma's cheek.

CHAPTER 19

A Scream in the Distance

NGADIPURO, ISLAND OF JAVA,
DUTCH EAST INDIES
NOVEMBER 1948

THE RAINS CLOSE IN AS November marches toward Christmas. Sam relives moments: Willem's innocent face floating away, the whack of bullets on water, Darma shouting two, the rebel's shredded body dangling from the bridge. In the three-way split that was Darma and the rebel and Sam, only Darma acted like a soldier. Darma did his job and walked away. And Sam? He'd convinced himself he was protecting Darma from judgment by the men. While Darma risked everything to stop the man from killing Sam, it was Sam who felt the hate. He was rescued from death; no one knows how much hate can possess a man when his life is given back to him.

It eats at him until finally he goes to the small chapel Brother Keenan assembled at one end of the mess tent. Aching to be close to something holy, Sam is drawn to the young deacon who believes enough to make the effort.

Arriving early for Sunday Mass, Sam sits on a chair in front of the makeshift altar, a confessional set up behind a teak screen the squad stole from a farmer's joglo while on patrol. The thing is massively heavy, and beautifully carved with images of Hindu gods and naked women. When not a confessional, it screens the men who have begun to bring local girls into camp for sex. No one misses the irony. Today, Sam listens to Keenan's whistling as the cleric sets up a small nativity scene and an Advent wreath, lighting the first of four candles to be lit each Sunday until Christmas.

"Sam." Keenan finishes his preparations and sits beside Sam, looking straight ahead. "You don't seem yourself. I know it's hard to keep perspective here. I'm struggling myself. But prayer can help."

"Yes, well, faith seems to have deserted me."

"Or maybe you've deserted it?"

"Maybe." The comfort of belief. Catholic, Buddhist, Muslim. It wouldn't matter; just a relief to have such certainty. But faith requires trust in a benevolent god, in a worthy humanity, in some kind of truth that doesn't require Sam to take sides, to judge, to kill. Such truth seems just out of reach. Maybe that's what hell is — simply never knowing the truth. Or never caring to know. Fuck, it's embarrassing, his hungering for truth. As though he's even capable of recognizing it. "I guess I don't know what to believe."

"It's not that simple. Truth is an ambiguous thing."

"Yes. But if we don't know what's true — here — how do we know we're doing the right thing?"

"There's not much truth in war, Sam. Each side believes what they need to believe in order to do the things war asks."

We'll all pay something in the end. "There was a priest on a train in Germany," he starts, but is overwhelmed by the memory.

"We've all seen too much," Keenan says quietly.

The picture of Father Pete blurs with a sudden image of his father, the beaten slump of Hendrik's shoulders as he waited for someone else to decide his fate, perhaps relieved to let the judgment come. If belief has nothing to do with truth, then truth has nothing to do with faith.

"A pathless land," Sam murmurs.

Keenan looks sideways at him. "Indeed."

Andre, Visser and a few others come in, genuflect and kneel. Keenan pats Sam's leg and goes to his side of the confessional to listen to the men unload their guilt. Sam wonders what they confess, if any of them speaks honestly anymore, or if they say only what needs to be said to keep from falling out of their minds.

Confessions over, the Mass begins. Sam watches the rituals, the physical preparation of the gifts, bread and wine made body and blood. He listens to the call and response of the liturgy, the familiar intonations settling his edgy heart. If nothing else, there is comfort in this repetition — if he can just reach back through the past few years to before the time war entered his life, back further to this ancient and solid thing, and hold onto it, perhaps he will reconnect to something bigger than himself, and this war. And he will survive the Indies.

On their way out, Keenan gives Sam the figurine of baby Jesus for safekeeping until Christmas Eve.

Ahead, Freddy turns to shout at Andre. "Did you tell him about Bonita?"

"Did you tell him you're a son of a bitch?" Andre counters. Freddy glares and walks away.

"Nicely done," Sam chuckles as they amble back to barracks. "At least we've got Jesus. Zwarte Piet won't be showing up here. After what we've done, he'd stuff *us* in his sack in place of the kids."

"Come on, Sam," Andre says quietly. "We're all right. We're just doing our job. It's not like we enjoy it. That would be different."

Enjoy it. The blood pulsing through his fingers when he shot the dangling rebel. Was that joy?

They've arrived at barracks where Darma and Taufik lounge in the shade. Sam flops onto his bunk and watches Taufik fling his arms about, explaining himself without words while Darma laughs at the boy's antics. Sam is startled by a twinge of jealousy, shakes his head and pulls out pen and paper. He owes Marie a letter and begins to tell her of Darma, of his friend's nature and his Javanese ideas around death and the afterlife, how Darma saved Sam from discovering the truth firsthand. He tells her of Marcel's resurrection and of his strangeness and uncertainty. Sam writes to Marie, knowing he's trying to understand it all himself.

Late afternoon and his efforts are interrupted by Andre slapping at his foot.

"Let's see if Cora has restocked the bar."

"Perfect." Sam goes to Darma. "The Jungle?"

"Think I'll stay here and teach him how to play permainan kadal," Darma says quietly, his long fingers tousling the boy's hair. "The Lizard Game."

Sam hesitates a second too long.

"What?"

"Nothing. That's great." Sam smiles at Taufik, who beams back. "I could stay," he says slowly.

"We'll be fine." Darma moves to stand in front of Sam and looks directly into his eyes.

Sam looks away in shame. "Let's go," he says to the others, jumping in the jeep and revving the engine as Stefan jumps in beside him, Andre and Raj in the back. Arriving at the bamboo tavern, he stumbles at the door and smashes into Cora.

"Jesus Christ!" she says as the tray of glasses crashes on the dirt floor. "Slow down, you stupid . . ." She stops when she sees Sam.

He flushes; the last time he saw Cora she was watching Freddy kick in a man's head. "Sorry, sorry, sorry." He drops to his knees, scrabbling to pick up the glass and pile in onto the tray.

"Okay, kid, get up." Cora sweeps the glass into a pile and together they load it onto her tray. She disappears out the back door, her round ass swaying in her tight skirt, a small crash into the trash bin. She returns, wiping her hands on her apron as she surveys the group. "Sit. Sit. Not like somebody died or anything."

Sam doesn't move and Cora guides him to a seat at the bar. "Right back," she says and serves Andre, Bart and a couple of other men who've come in, then returns to stand across from him behind the bar. "So what's going on?"

"Nothing." He didn't think he was so obvious. "I thought you might kick us out. After what you saw."

"I saw your face when that dickhead beat that poor man." She sets a whiskey in front of Sam, watching him blush. She taps his chest. "Means you still have something going on in there. Besides, wasn't that asshole in charge?" She glances toward where Raj drains his glass.

Sam doesn't tell her no one is in charge anymore. That perhaps it is not Raj who is the asshole. He crashes back another drink in one gulp, throat burning, eyes watering so Cora laughs and pours another. She bustles behind the counter while he sits silently drinking, the air thick with cigarette smoke. He thinks of his letter to Marie. Would she so easily forgive his sins? Perhaps Marie would agree with Marcel, wonder what this war has become, who Sam has become as a result.

"Leo would know," he slurs. Cora pats his hand as she whisks by. "I want to be like my brother." He sucks back another shot, wipes his mouth. "Brave. Good." Like Darma. It breaks over Sam so he almost weeps; Leo would have been proud to have Darma as a brother.

"Darma saved my life. I should stand up for him when the others . . . I'm a prick."

"Oh, for god's sake, enough of that. Darma can handle himself." Cora keeps up with his prattle, switching him to coffee, which he gulps down, like the whiskey and the coffee are just a different variety of lifeline.

"No, I'm a prick. No friend at all." To anyone. Brothers, friends, lovers — he lets them all down.

"Okay, so you're a prick. Not the first one. War does stuff."

"No shit," he says slowly. She's suddenly the wisest person he's ever known. "No shit."

She laughs then and the sound tickles him so he chuckles too. She's made him laugh. He reaches out as she walks by, hoping to whisk her onto the small space between tables to dance. But his elbow jabs into the softness of her breast.

"Ow, Jesus Sam," she curses him.

"Come on, Cora, just a dance," he mumbles, his head spinning, stomach churning.

Before he knows what's happened, Andre and Raj have thrown him out the door to puke up the night's offerings. He wipes his face with a rough hand and lies down in the dirt, imagining he is in a field of heather, Sari beside him. He stares up at a bright moon hanging over the perfect cone of a volcano in the distance.

"I don't deserve anyone," he whispers into the night, and starts to cry quiet tears as the earth spins under him and the constellations blur. A scream in the distance.

"Baby on a pitchfork." He laughs. He's too drunk to move. Road outside the bamboo bar, Ngadipuro village, East Java, Dutch East Indies. At least he knows where he is, talks to keep the dizzy spells away — Ngadipuro village, East Java, Dutch East Indies. Ngadipuro, East Java — again and again.

Another scream. His head clears for an instant and he pushes up to all fours, staggering to his feet as the sound sears through the night to pierce his booze-fogged brain. What the fuck? Lurching forward, he pulls his pistol from its holster. Another scream and another, unearthly, they drift from somewhere near the river. Sam runs, crashing through dark jungle, cobwebbed leaves slapping his head, a sudden hint of hibiscus, a silver flash of river. Hunched and running across the bridge, fear is a knife at the back of his throat. Spinning, spinning, he can't find the sound. There, a crushing howl somewhere between ecstasy and death. He runs, not sure if he now screams, or sobs, or is silent, his whole body convulsed with terror as he runs toward the sound he knows is Darma.

He reaches a clearing on the other side of the river and crouches behind a stand of bamboo stalks. A few feet away, a small figure, arms held behind his back by men in shadows. Beyond, a group has Darma standing in their midst, his ankles bound and a burlap sack over his head, body jerking in rhythm to the jab of their bayonets. Sam sees only shapes, bare-chested and wearing balaclavas.

Rebels. His heart lurches. A sliver of moon glances off light skin. He stands, stepping out from the thicket.

"Let him go." He doesn't recognize his voice. It startles those nearby and the small figure suddenly darts toward him. Taufik runs past, eyes wild, blood streaming from cuts scissoring across his face and chest. He stares at Sam an instant.

"Get help," Sam hisses. As Taufik sprints, Sam turns back to the group that faces him, rifles glinting in the dark, the rising sun a pink scar on the horizon behind them.

He hears only the slow drag of his breath. No response. No sound. Two rifles pointed at Sam's head, the other two slicing at Darma with bayonets, his agony puncturing Sam's ears. Suddenly he sees everything large and from beyond as his body surges toward the red rage of sunrise, his voice drawing up from some primal space inside as he screams and runs, flying toward the great energy he knows he will find, toward his destiny. He will save his friend.

Thrown sideways, he crashes to the earth as a body hurtles into him.

He wakes to a pounding head and gravel tongue, his body sore as one long bruise. And Raj standing over him, anguish on his face.

"What?" Sam croaks. "What happened?"

"You need to come."

Sam stares up at him from the ground, rolls to his knees in the dirt, all his senses taut despite a moment of vertigo. Raj thrusts Sam's rifle at him and throws him a canteen.

"Please tell me," Sam whispers, the silence terrifying. He has a faint recollection of a scream in the night and the images flash. No. Sam looks frantically for Taufik, and both men break into a jog, Sam following Raj down a small path away from the clearing and into the jungle.

"Andre and I came looking." Raj finally breaks his silence.

Sam can't breathe.

"We found Taufik." Raj's voice chokes off as they reach a small clearing to the right of the trail. Morning mist wisps the ground in front of a huge stand of bamboo where Andre sits cradling Taufik in his arms. Oh god. Sam runs to kneel beside them. The boy is covered in blood from gashes across his face and chest, but his eyes are open and he gives Sam a weak smile. Tears course down Andre's cheek as he glances toward the river's edge where a body lies splayed across a large boulder.

Hands on thighs, Sam leans forward a moment to steady himself. He walks slowly toward the rock, the outline of Darma's body blurring and then coming into too-sharp focus. He huffs quick breaths, anguish rising in his throat. Darma is naked, his face battered beyond recognition, hairless chest and arms and legs swollen and purple with bruising, cigarette burns, knife cuts, bloody rope marks round his wrists. So much blood, too much.

Sam convulses, turning to wretch up the sour bile in his stomach, spitting, wiping his mouth and slowly turning back. He forces himself to look again, searching for signs of why and how, as though such detail will help him to understand, to make this unreal thing real. His mind crashes into images. Darma stretched between ropes, the screams. Dear God.

A sob bleats up from somewhere deep in his gut, anger squeezing like a fist round his heart. There is no way to explain this ugly scene. Sam touches one of the long fingers, curls his fist round it as though he can squeeze an answer out of Darma's dead hand. He looks down at Taufik come to stand beside him, the boy's tears draining to mix with the blood seeping from the puzzle of cuts across his face and down his chest. The confused pictures whirling through Sam's head abruptly stop. The boy knows.

Sam kneels in front of Taufik. "Who did this?"

Taufik shakes his head.

A sound like a train rumbles behind Sam's eyes, the verdant green jungle reduced to a white-hot point. Moon glinting off naked chests.

"For fuck's sake, Taufik, you have to tell me." He grips the boy's arm, shaking him until a gutted cry pierces the air as Sam's fingers dig into a deep gash in Taufik's shoulder. Hot rage boils through Sam as he forces Taufik to stand over Darma's body. Someone else is shouting. Someone else lifts the boy's chin with the barrel of a rifle, ignores the tears streaming down Taufik's mute face. "Look at him." The train rushes in and Sam roars. "Tell me the truth."

Suddenly the ground comes up to meet him, Raj standing in front of him to shield Taufik behind as he backs away. "Sam, stop."

"The little fucker knows." He struggles to his feet. "He knows."

"No, he doesn't." Raj keeps moving away from Sam. "Darma's dead, Sam. It's not the kid's fault." Behind Raj, Andre carefully gathers the boy up and carries him away down the path while Raj continues to face Sam. "It's war, and they killed him. That's what happened."

Sam's mind flashes through what he saw, can't hit on anything concrete. He was too drunk to distinguish rebel from friend, can't let himself believe the thought creeping into his head, the memory of light skin. He'd vowed to keep Darma safe. Torn and mutilated on the rock, only fragments of Darma are visible in the slender hands and the skeletal outline of bloodied ribs round hollowed belly. Sam couldn't keep anyone safe. Not Leo. Not Darma.

An eruption flows through and around Sam's heart, the force finally cracking it, the aortic gaps filling with blind hatred. And the voice in his head that once screamed a reminder of what he wanted to be is pushed to the outside of that widening space, becoming only a whisper.

There is an urgency to Darma's burial, the locals whispering his violent death might conjure a hantu spirit to bring misfortune to the village. Sam can't help thinking that if Darma doesn't yet know he's dead, his spirit has a right to be angry, to shed the soft character he possessed in life for something distinctly harder. The women shroud the body in white cloth, the men laying him to rest with his head pointed east to Mecca, the Hindu village doing its best to respect Muslim tradition. Mostly, they hope to keep Darma's soul moving along.

At the graveside, the dukun recites prayers and the villagers respond. Taufik stands at the dukun's side, eyes down, face swollen and crisscrossed with stitches where Appeldoorn sewed up the worst of the slashing. Taufik works the back of one hand and then the other as he struggles not to cry. The ceremony over, everyone recites a few words before taking a handful of dirt and throwing it on the body. Sam does the same, trying to think of one word of comfort with which to send his friend off, one appropriate prayer, but his mind is blank. Darma will never get back to his grandparents' plantation to channel the water for rice paddies, pick tea leaves at just the right stage, roast coffee beans to perfection. He pictures his friend's joyful face, Darma in the hotel room, the hurt in his eyes when Sam was an asshole. This shrouded body only nurtures the hot rage threatening to shout out of him. He turns away quickly and smacks into Andre.

"Hang on there, Sam."

They follow a trail of rocks and sticks and other small obstacles scattered to keep Darma's spirit from following them back to the village. It's all too much. Mengeti, Darma called it, the connection between the two worlds, ancestors as guides for the living, history as prophesy. But if Darma's ancestors have control, if their actions in life shaped his future, then his ugly death is on their heads.

Sam walks away from Andre, unable to speak. Once again he is reminded of the impotence of words, the authority of silence. Leo hadn't spoken, hadn't even tried. Perhaps like Taufik, there was too much to share, too much pain and Leo only wanted to be where things were good, to relinquish himself to the cradling of Sam's arms and the soft bed of his childhood. To be at home. Sam had missed the point of his family's silence when their mother died, when they lost Leo. He'd wanted them to lay their emotions bare and writhing on the floor as indications of their truest feelings.

He'd been childish. Now, his anger at Taufik is replaced by a kind of envy at the dignity it takes for the boy to hold his peace.

He finally takes a gift of candy to Taufik. It's nothing, but all he has. Taufik's stitches pull at his chin as he smiles with relief, as though it is he who has been waiting for Sam's forgiveness, making Sam feel even worse.

"Was he able to teach you the Lizard game?" Sam asks quietly.

Taufik nods and heads toward a small clearing near the barracks where the men sometimes kick a soccer ball. Taufik places a stone in the center and searches the ground until he finds a small bamboo stick he balances on the stone so it overhangs on one side. Brandishing a longer stick, he whacks the small one, launching it ten meters. He motions to Sam to throw the stick back to the stone, and then bats it away with his hand, grinning wildly, motioning to Sam to throw the small stick at the stone again, batting it away so it lands even closer. Sam understands the goal is to somehow toss the stick past Taufik and back to the stone, where it began. He narrows his eyes, exaggerating his movements one way and then the other, until he throws the stick and leaps at Taufik at the same time. They land in a heap and wrestle, Taufik thumping on Sam's back and shoulders as Sam turtles. Looking up an instant, he's grateful to see Taufik smiling as he flails and pokes Sam in the ribs, tickling under his arms. Cradling the stick to his belly, Sam rolls onto his back, ready for the boy to wrestle it away, careful of the boy's stitched face and chest.

Instead, Taufik stands over him, his mirth turned to anguish, eyes streaming and mouth opened in a silent howl as he falls onto Sam, pounding Sam's head and face. Sam lets the boy hammer at him until Taufik is spent, weak and weeping as Sam holds him carefully, finally stroking Taufik's dirty hair and murmuring soothing sounds into his ear. Taufik's sobs subside and Sam slowly releases his hold, searching Taufik's streaked face, looking into brown eyes gone soft again. They stare at each other a moment. They don't need any words.

CHAPTER 20

Lost Souls

DECEMBER 1948

STARING INTO THE SPIRAL OF his grief, Sam is easily whirled into the vortex, the very brilliance and beauty of the jungle an affront. He knows what hides beyond the emerald foliage, and behind the hooded eyes of the villagers, his imagination pushing tension into his shoulders and neck, pounding into headaches. He is rescued by the war, his anger given a target by another massive police action launched just before Christmas. It will be a relief to march, walking the only way to ward off the explosion building at his core.

Hagen arrives to relay specific orders, telling them General Spoor's had enough of the rebel guerrillas who ignore the terms of the Renville Agreement and cross the demarcation line to conduct ever deadlier raids into Dutch territory. Operation Crow will push the rebels inward from the perimeter of Java, the ultimate objective to capture Sukarno's political base in Yogyakarta and end this thing.

"How long will we be gone, sir?" Andre asks.

"You won't be coming back to Ngadipuro, son. When we push west, the village will be secure. The squad will be needed elsewhere."

There is a hint of sympathy in Hagen's voice. "Say your goodbyes. We'll head out in the morning."

Andre stands erect, his face pale, eyes darting about. Sam looks away. Andre should have known better than to take up with Bonita.

They load transports, fuel jeeps, sort through the small touches collected to make their squalid barracks more of a home: river-burnished rocks, traditional masks painted garish and detailed, the tall penjor poles decorated with coconut leaves curving over the doorway. Sam throws it all out. He wants no reminders. Bundling only his letters from home, he crushes them together and ties them with bamboo strands, watches Andre quickly cram his things into his pack and disappear without a word. Where they would usually throw a harassing comment at his back, the men say nothing.

"Do you think he'll see her again?" Bart asks Raj.

"Maybe when this is over, but she might give up on him before then."

"Might be just as well," Sam says.

Raj looks at him, surprised. "What about Sari? She won't know where to find you."

"You saw the intelligence on Amir." Sari had only used Sam to get the clinic. To help her father. She'd made Sam a traitor. Even as he tries to convince himself, Sam steels himself to the memory of Sari's lips, her body pressed to his.

"Amir is dead, Sam," Raj says softly. "I just got word he was killed in Madiun. Wouldn't join the communists. Or he did. Who the hell knows?"

Amir dead, after all Sam had risked. Amir who wanted only to farm. Or perhaps that was all just bullshit too. "Well, I guess he deserved it."

Raj looks up quickly and meets Sam's gaze for a long minute. Then, as though he's made a decision, he vanishes quickly out the door. An hour later, Sam is summoned by Hagen.

"Sam, good to see you. Let's walk."

As they walk across the bridge, Sam wants to point to where Willem was shot, and Jesse so badly wounded he was taken to Jakarta in a coma — there and there and there — members of his squad picked off, to be replaced, again and again. As though it's Hagen's fault. It should be someone's fault. But Sam keeps his blame to himself. They arrive in the center of the village, where the women anxiously watch the clinic.

"I hear it's been a success." Hagen stops to watch as Raj gives orders to clear the supply shed of medicines and load the stretchers and trunks. "Appeldoorn says it's made a big difference."

"I think so. I suppose they'll go back to seeing the witch doctor now."

"I suppose." Hagen coughs, his eyes on a point somewhere in the distance. "Heard about your friend, Darma. So brutal." He turns to fix his eyes on Sam. "How you holding up?"

Sweat beads on his brow and under his shirt collar. His suspicions have been a tight fist squeezing his gut. He imagines telling the man everything. Let Hagen unravel the mystery of Darma's death, prove Sam wrong about the moonlit mirage of pale bodies. The ache to speak is palpable and he tastes the words on his tongue.

"War does things to people, Sam," Hagen persists. "Especially in this goddamn jungle. Never knowing where they are, who they are. Not everyone can handle it. So if you need out . . ." The words hang there as offering. "Maybe a desk job in Jakarta?"

Sam shakes his head even as he imagines the relief it would be to put his gun aside along with all the choices forced on him by carrying it. To shower every morning and walk to work. The army has done it for others; some men crying in their soup until transferred to shuffle paper, bad enough and they were sent home. Home. The word catches at his throat. He glances up at Hagen and leans forward.

"Raj is worried about you," Hagen says.

Son of a bitch; the madman is worried about him? As quickly as he thinks it he recalls Raj in the village and at the bridge, waiting for Sam to do the right thing, offering Sam a chance at redemption. Raj can't be the better man. Crumpling inside, Sam holds his peace.

"Sam?"

"I'm fine, sir. Ready to head out tomorrow and take on the bastards."

Hagen squints into the distance as though gauging the truth of Sam's words, then looks off to where Raj has stopped working to watch. Hagen turns to walk. "Alright, then. Let's take them on."

No one sleeps. Sam's sweat soaks his bedroll. He is happy when the sun rises and he can head behind the bamboo screen to pour cool water over his head, filling another pail and letting it trickle more slowly this time down his arms and chest to drip off his dick. Finally wrapping the towel around his waist, he steps into the small alley between the shower and the barracks. At the far end, Andre's long arms engulf Bonita's tiny figure, heads bent together as tears stream down her face. He kisses her then, long and deep, and she leans into him as though willing herself to be absorbed into his body. Watching the intensity of it stirs something in Sam. He's flooded with a quick panic; Raj is right. They won't come back to Ngadipuro. Sari won't know where to look for him. He shakes the thought away. She won't be looking anyway. He hurries to barracks to towel off and apply ointments, dress and head for one last breakfast.

When he gets there, Bonita is back at the canteen, no sign of tears, the flush in her face shrouded by Javanese composure as she slips a leaf-wrapped package into his pack.

"Terima kasih," he says, voice catching a moment in his throat.

"Sama-sama," she says, pausing to look up at him. "Tuhan bersatamu, Sam."

God be with you. He wants to say more to her, to thank her for feeding them, for treating their stinking laundry with care, for creating some semblance of home. For making Andre happy. But he feels suddenly awkward, instead giving her a quick peck on the cheek and turning away to look for Taufik. He has a moment to consider what will happen to the boy. The squad is Taufik's family, the village their home, all of them attached to the particular version of reality they've managed to carve out of this little part of hell. He wants to save the boy from his future even as he is anxious to leave the place behind.

Some of the women throw wistful glances at the squad, while the older village men shake hands. "Terima kasih" and "Selamat tinggal," Thank you and goodbye. The villagers smile tentatively, unsure of being left without protection from the pemuda in the trees. Taufik has still not emerged and Sam is first panicked and then left with the sickening sensation that he was wrong to believe the boy forgave him for Darma's death.

At 8:30 a.m., Spoor broadcasts his orders to the troops. "We will cross the Van Mook line and purge the Republic of unreliable elements." Spoor's voice is clear and confident.

Purge. Good word. Sam holds his gun high in salute. No one else does, some of the squad lowering their eyes from his. And they leave Ngadipuro behind, the village and the people, the bridge and the post. He's spent over a year here, killed a man, seen his mates die, welcomed new ones. Even imagined he'd fallen in love.

They are disappointingly late to the party. They haven't yet crossed the Solo River when reports come in that Yogya has fallen. Hagen tells them Sukarno and his vice-president along with several ministers allowed themselves to be captured and sent into exile on Bangka Island.

"They've convinced the Americans we're guilty of colonialism. As though it's a new concept." Hagen's laugh is raw. "Pearl Harbor and the atomic bomb and the fucking Americans think they know what history's all about. Like goddamn teenagers. Don't they understand the only reason this country has had any success is because we built it?"

The men shake their heads at the idiocy of those who would judge what they know nothing about. Sam recalls Amir's opinion about who built the country, but keeps his mouth shut.

It's Christmas Eve and there's no one to fight as they roll into Surakarta and down its wide streets, boulevards humming with people, local Indo running alongside the troops and reaching to press small gifts of tobacco or tea into their hands. In the midst of this support, Sam glimpses Dutch troops lounging against a wall, taking slow drags on cigarettes with one hand while holding guns trained on rebel soldiers lying face down in the dirt. One rebel's eyes bulge with fear as a soldier pulls his head back, threatening his throat with the bayonet of a rifle, the soldier's laugh callous, brittle. Interrogation? Torture? It doesn't matter anymore. This is just another day, another arrest. Sam feels the same deadness. While new recruits like Carl and Pieter are still moved by the gestures from the crowd, still believing in the cause, his own pinched heart pushes belief aside. What he believes doesn't matter.

"The whores here are as diseased as anywhere." Hagen breaks the spell as he dismisses them to wander the city. "And little kids are ready to pick your drunk-ass pockets. There might be a few resistance cells missed in the mop up. So team up and don't do anything stupid."

Sam squanders the afternoon watching artisans fire the city's famous silver into long threads they craft into intricate brooches and pendants, special hearts and flowers the men request for girl-friends and wives back home. He buys a silver powder container, hand-pounded hollow, its surface patterned with dimples he likes to run his hand over, the lid fitting perfectly. He will send it to Anika. He buys a brooch in the shape of a flower for Marie, then wanders Pasar Klewer, startled by batik sellers pushing to stand in front of him, their voices loud, claiming their fabrics display only original royal patterns worth much more than those from the vendors down the street who claim the same thing. It seems an eternity ago the girl showed him the batik process, the intricacy, the work and artistry.

As evening approaches, he buys noodle balls and bakso soup, hoping his guts can take what the street vendors serve from their warungs. He sits on a mat on a sidewalk, surprised when Raj joins him. They watch the tangled traffic, pedestrians and bicycles, army jeeps and becak taxis pulled by rope-muscled men or skinny ponies. The city is foreign and loud and bright after so long in the jungle. People pass on foot, chatting in Javanese, haggling prices, gossiping about neighbors. The people here go about the business of living as though the nature of the people in charge has little bearing on their lives.

"It has to," Sam says aloud.

Raj jumps, splashing soup on his legs. Sam finishes and hands his bowl back to the vendor, dropping a few rupiah into the man's hand. The soup is warm in his belly and his energy improves. He turns toward the sound of the river.

"Selamat malam," the man says behind him.

When Sam ignores the vendor, Raj jumps in. "Terima kasih," he says apologetically, before catching up and falling into step beside Sam.

"Think we'll see some action at Dieng?" Sam asks.

"Depends if Sukarno has any control left over his troops."

"You think he doesn't?"

"Sukarno wants the world to think he's being reasonable, that we're the only ones shooting people in the jungle. But his guerrillas have their own agenda now. I guess we'll find out when we get there."

They walk quietly, the sounds of the city fading as they reach a walkway at the river's edge. It is fringed by a concrete half-wall, small dwellings clustered along its length, Sam and Raj forced to duck under tin and plastic awnings stretching from the roofs of homes across the walkway.

"The Solo," Raj says and waves his hand toward the river wandering slow and brown, sluggish with islands of waste, the smell stifling. Near the river's edge, young boys fish bits of plastic and leather and fabric from the water, whooping and waving when they see Sam and Raj. Peering through the open window of a tin-roofed shack edging the walkway, Sam watches a one-legged man pound the sole of a shoe over his cobbler's bench. Ahead, an old man sweeps dust from the sidewalk in a rhythmic dance round the same spot. Over and over he sweeps, lost in the song he hums. Two young men round the corner to walk ahead, one slinging his arm over another's shoulder, ass swaying neat in tight red pants.

"All the weirdos are here," Raj says.

Sam knows they're both thinking of Darma, how different his life might have been in this river community. There is almost a gentle quality in Raj's gaze, changed, as though he carries himself a little more lightly since telling Sam of his father's death, since he talked Sam down from his anger while cradling damaged Taufik in his arms. Rage over Darma's death pushes behind Sam's eyes, threatening to blind him, but it seems to have made something clear to Raj. Something Sam wishes he could see.

There is sudden movement on the retaining wall a few feet away, and a giggle floats toward them. A small girl sits with her back to them, the tattered edge of her pink dress rippling as she swings her legs over the river below. Her head is covered by a white shawl and she hums to herself in a low voice as she hoists one skinny leg back over the wall, then the other, her movements excruciatingly slow so Sam thinks she must be crippled. Reaching one tiny foot toward the ground, she lets herself drop gently onto it, swaying and then steadying herself as the other foot hits. The girl is no more than three feet tall, too young to be out alone at night. Sam wonders if she is homeless. She moves bent but graceful, her face in shadow, her small form floating to stand directly in front of Sam as she lifts her head.

He recoils at the rivulet of wrinkles running down her withered neck, the fringe of hair a pure white halo. She is ancient. The light reflecting from nearby windows sparks her tiny eyes bright, her gaze moving across his face, memorizing his mouth and nose, his forehead. Suddenly her eyes are locked on his. He feels exposed, naked to her in some inexplicable way. He's not so much embarrassed as terrified, but can't look away from her deep brown irises narrowed with puzzlement, growing huge with alarm. She steps back quickly, eyes still on his face. Whistling out between small teeth, she leans forward again, waiting for him to bend toward her.

"Semangat hilang," she hisses into his ear.

And then she walks across the alley and enters a small home, the thin light from inside silhouetting her impossibly small, impossibly old body before she disappears. Seconds later, she emerges to set a basket on her stoop, incense wafting from it as she glances back at him with pity.

"I thought she was a little girl." Sam watches the old woman's bent form disappear into her home.

"What did she say?" Raj asks.

"It was something like semangat hilang."

Raj draws back a moment, quickly composing himself. "Lost soul," he says. "Prolonged yearning or discontent can loosen the soul and make us ill." He pauses, and Sam sees the philosopher Raj might have been. "Or even insane."

"Oh, come on. She's the crazy one."

Raj straightens up, barks a fake laugh, but the pity in his eyes is as deep as the old woman's. A shadow of fear stretches over Sam. As they walk away, he finds the baby Jesus figurine Keenan had given him forgotten in his pocket. He snorts, considers throwing it into the canal, but hears the old woman's voice again. Semangat hilang. He pushes the tiny Christ back into his pocket.

The squad is staying in an old hotel just outside the palace walls, the lobby filled with men sprawled drunkenly in chairs or coaxing local girls up to their rooms with offers of money and treats. Andre sits in a corner nursing a beer, eyes hooded, face pale; he has been drinking almost constantly since leaving Bonita behind in Ngadipuro. Sam takes them all in. Who are they? Any of them? Lost souls. No shit.

He hurries past, climbing the stairs to the second floor and his sparse room at the end of the hall. A small figure is slumped beside his door. A desperate joy rushes through him. Taufik looks up at him with a groggy smile and Sam's chest floods with feeling as he slides down the wall to sit, their shoulders touching. His breathing slows and he feels his senses return.

"How did you get here?"

Taufik smiles again, his brown and chipped teeth a welcome sight. Sam grins back. The boy's silence doesn't matter.

"I smuggled him along in the transport." Raj says from where he leans against the doorjamb of his room across from Sam's. "Kept him out of Hagen's sight."

"You?" It's impossible to hide his surprise.

"Well Andre's too fucked up about Bonita to think. And you weren't doing anything about it. So yeah, me."

Sam swallows hard. "Thank you."

Raj nods and goes into his room. Sam stands and opens his door, motioning to Taufik to join him. The boy sits on the only chair, watching as Sam undresses to his boxers and sponges himself off at a sink with unreliable water flow, applies what little ointments he has left and lies down on the bed. He waves at the sink. "Go ahead."

Taufik places his peci on the chair and shyly removes his T-shirt, leaving his tattered sarong round his waist, individual ribs visible amidst the flurry of scars across his chest. Sam can't take his eyes off them, staring so that Taufik rushes to pull his T-shirt back on.

"No, let me see." Sam gets up to stand in front of the boy, tentatively reaching to run his finger across the pink raised lines. He imagines a knife cutting the skin, the sick face of someone who could do such a thing.

"I wish I had been there." He searches Taufik's face. "That it had been me instead of Darma. Instead of you."

Taufik's eyes go wide in surprise and he shakes his head, glancing down at his body as though to indicate he is very much alive and there is no need for Sam's wish. Taking Sam's hand, Taufik places it on his mangled chest before spreading his own small brown fingers across the skin over Sam's heart, encouraging Sam with wide eyes to understand.

"Brothers?" Taufik thinks a moment, then nods so violently it makes Sam laugh. "Brothers."

Taufik spreads his shirt on the floor as though to lay on it, but Sam beckons him to the bed. It is big enough for two. Taufik resists.

"If we're brothers, we can share the damn bed. Come on, you could use a good night's sleep."

Taufik climbs in, clutching his side of the thin mattress. Sam remembers doing the same sleeping with Leo, afraid of the cuff he'd get if he happened to cross the invisible border between them, the occasional infiltration resulting first in wrestling and then full-on fighting before their father yelled at them to shut up if they didn't want a real beating. He smiles at the memory, watches Taufik in the slender moonlight through the window.

"Semangat hilang," he says, and Taufik's spine stiffens. "An old lady said it to me." Taufik rolls to face Sam, his breath shallow, eyes shining. "Never mind."

But the woman's pity stays with him as he listens to the night. Is he lost, his soul yearning? A drunk shouts from the lobby, a train horn rises in the distance, a gecko chirps from somewhere in the corner of the room. Taufik's breath becomes heavy with sleep and Sam is overwhelmed with gratitude for the boy at his side, Taufik's innocence, his child's faith there is something left in Sam to give. He falls into a troubled sleep and wakes to a cool towel wiping a feverish sweat from his brow, Taufik running the cloth down over Sam's chest, eyebrows raised in question as though about to run for help.

"I'm all right." Sam pushes him away, and when the boy frowns, he adds "thank you," turning on the dim overhead light, staring at it until Taufik's breathing becomes even and deep again. Sam fishes the notebook from his pack beside the bed. It's become a lifeline, a connection to a history he's lived beyond, a tether to the real world.

CHAPTER 21

The End of One War

A FARM, MUNSTER GERMANY
MAY 1945

THE VIOLENCE OF THE ALLIED bombings intensified through the spring, more lambs born, more of Germany destroyed. Emma slapped plates in front of me and barked orders as before. I was happy to follow her lead and pretend nothing had happened, though, when she caught my eye, I knew she hadn't forgotten. If I was honest, I'd imagined her coming to me for more, couldn't stop my hands under the blanket remembering what she'd done to me, how it felt to be inside her, how beautiful her body. In those moments I forgot where I was and let myself imagine the possibilities. But she left me to console myself with the guilty pleasure of no longer being a virgin. Holy Mary, Mother of God. The priests said one thing, Leo had told me another. He would be happy I hadn't forced anything from Emma. I couldn't wait to tell Leo.

And then on a morning in May she appeared at my shoulder on the porch.

"Hitler is dead." Her voice was flat.

I gaped at her, but she looked past me as though sizing up her chances in a world she didn't recognize. Emma was afraid of what might happen. What about me? If Hitler was killed, surely the Nazis would seek their revenge on people like me. But somehow I couldn't muster Emma's fear. Instead, a kind of space opened in my brain where dread collapsed in a whirl of dust. Hitler dead. Unbelievable, a man with such power, a laughable man really, a small man with a stupid mustache and ridiculous stiff-armed salute — heil this, heil that. Followed as though he were more than human, he was dead now as any other mortal.

Within days, Allied troops and tanks were on the road a kilometer from the farm, a truck finally turning in at the lane and a squad of men falling out the sides to amble up the drive. I watched from the porch step, heard a soft flutter behind me as Emma hung a white sheet out the shattered upstairs window.

"It's over then."

I dropped to my knees. I'd waited so long. For God. The Allies. Someone to save me. Eyes darting about, I didn't recognize the farm. It was as though I were seeing it for the first time: the wrecked barn, the joke of a fence I'd built, the pasture of bomb craters. Just like that, the place meant nothing at all. I stood. As the men came closer, I could see they were American. Compared to the German soldiers of late, these men were huge, their uniforms pressed, the sun sparkling off polished helmets. The swagger of their bodies seemed to expand the air around them, their easy confidence startling, as though bringing my freedom was not such a big thing. The bend in my back straightened and my shoulders dropped, chest bursting, lungs filling with air.

I sensed Emma behind me. She put her hand on my shoulder and, God help me, I shrugged it off, afraid now of any association. "Don't." I couldn't look at her, knew the disappointment I'd see in her face, the uncertainty as she waited to discover her fate, to learn if she was wife or widow. She stiffened beside me as we waited side by side for the Americans.

An officer in the lead walked up the porch stairs and pointed at me. "Kraut?" he asked.

I shook my head. "Netherlands."

Emma steeled her voice. "This is my farm."

Another soldier interpreted while the officer eyed my tattered clothes and dirty hands. Smiling a kind of pity, he nodded. "Go home," he said in English. I stood there stunned until the American laughed and pushed my shoulder, pointing west in the general direction of Holland. "Go. Home."

I wanted to throw my arms around the man, but I was afraid it was a mistake. Rushing to the porch, I stuffed my few things into a pillowcase ripped from the bed and heard the translator telling Emma her house would be commandeered for the men. She had three hours to collect her things and leave. She asked where she would go. How she might feed her children. The translator said that was not the Allies' concern.

"Let us stay upstairs. I'll do your cooking and cleaning," Emma begged as I came back to the porch. The officer pretended not to understand. "Please. My children."

The officer looked at her skeptically, but the translator barked. "Tell me, why should we help you? We've seen what you've done to men like him." He pointed at me. "And in the camps. My God. Nobody owes you a fucking thing."

Emma shook her head and looked at me, pleading. "I didn't do those things. I didn't know." She started to weep, pawing at my arm. "Please."

I froze. The Americans looked at me with raised eyebrows, waiting for me to betray my allegiances. Head down, I pushed past her. "I'm sorry," I muttered, looking up to see her eyes widen with recognition that I would not, could not, help her.

"I'll do anything," Emma whispered.

I couldn't watch this prostration and bolted down the stairs, running past the soldiers who waited in the yard. When I got to the road, I turned south and slowed to a walk, stopping after a hundred meters, doubled over and trying not to faint. I expected to hear a

shouted order or feel the singe of a bullet. Instead, I saw the dust
flying up from Father Pete's red hair, the little girl digging bunkers,
Leo's emaciated gaze when we'd parted. A great sound roared up
from my gut, plugging my ears, bursting out in a shout somewhere
between agony and joy. My stomach roiled up, vomit burning the
back of my throat as I glanced back to where Emma now suffered,
ahead to where jeeps and trucks wound down the road and others
like me emerged bewildered from farms or small shops. What to
do. Where to go. At the next junction I turned southwest, and
walked toward the Rhineland. Leo. I would find Leo.

The main thoroughfare was barely recognizable as a road.
Skirting deep craters, I hurried past women and children and old
men, a stream of people shuffling home, while German civilians
looked dazed, their years of righteous contempt now reduced to
the confusion of defeat. Slave laborers like myself walked alongside
released labor camp prisoners, clothes hanging from their bones,
angular and gaunt like the branches of the leafless trees along the
road, life's color blasted from both.

I walked, dozing in doorways through the darkest hours of the
night, slipping back onto the road at sunrise, ignoring moments of
pity when I thought perhaps I should help, hurrying toward Essen
and my imagined reunion with Leo.

I would see him first, standing broad-shouldered and sure like
he did at the mine an eternity ago. Strong and determined. We'd
clasp hands like men, embrace like brothers. Such a relief to let
him take control, to provide reassurances. My eyes teared at the
thought of finding Leo, of making the long walk home together,
how we would share our stories and make them funny and grand
to lessen their horror. We'd bring such joy to de Kruidenteelt, to
our sisters and Dad. There would be a party. And Hendrik would
be happy to see me despite what happened in Roermond. And
after. None of it would matter. The war was over. And I was bringing Leo home.

I reached the massive Krupps Ironworks to find it destroyed, while in the distance Essen still burned. Hurrying toward the city, I darted between people as the road narrowed to a path beaten through mountains of rubble, lifting my shirt over my nose to keep out the stench of burning rubber and flesh. Here a German soldier lay dead on a street corner, his helmeted head hanging over the curb and arms splayed to the side. There, the roasted forms of passengers in a burned streetcar. And down the road, bodies of dead German soldiers and civilians lined the way, set aside to make way for the Allied tanks and jeeps roaring past. I ignored the small children tugging at my sleeves, couldn't meet the eyes of girls gazing from blasted doorways, closed my ears to the crying of their mothers inside the shells of homes.

Served them right. I was only mildly shocked at my thoughts. These people should have known, they should have stopped, should have anticipated this exacting of a price. They'd let themselves be ugly, corrupted, and all who suffered for it could not be expected to be better than the sum of their pain. A brief flash of Emma's terror. Fuck.

Near the center of town my steps slowed, anger giving way to a terrible awe. Churches cracked, monuments toppled, bridges crumpled into the river below; ruins to the horizon. In the midst of tangled wires and buckled streetcar rails and debris, a garden bench, intact and with a small sign that read, Nicht for Juden. Not for Jews. I was suddenly afraid of what I would find at de Kruidenteelt. Even more for Leo.

I reached the munitions depot. The outside was a tangle of twisted metal and beams, the walls crumpled into gaping windows revealing the factory where Leo was sent. Upper floors had crashed onto those below, equipment scattered and burnt and broken. The building smoldered as ragged children scrambled amongst the ashes, pocketing bricks and small bits of metal.

I climbed through a window and wandered with these German children, who were just like those Dutch kids at the kolenberg so long ago. Lifting a slab of wood, I recoiled from a dust-covered foot before lifting the wood higher. It was not Leo. Poking behind a wall, I jumped as a rat scurried over a woman's body, her dress twisted up to her thighs and her face peacefully dead in the rubble. I wandered through one warehouse building, then another, came across the barrel of a massive siege gun, six meters long, untouched amidst the destruction as though still waiting for its war to begin. I felt heavy, growing slower with each hour until finally I was too exhausted to move and sat on a slab of concrete in the midst of the rubble, holding my head in my hands. If Leo was here, he was dead.

A small hand landed light on my shoulder and I looked up at a little blonde girl, eyes blue and honest like Anika's, face open and accepting in the way of children who see no more than what is in front of them. She smiled and held out a small chunk of bread. When I shook my head she insisted, holding it to my lips so I opened my mouth and she gently placed it on my tongue. I chewed and swallowed slowly. She nodded, and when I smiled she scampered off to join the others. Anika and Marie were counting on me to get home. I had to believe Leo survived and was walking just like me. Lunging to my feet, I glanced back at the girl, but she was gone.

I walked in a trance. It was almost dark when I reached the south edge of Essen and stuck my head into what was left of a storage shed from which others emerged tucking items under their jackets and rushing off. Searching inside, I found a tin of fish and a box of crackers and, to my delight, a half tin of matches. Sheltering in the doorway behind a decimated creamery, I started a small fire with some paper and wood from the collapsed building and before long was curled up on the floor, sleeping as though dead.

In the morning I finished the crackers and headed out. As the sun rose, the road opened into countryside, flowing again with a river of human flesh and goods and sorrow. Mothers pushed prams loaded with belongings, their children scurrying about, while old men and women moved in a dazed shuffle. Laborers like me created a babel of languages, Dutch and Belgian and French heading west, Russians and Poles east, everyone going home to a place they would not recognize. American trucks passed by with load after load of surrendered German soldiers who sat stony-faced, resigned to their fate, perhaps even a little relieved, their look one more of exhaustion than defeat.

I wanted only to step onto Dutch soil, but the border was still two days' walking. Skirting past the old and slow and lame, I stumbled across fields at times, striding down the road at others. I found an unprotected American jeep, its occupants standing at an intersection of some rural houses where a German woman stood outside the door of her home, coat open to reveal her naked body as she held the hand of an American GI and tempted him to come inside.

"Goin' fratin'," one of the men called out to applause and whistles from the others.

"Jesus. Easy as that."

"Hope he don't get caught. Sixty-five-dollar whore right there."

The soldier grinned at the other men as he handed a sandwich to a small child on the porch, then whipped the woman's jacket off as they entered, her backside revealed a moment before disappearing inside.

I felt slightly ill imagining Simon and Martha watching their mother do the same. Quickly snatching cigarettes and a ration kit from the glove box of the jeep, I ducked into nearby trees to savor the first chocolate I'd tasted in years, letting each piece melt on my tongue before rolling it around in my mouth and swallowing. Small chunks of heaven.

The Lucky Strikes were like gold. I traded them for cheese or bread, and otherwise smoked them to stave off hunger. Further south and west, women foraged in the fields for potatoes as I once did, their children listless beside them. The Germans seemed to be starving while in the next small town a Red Cross worker, crisp in her dark blue jacket and cap, offered coffee and donuts to Allied soldiers from a street corner stand. The men flirted, but she only smiled slightly at each before serving the next.

The Americans laughed; they were loud. Confident. Europe had been whispering for a very long time, deference become a way of life, a way to stay alive. I didn't trust the volume of those new voices, didn't know how to respond. I walked, shoulders hunched against the rain that had started again. I was so cold, my jacket thin. I just wanted to get home, the longing more than I could bear at times, my steps too slow, the distance too great.

Finally I neared the border. A massive field ran alongside the road, fenced and re-fenced, like paddocks for livestock, but with a hash of barbed wire reaching three meters high. Instead of cows, the pens held hundreds of German soldiers. The road was raised so I looked down on a sea of faces. Men and blond boys stared back, holding their collars up against the rain, eyes deadened like none of it mattered. Some smoked, but mostly they just stood, packed together in muddy, treeless pens. Waiting. I tried not to look at them, heard nothing but the sound of my boots.

In the last pen, in the corner nearest the road, I saw a familiar form. Drawn toward him in spite of myself, I slipped down the roadside into the ditch, startled by the others inside suddenly clamoring for cigarettes or food. But I kept my eyes on the lone figure, ignoring my fluttering heart as I slowly came to stand across the fence from him. Rudy sat on a small stump. He wore the same up-turned officer's cap he'd worn fishing, an undershirt, suspenders hanging loose over his shoulders and jacket thrown over a young boy lying beside him just out of the mud. Rudy did nothing to protect himself from the rain though he shivered uncontrollably, sitting with hands between his knees, head down and rocking ever so slightly as he murmured to himself.

"Mr. Konig?" No response. Maybe I'd made a mistake. "Rudy?"

He looked up with eyes empty of light. Those blue irises had once danced with hope as he sat on the edge of the canal and dangled his hook into waters blasted to sludge by bombs, jigging for fish that weren't there. Now Rudy's eyes were like wells he'd turned inside himself. I scanned the fence quickly for someone to tell, to convince of their mistake, to explain why he was not like the others and shouldn't be kept there. An American uniform started to move toward me from the other end of the pen, rifle ready.

"It's me. Sam."

Rudy's eyes cleared an instant. "Sam? Ah, yes. Did you find your brother?"

"Yes. He's alive. Or at least he was."

"Good." He went back to his rocking and muttering. "Good then."

"I'll get you out of here." My voice was low, face close to the fence. I glanced to the approaching guard. "I'll tell them what you did for Leo. They can . . ."

"No!" He shouted and I jumped back, the other prisoners looking up in surprise. The guard quickened his pace. "They won't release me," Rudy said more softly and let out a long sigh like a moan, dropping his head again as though it held too much, his voice barely audible. "I've done things."

I was stunned, throat closing with what I couldn't do or say.

"Go home to your sisters." He looked up at me through hooded eyes, smiled slightly. "Go fishing."

"What the fuck are you doing?" The American was at my elbow, pushing me back up toward the road. "Get the hell out of here."

"Tell Marie . . ." Behind me, Rudy's voice was soft with affection.

What the hell? He didn't finish or I couldn't hear him, and the American was pushing me again. I walked away, walking one foot in front of the other as the German POWs faded behind. *Tell Marie* — it echoed in my ears as I trudged forward. Home would make sense. Home would comfort my nervous heart.

At the border, I crossed through a Canadian forces checkpoint and was suddenly in Limburg, breathing deeply as though the air had changed form and would purge my lungs. My shoulders slumped down from where they'd been hunched up around my ears and I dropped to the ground and kissed it, ran the dirt and loam through my fingers, Dutch soil free now from its long occupation —

the air, the soil and me, released from our waiting. I stood again. Walked again.

Approaching Roermond from the east, I joined the stream of hundreds walking toward town, more quickly now, sure-footed on our own soil, anticipating reunions and welcomes, nervous excitement rippling through the air. Around me, every single building was damaged or destroyed and I wondered if there was anyone left for these people to come home to. In the distance, St. Christopher's was a lonesome landmark, its saint toppled, bell tower split in half. I searched for glimpses of war's end. Dutch flags flew from every post or pole or building left standing, as though the sheer numbers would make up for lost time. Canadian and American flags too. In one doorway, an old man watched me pass, nodding solemnly as though he understood what I'd been through. Maybe he did. I nodded back, chest tightening as though I might cry. I'd been invisible for so long.

I was still alone, though surrounded by a tide of humanity. My thoughts wandered because they could, because for the first time in five years I was not afraid. The horror remained, but the fear was gone. Its loss left me so weary my bones ached and my feet slowed until I was almost stopped in the road. My temples were pounding. I could feel the hard callouses on my feet and knew they bled from rubbing against the cracked leather of the old boots I'd managed to hang onto all this time. It was a small wonder. Someone bumped me from behind and I grunted. A child's wagon crashed into my knee and it buckled. A hand reached toward me as I fell into sweet blackness.

I woke to cool fingers stroking my temple and forehead. When I opened my eyes, the hand was quickly withdrawn, a girl of about fourteen gazing at me through lowered lashes, her face eerie in the soft lantern light.

"You fainted in the street," she said. "My father brought you to the church. He's the caretaker here."

I tried to sit up, but swooned again.

"Have some water," she said, holding out a tin cup. I gulped it down greedily, so she dipped it in the pail next to her and gave me another.

"Thank you." My voice cracked and she laughed. A few lamps dotted the inside of St. Christopher's. Their faint glow outlined bricks piled against damaged walls where curled human figures slept. Lying back again, I looked up to where frescoes had once shimmered and saw half the roof gone, the spire above pointing accusations at the stars.

"Everyone is coming home," the girl said. "Finally. There are so many people just like you. Were you in a camp?" She waited only a second. "Forced to work? How awful for you. What's your name?"

"Sam." I closed my eyes, hoping she would stop. I couldn't answer her questions, there was too much to say or too little. I wanted the forgetting to start.

"My father says you'll want to talk about what happened to you," she said knowingly, as if she and her father had rehearsed what must be said to one so fragile.

"Not now."

She stood, offended, and I let her go, watching her take her bucket and cup to the next boy who sat a meter from the wall with his back to the church. Maybe he would make her feel better, tell her what she wanted to hear.

I slept again and woke only when light streamed into my eyes through a broken stained-glass window. Colored patterns danced on the wall, glimmering deep, then pastel, fading as the sun rose and shone through the hole in the pane. I sat up and stretched the ache from my back, stood to test my legs and walked out of the church toward home. One foot in front of the other, keeping time to a childhood tune: "Vader Jakob, Vader Jakob, Slaapt jij nog? Slaapt jij nog?" Sleep you well? Not yet. But soon. Maybe.

CHAPTER 22

The Beginning of Reckoning

MAY 1945

A SCREAM AND CRASH FROM inside the house startled me, but no more than the tiny figure hurtling down the broken porch step, running and throwing itself without stopping into me, sending us rolling onto the grass as the roadside flowers I'd picked sprayed out of my hand. Anika clutched at my arms and neck, pushed away to look again as if to make sure I was real, squealing and hugging me again. Laughing, I looked into her clear blue eyes. Finally she lay beside me in the grass and sobbed, pushing her fist into her mouth to stem the great gasps lurching up from somewhere deep inside her.

I stood and took her hand, pulling her up and clasping her hard. "Leo?" I asked quietly into her hair.

She shook her head. "Not yet." She tipped her head back to give me a small hopeful smile before turning to the house. "Marie," she called, gulping down her tears. "Marie!"

Anika squeezed my hand just as Marie emerged from inside the door, so thin it was as though her dress was held up by a wire hanger. I stopped. Her hair was gone. And her bald head was painted orange.

"Marie." I could hardly breathe. "What the hell? Who did this to you?"

My eyes fired around the farm. The shed where Dad kept Netti and his cart was a blackened heap, the barn where I'd spied on the German command center flattened, the chicken coop the only outbuilding left standing. I looked back to Marie. Her face was unreadable.

"Our neighbors," she said quietly and disappeared into the house.

I rushed in after her. She stood leaning into the table, hands clenching its top, shoulders thin as brittle filament as I reached to hold her. Turning quickly, she pushed her naked orange head against my chest.

"Don't ask," she said. "Not yet. You're home. That's enough for now."

Out the window I saw Dad arrive riding Netti. I touched Marie's shoulder and went to the porch as Dad stopped at the corral and slid to the ground, crouching there an instant before straightening slowly and looking up to stare at me.

"Leo?" The hope in his voice was unbearable.

"No, it's me. Sam."

"Holy hell, Sam." His face shifted and he hobbled toward me. "You made it."

"I did."

"Look at you." He clasped my hand in his own, hugging me briefly before stepping back to look around like I might be mistaken. "No Leo, then?"

For Christ's sake. I could barely stand it, shoulders stiffening for a fight. But the anger left as quickly as it came. He was so small. No more than fifty years old, the war had made him an old man, hunched into himself, face cracked like the leaves of a drought-stricken plant, hands parged the same.

I shook my head, searching for something to say. "Netti survived."

"Yeah, she's tough."

"Like you."

He snorted.

Marie joined us. We watched Dad wrestle the hackamore from Netti's neck and turn her loose in the pasture. "He's not well," she whispered.

Dad returned to hang the bridle on a broken corral post. I swallowed hard. They needed to know.

"I saw Leo."

Marie stared, her knuckles at her lips. Dad turned slowly.

"I was with him for a few months, in a camp up north before they sent me to a farm near Munster. Leo went to build munitions in Essen. I went to the factory before I came home. I looked for him, Dad." My voice broke as Marie took my hand. "I couldn't find him."

We stood silent a moment.

"He'll come home," Marie said finally, standing tall and nodding vigorously, her orange head like a beacon.

I nodded, but what I remembered was Leo's frail body hobbling away.

The girls nursed me for ten days. Marie maintained her silence about what happened with the neighbors but kept me always in sight, until I became strong enough for impatience and snuck out for a foray into Heibloem, where mocking voices at the grocer sent me quickly home.

"Is it true?" I towered behind Marie who sat at the kitchen table, stitching. The needle stopped and she folded her hands on the table, her silence infuriating. "You slept with one of those bastards? Jesus Christ."

"No, not Jesus. Just a German." She chuckled dryly, inviting me to soften.

I raised my hand, imagined slapping her hard across the back of her bald head so it swiveled and her neck cracked. She tensed as though expecting it, and shame rushed over me. How quickly I'd left thoughts of Emma behind.

"But a Nazi? Marie, what the hell?"

She turned. "So you've let others convince you of my guilt."

"For God's sake . . . and Leo, what would Leo think?"

Tears sprang to her eyes, but she held her head high while her shoulders heaved with anger. "You don't know anything."

I searched her face. "Tell me, then. Tell me they're wrong."

"I'm lucky they didn't kill me. They have killed some you know. Hanged them in the streets. But women like me, the Moffenmeiden — whores by another name — they humiliated us instead. Painted us flag orange. Paraded us around the neighborhood." She touched her head, gazing at me a moment before she shrugged, lips trembling in a weak smile.

I staggered back. They had shaved Leo. In the camps at the hands of the Germans, and now Marie at the hands of our own.

"Most women did it for favors, extra rations so their kids didn't starve, that kind of thing," she said quietly. "Most were desperate."

I thought of the American soldiers and their German frat lady handing a sandwich to her little girl. While I'd been gone, my sisters had suffered too. "And you?" I asked finally.

"It doesn't matter what I tell anyone, they won't believe me." She sighed. "Do you remember an older officer? He came here just after Leo disappeared. His name was Rudy." Her face softened a little and she dropped her head so she didn't see my face collapse, couldn't hear the hard beat of my heart in my throat. *Tell Marie.*

"I met him, yes."

She looked up again and went to the window. "Rudy showed up at the door one night when Anika was away helping Oma Jeanne in Heibloem. He asked if I could get a message to the Janssen place, to warn them that the Nazis knew about the Jew they were helping. I was stunned. He obviously knew we were with the resistance all along. I was so afraid it was a setup. But what could I do? When I got there the Gestapo were already raiding the house." Marie shook her head hard as though trying to dislodge the picture in her brain. "I hid in the trees. They executed the Janssen boy in front of his mother, the whole family dragged away. Rudy cried when I told him."

"And you think that makes him a hero? He made you do things, Marie . . ."

She turned from the window and raised tired eyes to mine, shaking her head at my ignorance.

"He didn't *make* me do anything."

And in the cellar, with the bombs falling, and the fear in my nose and mouth, Emma never made me do anything either.

Marie straightened her shoulders. "He disappeared just before Germany surrendered. Knew it was coming. Knew he'd face what I face now. Our neighbors won't believe me on the word of a German. The Allies wouldn't spare Rudy's life on the word of a whore, now would they?" Her voice broke and she whispered. "I haven't seen him since."

Rudy helped Leo, and now the Janssen family. But Rudy had done other things too. Had said so himself. For a moment I thought Marie should know Rudy was a prisoner and would die. But I also remembered Rudy's eyes just beyond the fence, his body bearing the exposure that would kill him so a sick boy might be warm. And his voice, the soft lilt when he said her name. I was mute with confusion, arms hanging useless by my side.

"I met him once. He liked to fish."

"Yes, he told me." She laughed a sad laugh. "Never caught a thing."

"I asked him why he wasted his time." Hesitating, I touched her head softly. "I'm sorry."

She nodded. "Me too."

I left the house and crossed the yard, sticking my head in at the chicken coop. The cages were empty, the chickens long since eaten. Dust and cobwebs laced everything, the hidden door wide open, scoops and pails scattered across the floor. The space inside was musty, a blanket and pillow still rolled along the length of one wall, a cup on its side in the center of the floor. Anika told me Daniel made it to the underground shortly after I was picked up. With so many in need of hiding, she'd had to pay. And now stories were coming out about the Jews. Pictures of camps filled with walking skeletons, gas chambers and ovens, the dead piled up like cordwood. Shuddering at memories of rail cars and waving women, I looked around, reaching out so my fingertips almost touched the walls on either side. Such a small space. It hadn't seemed so small when it was safe. I walked out and quietly shut the coop door behind.

Past the burnt-out shed and torched barn, I headed to the canal to sit on the bank where I'd sat with Rudy. Slumped with the weight of my head in my hands, I couldn't help thinking of Rudy's words, wondering if a man can be two people at the same time. Part saint, part monster. Beautiful and ugly. I'd been convinced the Germans were all guilty, should all be punished. But how to reconcile Marie with Rudy and Rudy with his uniform. And with those words: *I've done things.* Rudy would die for what he did, but he would die of exposure or starvation because the Allies with their white hearts chose vengeance. I was a hypocrite, had hesitated to help Daniel, still dreamed of the women in Roermond we'd abandoned to the Germans. Emma flashed through my head. At least Marie had loved Rudy, or thought she did; at least she had risked something.

Dad walked toward me along the canal. Always walking. Since I got home, he only worked and walked, the girls sharing sorrowful glances and shaking their heads in pity for him. But I hung onto my resentment. I thought I hated Dad. The little girl, the women, the train, they came unbidden to my mind so I couldn't fathom Dad's weakness, couldn't conjure any excuses that would let me forgive him. I watched him throw bits of something to the few ducks trying to navigate the slurried water, finally coming to sit beside me. He was tentative, shy somehow. We were silent, strung tight with awareness of each other.

He clenched his shaking hands. Released. Clenched again.

"What happened when I left?" My breath shook as I finally realized the position I'd put them all in. "The girls? They didn't . . . ?"

"No, they left the girls alone. Interrogated me for a while. Beat me up. But Netti wouldn't move for anyone else, so they had to bring me back home." He laughed a little. "Imagine that." He hesitated as if to say more, but stopped, sighing heavily.

I wanted to fill the air with words to hurt him, with questions he couldn't avoid. Why and how and who. They screamed in my head, but I was suddenly overwhelmed, throat blocked, chest aching. It was too much.

"It's over, Sam. And we're alive."

I knew we were both thinking of Leo.

"You look like him now." Dad waved his eyes up and down the length of me, eyes tearing. "Shit, can't seem to stop crying these days. Like a goddamn girl."

"It's okay, Dad."

I wanted to mean it. Could have wept too, for all of it, exhausted with trying to understand what had happened. I wanted to sleep. For days. And then to wake on the other side of this thing, to look back and say *yes, yes that happened*, and to look ahead and say *that, that is my future.*

CHAPTER 23

One White Man Amidst the Brown

YOGYAKARTA, ISLAND OF JAVA,
DUTCH EAST INDIES
JANUARY 1949

WALKING HAS BECOME SAM'S LIFE. That and the searing pain in his feet as he marches toward Yogya, the clarity of putting one foot in front of the other a gift in this place where so little can be predicted. Maybe that was his dad's obsession, to walk back to something he could recognize. Or toward forgiveness. But what needed forgiving? His father had done his best, had rescued many according to Marcel. Yet his dad walked, even after Sam came home and his sisters moved beyond the war, walked just as Sam does now.

A few wisps of rain cloud float away and across the smoking cone of Mount Merapi rising in the distance. It backdrops the spires of the Hindu temples at Prambanan, their jagged stone walls soaring forty meters into the blue sky, every surface carved into perfectly etched reliefs, small enclaves housing the gods within — Brahma, Vishnu, Shiva.

"They say if you touch the statue and then your head, three times, you will be given wisdom or beauty or health. Depends on the god." Raj grins, and Sam wonders again at this philosopher-soldier.

Made silly by the thought of wishes granted, the men run from one temple to the next, climbing the staggered walls and rushing like children up steps glossed by a millennium of feet, hoping to beat the others to touch the foot of Vishnu, or linger suggestively over the breast of Durga. Sam wonders what Darma would think of such irreverence, imagines robed men walking the steps to pray or pilgrims running pious fingers over the intricately carved reliefs of man and god and beast. He wonders what those who built this place hoped their work would mean. Or if the meaning was in the work itself, their sweat dried into the stone as their raw hands etched stories for future worshippers. So many stories, so many gods, real and imagined, so many choices. He can't think straight for all the choices.

"You okay?" Andre peers out from an enclave above, bringing Sam back to where he leans against a wall in the shade of one of the temples. Suddenly overcome with fatigue and heat, he sits quickly.

"Yeah." He waves Andre away.

But he is not okay. His gut roils and he quickly finds a pit toilet at the edge of the temple complex and sits, head spinning while his insides explode out of him. Sweat pours down his face and under his arms as he braces himself, hands pressed against the walls on either side until finally the spell passes and he can stand again. He drinks his canteen dry, the warm water like a saving grace, wanting more.

Raj hollers. They march again.

Smoke spirals from Yogya in the distance. Both the Republican headquarters and airport have been set afire, the first by retreating rebel forces, the second by Dutch bombs. The battalion marches through, the vibrant city distracting Sam from his nausea. Whitewashed and pillared buildings of the Dutch administration, the squat homes of government officials, the Dutch architecture is infused with practical Javanese influences — large bamboo-shuttered windows to ventilate the country's heat, overhanging eaves to shed its rains. In the kraton, the sultan's walled city, the streets wander through and around the residences of those lucky enough to live within. Massive gilded gates separate them from the sprawling palace beyond, its marble pillars studded with gold and jade trim above the gleaming tile floors of a grand esplanade stretching under peaked red roofs, delft flower pots cascading down the steps. A suspended golden umbrella twirls above it all. Gamelan music floats from the courtyard, where slim women in richly colored sarongs dance, floating across the grass as though levitated, mesmerizing Sam with hands that trace synchronized patterns in the air.

Most local officials, adipati loyal to the Dutch, have been killed by Sukarno's troops, but the Sultan of Yogya has both fought the Dutch and provided sanctuary to Sukarno. Each side chooses to leave him alone, his popularity so great they are afraid of what will happen if they take him on. Even Hagen sounds impressed. Looking back at the palace, Sam can't help wonder if the sultan protects the people only to keep his power and wealth. Is that what Sam is fighting for? So those outside the palace who shuffle and bow and prostrate themselves at the gate can keep a sultan in gold?

The squad moves out of Yogya toward Wonosobo in the Dieng Plateau, where Hagen and the rest of the battalion will meet them with the transports and jeeps. Hoping to flush the rebels out, Raj steers them away from the roads and the calming patterns of civilization, plunging the men back into jungle so heavy it's like a vise wrapped around Sam's head.

They walk for days. Machetes slash as the men slip down steep ravines to trudge up the other side, crawl on their bellies through razor-sharp lemongrass. The landscape rises with the volcanic terrain, their bodies and gear weighted by January rains that rot their feet in their boots while their skin absorbs the jungle maladies. Visser keeps Taufik busy helping him to treat those with fever, dysentery, bouts of trachoma. No one speaks. They only march, as though words might eat up too much energy, as though once the words start, they will become a single chorus of bitching complaints so loud the men will succumb.

Sam thinks his fever might be worse and wonders if the anti-malarials have failed. His shoulders ache with tension and his head pounds with dehydration from the diarrhea visiting him again. He is so tired. He imagines a tropical bug no one's ever heard of, terrified he'll die out here from some unceremonious leaching of his insides. He walks, putting one foot in front of the other, hoping the act will keep him present.

They've managed to scare up a rebel pod or two, taking sniper fire and responding with the staccato of machine guns. But the rebels are always one step ahead, disappearing into the jungle's depths to reappear in the form of a blown bridge or a torched plantation warehouse. Finally Raj receives radio intelligence of suspected rebels in a village a little to the north. They push toward it, machetes hacking at the undergrowth and senses alert as night curtains the jungle.

"Stop."

The sweep of Raj's headlamp reveals an abandoned campsite, remnants of a cooking fire with a pot still suspended above it on a bamboo tripod. The tall grasses nearby are flattened into body shapes. Sam clutches his gun and crouches near the tree line with the others, straining to hear over the nighttime din. A sudden quiet as though the jungle knows to listen.

"Cover!"

He dives behind a tree just as the grenade erupts, showering him with dirt and tree roots and rocks. Bullets whizz past his head. Shapes run and duck in the gloom. Suddenly he's firing and running, everyone firing and running. Raj lets go a rattle of bullets from the semiautomatic, the roar corking Sam's ears so he hears only a muffled scream, then another. Up again, legs churning. A tree branch cracks across his helmet, knocks it back, and he feels a sharp tear across his forehead. Roots and rocks trip him up. A shot. A gasp from behind. Bart has been hit.

"You okay," Sam yells.

"I got him," Visser shouts. "Go."

He crawls forward, the jungle scraping his knees and belly as he moves and shoots, ducking and running, shapes around him doing the same. Until he realizes the noise is gone, the guns are stopped. Absolute silence. Breath heaving, he squats alongside a tree. And then a moan in front and to his left. He moves in a crouch toward the sound, fixes his bayonet, straining as though his ears and skin will see what his eyes cannot. A grunt as he stumbles over a rebel whose blood-soaked chest glistens in the night. Sam kneels and takes the man's rifle from his hand and the grenade from the belt around his waist. He should tie him up, make him into another POW, but that's not what Sam wants.

The man is an outline on the dark ground, his breath gurgling blood. A whisper in the dark. *I'd hate to see it make you ugly.* The hair stands on Sam's neck. Amir? No, Amir is dead. But the whisper roars in Sam's head.

Shut up.

He raises his gun and points it at the man's head, tries to slow his breathing. Another sound, softer than the first. He needs to shut the man up. If he can shut the man up, he can shut out the war. The ache of fear pulses through to a single point of relief — his rage — his finger on the trigger. Squeezing slightly, he breathes out slowly, expelling doubt, eyes wide open staring at the man on the ground. A shove from behind and Raj pushes past to shoot the rebel between his surprised eyes.

"What the hell?"

Raj turns and walks away as he orders the squad to return to the clearing. Sam follows, thrusting the rebel's grenade into his own belt and throwing the rifle over his shoulder. He is shaking. Not with relief, but with anger and disappointment. He'd been ready. So close. He moves quickly to catch up to the others. They retrace their steps, stumble onto the dead rebels and relieve them of their remaining weapons.

"Pleasure is all mine." A young replacement named Kurt shakes the hand of one dead body. He takes the grenade from the man's belt. "Kinda ugly though." Half the rebel's face is gone. Mocking the dead. Others direct their pent-up anger at the bodies, perhaps a boot to the head as repayment for having been forced to kill them in the first place. Seven dead rebels. Raj closes their eyes, crosses their arms.

"Holy shit," Andre whistles loudly from the side of the clearing.

Dug into the ground and camouflaged by palm leaves and tree branches, Andre has found a rebel stash, twenty Japanese- and Dutch-issue rifles, a handful of grenades and a submachine gun. The rebel grenade is suddenly less heavy in Sam's belt, the gun across his back less cold. He adds his loot to the pile.

A curtain of cloud drops, the torrential rain warm on their heads as they lug the arsenal they've recovered back along peasant trails, bodies scoured with fatigue, eyes bright with the certainty of guerrillas in the bush. They return to the clearing where Visser has covered Bart with a body bag. Sam is stunned. Bart is dead. Stupid, unlucky Bart. Dead. Sam remembers the cry, the crash of a body, Visser telling him to go on.

"He was already gone," Visser says, as if reading his mind, turning away to wrap a tourniquet around Marcus's elbow to stop the bleeding from a clean bullet hole right through the forearm. Marcus laughs and calls it a flesh wound, "all in a day's work," but his voice is loud with shock as Visser binds the wound.

They slip through the jungle to another clearing that opens into a rice field, crawl forward to lay tense and listening at its soggy edge. The jungle resumes its nighttime overture as some of the men whisper glorified stories of the night's work, fade into crude jokes, chain smoke, pull on flasks. Sam leans against his pack and removes one of his boots to plaster ointment and a bandage over a deep and weeping blister on his heel. His sock is soaked with sweat and resists his foot, a moment of searing pain as he finally pulls his boot back on.

He gingerly explores the gash from the tree branch. Visser comes from where he and Taufik have the medical supplies and stings the cut with alcohol before bandaging it lightly. "Just a scratch," Visser says to reassure Taufik, but the boy hovers until the night begins to fade and the volcano peaks in the distance turn blue with dawn.

Each day they march until dusk feathers the treetops and the air inflates with frog song and the katydid's ratcheted hum. The night heron screeches and chuffs, macaques swinging overhead, their shrill bark turning to a growling pant that raises the hair on Sam's neck. He stumbles and the monkey chorus sounds like ridicule. Each night they clear a camp by hand and, if no shelter exists, they dig a bunker and wait for the sun to drop. The dark fires Sam's imagination, the jungle's impenetrable vibrations become a haunting, while his eyes see shadows of beasts, pemuda waiting just out of sight. He fingers the trigger on his gun, leaning his whole body into the night. He doesn't sleep. No one sleeps.

They capture a few bewildered men in a small village, suspected rebels who seem unsure how to use their weapons. Kurt and Freddy throw a rope over a beam and haul a local up by his bound feet so his head hangs. They take bamboo sticks to his ribs and the back of his thighs, threatening more. Sam watches, stomach churning into an urgent coil. He's afraid he'll pass out as he squats beside a long, low house, groaning with the red-hot agony of his rectum. Finally relieved he comes back to the street to see the prisoner slammed on his head with a sickening thud. Another man watches, crumbling, begging them to stop, admitting the guns came from a white man moving with guerrilla rebels just ahead of the Dutch squad. The white man walks in threadbare shoes handing out medicine along with weapons, telling the villagers to defend their property and families against Dutch colonial abuses.

The White Rebel. The man says it reverently, and at those words Freddy torches the man's home, the squad walking away as the village burns. They pick up the pace, hoping the traitor isn't too far ahead, hoping to be the first to take the fateful shot that will be the only justice he deserves.

Raj radios coordinates to let Hagen know where Bakker might be. Within an hour, a prop plane drones in the distance, dropping leaflets that flutter in the sun. The prop is followed minutes later by three Dutch fighters, flying low, strafing the treetops. Seconds later, Sam hears a blast, smoke rising in the distance, the squad hurrying toward it, the jungle dense and the path narrow.

The screaming reaches him as they stumble round a corner and into the carnage. Son of a bitch, the rebels were traveling with their families? The stench of burning flesh overwhelms him even before he sees the women's charred skin, men impaled by bamboo or teak branches become shrapnel. For a moment he is back in Essen, stunned by the revenge the Allies thought it necessary to inflict on the Germans. A small boy sits against a tree, eyes swimming in a scorched face.

Sam picks up one of the leaflets dropped from the plane. *Wanted. Bakker. 50,000 guilder reward.* He smooths the creased paper, wipes at the smudge over the picture, trying to smear away the image of Marcel. It is Marcel. *Do you ever think we might be to these people what the Nazis were to us?* Marcel's words screech at him. Marcel thought too much, they'd said. And laughed. But Marcel had thought his way into a whole new choice. And he didn't choose Holland. Or his mates. Or Sam. And now this scorched boy in front of Sam is dead because the Dutch will do anything to kill Marcel for making the wrong choice.

Even as he stares stunned at the picture in his hand, several of the men scramble among the victims, oblivious to the horror, hoping only to find the body of one white man. Sam moves forward, numb, the corpses and the living become one mass of flesh writhing amid inhuman whimpers, gut screams, gasps and moans. He's never heard such pain. Dropping his Sten, he leaves it to dangle at his side, moans a little and puts his hands over his ears.

He breathes noisily through his mouth. Andre looks over, but Sam can't explain the panic building in his chest. *Do you ever think . . .* He wants to drown out Marcel's voice, keeps his ears covered, trying to block the sounds of suffering. And he moves, walking faster as the jungle path opens to a road out of the horror. He is almost running, brought up short by Andre calling from a few meters back.

"Wait, Sam."

He spins around, suddenly terrified, drops to sprawl on the ground, rifle waving back and forth at the nearby jungle, scanning the trees, their dappled leaves a perfect camouflage. Marcel's aim could be trained on him right now. Andre catches up, the other men not far behind.

"Sam," Andre says it gently, helping him to his feet. "We're getting out of here. They say Bakker is with another group of rebels that came through here an hour ago. There's still time to catch the son of a bitch."

"Son of a bitch," Sam repeats softly. The death-drunk eyes of the small boy stay with him, asking him for answers. Leo would know, if only he were here. Sweat pours into Sam's eyes. He is so cold.

"Command says the next village is friendly," Raj shouts. "We better hurry."

They march another hour and arrive at the kampong. But this time, the rebels have been there first. They've blown the north half of the bridge so the south half sags over the river where the water runs hard below. Wading across, the men push their feet against the rocky bottom, guns overhead, watching the trees for snipers. Raj enters the first house he comes to, hollering so Sam and Carl rush in behind him. It takes a moment for Sam's eyes to adjust to see two men and a woman twisted in a pile, a baby on a mat in the corner, all of them with bullets through their heads. The reek of death fills Sam's nose as he recognizes the black distortion of the baby's face is a mass of flies.

"Oh, Jesus." Carl bolts back outside to retch.

But Sam is mesmerized. He wanders the room. Sleeping mats on the floor, pots hanging, clothes strung to dry on a line across one end of the kitchen, where a two-burner hot plate sits beside a bag of rice and a bowl of rotting vegetables. A crude rattle made from hollowed teak and filled with dried beans pokes out from under a rug. Sam picks it up and places it beside the baby, chasing the flies away with a wave of his hand, but they settle right back and he leaves them. The men are silent, and he wonders if Marcel did this, if his friend found enough truth in the rebel cause that he would murder a baby because his parents chose the Dutch.

"What was he thinking when he did this?" Sam asks.

"Who?" Raj gives him a confused look.

Shit. Sam clamps his mouth shut and they head out to meet the rest of the squad. Sam hears a wail, wondering for a moment if the baby is crying.

"Incoming!" Andre yells and they scramble.

An explosion rocks the air. Sam crashes into the ditch, water filling his boots and soaking him. He pokes his head up to see the house he just left engulfed in crackling flame. Another wail as mortar fire hits too close.

"Fuck, artillery. North side!" Pieter yells.

The men cover each other as they run toward a storage shed, sheltering finally on its south side. Sam's ears ring with noise and adrenalin. He races east in a series of slow-motion sprints between buildings, behind trees, finally tucking himself behind a large bamboo crate balanced on a two-wheel cart. Its hitch is on the ground, the lone sheep inside forced to balance uphill. It stares dumbly at Sam until a bullet grazes its right side and it quietly tumbles over and back to rest against the green struts. Sam reaches out to stroke the animal's soft nose and limp ear. Poor thing. For a moment, he's back in Emma's barn.

Andre hollers and he startles back, machine gun fire bursting round his feet as he runs and dives in beside Andre. They look at one another and sprint east again, up side streets where women and children huddle in doorways. Adrenalin and fear and a kind of out-of-body determination propel Sam forward. The men yell coordinates, warnings, encouragement. They race forward but the enemy has disappeared into the gaping holes of windows, the jungle perimeter, the air. Finally, the two units meet at the north end and neither can claim a single rebel sighting.

"Burn 'em out," Freddy chants, excitement in his eyes.

"No," Raj says. "The women and kids."

"Fuck them."

"They're hiding in the north end."

The squad fans out, scouring every home, pushing pubescent boys and old men toward the grass at the side of the wrecked bridge, until fifteen men are lined up. Freddy kicks them in the back so they topple face-down in the dirt, hands covering the backs of their heads, Andre demanding they tell him who blew the bridge, where the rebels are hiding.

Sam watches. It's the same old game. No one knows who's playing. But everyone could die. Even babies. The faces of the enemy bleed together, skin and eyes, small hands and feet, all suspect, like the jungle and the rivers and the plantations, the whole place just one enormous, confusing threat. Sweat in his eyes, white heat like a knife in his belly.

A flash of something to his right.

"Hey," he yells and runs toward where it was. Easing himself around the corner, he hears the slap of sandals running away, the crack of branches as a figure disappears into the jungle beyond. Sam sprints after, hiding behind a stand of bamboo, ducking palm leaves. Ahead, the rush of a waterfall cuts off all sound, its spray misting over him as he slips across wet rocks to cross the stream below. He makes his way up a narrow path fringing the waterfall's edge, sees a glimpse of white ahead. He scrambles forward, holding the Sten awkwardly in one hand as he gropes for a hold with the other, hauling himself up and up. Another arc in the path and he is at the top, the waterfall roaring beyond where the man in a white tunic looks over the edge. Nowhere left to go.

Sam's breath rattles, the man a blur as he turns to face Sam. Blue eyes stare from a face browned with sun, hair tucked under a headscarf, a white scar running down his left arm. The water thunders behind the White Rebel, the fucking traitor. Marcel.

Sam raises his rifle and points it.

"I'm unarmed, Sam," Marcel's voice wavers. "Dropped my gun in the damn river." He barks a short laugh and bows his head a moment before looking up into Sam's eyes. "What are you going to do?"

"What should I do, Marcel? You tell me. What the fuck. Does friendship mean nothing? Loyalty?"

"Loyalty to what, Sam? To keeping people poor and miserable? Jesus, grow up."

"Grow up?" Sam's stomach roils. "I haven't been a child since Hitler invaded. What makes you think you know the truth any better than I do? Grow up. Fuck you."

"What are you talking about? Truth? This isn't about truth. It's about right and wrong."

Leo's words haunting him all the way to this moment.

"Look around you, Sam. Anyone can be a Nazi. The right circumstances, the right crazy fuck leader, create enemies out of thin air. Anyone."

"We're better than that."

"Are we?"

"Shut up." He can't see for the sweat running in his eyes, anger pounding in his head. He thinks of the small, scorched boy, the fly-covered face of the baby. "You think your choice is better than mine, but we're all ugly."

He walks forward to poke Marcel with his rifle. Marcel's eyes dart about as though calculating Sam's next move, as though he might still have a way out, a way to live. Sam laughs, prodding Marcel again, pushing him backward until they stand on the jagged rocks at the edge of the waterfall. It is a silent film in Sam's head, everything large and slow. He sees Marcel's bare toes clenched to grip the edge of the wet rock, calf muscles straining so hard the veins pulse beneath the flesh. Sam leans in so close he can see the wrinkles round Marcel's mouth, the crescent scar on his left arm.

"Did you kill that baby?" Sam asks quietly. Marcel looks confused. Sam needs an answer, says the words again, loud and slow. "Did you kill that baby?"

"No."

Blood beats in his ears. "Yes, yes I think you did. And my friends too. Sniped them from the trees. And Darma." He chokes a moment. "You sick son of a bitch. What the fuck was that? What kind of a man does that?"

Marcel shakes his head. "But I helped your friend, Sam."

But the fire in Sam's gut won't let him listen. He draws himself tall. Marcel sickens him, this coward contorting the truth to save himself. Sam pats his rifle.

"Fuck you, Amir," he shouts. It's not wrong to avenge the death of a baby, the men of his squad, to show Marcel his loyalties are wrong. In fact, there is redemption in ticking off the names on a list of the dead, an eye for an eye and all that. Righteousness surges in his chest. Fear is gone. Even hate is gone. He doesn't hate Marcel. He only needs him not to exist, so things will be right with the world. He looks around at the jungle, closes his eyes to hear the water bubbling below. The knife twists in his gut.

"Sam," Raj says loudly. He stands meters away down the path.

Sam's eyes flash open. "They killed your father, Raj." He can barely speak over the buzz in his head. "Took off his fucking head. The people's sovereignty they said, like it was some kind of game. You won't avenge your father?"

"Not like this." Raj's voice breaks. "Not anymore."

Sam stares at Raj a moment. Coward. He turns back to Marcel, sagging now at the lip of the waterfall, stares into Marcel's eyes.

"Dendam." His voice is loud and strong in his ears. Revenge.

Marcel's irises widen and Sam chuckles. Marcel knows what it means, has known all along. Marcel mouths something Sam imagines is a prayer.

"That's right. Pray, you goddamned traitor." This too will prove something to Amir; they all want heaven. He raises his gun. "Dendam."

Breathe. Slow squeeze on the trigger.

"Stoppen."

A small voice, a voice buried in silence for so long it barely sounds. A voice Sam knows, though he's never heard it. He turns to see horror slashing Taufik's scarred face, anguished eyes pleading as though he too will die if Sam does this terrible thing.

"Stoppen," Taufik gasps it out again, collapsing as though this one word is too much.

Sam looks at the boy on the ground, whirls to see Andre and Raj and the arriving squad. Everything slows. His weighted body, his hands as though distant, the gun he holds, all like something beyond and apart from him. Marcel stares. And a parade of men dances in Sam's head. Darma and Willem and Bart; Rudy and Father Pete; a dangling rebel and a terrified miner. Amir.

I've done things.

Anyone can be a Nazi.

We'll all pay something in the end.

An ugly wave.

He sways, panting, sweat pouring to mix with his tears. A moan rises, bubbling up from the dark space of his anger, a volcanic roar screaming out of him. And suddenly Sam knows the truth.

He is the rebel who put a bullet in bespectacled Willem's head, who killed a baby. He is the American watching Rudy die, Freddy who kicked a man's head until it spilled, the Dutch bomber who wiped out families and scorched a small boy. He is the pemuda who killed Raj's father, the communist who killed Amir. He is the Nazi who put a bullet in Father Pete's red-haired head. The men who mutilated Darma. Sam looks at the gun in his hand, legs quivering, chest caving so he can't breathe. He sinks to his knees in front of Marcel.

They are all killing each other. They are all dying.

Andre's voice. "Take him."

Sam looks up to see Marcel's face stilled by grief, sad eyes recognizing all they have come from and the things they can no longer be. A small smile. Sam reaches, Marcel jumps, and the water's roar fills Sam's head.

Freddy rushes to the edge of the waterfall, beckoning the others, chattering about a search, asking loudly why Sam didn't kill the traitor.

"That's enough," Raj says quietly. The men's voices continue to hammer, and Raj roars, "Enough!" Andre and Freddy step back. Voice shaking, Raj orders the squad to form up as he sends Taufik with Visser to the back of the platoon.

Lips twisted, nose flaring, Raj comes to Sam's side and helps him to his feet, taking his arm as they wind their way down the path from the waterfall, find the road and march again. Sam can barely feel his legs, his head spinning. Sweating. Shivering. Raj stays by his side while the rest of the squad stare tight-lipped, giving him a wide berth. Except for Freddy, who dog-trots alongside Sam, prodding him with questions.

"Fuck off, Freddy," Raj hisses, then leans toward Sam. "We'll be in Magelang soon."

That doesn't help. Leo won't be in Magelang. Sam has to walk. One foot in front of the other. The path narrowing.

"Whoa Sam, where are you going?" Raj calls.

"Home." He looks around, confused. He's wandered off the road and thirty meters into a rice field. "I have to find Leo."

A hand takes his elbow. Blurred faces hover.

"Holy shit, he's on fire."

The voices fade.

CHAPTER 24

One True Thing

IT IS THE SWISH OF a broom that wakes him, its rhythmic scratch flaking away layers of calcified dust from his mind so he can finally rise to the surface and open his eyes. A spider stares down from its patterned web, its pincers opening and closing on the air above. Large even as tropical spiders go, its eight legs are jointed in three places and extend well beyond its body. Somehow it has managed to make a home inside the net lacing the bed. Mosquitoes out, spiders in. On the ceiling above, a gecko is frozen in place, its four feet turned slightly inward like a pigeon-footed child. Only its eyes move. Suddenly, its excrement falls on the netting above and Sam jumps, sending it scooting into the crevice between ceiling and wall beam where it tut-tuts its indignation.

"Sure, give me hell." Sam's voice is hoarse, his throat like gravel. "You're the one who shit the bed."

He sees Taufik then, the broom suspended in the boy's hand. Taufik turns slowly as though expecting a ghost, eyes filling with gratitude. Sam smiles and pushes himself up on his elbows until dizziness forces him back down. Before Sam can say anything,

Taufik rushes out. Looking down, Sam sees an angry raised rash covering his arms and legs, an intravenous needle in the vein of his left hand fed by a small hose connected to a bag of fluid strung from a bedpost. A slow drip into his body. He shivers in the chill of damp sheets. Minutes later, Taufik returns with a dark woman in a nursing cap.

"You've come back to us," she says, peering at him through the netting. She pulls it aside and steps closer, resting her hand against Sam's forehead and shining a pen lamp back and forth at each eye in turn. Sam squints and pushes it away.

"What do you mean?" He peers around. "Where am I?"

"Near Magelang." Her accent is thickly Javanese. "You collapsed and your squad brought you here. Keep it under your tongue," she says, sticking a thermometer into his mouth. She busies herself, pulling the netting back and adjusting his sheets, finally retrieving the thermometer and holding it close to her face. "Your fever has broken." She disappears out the door.

He remembers Taufik sponging his forehead, the men forming up to march, but not much else. He waits, but is suddenly impatient, slowly sitting, carefully swinging his legs over the side of the bed and retrieving the bag from where it hangs. Taufik rushes to wrestle the hose out of the way and help him stand. The room is large and square and contains only the bed and a small nightstand. Bamboo walls reach to a foot from the red tile ceiling. His pack rests in one corner, his rifle against the wall. As Sam opens the door, a brown toad gulps at him from where it perches on the top of the wall, jumping to bounce past him out the door and into the sunlit jungle.

Sam wanders a shaded rock path toward the river visible just beyond the trees. It is dreamlike, luring him forward a few tentative steps, barely conscious of Taufik's hand guiding him. Half walls of stone line the path on one side, small Buddha heads and bird reliefs carved here and there. A tall, streamlined rooster struts his yellow and red, crowing a strangled intermittent sound, muttering hens

pecking in pursuit as their young hurry to keep up. The path reaches
the edge of a thirty-meter drop where faded wooden tables and
chairs look out over the river sparkling below. The few steps have
left him exhausted, and he sits to watch the water, body flaccid with
relief even as he scans the jungle, deciding that somehow he is safe
and will not worry. Barely aware of Taufik waiting nearby, Sam nods.

"There you are." The nurse is back with a man, an astonishing man, thin black hair spiking out around his face, while at the
back it is so long he has wrapped it in braided cords around his
neck. His white T-shirt is tattered and stained with red-painted
patterns, sarong flapping carelessly, bare feet saturated with dirt and
calloused hard. Sam is mesmerized by the man's feet, imagining
them shoeless for all time, navigating every sharp pebble or the
silky volcanic loam. To touch the earth at every moment. Imagine.
The man sinks into the chair across the table and squints at Sam
through bright black eyes. "You gave us quite a scare."

"What happened?"

"You collapsed from fever and dehydration, broke out in a
rash and then went into a coma. And now, suddenly, you are with
us again."

"How long?"

"Two weeks. The doctors did tests, but they have no idea."

Two weeks. He'd thought perhaps a few hours. "Where's my
squad?"

"Dieng. Your commander couldn't wait."

"What is this place?"

"A hospice of sorts. Run by Catholic Mission sisters, but staffed
mostly by locals."

"It's beautiful." Sam waves vaguely toward the river and the
jungle.

"Hmmm . . ." The man with the braided hair gazes out over the
river and smiles. "A sacred place."

Sam barely hears him, so tired he suddenly rests his head on his
arms on the table. Out of the corner of his eye, he sees the man pad

away on his tattered feet, the nurse wringing her hands a moment before hurrying after him, Taufik curled up in the chair across from Sam and watching over him as the river tumbles below.

It might be the same day, or the next, or a week later when an insect's buzzing hums him awake. He's never seen a bee so huge. It bumbles to hover over the white jasmine, crashes into an orchid before settling on the wide mouth of the red hibiscus. Sam can see its tongue working to drink the nectar, the weight of the load making the bee cumbersome in flight. Another joins the first and soon a small swarm wreathes around the flowers and shrubs near the table. Sam doesn't move, head on his arms. He is not afraid to be stung, in fact remembers as a boy how he marveled at the bees' frenetic efforts to pollinate the tiny pink flowers of the heather. Memories from before the war. Such a relief he is able to remember a time before war. Tears wet his cheeks.

A pair of sensible white shoes appears beside the table, their surface dusted gray. Above the shoes, slim brown ankles curve toward small fire-scarred calves that disappear into a white dress. Still he does not raise his head, instead letting his gaze wander past the small waist and curve of breast to her neckline. He's not embarrassed by this slow ascent to her face, merely curious. Until he sees a pink mole against the dark skin of her breastbone. Until he sees the small scar on her chin that extends to her lip. And looks finally into deep brown irises. Sari.

"Hallo, Sam."

Something wrenches open in his chest and relief floods into the space, so utter and overwhelming that he is strangled by a moan, the tears now a river flowing. Sari stands close and he clutches her waist, pushing himself into her so she puts her arms round his head, cradling it there to her pelvis, waiting as he weeps great gulping sobs. He cannot speak when he finally looks up. He cannot speak because he will never stop, and she will know the names of his anguish. He moans again and she gently pulls herself away, pushing his hair back and running soft fingers down the side of his face to hold his chin cupped in her palm. And she smiles, slow and lovely and warm, the tenderness reaching past the months of pain to where he catches a glimpse of himself in her eyes.

"It's okay, Sam."

He opens his mouth to protest, but closes it again, shaking his head. She sits in the other chair and holds his hand as they watch the river in perfect silence. The other nurse brings food and water, tapes his intravenous needle more securely while throwing questioning looks at Sari, who ignores her and continues to sit with him, listening to the birds and watching the river until dark drops on them.

"I'll take you back now, and you can sleep. I will come again tomorrow."

He lets her lead him to his room, panicking when she moves to leave, grasping at her hand like a child. He is embarrassed by his actions, mortified, but he can't stop himself.

"Trust me."

And he does, his heart leaping when she comes the next day to hang a new bag of electrolyte solution and adjust the intravenous rate. He learns it is Raj who got a message to Sari through Bonita. Raj who asked Sari to come to this strange place from Madiun where she'd gone to help her mother bury Amir. Amir, who was killed by Sukarno's forces, though he'd never pledged allegiance to anyone, killed just the same. For wanting to farm.

Sam was wrong about so many things. But Sari is here, after everything. He blushes, clumsy and awkward as she helps him to bathe, skin tingling at her touch. She washes his back and chest, kneads soap through hair grown past his ears before turning away so he can do the rest. When she is through, she holds his hand a moment, then smiles and leaves to change the dressings and hold the hands of others like himself.

He knows nothing of them. Without uniforms, they are all just men, and he doesn't want to know their stories, wants only to keep memory as distant as home. A reckoning will come, but he's afraid these others will force it on him too soon, demand a sharing before he understands what happened. To say the words out loud might send him back to that dark place.

Each morning after Sari leaves, Taufik leads him to the riverside table, where Sam's restless mind stills among the scattered bamboo huts, rock pools and stone carvings, benches with twisted driftwood arms. The rippling play of finch and shama and lovebird fills his ears, the chirp of gecko and hum of insect a chorus of sound, a dissonant melody. He takes notes, hoping his descriptions can somehow capture the joy of such sound.

Each day, a young woman comes down the path to bring him food, sky-blue boiled eggs and mango, cones of sticky rice, thick black coffee with milk. He cannot get enough. The woman is slight, always approaching him with her head down and carefully placing the tray so as not to disturb him, walking away without a word exchanged between them. She hums softly as he watches her take the baby from the sling on her back and set the child onto a low table to change his diaper. Just old enough to sit waving chubby arms, the child squeals his delight as his mother peels a banana and hands it to him. The child gums the fruit, watching the river below or staring at the jungle beyond.

Sam wonders what this small boy sees, what he thinks, how the sound of the river and the rhythms of the jungle will mold him, how different his character from that of someone shaped by the clang of streetcar and the tick of a clock. Everything in Holland is square and correct and purposeful, its streets, its ideas, even its water subdued by dikes and dams. The Javanese jungle is wild, all round corners and impulse. He dares to imagine a life here with Sari, their home, their child. But he wonders if he could ever get used to nature's chaos, if the jungle could ever become a home he would stop trying to tame.

The hour with Sari is a salve he awaits every day, anticipating the rhythm of their day; the coffee she brings, the way she crosses her legs, the slow swing of her foot as they sit quietly. Day after day until, finally, he begins to speak. It comes in fragments, quick and guttural. He hears the wanting in his voice and she doesn't let on that she knows his desperation to speak a complete thought to her, to tell her she is cantik, beautiful, to take her small hand in his own and touch each finger one at a time. She expects nothing from him and he loves her for this generosity, abhors his inability to ask about her. But he is without capacity, his exhaustion stifling.

Dutch doctors come to examine him, one after another saying they don't understand. They are astounded he is alive, given the length and intensity of his fever. They speculate the coma helped, they speculate on tropical diseases, they speculate but no one has an explanation for what he's had, let alone a name. They use different creams and ointments on the rash, but nothing seems to make much difference until over the course of two days it finally disappears on its own. A different, aged doctor is brought from Yogya. He asks questions, pokes and prods and examines the test results.

"You had the fever."

Sari sputters beside him and Sam bursts out laughing, the first time he's laughed since waking.

The doctor is impatient. "I've been here a long time, seen some strange things, but this only once; some kind of bug or virus, the rash and days of fever, coma, full recovery. No real explanation. These young doctors can truss you up and do tests. Won't make them any the wiser. The fever. That's it."

The doctor gathers his things. "Needs lots of rest," he says to Sari. "Keep him hydrated. He'll be fine."

When the doctor is gone, they sit alone again, and he listens to the hush of the river, its murmur mirroring the beat of his heart. His aching heart. His lost soul.

"Semangat hilang." Sam waits for Sari's reaction. "An old woman said it to me."

She only nods gently, as though she's known all along. He cries again.

"It's red garbage tea. Ginger, cloves, cinnamon. They throw a wooden cup in while it brews. Invigorates the body and keeps you warm." A mug slides toward him across his riverside table and someone sits down. Sam knows the man by his calloused feet.

"Banya," the man says, reaching out a firm hand, the fingernail of his index finger long and curved. "We met earlier. I've come to help you."

"The doctor tells me I just need rest."

"Sari believes you are lost."

He feels a moment of betrayal. "Well, I'm not exactly sure where Magelang is in the big scheme of things." He tries to smile.

The small, strange man gazes back at him unperturbed. "When you came to us you muttered things in your sleep. Dark things."

Marcel, the whites of his eyes grown huge, the hallucinations. Sam is hit by a wave of nausea remembering the intensity of his anger in that moment, his desire to kill his friend. If it weren't for Taufik, he'd have done it, watched Marcel's pupils roll back, the body crumple and fall twisting into the river. He'd been ready for the satisfaction. The pure joy. He didn't kill Marcel, but Marcel is dead anyway; he couldn't have survived the rocks at the bottom of the falls. Sam hunches into himself, struggling for control, wondering with sudden anguish if Sari heard his utterings, if she knows the truth about him.

"Sari says you are a good man," Banya says as if hearing his thoughts.

He cannot stop his weeping. "I don't know what I am," he whispers, gripping the arms of the chair, clutching them as though if he doesn't hang on, he might drift away entirely.

"Come with me."

He follows Banya's mangled feet, watching the easy sway of the man's walk as he pauses to pick a hibiscus flower and suck the juice as Darma once did, squeezes a jackfruit on the tree to test its readiness. It is as though they are going for a stroll, not looking to find

Sam's lost spirit. Exhausted, Sam stops to lean against a rail and the man waits, taking Sam's arm as they descend stone steps to a path that follows the river past women working small gardens, ascending again to look down at where two rivers meet.

"The Elo is male," Banya points to the white-crested river tumbling wildly in from the northeast. "And the Progo female." He nods west to where another river wanders in, tranquil, untroubled it seems by time or distance. Where the two meet, the Progo's brown stillness becomes a wall, determined through its sheer calming force to slow the reckless rage of the Elo thundering toward it. And the Elo succumbs.

"She's strong," Sam says. "Stops him cold."

"Not quite." Banya gestures south to where the rivers are merged into one, to where the water flows in an uneven dance, swirling in eddies and rippling rapids in its center, drifting languid and serene under the flowered rambutan leaning out from shore. "They take the best of each of their natures and become one true thing. Sacred."

Sam watches the rivers force themselves on each other, arguing their separate passions, taking and giving until joined downstream into a single flow of water at peace with its new, uncertain character.

"We can learn from the river," Banya says.

"It might be too late for me."

"Only you know the answer to that."

Who but yourself can tell you if you are beautiful or ugly within? Who but yourself can tell you if you are incorruptible?

Each day he is a little stronger, his body recovering, his stormy dreams soothed by the serenity of this jungle sanctuary. Every morning he walks with Sari a little further, until they finally come out of the jungle hospice and into the village to see the people, everyday people living everyday lives. He is hungry to know them, to see how they live, what they care about, who they love. He wants all their stories. He speaks with locals in halting Javanese, takes notes, writing words and phrases about everyone and everything he sees, trying to fix a little of his brokenness.

When they get back, he rests, Taufik always on hand. The boy maintains his silence, but seems happier moving through the routines of each day, fishing with some of the local children or splashing with them in the river. Sam and Taufik spend their afternoons with the congklak board, moving shells quickly through the dragon-carved teak, the boy scooping up Sam's and laughing at Sam's slow strategy that never wins him the game.

Finally able to walk alone, Sam wanders the market in Magelang, passing cages of chickens and ducks, rabbits and songbirds, merchant hands flying as they cut their deals. Another street is filled with carts and tables of produce, peppers of myriad colors, string beans and cassava root, banana and mango. The women eye him, their bright headscarves flashing. His walking takes him past two old ladies on a verandah who smile toothless grins and wave. "Selamat sore" he calls, and "Hari baik." They laugh and return to their gossiping. He's seen these women.

At her warung on the corner, a Chinese woman ladles chicken and broth, noodles and vegetables into a bowl, finishing with a shot of sambal that makes his forehead bead and tongue rage. It is the first thing he's actually tasted in weeks, the best soup he's ever had. He looks up to see a man watching from across the narrow street, eyes sunk into a face covered in white patches ridged by fiery red. The man hobbles on crutches, his right leg missing from just above the knee. This too he has seen before.

He walks, one foot in front of the other, convinced somehow his walking will take him back to who he once was. He understands his father now. But it is a slow reckoning, as slow as the pace of a nation defined by relentless heat, the stoop and rise of workers in the sawah matching his slow walk to recovery. So too his mind, his tics and bodily functions, everything slowed to the rhythms of the sun and the heat, his anxiety lifted a little more each day by the shy opening of Sari's smile, the dip of her chin as she enters his room to prepare his medicine and fix his bed. Every day she sits with him awhile. And each day, he trusts a little more.

CHAPTER 25

The History of the World

FEBRUARY 1949

A MONTH SINCE HE WOKE. Banya shows up in the chill dark and presents Sam with a walking stick, the top perfectly carved into a dragon head so Sam's hand grasps the beast's smooth throat.

"I think you are ready for the temple," Banya says, gesturing to where Candi Borobudur's massive bulk looms black against the murky blue of near dawn, the Buddhist monument built and abandoned a thousand years ago.

Outside the gates of the hospice, Banya helps Sam onto the canopied seat of a waiting becak, watches Taufik climb in and waves them off. The grizzled old man in front pedals slowly at first, building momentum as they glide down the hill and through the empty streets of town. Halfway up the hill on the other side, they slow to a crawl and the man gets out to push, jumping back in to pedal again as the land flattens out and they emerge from the jungle at the temple's base. Its dark bulk rises eerily into the morning gloom. Taufik climbs quickly up black, foot-worn steps and through stone arches. Sam lags behind in the dark, huffing as they reach the top, where he can just make out a shadowed Buddha inside each rounded stupa.

They find a spot to sit on a ledge facing the skyline, watching as it turns blood red, light leaking over the horizon to outline the cone of Merapi in the distance, the plume of smoke drifting from its peak a constant reminder of its inclination to blow. Merbabu stands dormant alongside its twin. Rage and calm. Elo and Progo. Leo and Marie. Fog hangs suspended like a great bread roll to cloak the jungle in the valley between volcano and temple. As they watch, the horizon fades to purple and pink, finally orange and then yellow, the colors bouncing off the stupas and spires, dissipating the fog so the valley below comes alive. Sam has been holding his breath, thinking a chorus of angels might burst into song. But there is only the sound of Taufik's silence blending into the hushed breeze ruffling Sam's hair. The notebook is clutched in his hand, the moment too perfect to capture in words. He simply watches until the sun has risen to completely bathe the temple and valley with its heat.

"Wow," he says, finding his voice. Taufik smiles wide before taking his hand and leading Sam back down to the foot of the monument now lit by sunlight. He gapes at the size of the thing, the nine terraced tiers of gray volcanic stone carved and assembled piece by heavy piece, rising so even craning his neck he cannot see the top.

He runs his hand over the stone as they move clockwise around the lower terraces, the walls and balustrades covered in fine reliefs depicting all of nature: fish and turtle, bird and beast, trees and flowers in bloom. Up another terrace, and people emerge into the world, carved from the stone as full-faced, near naked and smiling souls who work and dance and eat, all they might desire at their fingertips. But moving up the terraces, human desire meets with consequence, one relief picturing proud hunters skewering turtle and deer on the left, while on the right those same men are boiled alive in a pot over an open flame. In another, women and men are wrapped in various stages of seduction and sex, their reward the persecution by the gossip of others. Each of the square terraces is hundreds of meters of pathway and wall filled with reliefs. The next introduces civilization — fancy clothing, tools and horses, the machinery of war. Worry is now etched into the eyes of the people who stand subservient at the feet of the powerful. More belongings, more structures, less joy.

There are no carved reliefs at the top, only the round stupas, each housing an individual Buddha escaped it seems from all that came before. They look out over the valley, oblivious to the desire and worry and power and grief in the tiers below. Sam wonders if he's lived the end of times, all this fighting for earthly things as the gods laugh. Maybe that's what Darma is doing now. Laughing. And Amir and Rudy. Muslim, Hindu and Christian, spirits released from their own history, from this earthly segregation to share a beer and shake their heads at the foibles of the living.

Sam lifts his face to the sun, watches the small dots that are workers in sawahs carved out of the jungle valley below, the volcano cones black against stark blue sky. He is exhausted as they make their way back down to the becak, head nodding as it returns them to the hospice, where he collapses onto his bed. For the first time since coming out of the coma, he does not dream.

"What did you think?" Sari asks later as they sit again by the water.

"First the convergence of the sacred rivers, and now the temple. I think Banya is trying to teach me something."

"And?" She grins. "What did you learn?"

"Only the history of the world."

Sari laughs a low rich sound, crinkles brightening the corners of her eyes as her cheeks dimple. Oh, how he loves her.

And as if she knows, she finally begins to tell him of her life after Ngadipuro, of how her mother arranged for her to be tucked away working at a hospital in Madiun, where she pretended her devotion to Christ and the Dutch by nursing soldiers back to health, protected by the nuns from the forces who killed her father. Fatil continues to work with the women's groups, nationalists threatening to fold the demands of the women's movement into the greater cause. Sari tells him the Dutch have turned on women like her mother, imprisoning them for their efforts toward independence without considering the colony's former support of women's equality and an end to child marriage.

The Dutch turned on the women. Sam cringes, wondering at Sari's tiny mother, standing up to all comers with her fiery eyes and fierce tongue, willing to die for the cause and leave Sari alone in the world. Perhaps as his dad had been willing, protecting Sam the same way Fatil now tries to protect Sari from the consequences. It is a startling thing, that kind of courage, that kind of love.

"I heard about Darma," she says finally. "Such a gentle soul to die like that."

Grief too is startling, the memory so near the surface that the taste of blood springs metallic to his mouth. He looks away, wondering what else she's heard, his tongue weighted by all he cannot say.

"I'm sorry, Sam." She puts a hand on his arm and he is back in Ngadipuro before Darma died, before the fever, before his mind left him. Back when he thought he loved her. And he does. He wants to know her deeply and protect her absolutely. He leans toward her, a stirring deep inside, but sadness confuses her face.

He leans away again. "What is it?"

She pauses, gathering herself, looks him in the eye. "Did you see my father again? Before he died?"

They haven't spoken of Amir. He thought it was because it was too painful for her. Now he realizes it's because she was waiting for him to regain his strength. He's ashamed at his selfishness, wondering how long she has been wanting to ask.

"I'm sorry, Sari. I never saw him again after the last time in Ngadipuro."

"Neither did I. Your men raided our home and he barely escaped." She looks at him hard and he leans away, confused and then horrified as her words hit him. *I think you will do what is right*, she'd said. *I think you are a good man.*

"Sari. No. I didn't send them." He shakes his head. "It was Freddy. I didn't know he'd followed me. Oh god." He can hardly breathe round his heart racing in his throat. "Please believe me."

The stiffness leaves her shoulders and her face crumples. "I thought that . . . I thought after everything, you still turned him in." She wraps her arms round herself. "I didn't want to believe it, but what was I to think?" Her nose flares, tears at the edges of her eyes.

"No, Sari. I couldn't hurt you." But his men did. They'd chased her father into the arms of the communists and Amir was killed for it. So many people dead. "I am so sorry."

He moves closer to her and, when she does not back away, gathers her into his arms. She rests her head on his shoulder and weeps. He doesn't move, willing her to believe him, heart surging as he feels her grief mingle with his own, to feel such pain a sweet relief. Because pain means he cares again. Because he finally wants more than anything to be what Anika thought he could be, what Sari wants him to be. He caresses her hair, runs his fingers through the tears on her cheek and down her arm. She looks up at him, eyes shining with trust. And love.

Taking his hand, Sari leads him past the sacred confluence of rivers to his room. In one motion she shrugs off her kebaya, steps out of her skirt and turns to face him, a small pride in her eye. She knows she is beautiful. He stands a meter away, taking the time to see her fine neck, round of breast, taut stomach, curve of hip. Back to her eyes, daring him now. He smiles and slowly lifts his shirt over his head, drops his shorts. And the space between them is gone as they fall onto the bed, fall into each other. Not desperate, or euphoric, or fearful. A beautiful falling.

The next day, Taufik excitedly thrusts a package at him, waiting as Sam props his pillows and opens the attached envelope. It is his father's cramped handwriting.

Dear Sam,

I don't know if you will ever wish to speak to me. It seems nothing about the war is forgotten, nor forgiven, but the effort of trying to understand is so exhausting people are afraid they will never recover. And so they don't say a word. Maybe that's how terrible events finally end, unresolved, but left behind so people can move forward. I found these in the wall behind your headboard. But this is only part of the story. I hope you write the rest.

Love, Dad

He stares at the letter in his lap, slowly opening the package and pulling out three small notebooks, the edges slightly curled in the humidity; Nazi occupation there in his lap.

Flipping them open one by one, he reads his own words describing the perfect line of goose-stepping parade boots, Mr. Vanderveen's raised arm flashing in salute. Beyond the boots, the ache of sadness on an old man's face as he squints at the spectacle from under the brim of his fedora. Women in line for rations, the young one with honey skin and sensible shoes absently smoothing her hair as she looked directly at Sam.

He reads about Anika and Marie standing in the door of the chicken coop, their limbs dwarfed in men's overalls, arms thrown round one another as they laugh. Beyond them that other door, disguised as a wall to hide all their secrets. And Hendrik, harnessing Nettie to the wagon, the slump of his shoulders evidence of the man's hard nature, the truth Sam now knows was the pain of his choices.

He sees the inadequacies of his words, his notes about the miners, their skinny bodies blackened by coal dust, shoulders bent as they wrapped arms round each other in their moment of rebellion. Their moment of courage. And Leo, face darkened by coal, light hair lifted in the wind. So young. Three years younger than Sam is now. Only now does Sam remember how tentative Leo's raised fist, his pinched grin and worried eyes, the flared nose and tightness in his jaw. Dear god, how afraid Leo was.

"What if we do nothing and we die anyway?"

Brave words. Or just a teenager's bravado. Sam has spent these years measuring himself against Leo's words as though his brother's was a singular courage. But Leo and Hendrik and Rudy were dead or destroyed for their noble efforts. And now in this new war, so many others. They'd all been courageous. But they'd all failed at courage too. It was Darma alone who was truly brave. Darma who held the truth in his kind soul.

Another notebook. Marcel asking about pubic hair, worrying over his father's disappearance and his mother's anguish. Evidence of Sam's love for his friend in these pages. And now in this strange place, he is supposed to hate Marcel, pretend he doesn't understand the nature of his friend's convictions, Marcel's history and motivations. But he does know Marcel.

He has the words now, will send the stories to his father, explain how he's managed to see the Nazi occupation from a distance, to see what really mattered in the determination of his sisters to endure, in the sacrifice of his father's bent back. He'd thought his dad guilty, hadn't trusted Hendrik might be making his own choices in his own way, that he might be doing the right thing. A desperate ache engulfs Sam, his heart collapsing with wanting to go home and ask the questions that will give his father permission to grieve his choices. He wants to hold his father and beg his forgiveness, to rewrite that story. Tears slide from his eyes.

He picks up the embossed notebook he's used in Indonesia, the notebook his dad gave him. He will send the stories to his father. But there is one left to write.

CHAPTER 26

Walking Leo Home

JUNE 1945

WE WAITED FOR LEO. AND while we waited, we worked, fixing the house, salvaging what we could from the rubble of the shed and barn and clearing away the rest. Dad surveyed the fields to see what could be replanted in time to squeeze out a crop. We sought to return to some kind of normal. But despite our efforts, normal was an illusion, the country devastated and the Allies, mostly Canadians now, doing what they could to restore electricity and water, to supply enough gas for heaters and food for the hungry.

Wanting to go back to school, I biked to Eindhoven on a June morning to ask about starting the agriculture program there. I'd found some rubber tires for one of the bikes and the wind rushed past my ears as I held my head high, arms straight out like I might take flight. I'd always loved the countryside of Noord Brabant, its orchards and vegetable plots, its small flocks of sheep and lambs. It was pastoral. Romantic. Limburg's farms were functional — oats and potatoes, barns full of hogs. But the romance I remembered in Brabant was shattered, cherry trees broken and scarred, fields bomb-pitted though plows and men now worked to restore them.

I paused my pedaling to coast through a meadow of tiny white wildflowers, their survival giving me hope as I rode into town. At the college, they took my name and told me the school would be ready for fall session.

Wandering through town, I jumped as Canadian trucks roared past, children everywhere latching onto the soldiers like they were heroic big brothers, and girls waving at them from where they walked or sat in sidewalk cafés sprung back to life in a thriving black market. Cigarettes for a coffee, a sandwich for a blanket. It was said the women were throwing themselves at Allied soldiers, not in exchange for food or safety as I'd seen in Germany, but because they'd forgotten their churches and families in the frenzied joy of liberation. Entire households extended gezelligheid, coziness and companionability, to the soldiers. It made me uneasy, this affection. I'd seen too much to trust in the good intentions of those men, those loud men with their invectives about the war, claiming a moral superiority, as if they understood occupation and internment and the impotence it created, let alone my country, my people. I was grateful and yet resented them at the same time.

And then I saw Petra sitting on a small bench with some other girls, their heads bent together, chattering. I walked by to make sure it was her. She was thin, her hair dull, and she wore a simple housedress that had seen better days. And heels. Always the heels. Even at the height of the occupation, the girls wore their heels as if the fashion statement might ward off complete capitulation.

"The Canadians look delicious, don't they?" said one of the girls.

A thrust of anger and I realized I might be simply jealous of the soldiers and the place they'd taken in the hearts of Dutch girls. I watched Petra closely to see her reaction to the comment, if she too was in love with the soldiers. Just then she looked up, her blue eyes snapping and widening like sky and I forgot everything else.

"Sam!" She came to me, suddenly shy as the other girls watched curiously. "What are you doing here? I mean," she stuttered, "you're home?"

"Yes, after I was picked up from Mr. Abel's field I went to a camp. Then sent to a farm in Germany. And now, I'm home." It didn't sound like much wrapped up in so few words. Maybe that's how I'd address it, like a series of unfortunate events I'd lived through, but which were thoroughly behind me. "What are you doing in Eindhoven?"

"I've started nurse's training. They started the program early with so many wounded and sick."

My heart skipped. "I'll be starting here in the fall. Agriculture."

She smiled broadly, looked back to the girls still watching and gave a small wave. They smirked and closed the circle, giggling as we walked away. Deep breath. I let my hand brush against hers and she smiled at me, linking her arm through mine.

"So you were in Germany. What was that like? Everybody heiling Hitler and teaching their children to hate the Jews?"

"Something like that." I didn't want to bring that to this street with her on my arm. "I hear you were liberated early."

"It was so exciting. Everyone went wild when the Canadians came through." She flushed with the memory, eyes shining. When I said nothing, her voice rose. "I'll admit, some girls go too far, throwing themselves at any soldier who looks their way. But I understand it. Those first days were unreal. To finally fly the flag, to walk down the street. The feeling of freedom — incredible."

Images flared in my head. "I was in a camp and forced to work in Germany. I think I get it."

Pulling her arm from mine, she stopped and stood back a little. "I met one of them, a Canadian who helped my dad rebuild the storage shed and get water back to the house. His name was Adam." Her voice went soft as though the name conjured a memory she could barely contain.

We'd all bent the rules, hushed warnings from mothers and priests made irrelevant in a world gone mad. Had any of us loved — truly — or had we only been compassionate, or desperate, or euphoric? I barely knew Petra. Who was I to judge? I decided not to speak of my time in Germany again. We would start anew like the farms and neighborhoods, the entire country mucking its way back to normal. Linking arms again, we walked to the boarding house where she lived. An old man sat on the porch swing, his face gray, eyes lost to thoughts beyond what anyone could see.

"Doorman," Petra said with a smile, raising her eyebrows to acknowledge what I was thinking; the man did nothing at all. "Hello, Benny."

Petra reached to rest her hand softly on the man's shoulder, letting it sit there until he covered it with his own, rheumy eyes focusing a moment to smile at her. It was so gentle, this small thing. This was a girl I could love. A flock of finches swooped in, their chatter swelling the air with their light energy.

"I don't know when I last heard the birds," I said.

She glanced to where they flitted round the shrub by the porch, and smiled. "They just came back today."

Sparrows greeted me when I got back to de Kruidenteelt, their return finally filling the silence left when the guns stopped.

The next day, it was Leo's turn.

Alone at the farm, I stood a moment watching the staggered steps, the sway of a wafer-thin body stopped as if to wager how much farther it could go. I didn't want this skeleton to be my brother. But I knew it was. I held back a sob, rushing down the lane to Leo, helplessly afraid to hug him, afraid he would break. We stared at one another, a faint smile of recognition and relief round Leo's cracked lips before he swayed, wrapped his arms around my shoulders and fainted into me.

I lifted him in one movement and carried him to the house. He weighed nothing at all, smelled of stale sweat. But of something deeper too, something strong and potent. Upstairs, I laid him on the bed in our old room. Marie had kept everything exactly as it was in hopes of his return, as though changing one thing would mean she'd given up. Now her twin lay limp on the bed, filthy clothes stinking and worn to a thread, closed eyes sunk into hollowed dark sockets, and cheekbones so sharp they might, at the slightest touch, break through the surface and escape his face.

Oh god. Breathing hard to squash the panic, I ran downstairs to the tap. Cold. No fuel for the heater. Shit. Kindling a fire, I pushed the kettle onto the stove and ran back up with the scissors to cut off the rank clothes, sucking breath as his naked body emerged. He was shrunk to half the man I remembered, opaque in the sunlight lapping through the open window. Like the dead Jew in the railcar, limbs like the delicate humerus of the sparrow's wing, his birdlike lightness. Pocked with sores, Leo's skin was blistered and scabbed. I could just make out the shadowed lift of his ribs as he rattled a wheezing breath.

I forced myself to move. To fetch water from the stove and dip a towel into it, squeezing it onto Leo's chest, wiping his neck and shoulders as gently as I might a newborn. Dip, squeeze, wipe. Stomach, arms and legs, the soft wilt of penis and scrotum. I turned him over. A soft moan. Wiping Leo's back, I uncovered the yellowed evidence of bruising across the shoulders, dipped and squeezed and wiped some more. Over and over, until the grime and sweat and the ooze erupting from the sores was gone, leaving only blanched skin. I hummed softly as I worked. Otherwise I'd have shouted. How dare this happen, this cruel return after so much and so long. I thumped the mattress and Leo stirred a little. I rummaged for a clean nightshirt among my own things, glancing out the window, hoping to see Marie and Anika coming down the lane. They needed to be here. I needed them here.

Leo was dying. A bubble of grief blocked my chest. Bent over, I clutched my arms round myself, holding there briefly. Inhaling deeply, I returned to the bedside and lifted Leo gently by the shoulders to slide the nightshirt over his head and lay him back, threading his arms through the holes and pulling the shirt down to his knees. Leo's skin prickled with goose flesh. In the closet, I found a heavy quilt Mom made before she died, inhaled its musty scent, hoping she was somewhere there to help me be in this moment what Leo was for me in the moment of her death. Pulling the quilt to his chin, I knelt beside the bed. I thought I should pray and pulled the bedside drawer open. Draping the rosary beads through my fingers, I couldn't think of the words. Reaching under the covers, I took Leo's cold hand in my own, ran a finger across the raised scars, the curled fingers.

"Dear god, please. Please." I stared at Leo's pale face, put my ear to his mouth and found only a hint of breath sound. Resting my head beside Leo's, I whispered. "You were right. I didn't know anything. I still don't."

I thought I'd seen and endured so much, had even started to take a certain pride in my survival, imagining the stories I'd someday tell my children about Rudy and the camp and how luck of the draw got me out of there. Thought one day I'd even speak of Emma, like I understood what happened. I imagined my tales of the camp and Germany and the long walk home would be important to someone, my listeners knowing I'd moved beyond the tale. Leo was supposed to be part of his own story. I wanted an accounting of my brother's life — a girl he loved, a friend he found, the meaning he managed to glean from it all. I needed to know Leo's war, needed it to be more than a sad story, an unfortunate life, a disappointing end.

I shook him in one sudden movement, the lack of resistance frightening. His arm slid free to hang off the bed, his head rocking back and forth as though fluid. With mouth gaping, a faint moan, he opened his eyes slightly and gazed at me, a smile of recognition and gratitude touching his lips.

I held his gaze, willing him back into the world. "Stay. Please."

But he drifted away again.

Tucking his arm in, I climbed under the covers and stretched out alongside my brother, wrapping him in my arms and gently rocking with him, back and forth, back and forth, as though somehow I could stop what was coming. I held him and rocked him as his body cooled, on and on, first humming, then words whis-per-sung into his ear, "Now I lay me down to sleep. I pray thee Lord my soul to keep . . ." I felt hollowed, mind a fissure, regret fluttering in the cavern of my stomach. I hadn't protected Leo the way he'd protected me. I lay there long into the afternoon, the shadows of the tree limbs outside the window entwined with the patterns and leaves on the quilt.

Dusk, and I heard Dad's gruff voice and then the girls' chatter floating through the open window. I wasn't ready, wanted to hang onto the secret a bit longer. Sharing it would mean explanations and expectations and grieving. Saying it aloud would make it real. I couldn't bear the thought of making it real. Marie laughed. Oh god, Marie. Slowly I released Leo from my arms, rose from the bed, and pulled the covers to Leo's chin, searching the haggard face once more for a reason, for forgiveness. Knees giving way, I sobbed once, cheek pressed to his. "I'm so sorry."

I stood and stretched the quilt up over his mouth, nose, eyes, the few spikes of hair, until my brother was only a small form out-lined by our mother's embroidery. Straightening, I rubbed my hand across my forehead and down over my face. And forced my legs toward the door.

Grateful tears stream from Sam's eyes as he lowers the pen. Leo is dead. It's there on the page, Sam's brother a part of history now, released to whatever is out there, heaven, a whirl of energy or noth-ing at all. It doesn't really matter. Leo will be with all those others Sam has lost, their individual histories shaping the future as Darma believed. Mengeti. Sam has written the story. It is for others to glean prophesy from it.

But there are more stories to be written, more souls to be released. Amir and Darma, Bart and Willem. Sam picks up the embossed notebook again, thinks of what he might write about this new war.

Darma's slender hands picking a wildflower, Andre fingering the beads of the rosary, Raj sharing the pain of his father's death. Boats in the harbor, goats in the market, skinny boys soaping their hair under a waterfall, women in wide-brimmed hats shuffling through rice laid out to dry.

But beyond description? Glimpses of small dark men on the forest floor with Dutch rifles trained on them. A bapak with pissed sarong and feeble eyes begging for mercy, villagers watching these young and stupid soldiers with their guns and torches and single-edged klewang who believe they are better than the Nazis because of the nature of their cause. Another kind of occupation. Another ending.

Stories are like the stone reliefs at Borobudur, the grand sweep of history in the background, individual lives woven through the narrative to shed light on the truth; first the recognition and then the reckoning. And then, finally, the moving forward. He will wait to make these new words into stories, wait until he can see his time in Indonesia from a distance. Wait until he is strong enough for that kind of honesty.

If We Only Knew the Beginning

MARCH 1949

HE IS JOLTED FROM HIS thoughts by a voice. Raj stands just outside the doorway talking to Sari.

"I don't know," Sari says. "He's only just strong enough now to walk into town."

"He could rest on the train."

Sam's heart slows to a dull thud. He sits up, pulls the mosquito net back and swings his legs over the side. Raj's face lights with relief as he comes to sit on the chair beside the bed.

"How are you, Sam?"

"Better all the time."

Raj looks unsure. "Walk with me?"

They make their way to the edge of the bank high above the river, stopping in the shade of a huge bamboo stand. "This is quite the place." Raj gazes out a while and takes a deep breath. "Sari tells me you're on the mend."

"They've taken good care of me, here. She's taken good care."

Raj nods. "I've arranged for you to go home, Sam."

His gut twists. "I thought I'd come back to the squad."

"You've already been replaced." Raj moves to the edge of the riverbank and looks down. "The doctors are concerned about your fitness. Look at you. You're a bloody toothpick. And they're worried about you. Mentally." He says the last carefully.

But Sam only smiles. He's not been stable, but how does he tell Raj his mind has been steadied by river myth and temple story?

Raj speaks quietly. "When my father was murdered, I thought it was simple. If I just killed them, everything would go back to the way it was before my dad died. But I was wrong. I can't bring him back, and we're not going to win this thing. Everyone knows it. They're planning a ceasefire as we speak, withdrawal, everyone talking about an Indonesian Republic like it's a real thing. Holland is bailing on us, and it's every man for himself out there."

"I think maybe it always was."

Raj nods. "It'll be over in six months. You'll just go home a little earlier than the others."

Going home. Weeks ago he'd have given anything. But now his mind whirls. Taufik watches from where he squats under a tree twenty meters away and, in the distance, Sari speaks with Banya, gesturing with her hands in her quiet, intense way.

Raj follows his gaze. "I've made sure they'll keep her on here until it's over."

"What about you?"

"I seem to become whatever helps me to survive. But you should go back to Holland the person you were before . . ."

"I was just a kid. A kid who liked to write stories."

"Then go home and write stories, Sam." Raj smiles. "I've already sent in for your discharge and made arrangements for tickets to Bandung. You'll be quarantined there for a bit before you can ship out. Andre's going with you to work in Bandung. He's been wounded. He lost an arm, Sam."

"Jesus." Not Andre, jubilant and loyal.

"He's lucky, actually. A grenade landed right in front of him. It could have been a lot worse. So he's going with you. Bonita too.

She's pregnant. And now, well, he'll need her." Raj suddenly peers more closely at the water. "Well look at that, one river slows the other right down."

Sam lets the relief wash over him. No more jungle, no more killing. The last of the knot in his gut unfurls even as his heart tightens. Sari.

She is her reserved self when he tells her, declining his invitation to see him off at the train station. Instead, on his last night at the hospice, they meet on the bank where the Elo meets the Progo, the whir of cicadas and chorusing frogs ringing together in tones and semitones around the river's tumbling bassline. They stand side by side without touching, as though formal behavior will dispel their anguish, until finally he turns to look at her, silently gazing as the gathering night gives soft edges to her profile.

"You're so beautiful."

She makes a soft sound, like her beauty is a given, like she wants more.

"And I love you." The words surprise him even as he knows they are true.

"But you will leave."

"I don't have a choice. I'm still a soldier."

"And I am my father's daughter."

Do you think I will give up my country because you are a nice young man? Amir would not. And neither will Sari. And no matter how he grieves Dutch actions or is seized by regret for his own, Sam can never be like Marcel. They all have to choose. Like the batik artists who envision the end and create something beautiful with their million bits of wax. Perhaps it's the only thing he's learned, to trust himself to make the right choices.

And Sari? She will choose Indonesia. He stares into the dark, listening for words he knows she will not say. *I will come with you. I will be your wife.* Instead, her sigh is long and full of all the riddles they cannot solve without changing the world.

"I love you too," she says finally and grasps his hand.

They stand, all the unsaid words heavy on his chest, the ache to speak so great he moans a little and she turns to him. They cling to one another, Sam folding Sari into him as though he might contain all of her body in his, all of their shared past and unknown future, willing time to stop. In the moment, love is simple, the only word they need to give faint voice to the joy and desolation sharpening each measure of the jungle's night song. A cock crows nearby and she pulls away, staring hard into his eyes, all the questions he'd seen in them when she'd looked up at him from her bicycle months before still unanswered. Except perhaps one — who he is. She smiles and kisses him so deeply he cannot tell what separates them.

The next morning, he waits with her outside his room at the hospice, watching Andre and Bonita make their way down the path, his breath catching at the sight of Andre's shirt sleeve tied and dangling empty from the elbow. Their embrace is awkward as Sam feels the absence of his friend's arm gone at the bicep. Bonita and Sari hug intensely, as women do. Andre catches Taufik in a one-armed bear hug and tousles the boy's hair. "He's grown."

"Yes." Sam clears the lump from his throat.

Andre glances around and then back to where Taufik beams, a boy with a future in which everything is possible. Taufik examines Andre's arm, unfazed by the missing limb, perhaps a small casualty in all that's been lost. And where Sam had expected to see pity in Bonita's eyes, there is only a deep love for Andre. He sees it in them both. Raj is right — Andre needs Bonita but not because of his handicap.

"It's a hell of a thing," Andre says, nodding his chin at the missing arm. "Worst is the phantom pain, and figuring out new ways to wipe my ass."

Sam's laugh is forced. He'd expected Andre to be angry, but instead Andre nudges Bonita in front of him as they move toward the hospice gate, pinching her so she swats at him with her free hand, glancing back to wink at Sam, giving him permission to accept Andre's loss, to behave as though a one-armed Andre is normal. Taufik bounds alongside Sari. Sam hangs back and watches these people he loves. He knows Andre will stay with Bonita and their baby, Andre's black-and-white world a blessing in complicated times. And Taufik. As though he knows Sam's thoughts, Taufik turns and stops, looking up with a bright smile as he puts his hand on Sam's chest. Brothers.

They clasp each other, hanging onto the hug so Sam feels all of it, their shared trauma and joy and love. He will leave Taufik in the jungle with Sari, who will mother the boy out of his silence and into the world. Sari who moves through her days like water choosing its rhythm. They've reached the gate. She stands with her head high, nose flaring as she smiles and dips her chin to him. He tilts his head and returns her gaze.

Sam turns and walks the road to Magelang, where he will catch the train first to Bandung and then Jakarta, lay aside his weapon and sail for home.

AUTHOR'S NOTE

AS DARMA TELLS SAM, MENGETI is Javanese for "this writing of history" or "history as prophesy." Official Indonesian history remembers the war of independence in nationalistic language, while in the Netherlands it was dood zwigen, silenced to death. This novel, then, is my interpretation of a somewhat limited historical record, and I've tried to navigate the space between nationalism and silence to reach the kind of middling truth fiction allows us to consider, while recognizing that no absolute truth exists.

Beyond documented political and military figures and events, and those events my dad actually experienced under occupation, the characters and events of this story are entirely fictional. Sam is a composite of those vets I read about and my imagination. The character of Marcel Bakker is based on Poncke Princen, the White Guerrilla, a Dutch conscript who deserted to join the independence forces because he believed Indonesians should determine their own future. Most of the story's characters are Dutch or Eurasian with the exception of Amir, Fatil and Sari, who are, I hope, representative of those Javanese caught in the middle of the conflict and forced to make impossible choices. Otherwise, I felt it was not my place to tell the story of the revolutionaries who fought colonial oppression, except to include known historical events such as the Bersiap period in Surabaya and instances in which some independence forces victimized those who supported the Dutch.

A note about language. I recognize the racist roots of colonialism and, as a descendant of the oppressors, it is my fervent wish to avoid further harm. In that spirit, I've used what we know to be offensive colonial terms and language only as necessary to place this story in the context of the history in which it happened. The language used by the Javanese characters in the novel is a mix of pre-independence Javanese and Bahasa Indonesia, the national language of the entire archipelago post-independence. And finally, as many would know, the Catholic Mass was said in Latin until the 1960s, but for ease of understanding I've used English.

Mengeti, this writing of history, will not be perfect, and any mistakes are entirely mine.

ACKNOWLEDGMENTS

I'LL START WITH MY DAD. This story would not exist but for his willingness to dive back seventy years and remember both the occupation of Holland and his time in Indonesia with an honest and open heart. While he had a desk job in Jarkarta and was not part of the Police Actions, at ninety-six my dad continues to be reflective about what happened in the East Indies, understanding the difference between what he believed at the time and the historical realities for those colonized. Volumes could be written about my mom and dad. Thank you both.

I am indebted to my editor, Susan Renouf, for both choosing this book and for her intuitive understanding of what I hoped to achieve with it as she offered astute suggestions. To Jen Knoch for her careful copy edit, art director Jessica Albert for book design and Caroline Suzuki for a superb cover, Pia Singhal, Shannon Parr, Elham Ali, Cassie Smyth, David Caron and everyone at ECW Press, thank you. It's been a joy to work with you.

So much gratitude to Leeann Minogue and Sandra Birdsell for their sound suggestions, and especially to Lawrence Hill for his careful reading and support of this book. To Helen Humphreys and Guy Vanderhaeghe for the insight they shared as faculty at Sage Hill Writing, and to the cohorts I worked with in that wonderful space, thank you. To the Saskatchewan Writers' Guild and the Saskatchewan writing community — you keep me going.

Thank you to my sister, Wilma Groenen, for being my stalwart travel companion as we navigated our way across Java. Two "intrepid dorks," we had so many people help us on our journey. I am indebted to guest house owners Jordi, Sony and Bowo, who shared their space, knowledge, neighbors and music with us; to Mr. Zul and his wife, Fatil, for their persistence in finding my uncle's grave in Depok; Tatang Wibowo, filmmaker and seventh-generation batik artist, who shared his art; the Muslim school children who toured us through the Hindu temples of Prambanan; Jimbaran Bay in Bali for simply existing.

A huge thank you to SK Arts for funding my travel, the Canada Council for funding time to write and to the Saskatchewan Foundation for the Arts for an award supporting this book.

A complicated history is impossible to write without the research and writing of so many. Among the array of books, articles and online work I consulted (for a more comprehensive list see annelazurko. com), I am particularly indebted to the writings of the late Pramoedya Ananta Toer. Despite having fought with independence forces, he was later exiled by Sukarno to a penal colony on Buru Island for his criticism of government human rights abuses and state-sanctioned killings. Translated and read worldwide, his work is still largely banned in Indonesia, yet Toer is considered one of the country's finest writers, among his work the *Buru Quartet* and *The Mute's Soliloquy*. Benedict Anderson's "Reading 'Revenge' by Pramoedya Ananta Toer" was invaluable in my own exploration of the nature of dendam and the ways in which words are weaponized when language slips the knot that ties it to meaning.

Stef Scagliola's essay "The Silences and Myths of a 'Dirty War'" was instrumental to understanding both how the Dutch view of the war affected returning soldiers, and the country's collective silence around this history. Anthony Reid's comprehensive book *The Indonesian National Revolution, 1945–50* was invaluable and Raj's account in the novel of dogs with "bellies collapsed like bicycle tires because no one thought to feed them" (page 197) is from Idrus's story "Surabaya," translated by Nababan and Anderson. The words of Dutch veterans are given voice in "The Decolonization War in Indonesia, 1945–1949: War Crimes in Dutch Veterans' Egodocuments" by Gert Oostindie, Irene Hoogenboom and Jonathon Verwey. Elizabeth Pisani's *Indonesia Etc.* is a wonderful guide to the country and its history. Thank you also to those journalists, filmmakers and poets whose work gave mine credibility. A 1947 article by the late Tom Gurr about Dutch soldiers in Ngadipuro inspired so much in this book, and Bart Nijpels's film *Poncke Princen (The White Guerrilla)* informed the character of Marcel. David Stafford's *Endgame, 1945: The Missing Final Chapter of WWII* gave structure to Sam's end-of-war experiences, while the lack of empathy for the Jewish experience expressed by Daniel, "No one allowed to die too late" (page 56), is from an untitled poem by Wim Ramaker. Much appreciation to Jiddu Krishnamurti for his teachings on the nature of truth.

Thank you to those Dutch soldiers who, through writing, photographs and interviews attempted to tell the truth about some of the atrocities they saw and were a part of: Joop Hueting, Gus Blok and Maarten Schaafsma to name a few. Many Dutch scholars and citizens are currently examining and writing about Holland's colonial past. As we have discovered in Canada, the act of recognizing and reconciling with those harmed is difficult but necessary work.

Thank you to my cousins in Holland who encouraged my writing of their history despite my having been born and raised in Canada. To my adult children, Sara, Anita, Logan and Madelana, you inspire me every day. Finally, to David, my partner in life and love for over thirty years, you gave me the gift of time. Thank you.